# LIES
# ARE
# FOREVER

## C. JEAN DOWNER

## About the Author

C. Jean Downer writes traditional whodunits with a magical twist. She's a self-proclaimed expert in the field, with thousands of mystery books, television episodes, and movies to her reading and viewing credit. Even her family refuses to watch mysteries with her because of her gifts of deduction unless she zips it.

If she was younger and braver, she'd trade her Ph.D. for a PI in a heartbeat! C'est la vie.

Downer is the author of *Lies Are Forever*, the first book of the Sloane West Mysteries, and a published poet. She lives in White Rock, British Columbia, with her wife of twenty-plus years, their two fabulous daughters, two lazy dogs, and three chill cats.

# LIES
# ARE
# FOREVER

## C. JEAN DOWNER

2023

Bella Books, Inc.
P.O. Box 10543
Tallahassee, FL 32302

Printed in the United States of America on acid-free paper.

First Edition - 2023

Editor: Cath Walker
Cover Designer: Kayla Mancuso
Photo credit: Adrienne Thiessen, Gemini Photography

ISBN: 978-1-64247-489-3

## PUBLISHER'S NOTE

## Acknowledgment

A special thank-you to Bella Books, my publisher, for bringing me into their family of talented authors and believing in my story.

To my brilliant editor, Cath Walker, I so enjoyed working with you and learned so much from your guidance. Thank you for bringing out the best in me.

To my beta readers, especially Sharon, my bibliophile mom, thank you for your thoughtful and perceptive feedback on my writing.

And to Theresa, my wife, Hayden and Hadley, our daughters, thank you for your constant support and love and for talking endless hours about murder mysteries with me.

# CHAPTER ONE

Sloane West walked to a cramped kitchen and dug out an old Dupont lighter from a utility drawer. It was engraved with the date she stopped smoking, a gag gift from her ex that wasn't funny anymore.

One flick of the spark wheel and a flame shot up, releasing white spirit and memories of past camping trips. She held it under an ivory envelope with handwritten calligraphy until the fire caught hold and spread, licking at her fingers. Then she dropped the burning paper into the sink and gripped the counter. How did she fail to realize Jess was falling out of love with her and in love with him? A dark, long-haired cat appeared beside her and meowed.

"Jesus, Bear. You scared me."

She rubbed her head against Sloane's legs and jumped onto the kitchen counter.

A tinge of guilt spread hotly across Sloane's face, and she stroked Bear's back. "Don't worry about the fire. I'll put it out." The stream of water sizzled as it hit the flames, releasing a puff of smoke.

Bear leaped down and led Sloane to the bay window. Across the street, the sun had lowered behind a row of dilapidated brownstones. Her neighbors would flow out soon into the dusk, milling around buzzing streetlights. Trading. Selling. Getting whatever they needed.

Her upstairs neighbor leaned against a gargoyle-headed newel post that flanked their stoop. She locked eyes with him and lifted her chin. He reciprocated, dragged the last of his cigarette before flicking it to the gutter, and lit another.

Sloane bent down and nuzzled her face into Bear's long fur. "They've got some nerve sending me an invitation, right?"

Bear meowed.

"Exactly. Screw them. I knew you'd understand."

A knock at the front door brought her back to the present. Sloane unlocked the bolt, slid off the chain, and yanked the door open. "What do you want?"

An elderly man stood before her. He removed his gray trilby and stared at her, open-mouthed. "I'm so sorry." His deep voice caught. "I'm Harold Huxham, a solicitor. I have a four-thirty appointment with Ms. Sloane West."

She glanced at her watch and rubbed her forehead. "You're at the right place, Mr. Huxham. But it's only ten after."

"Call me Harold, please. I'm terribly sorry. I thought your office would have a lobby. I can wait outside if you'd like."

"I can't let you do that." She backed up and gestured for him to come in. "And you can call me Sloane." She bolted the door. "Assuming was your first mistake, Harold. I work from home. If you don't arrive on time, you might find me in the shower or not here." She pointed at two overstuffed armchairs facing an antique secretary. "Have a seat."

Harold sniffed the air. "Have you had a fire?"

Sloane chuckled and opened one of the bay windows. "No. I had a cleansing."

"I see." Harold placed his briefcase on the floor, set his hat on it, removed his dark-blue wool coat, folded it, and draped it across the back of the armchair.

Sloane gave him a once-over. He was tall and robust with a body that seemed to have survived well into old age, neither frail nor cumbersome. The type of body she wanted if she ever got that old.

She sat on the corner of her desk. "So, how'd you get past our security door? I thought you were my neighbor."

"A gentleman on the steps insisted he buzz me in. I believe he was annoyed with my presence."

"Was he short, bald, and rude?"

"You know him then?"

"Gary Prence. He lives upstairs. One of these times, he'll let the wrong person in and be sorry." She pushed off the desk. "Can I get you coffee, tea, whiskey?"

"If it isn't too much trouble, a cup of tea with milk would be splendid."

"No trouble at all."

Ignoring the charred mess in the sink, she started a teakettle and filled a tray with cups, a carton of milk, and a bottle of whiskey. The cups had belonged to Jane, her mother, and the whiskey something special she had brought home from a distillery tour in Ireland.

She returned to Harold surveying her apartment. His gaze had settled on three paintings hanging in a row across her living room wall, and the corners of his mouth had turned up.

"You like the Impressionists?" he asked as she set down the tray.

"Yeah, but these are hand-painted reproductions." She pointed at each. "A Morisot, Renoir, and Cassatt." Sloane placed a cup in front of Harold and one in front of her chair. "I didn't buy them. I inherited them."

His smile disappeared as he studied each painting.

Bear lifted her head and meowed.

Harold turned to her, and his eyes widened. "My heavens. It couldn't be…"

Sloane opened a box of Earl Grey, dropped a teabag into each cup, and sat. "Couldn't be what?"

"Oh, it's nothing. I was just admiring your cat. I knew one that looked exactly like it. Same distinct eye color."

"Yeah, not surprising. Bear is a plain old, American long-haired cat. There are probably ten more like her on my street alone."

Bear bristled and flicked her tail.

Sloane laughed. "See, now I made her mad. There's no telling what she'll do."

The kettle whistled, a trill turning into a screech. "Jesus. Just one second. I don't know why I keep that thing." She hurried to the kitchen and made their tea. "Would you like a splash of whiskey in your tea?" she asked, holding out the bottle.

He settled into his chair. "No, thank you, it's a bit early for me."

"Are you sure? It's five o'clock somewhere." She checked her watch. "Hell, it's a cocktail hour here."

He covered his cup with his hand and shook his head.

"Suit yourself." She poured herself a healthy shot. "So tell me, Harold. Why does a distinguished lawyer make an appointment with a PI in the Bronx without telling her that he's from Vancouver Island?"

He straightened. "How did you know? Are you an expert in accents?"

"I've read a few books. Yours is easy, though. Hints of British etiquette with Western Canadian patterns. Also, New Yorkers don't apologize. Unless we need to. Then we still don't. But you Canadians are famous for it." She took a long drink. "That. And I read Victoria, BC, on the boarding pass in your coat pocket."

"Hah. You're devilishly clever." He glanced at Bear, who was looking back at him, and the joy in his voice trailed off. "How old is your Bear?"

Sloane thought for a minute. "She's been with us from the time I was in high school. Sixteen, seventeen years old." She glanced at Bear. "Jane gave her to me about seven years ago when I moved in here. She thought I needed company." She watched Bear curl her tail around her body and turned back to Harold. "Listen, you've piqued my curiosity, and lucky for you,

I need a distraction. So I'm all yours. How can my services be of help?"

"Well the truth is…" Bending over the chair's arm, he retrieved his briefcase, placed it on the desk, and flipped the locks open. "I'm not here for your private investigative services." He inched open the leather top. "I'm sorry to say, my business with you is personal."

Sloane leaned forward and slipped her hand under the desk, watching every movement he made. "Tell me you're kidding. Because I swear to God, Harold, I'll throw you out if you're here to sell me something."

"No, no. I'm not peddling." He turned his briefcase around. It was full of files. "I'm sorry for my secrecy. But I feared you might refuse to meet with me if you knew the true nature of my visit."

"So you're here under false pretenses." She let go of the Beretta on the underside of her desk and pulled her hand back.

"I apologize for being vague. Please allow me to explain. What I have to say will be difficult for you. And I wanted you to hear it in person."

"Vague? Is that what Canadians call lying?" She sat back, hard. "It's your money, boss. So go ahead and tell me. But you're still paying my consulting fee."

"Of course, I understand your time is valuable." With a trembling hand, Harold removed a manila folder. "I am the executor for the late Nathaniel and Mary West. Do you know who they are?" He searched her face.

"Never heard of them."

"That's what I feared." He opened the file and handed her a piece of paper. "Nathaniel and Mary West were from Denwick, a small town on Vancouver Island, British Columbia. They left their personal estate in a trust to their only child. That is Jane West's birth certificate, their daughter."

"Jane West?"

"Yes, your mother."

Sloane read the document and tossed it back. "Same name. But we both know that doesn't mean anything. I can't imagine you traveled all this way on that assumption. What else do you have?"

There was an urgency in her voice she could not hide. Jane had died a month earlier, and she discovered her mother had lied about many things. Jane's life had become a mystery to her. Full of secrets. And Sloane's sleuthing had hit a dead end. Harold removed a stack of envelopes from his briefcase and slid them across the desk. "I have these."

Sloane stared at the stack. Her heart pounded, and she grabbed a letter off the top. The address was written in Jane's hand, her distinctive cursive loops. She opened the letter and read.

"I am deeply heartbroken about your mother's death," Harold said. "I'm here to share my condolences. But I'm also obligated to tell you the West estate, therefore, goes to you."

Sloane looked up, silent. "Where did you find these?" she asked, pushing the letters back to him.

"In your grandparents' effects. What I don't understand…" He coughed. "…is why your mother never once mentioned you to Natty and Mary. Or at least, I believe so, as they never told me about you."

Sloane downed the rest of her tea. "Yeah? Jane never told me about her parents, either. Who knows why? She lied about a lot of things."

Harold picked up his cup and leaned forward. "On second thought, I will take a shot of your whiskey."

She poured him a generous amount, and he tossed it back. "Seems you're more upset to tell me about my long-lost family than I am to hear about them."

His shoulders rounded. "Natty and Mary were my closest friends. I was at the hospital when your mother was born. Held her in my arms right after your grandfather did. She was the daughter I never had."

"Divorced?"

"Oh, no, no. Never married."

Sloane's brow arched. "I see. So Jane grew up in Canada?"

"Yes. On the Island. Left us when she was eighteen. If your grandparents knew why she did so, they never told me." He tapped one of Jane's letters. "This PO box is the only thing about your mother I could find." He sat back and sighed. "I can't imagine why she hid both of you from us."

Sloane poured a shot into her empty cup and drank it in one swallow.

The sun was setting, and its amber light squeezed through the row houses, throwing striped shadows over the hardwood floor. Her mind raced. All the lies. All the questions she had. It was time for some damn answers. "What makes you think Jane hid us? Her parents had a PO box address. Why the hell didn't they find us?"

Harold wiped his watery eyes with a handkerchief and stuffed it back in his pocket. "You have every right to be angry. But your grandparents told me they did attempt to find your mother. They hired private investigators. But always without success. I don't know why." He spread his aged hands over his knees. "Then we lost Natty and Mary this past January. I was packing up their office not long after and found Jane's letters with the PO box. So I wrote to your mother right away. I waited for a few weeks but didn't hear back. That's when I searched for her online. And after all those years of trying, I found her obituary on my first search. Your name was given as her only relative."

"Just like that, huh?"

Harold nodded, pulled out his handkerchief, and rubbed his nose. "Yes. Just like magic."

Sloane arched an eyebrow slightly. "How did Jane's parents die?"

"They were killed in a terrible car accident on Highway One. Single-vehicle crash. Their taxi driver lost control, leaving the road." He paused. "All three died at the scene."

"Jesus. And a month later Jane dies in a car accident." She shook her head.

"My God. What happened?"

"She drove her MG once or twice a month. Just to get away from the city for a few days. I don't know where she was headed, but she didn't get far. A sanitation truck T-boned her before she got past 78th Street. He lived. She died."

"I'm so sorry. This must be terribly difficult for you." He removed a framed photo from his briefcase and handed it to her. "This is your family. Your mother and your grandparents. I suspect you've never seen a picture of your mother so young. Your hair is just like hers. You could have been twins."

The photo was taken at some sort of party in a backyard. Jane had her father's eyes, round and dark, and her mother's long black hair. Sloane recognized herself in all three. Except no one had her ice-gray eyes. She picked up a photo from the window seat.

Bear meowed and stood on all fours, arching her back in a stretch.

Sloane handed the picture to Harold. "This is how Jane wore her hair, during my entire life, dyed blond in a chin-length blunt cut. I always thought my dark hair came from my father. Assuming was *my* first mistake, huh?"

Harold studied the photo. It was wintertime. Jane and Sloane stood in front of a lit-up Christmas tree. "Sometimes assumptions are all we're allowed." His trembling hand placed the photo next to the other.

"Only if we give up on the truth." She looked at the older photo again. "When was this taken?"

He closed his eyes, his index finger tapping through memories. Then his eyes opened. "It was Jane's going-away party. She was two years behind my nephew Charlie, so it was the summer of 1988. They were very close." Harold spooned the teabag into his cup, and Sloane handed him the kettle. "She was coming here for a holiday before university."

"In 1988? Are you sure?"

"I have no doubt. Your mother was supposed to attend McGill in Montreal that fall. She was a brilliant girl. She could understand people with a kind of wisdom beyond her age. We were all so proud of her." Harold looked away, his gaze landing on Bear.

Sloane scooted back in her chair. "While I can appreciate your need to find me, I'm afraid you've wasted your time. I didn't know the Wests. And I'm not interested in their estate."

"You are under no pressure to decide today. The West estate is your birthright. At least allow yourself some time to think about it. There's no hurry."

Sloane rinsed out her mug and poured another whiskey neat. "Look around, Harold. This stuff isn't mine. Jane left me everything. The paintings, the furniture, all of it."

"Then her trust passes to you, too."

"My apartment is tiny. I don't want their things as well. I owned a sofa and a bed before she died. I keep it all for Bear. I think she likes having Jane's things around."

Harold stared at Bear, his brows drawing together. "Your cat is lucky to have such a lovely home."

Sloane leaned against the half wall. "Listen, you seem like an upstanding guy. And I can tell your heart is in the right place. So, I want to help you finish your work. Who's the contingent beneficiary?"

He hesitated. "Your grandparents did not provide one, except for the property they hold in common with others in Denwick. It is complicated. But in simplest terms, after you, the land and building in which they have their business passes next to your grandparents' three closest friends."

"Then I'd be honored to sign over the entire estate to them."

"Of course, you can, but I know they would rather you accept your legacy."

"Seems I only have one of those friend's word for that, Harold."

He tapped his nose with a crooked finger. "Cleverness is a family trait. You're right. I am one of the three, but I assure you that the others agree with me. Knowing you are here, alive, has helped our grieving. Knowing the West family lives on in you." The affection in his voice lingered, and he picked up the photo of Jane and her parents. "But if your final decision is no, I'll draw up the paperwork. I must ask, though, would you consider doing an old man one favor?"

"Am I about to hear your superior rhetorical skills? Because they've been pretty good so far."

He chuckled. "No, no. I have only an honest plea. Come to Denwick, sign the papers and stay for a weekend. I will show you all the places your family loved. The cottage where your mother grew up. Old Main Street, where your grandparents ran a gallery and I have my law office." His voice was full of nostalgia. "And there is one estate item I insist you accept." He pointed to the three paintings on Sloane's wall. "Your mother got her love of Impressionist art from her parents. To nurture her enthusiasm, Natty and Mary bought her an original Degas for her sixteenth birthday. Natty said it was an investment for her future. And, oh my, sweet Jane could enthrall you with her interpretation of that painting." He smiled at the fleeting memory. "It hung above their mantle. But now it's in my office safe."

"Jesus. An original?"

"Yes. It was her prized possession."

"Makes me wonder why she left it in Denwick then." Sloane looked at the reproductions Jane had hung in their home. What else had she left behind? She tapped the heel of her shoe against the wall. "All right, Harold. How's the weather on the Island right now? I'm due a few days off. But only if you promise to be my chaperone."

Harold patted his knees. "Wonderful. I would be honored to escort you around our humble village. When would you—"

Someone tapped on the door.

"Hold that thought."

The knocking grew louder.

Bear hissed and leaped on top of the bookcases, the pupils in her fluorescent yellow-green eyes shrinking into slits.

Sloane set her mug down and pushed off the half-wall. "Give me a damn second, Prence. You're scaring Bear." She unlocked the bolt and was about to slide the chain when a voice in her head shouted.

*Move!*

Before she could step away, someone kicked the door, breaking it off its hinges. The force slammed her against the wall, and the door struck her face. Her nose cracked. Everything went black for a split second. Then an intense heat surged through her body as she filled with rage.

A man rushed inside, gun first, and a shot pierced the air.

Sloane lunged at him as a dark shadow flashed over her.

The man turned the gun on her. She grabbed his shoulder and wrist, driving his arm into her thrusting knee. The bones in his elbow cracked and snapped upward. The gun hit the floor, and Sloane kicked it into the living room.

The assailant clutched her throat with his good hand, shoving her against the wall and lifting her off the floor. He snarled, low and menacing.

Hot breath hit Sloane's face as his mouth drew closer. She pushed against the wall with her feet, scratched at his eyes with one hand, and jabbed her fist into his throat with the other. He dropped her and stumbled back. Sloane quickly landed a kick to his abdomen, sending him crashing into the bookcase across the room, where he crumpled to the floor.

She bent over, coughing and catching her breath as the man leaped to his feet and ran for his gun. Surprise slowed her reaction, but she raced him to the firearm. Before he could pick it up, she jumped, striking the side of his knee with a front kick.

The shooter gave a guttural cry.

Sloane landed a roundhouse kick to his head. He fell at her feet, silent, motionless, his arm and leg bending unnaturally.

Bear appeared at her side and sniffed the stranger.

"Harold!" she shouted and ran to the old man.

# CHAPTER TWO

Harold Huxham's body slumped over the chair's arm.

"No…no, no, no."

The single gunshot had struck the center of his forehead. A clean entry. An assassin's kill. The fatal damage was only visible in the back of his skull, where the bullet left a ragged, gaping hole.

"I'm sorry. I'm so, so sorry." Sloane's eyes teared. She turned to the shooter. He still hadn't moved. His face was pointed in her direction, and she studied it but had no idea who he was.

What the hell was going on? Sloane fell to her knees, replaying the fight in her mind, perhaps the most terrifying of her life, worse than any scrapes she'd got into as a cop.

Bear leaped on the desk and meowed.

"Yeah. I agree. This is messed up." Her hands were covered in blood. She wiped it on her jeans and got to her feet. Her phone was on the clean side of the desk, sparing it from the blood spray and brain tissue that covered the other side and the wall behind.

After calling 911, she knelt next to the shooter. She had avoided using a rabbit punch and expected to feel a pulse. But the force of her final kick had done the same damage. He was dead.

"Holy shit, what happened?" a startled voice came from the hallway.

She turned. "Damnit, Prence, don't skulk around my door."

"I ain't skulking." Gary shifted from one foot to another. He had an unlit cigarette dangling off his bottom lip and a grocery bag in each arm. His eyes were fixed on the shooter's body. Then he looked at the bloody mess behind the armchair. "Oh, man. Is that the old guy in the chair?"

Anger flooded Sloane's body. She jumped up with clenched fists. "Yeah. His name's Harold Huxham." She got in Gary's face. "Did you let the other guy in, too?"

"Nah, I swear. I never seen him before, Slo. Jimmy took me to the bodega on 120th right after I let the old guy in. I even got you that cheese you like. But it's ahight. I'll give it to you later." He shifted the bags, and his voice lowered. "I guess the guy was in trouble, huh?"

"He wasn't here about a case."

"That one must've had it out for him, anyways, right? Nobody's gonna break into your apartment." Gary tilted his head to one side, staring at the shooter. "He's really messed up. I thought you weren't supposed to go all hocus-pocus in fights no more. You really screwed the pooch, huh?"

"Jesus Christ, Prence. He killed Harold and tried to kill me. I had to defend myself."

"Okay. Okay. I just don't wanna see you get into no more trouble."

Sirens shrilled and wailed as they drew closer.

"You better get out of here."

Gary backed up. "Ahight. I'm goin'. But your face. Do you need a washcloth or something? Some ice?"

"No. I'm fine. Leave. Now."

"I'll be upstairs if you need me."

"Yeah, sure. Go."

The stranger in her living room wasn't the first person she had killed or the only time she had heard a voice in her head. The last time she was NYPD. It had happened during a drug-house raid. She had heard a warning voice and took cover, but her senior officer hadn't. Watching her get shot filled her with an anger so overpowering, she ran down the shooter a mile away from the scene and broke his neck with her bare hands. Their supervisor placed her on administrative leave. After FID cleared her to return to duty, she couldn't. She knew it would only be a matter of time before rage consumed her and she killed someone again.

Sloane took a picture of the dead man's face with her phone and rifled through his pants pockets. No ID. Nothing. She searched the inside pockets of his black jacket and pulled out two one-inch headshots. One of Harold and one of her. They'd been targeted.

She looked at the back of the photos. Harold's was blank. Her address was written on the back of hers. She flipped them over again, and with a flash of green light they disintegrated in her hands. "What the hell?"

She got to her feet and backed away.

The sirens outside grew louder.

The assassin was a professional, armed with a weapon and pictures of his marks. No money. No identification. But who hired him? Possible suspects ran through her mind. Perps she had brought to justice? Members of gangs? No. It couldn't be. He had shot Harold first.

The police siren was right outside. She moved to the window. A patrol car drew to a sudden halt, and two beat cops got out. The shorter officer aimed the car's floodlight at the front of the row house, even though it was still dusk. She turned from the harsh light and walked to the front door.

The taller cop barged inside, gun drawn. "Hands where I can see them. On the ground!"

Sloane knew the drill. She clasped her hands behind her head and kneeled on the floor. Then she lay on her stomach with arms spread eagle.

"Is anyone else in the house?" he asked.

"No."

"All clear," the shorter officer called from the back of her apartment.

She stayed completely still and spoke. "I'm Sloane West. This is my apartment. I called in the shooting."

The taller cop withdrew his revolver, and the shorter one returned and shoved a pair of shoe covers into his partner's chest before helping Sloane to her feet. "I'm Constable Bryant. He's Constable Gordon. What happened here?"

"The deceased in the chair is Harold Huxham. He arrived today from BC to meet with me. The deceased on the floor broke in and shot Harold. Then he turned the gun on me."

Gordon struggled with the shoe covers, hopping on one leg at a time. He walked over to Harold, examined his body, and flipped open a notepad. "Why was Mr. Huxham here to meet you?"

"He made an appointment with me last week. I'm a PI. My license is in the desk. Top right drawer." She nodded at the shooter. "He broke through the door about half an hour into our meeting."

Bryant returned and handed Sloane a damp dishrag full of ice. "Do you recognize the shooter?"

"I've never seen him before." She wiped the salty taste of blood from her mouth, chin and neck and put the cold pack on her nose.

Gordon examined the man's twisted limbs. "What happened to him?"

"He turned the gun on me, and I disarmed him. In self-defense."

He smirked. "You did this?"

Sloane stood eye-to-eye with Gordon. "Yeah. Mr. Huxham and I were alone."

"Maybe you forgot he brought someone with him? Or your boyfriend was here?"

His voice was accusatory, and she glared at him, stepping closer and daring him to double down. "I said we were alone."

Bryant moved between them and walked Sloane a few paces back while two more patrol cars arrived, sirens screaming.

"Homicide's gonna have more questions for you," Gordon said, stepping around Bryant.

Sloane met him straight on. "Yeah, I know."

Bryant pulled her back and led her to the front door. "Thank you for your cooperation, Ms. West. I need you to wait outside now. Do you want to call someone to sit with you?"

"No. I don't need anyone." She nodded. "Thanks for the ice."

Sloane walked down the narrow hallway toward the row house's front door. There was a split staircase off the entry. It led up to Gary's place and down to an unoccupied basement apartment. She sat on the up treads and picked at the beige patterned carpet, the worse for wear.

Across the street, neighbors milled about, trying to figure out what was happening inside 194b East 140th Street. She expected the audience. Everybody loved drama.

A door creaked above her, and she smelled Gary's cigarette before hearing his footsteps. "How you doin', Slo?" he asked with a hushed voice. "You want more ice for your face?" He wore evening loungewear, a silk set straight out of *The Godfather*. His cigarette smoke curled up and over his bald head.

"I'm fine, Prence."

"Okay, okay. But I was thinking the cops are gonna be at your place all night, right? So you need to crash on my couch tonight or what?"

"I figured you were making Jimmy dinner tonight?"

"Nah, I'm stayin' at his place tomorrow."

"Yeah, thanks. That helps. We'll come up after I talk to Homicide."

"Uh, okay. But do you gotta bring the cat? It gives me the creeps."

Sloane cocked her head. "Are you kidding me right now?"

"Ahight, ahight. But bring one of your bottles then. A fancy one. It'll mellow me out." He winked and hurried back up the stairs.

A voice boomed inside Sloane's apartment. She turned and stuck her head between two paint-chipped spindles in the banister. "Why haven't you secured the area?" the man yelled. "How the hell did you get through training? Get out there and set up a perimeter. Front and back. There's no telling what evidence we've lost."

Sloane recognized the voice—Borough Chief Detective Jacobson. She knew him well. When she was on the force, he was her supervisor. And he had been one of Jane's oldest friends. He was a real throwback, a *Law and Order* type, intelligent, intuitive, and all his moves a clichéd performance.

Constables Bryant and Gordon sulked past her. She wiggled her head free and watched them in the harsh spotlight as they taped off the front door. It was a shame Bryant was stuck with an ass of a partner.

A darkened silhouette approached them and ducked under the caution tape.

Sloane groaned. "Jesus Christ. Why are you here?"

"Seriously, West? I hear a 10-10 at your address. I'm going to come. Thank God you're okay." Thomas Hanson sat next to her. His cheeks were flushed, and he reached toward her face. "Let me see your nose?"

She batted away his hand. "There's nothing wrong with it. I don't want you here, Tom. If you need to, go talk to Jacobson. He's inside. Otherwise, leave."

Tom rubbed his hands on his thighs. "C'mon. How long are you going to punish me? At least talk to me. To us."

"Punish? Please. I'm not talking about it. Not now. Not ever." Her voice was steady, but her hands shook, clenched into fists. To her relief, heavy footsteps stomped down the hallway, and Chief Detective Jacobson rounded the staircase.

"Hey, you okay?" he asked her.

She glared at Tom. "I've been better."

"Yeah. I guess so. It's a mess in there." Jacobson leaned on the banister. It groaned and bowed under the bulk of his muscular body. "It was easy to tell which one you killed."

"Bad form, sir."

"Who asked you, Hanson? She knows I'm messing with her."

"Yeah. Hiding my amusement deep down with all my other buried emotions."

He chuckled, then turned to Tom. "Why are you sitting here anyway? We need to identify the shooter and get contact numbers for Mr. Huxham's family. And notify the Canadian Consulate. We're gonna have a shitload of red tape." He pointed to the door. "Go on. Get outta here."

"Yes, sir." Tom turned to Sloane. "Don't be a stranger. You can call Jess or me anytime. I know she would like to hear from you, too. And we aren't going anywhere. So when you're ready to talk, let us know."

As soon as he disappeared into the light, Sloane released an exasperated breath, saying, "Give me a fucking break."

Jacobson shifted his weight. "You sure you're okay? Do you want a medic to take a look at your nose?"

Sloane leaned back against the stairs. "No. I'm fine, thanks, Jac."

"Oh, sure. Now I'm worried. Your mother told me what fine means. Fucking Insecure Neurotic and Emotional."

Sloane laughed sardonically and stared at the worn carpet.

"All right. No medic. Just tell me what happened."

"I don't know. I'm still trying to make sense of it." She looked up. "The victim's name is Harold Huxham. We had an appointment today."

"Did you know him?"

"Never seen him before. He's from Vancouver Island. A lawyer. But he didn't come to see me for my detective work. He knew Jane and her parents. Seems Jane was born and raised there, in a village called Denwick."

"In Canada? Your mother said she'd never traveled out of the country."

"Yeah, well, she lied. He had letters she wrote to her parents and a family photo to prove it. They're all inside my place. Jane lied, Jac. I doubt she ever told us the truth about anything, ever." She felt terrible for the callous way she was sullying Jane's memory, but it was obvious they never really knew the woman.

He looked down and planted a foot on the first step, his shoulders slouched.

Sloane knew he had loved Jane and still grieved her death. He had been in her life for twenty years since the first time the FBI asked her to profile an unknown subject. He had been in the front row next to Sloane at Jane's memorial.

Jacobson rubbed his foot back and forth on a blackened spot of chewing gum. "I suppose Jane had her reasons." He straightened. "What did Mr. Huxham want?"

"He traveled all that way to tell me her parents left her a trust, and I guess it's mine now."

"And when did the shooter arrive?"

"About twenty-five minutes after Harold."

"Did you hear or see a car?"

"No. He banged on the door out of the blue. I don't even know how he got past our security door. And as soon as I turned the lock, he busted in. The door hit me and dazed me a little. I heard him shoot once before I got my bearings. Then he turned the gun on me." She hesitated. "I tried not to use lethal force."

Jacobson leaned into the hallway and glanced down the hall. "Do you recognize him?"

"No. But clearly he's no beginner. And he's not from around here. No one in my neighborhood wears bespoke tracksuits."

Jacobson raised his chin, making eye contact with her again. "I agree. That was one helluva shot. What about your investigations? You got any enemies out there?"

She again thought about her past cases, everything from missing persons, wrongful deaths, and organized crime to insurance fraud. "Maybe, but no one willing to pay for a shooter with a custom Nighthawk."

"Yeah. It's a beauty." Jacobson straightened. "Did Mr. Huxham mention anyone angry about him coming to see you?"

"No." She lowered her voice. "Listen, Jac. I know someone hired the shooter to kill Harold *and* me."

Jacobson's brow furrowed. "What makes you say that?"

The Chief Detective was a friend but had clear boundaries around investigations with her since she left his squad. And she had crossed one. So she measured her words. "Okay. This is going to piss you off. I checked the shooter's pockets before Gordon and Bryant arrived."

"Jesus, West. You're killing me."

"I know, Jac. But he had just killed Harold and had tried to kill me. All I could think about was why."

Jacobson looked away.

"There's more. I found one-inch photos of Harold and me inside his jacket." She waited for a stronger reaction, but he stared straight ahead, listening. "You're going to think what I'm about to say is ridiculous but hear me out. As soon as I had the pictures in my hand, they just disintegrated."

He shook his head and looked at her as though the door had done more than bloody her nose. "What're you saying?"

"I saw it happen. And you know I don't lie. He had our pictures. I've been sitting here thinking about it, and the only thing linking Harold and me is my inheritance. Only someone in Denwick would know about it, Jac. That's where we'll find who hired him."

She expected him to blow off her hunch, especially since the disappearing photo evidence seemed so implausible. But he patted the banister with his hand a few times and seemed to consider the connection. "All right. But let us find out who this guy is before you start anything." He pulled his foot off the first step. "Do you have somewhere to spend the night?"

"Yeah, with a neighbor."

"If you think of something else, call me. Otherwise, get some sleep. I'll call you tomorrow. And don't go off trying to track down the shooter's identity. Leave that to us."

# CHAPTER THREE

There were no tables at Stella's, only a long narrow bar. Sloane sat on a black plastic-covered barstool, tossed Jane's keychain next to her, and rubbed her shoulders. Gary's sofa had seen better days. Every few minutes, she glanced up at the other regulars' reflections in a grimy mirror. They were a stoic crowd, eating their lunch while they drank a noontime nip, never maudlin or offering more than a head nod as a greeting or farewell.

"Your usual?" a voice seasoned with tobacco and age asked. It was Mel, Stella's granddaughter and current proprietor. She was an old-school barkeep with a perpetual tan and flaxen hair out of a bottle cut close on the sides and spiked on top. Sloane came to Stella's for Mel's low-key personality and her discretion. She placed a setup and glass of water in front of Sloane.

"Yeah. Thanks." Sloane had returned from an early trip to Manhattan, where she had tracked down Jane's PO box at an upscale mail shop off Fifth Avenue. And the only thing she could think was why weren't the Wests' investigators able to find them? Stake out the mail shop. Find Jane. It made no sense.

Unless Harold had lied. But he hadn't. She could read a person's tell. Well, everyone's except for Jane's.

She rubbed her thumb over a pendant attached to Jane's keyring, a silver Tree of Life with intricately carved roots, limbs, and leaves. Two branches held a transparent bead with a five-sided star at its center. A pentagram. She had admired it since she was little, but Jane never let her play with it.

"Here you go, doll. One hot pastrami with fries." Mel set down a plate and leaned against the bar. "I heard what happened yesterday. Lunch is on the house."

"You don't have to do that, Mel."

"I know. But I'm going to." She winked. "Let me know how I can help."

Sloane kept her head down, ate her lunch, and replayed the events of Harold's murder in her head. Their meeting. Who knew about it? His nephew. What the hell was his name? Charlie. That's right. What did he know? Did he benefit from their deaths?

She smeared her fries in a ramekin of ketchup and thought about the shooter. Who was he? How'd he get in the building? And how the hell did he shake off her first kick?

She thought about Harold. He had seemed genuinely kind and to have cared about the Wests a great deal. Enough to get her to come to Denwick. He knew about Jane's past. Hell, all she had were some old journals she found when cleaning out Jane's apartment. She read the leather books from cover to cover. She had hoped they would hold a history of Jane's past. Clues. But instead, they were records of every patient Jane had in her psychology practice and all the criminals she had profiled for the FBI. The only entries about Sloane were instances Jane had had to calm her. Jane called it her escalating anger.

"You done here?" Mel asked, bringing Sloane back.

She pushed her plate away. "Yeah."

Mel turned, grabbed a whiskey bottle off a shelf behind her, poured a double, and slid the tumbler across the bar. Then she picked up the empty plate.

"You got a second, Mel?" Sloane asked.

"Anything for you, doll."

"I took a photo of the shooter." She pulled up the man's picture on her phone. "Have you ever seen him before?"

Mel squinted at the screen. "No. Never seen him."

"Could you ask around?"

"Text me the picture." She rapped the bar with her knuckles. "Oh yeah, the missus says you need to come to dinner again. You know she likes to have the young ones around." She laughed a throaty laugh.

Mel was Sloane's best and most trustworthy informant. She had ears and eyes spread out across the five boroughs. So if she didn't recognize the shooter or know someone who did, he wasn't local. Her phone rang. No phone conversations at the bar. House rules. She gulped her whiskey, laid a twenty for a tip, and gave Mel a nod goodbye.

Outside she answered, "West speaking."

"Hey. It's Jac. The CSIs are done at your place. You know they don't clean up, right?"

"Yeah, I know."

"We got contacts for bioremediations. I can put in a call for you."

"No thanks. I'll take care of it." The afternoon sun glared off the concrete, and she dug through her tote for her sunglasses. "Have you identified the shooter?"

"Nothing yet."

"No fingerprints? DNA?"

"The ME's backed up, but they're working on it. And before you ask, we're jammed up with the Canadian consulate and Mr. Huxham's next of kin."

"Any leads?"

His voice rose. "You know I'm not gonna tell you that."

"Are you at least looking at the Wests' will and the beneficiaries in Denwick?"

"We don't even know who the shooter is." His voice calmed. "You know we gotta rule out local before involving the Canadian authorities."

"You're wasting time, Jac."

"And you might hold more sway if you were back on my team. But right now, I need you to stay out of it. Remember, he tried to kill you, too."

"C'mon, Jac."

"I mean it, West. You need to be careful until we know you're safe. I'll call you when I know something."

Sloane rounded the corner and walked the two blocks home.

Gary and a couple of his associates stood on the stoop. When she approached, they stopped talking. "The cops are gone," Gary said. "I took the tape down and tossed the cat back inside. But your front door ain't shutting." He flicked a cigarette butt onto the sidewalk. "I got a guy coming to fix it tomorrow, ahight?"

"Yeah. Thanks. And thanks again for last night. You're a regular Martha Stewart. The extra quilt was the perfect touch. And Bear loved her satin pillow."

The other guys fell about laughing. Gary threw up his arms. "What's so funny? I'm a good host." He followed Sloane up the stairs. "You felt at home, right?"

"Yeah, Prence. First class. The homemade crumpets with our tea were"—she kissed the tips of her fingers—"delicious." She could still hear the guys howling in laughter as she walked down her hall.

The apartment smelled like homicide—a mixture of body fluids and forensic chemicals. She opened the bay window. Bear appeared at her feet, leaped onto the window seat, and meowed.

"Don't worry about any of this. I'm cleaning up right now." She scratched Bear's chin until she purred and curled up in the afternoon sun.

Sloane laid Jane's mail from her secret PO box on a side table next to the sofa. She stared at her mother's armchair, soaked with Harold's blood. Her face flushed hot as she kicked the chair on its side and shoved it into the hallway. Then she slammed her front door shut, but it swung open, hanging askew on broken hinges. She kicked it repeatedly until it jammed into its frame, shutting out the chair, blocking out the murder. Sliding to the floor with her back against the wall, she buried her head in her knees.

The bastard killed an innocent man. A kind, thoughtful man. For what? And Jacobson was wrong. Harold was not an unfortunate victim caught in the crosshairs of some vendetta against her. But he was right about one thing. She was in danger. Because whoever hired the shooter only got half of what they paid for.

Over the next four hours, Sloane cleaned her apartment with a stack of torn-up T-shirts and a bucket of diluted bleach. Harold's blood had splattered as far as the kitchen and as high as the ceiling, and a film of fine black dust left by forensics covered every surface from the front door to her desk.

After removing all traces of the crime scene, Sloane took a hot shower and wrapped up in a thick cotton robe. She opened a diet soda and sat on the velvet sofa. The setting sun illuminated the reproduction of Morisot's *The Garden at Bougival*. Its effulgence emphasized the delicate brushstrokes that made the painting dance. Sloane was a child the first time she noticed the movement. She had brought a science project home and needed her parents' eyes and hair color.

Jane said, "We'll have to make something up for your father's features."

Sloane cried, "I don't want to lie. If I don't tell the truth, my experiment won't be valid."

Jane walked around her desk and held Sloane in a tight embrace, swaying them side to side in front of the Morisot as if they were two of the dancing flowers. "You aren't lying if you don't know. I could tell you something fantastical about witches, Demons, and other mythical beings or about a boring man from California. But instead, I'm telling you the truth. I simply can't say, pet. Someday, you'll understand. But not today."

Bear pawed at Sloane's leg, and she returned to the present.

"Hey. You hungry? Me, too. Let's have some dinner and go to bed. Tomorrow we identify the shooter."

# CHAPTER FOUR

Three days after Harold Huxham's murder, Borough Chief Detective Peter Jacobson left a message on Sloane's phone to meet him at the 78th Precinct at two p.m. She had failed to get a lead on the shooter's identity and had just called in a favor to her contacts on Jacobson's team. Jac had either figured out the shooter's name or discovered Mike Garcia and Katie Chen had side gigs, slipping her information.

She walked the six blocks to the station, a three-story brick building with solid wood doors, arched windows, and an antiseptic interior of linoleum floors and white tiled walls. Behind the front desk, officers and plainclothes detectives scuttled in and out of doors and stopped at the watch lieutenant's desk. A Dutch door separated them from the offices.

At two p.m. sharp, Jacobson appeared. "Hey, West. Let's go." She followed him to the end of a sterile corridor into an interview room. "Have a seat." He dropped a manila folder on the table. "We got the shooter's name and possible motive." He sat, opened the file, and slid it in front of her.

"Liam Morris. He lived in Manhattan. Ran a security consulting business. No priors."

Sloane continued to read. "Security business? And you failed to get a hit on his prints?" She looked up. "C'mon, Jac."

"Yeah, well, the first attempt had a glitch or something. But the ME reran AFIS yesterday and got a hit right away."

Sloane pinched her brows together. "Glitches?"

"It happens." Jacobson motioned for her to turn the page. "We have Morris on CCTV thirty minutes after Mr. Huxham arrived at JFK. He hired a taxi. It dropped him off at 140th and St. Theresa's."

"Stella's?"

"That's right." Jacobson leaned forward, resting his arms on the table. "We searched his apartment. Turn the page." He waited. "We found that." He sat back and crossed his arms while Sloane read the rest of the file.

Sloane's jaw clenched. A dossier on her. He had no visible employer. It didn't make sense. She tossed the file at Jacobson. "Let me guess, the file on me was just sitting out in the open."

Jacobson shifted in his chair. "Evidence pictures show it on his desk."

"Morris was a professional. He would have hidden that."

Jacobson shrugged.

She threw her hands in the air. "C'mon, Jac. He had photos of me and Harold. I swear. Have I ever lied to you?"

"No." He held her eyes. "I know you think you saw two photos. But maybe the shock of the attack affected what you think you saw."

"Whatever. Since when do you think I wilt under pressure?"

"I know. I know." He slapped his hand on the table. Listen, I'll consider the Canadian angle if you can get me something concrete."

Sloane pushed back in her chair and stood. "Fine. I will."

"Oh, yeah. Another thing. We got a hold of Mr. Huxham's family. His nephew arrived this morning. Hanson's taking him to the morgue this afternoon."

"Nephew?"

"That's what Hanson said. Mr. Huxham's only family is one nephew, Charles Huxham." Jacobson got to his feet. "That's all we got. I knew you wouldn't like it."

"Did you come to that conclusion all on your own?"

"Ouch." He opened the door and closed it again. "One more thing. The ME ruled Morris's COD as blunt-force trauma. Your statement stands. Self-defense. But you have to stop walloping people." He put an arm around her shoulder. "I could use you on my team again. Not that I condone kicking someone's ass, but I wouldn't worry about you taking care of yourself, right? You could be back in plain clothes in less than a year."

"Give it a rest, Jac." She tapped the file in his hand. "I couldn't work under these conditions."

She left the interview room and stopped in the corridor. Tom Hanson was at the end of the hall, standing at the Dutch door. Until three days ago, she hadn't seen him for over a year since he and Jess confessed undying love and her life had fallen apart.

Tom opened the bottom section, and a man and woman entered the office area. Sloane hurried toward them. Tom might put them in an interview room before Charles Huxham could see her. Even brief interactions revealed a lot.

The three approached. The man was Charles Huxham. No doubt. His eyes and build were similar to Harold's. He had dark-brown hair, graying at the temples and looked to be in his early fifties. When his eyes met Sloane's, he quickly averted them.

The woman with Charles had her arm around his, dabbing her eyes with a tissue held in her free hand. She was thin, almost gaunt, with graying, brown hair, a sharp pointed nose, and a smile too big for her sunken face. When she looked up and saw Sloane, she looked shocked and reached out as if to get Sloane's attention.

But the man grabbed her hand and nudged her along. Were they married? Neither wore rings. But she sensed they had been close for a long time. And they must have both known Jane. Why else had the sight of her daughter nearly stopped them in their tracks? Sloane watched the couple disappear into an interview room. Tom stared back at her with an injured look, and she turned away.

As she walked back home, she considered the couple's reactions. Was it seeing her, Jane's look-alike, a friend they had lost so many years before? Was it because she was supposed to be dead? Were they disappointed? Guilty? Whatever it was, they had both earned a spot on her suspect list.

Inside her apartment, the smell of crime had gone, but death lingered. She lit sage and lavender incense sticks and opened the bay window. Bear brushed back and forth against her legs and meowed. "Are you hungry?" Sloane picked her up. "Me, too. How about an early dinner?" She placed her on the kitchen counter.

Bear paced, watching Sloane.

"Give me a second. Gourmet food takes time."

The cat meowed.

Sloane chuckled. "Don't mock me, or you're only getting dry kibble." She took out half a takeout burger from the fridge and stuck it in a microwave, the most sophisticated appliance in her kitchen. Not that she cared. The best bodegas and takeout restaurants in the Bronx were within a ten-minute walk, and she had mapped out her favorites years ago.

Sloane fed warm pieces of the beef to Bear while she polished off cold fries with ketchup. Then she opened a can of tuna. "Don't say I never spoil you."

Bear stuck up her nose.

"Yeah. It's not fresh fish, your majesty."

Sloane poured herself a whiskey neat and left Bear to her dinner. At her desk, she picked up the photo Harold had brought. Blood spatters had soaked into the wooden frame. She undid the back, removed the photo, and threw the rest away.

A streetlamp sputtered to life. Its hum and soft glow reached into the living room. Sloane walked to the bay window, lowered its blinds, and sank into the sofa. She propped the photo against a lamp on the side table and grabbed Jane's mail.

Harold's letter was there like he said it would be. He had included two business cards, his and Charles's. They were the principals of Huxham Law.

As she read the letter, his deep, concerned voice sounded in her head. He asked Jane to return home and settle her parents' estate and to comfort someone named Dora. Finally, he expressed his love and admiration for Jane and her parents.

Sloane folded the letter and stuffed it back in its envelope. She stared at the Wests' blood-spattered will. What had Jane left behind? And why did Harold say the will was complicated? Reading through the legalese was frustrating, but eventually she understood that the Wests' art gallery was on land owned in common with three other Denwick families. Purchased originally from a holding decreed by a Royal Charter Grant to a Reginald Gildey in 1850. Bear leaped onto the sofa and climbed the back cushions, curling up next to Sloane's head. Her tail swished back and forth.

"Listen. I have to make a phone call. Then I need to run some stuff by you, so don't fall asleep," she said, folding up the will. She dialed Tom Hanson's number. It rang only once.

"Sloane?"

"Yeah, it's me. Listen, I need some information. Were you with Charles Huxham this afternoon?"

"When we passed you in the hall? Yeah, that was him."

"How did he act at the morgue?"

"He didn't seem too upset, but the woman with him had a hard time. Why do you want to know?"

"I'm not sure yet."

"What were you doing with the Chief?"

"I was following up on a hunch. Thanks for your help."

"Wait. Don't hang up. I've got more." He sounded desperate. "Charles Huxham was distracted the entire time I was with him. And I'm pretty sure it was because he saw you. He asked if it was you in the hall. If you were in any sort of trouble. But I didn't tell him anything."

Sloane let her head fall against the sofa and got Bear's tail in her face. She recalled Harold's voice. "She was two years behind my nephew Charlie. They were close."

"He knew Jane. I just reminded him of her. That's all. Did he want to know what happened in the apartment?"

"Every detail. He was pissed. Kept saying his uncle should've never come to New York."

"What about the woman?"

"She just cried the entire time. Never said a word."

"All right. Thanks for the information." She hung up before Tom could respond and settled into the sofa, twisting a white-gold ring on her finger. Tom had probably seen it. Likely already told Jess she was still wearing it. At least the band wasn't on her left hand any longer.

She scratched Bear's chin. "Time to wake up and brainstorm."

Bear lifted her head and mewed softly.

Now Tom was no longer in her life, she briefed her cases with Bear. They didn't sit in front of a case board late into the night. Or build a solid line of inquiry from each other's hunches. But it worked well.

"Huxham took this photo after Jane's graduation in June of eighty-eight. I was born in January. So that means Jane was pregnant when she came to New York. What does that mean for the case? I don't know yet. But personally, it probably means I've been searching for my father in the wrong country."

Sloane traced her finger over Jane's image. "Did her parents know she was pregnant? Did they drive her away? Did she run because she couldn't face them? Or did she run from the man who got her pregnant?"

Bear meowed, seeming more alert.

"Yeah. I agree. Why would she stay in contact with her parents if they drove her away? But why didn't she tell them about me? They left their money to her. Not the action of angry estranged parents." She put the photo against the lamp again. "I haven't found anything else about her life other than her journals. If Jane's parents had hidden their lives as much as she had, I doubt we'd find anything in Denwick either."

Bear slipped down next to her, meowing.

"Yeah, I know. Whoever hired Morris is there. And they're desperate enough to kill for the land—Harold's and mine. Which means they might not stop until the job is done. I wonder who else owns it."

Bear yowled.

"Whoa, big girl. No worries. Nothing is going to happen to me."

Sloane dialed the number on Charles's card.

"Hello."

"Charles Huxham?"

"Who's calling?"

"Hello, Mr. Huxham. Sloane West here. I wanted to extend my condolences—"

"Well, you saved me a call, Ms. West," he said, interrupting her. "We have unfinished business. I will need to finalize the paperwork he gave you."

His voice was angry. Was he masking his loss or guilt? "All right. Harold and I talked about my inheritance. But I haven't decided if I want their money."

He paused. "I'd appreciate a decision as soon as possible. Now I must file Harold's will for his beneficiaries." He scoffed. "With the Wests and your mother dead, you've come into quite a bit of money, haven't you?" His words stung like the accusation he meant them to be.

Adrenaline surged through Sloane. "You're in luck, Mr. Huxham. I just made up my mind. I'll accept my inheritance, and I'll sign the paperwork in Denwick."

Charles coughed for several minutes. "That's fine," he replied, finally catching his breath. "I'm returning in a few days. Let me know when you plan to arrive, and I'll have the paperwork ready." He abruptly ended their call.

Bear purred and slipped onto Sloane's lap, climbing up her chest. When Sloane opened her eyes, their noses touched. "All right. Pack a bag, Bear. We're going to Canada."

# CHAPTER FIVE

Sloane's taxi drew to a halt beside a stone fountain in the circular drive of a storybook house with a caramel-brown stone exterior, a green slate roof, and beehive chimneys on each end. Three stately windows on the main floor and four gabled ones on the second floor finished the façade.

"333 Mallow Avenue," the cabbie said. "Mallow Cottage."

The Wests' house stood among a handful of gnarled and knotted mature trees and flowerbeds undulating along the sides of a lush, green lawn. "This is not what I expected," Sloane whispered. She lifted Bear's carrier and alighted while the driver popped the trunk and removed her bags. The air was heavy with winter jasmine. Its blooming vines crawled over the entire left side of the cottage.

Something moved behind a rose hedge separating Mallow Cottage from the neighbor's hobbit-looking house, moss growing over its sloping roofline. Sloane peered into the dense foliage.

"May I put your luggage inside?"

She turned back to the driver and set the carrier down on the drive. "No, thanks. I've got it."

The cabbie reached out his hand. "My card for when you're ready to return to the airport. It would be my pleasure to take you."

She shoved his card into her back pocket. "I'll give you a call in a few days."

As the taxi pulled away, Sloane felt a vibration inside her body. She rubbed her arms. The start of a new job always excited her, but this was different, and so was this case. None of her past work involved an inheritance or finding lost family and a murderer in another country.

She bent down and peeked under the blanket covering the carrier. Bear was sleeping off the travel tranquilizer. She whispered to her anyway. "Questions lead to answers, Bear. So let's start asking."

The Wests' front door opened, and Sloane straightened. The woman who had been with Charles Huxham at the 78th Precinct walked out of the house, waving enthusiastically. She joined Sloane on the paved drive. "Hello, I'm Lore Reed. Charlie Huxham's friend. He's in a meeting and asked me to open the cottage for you. But he'll be here soon."

"Thanks. I'm Sloane West."

"I know, dear. I would recognize you anywhere. You look exactly like your mother. We were close friends growing up, like sisters, really. Tends to happen when you're the same age in a small town." She looked down at the carrier. "Who do you have there?"

Sloane pulled back a corner of the blanket. "This is Bear."

Lore peeked inside. "Well, well. Hello, Bear. I've never had cats, even though I adore them. But I'm allergic." She straightened and extended the handles on Sloane's luggage.

"You don't have to do that. I'll come back for those."

"After your long flight? Absolutely not. Let me help." Sloane picked up the cat carrier and followed her inside.

Lore led her through a living room and breakfast area. The familiarity of the place overwhelmed Sloane. It was a bigger version of her childhood home, with dark wood furniture,

Impressionist paintings randomly hung about the walls, and the heavy, enduring smell of the past. She held the carrier tighter to her chest and thought, why would Jane want to replicate what she ran from?

Lore passed down a hall and opened the only door on the right. "Here we go. I made this guest room up for you. There are two more on the second floor with the family bedrooms. But I thought you would be more comfortable down here."

Sloane placed the carrier on the bed. It sank inches into a plush duvet, and for a moment, she wished she could join Bear, who was still asleep. "This is great. Thanks."

"Wonderful. I hope you like it here. Your grandparents' cottage is lovely. I've been taking care of the plants since..." Lore's voice trailed off, and she turned away, putting Sloane's bags in the closet.

"That's kind of you."

Lore turned back and gave her a faint smile. "If you don't mind, I'd like to get something off my chest." She clasped her hands. "I apologize for not saying hello in New York. It was a hectic day. Charlie was in a state, and I was devastated and nervous. I'd never been there before, and I nearly fainted when I saw you."

"Don't worry about it."

"I've been reminiscing about sweet Jane ever since. I would never forgive myself if she knew I didn't introduce myself to her daughter." She bit her lip and straightened a throw pillow in a navy-blue recliner. "I asked Charlie what he thought when he saw you, but he said he didn't recognize you. Which was ridiculous. You really could be your mother."

"Yeah. That's what I've heard." Sloane put her toiletry bag in the en suite.

Lore managed another smile. "You must be exhausted. Come with me to the kitchen. I brought some things to help you relax. Hopefully, they'll help you feel right at home." She scurried out of the room.

They passed through a brick archway into the kitchen, and a pungent odor overwhelmed Sloane. A stunning floral arrangement with trumpet lilies sat on a long, white granite island. She read the card attached to the arrangement and looked at Lore. "Thanks for the flowers."

"You're welcome. It's the least I could do." Lore doted on the blooms as if she were preening a child for a portrait. "If you want to keep a fresh arrangement during your stay, I own A Different Petal on Old Main, and I'd be happy to order your favorites."

"No thanks. I won't be here long enough." Sloane moved the vase down to the opposite end of the island.

"Of course. What was I thinking? New York is your home." Lore removed three wineglasses from a cupboard, uncorked a bottle of red, and filled two of them. "This is pinot noir. I hope you like it. I brought you a cabernet sauvignon for later if you don't."

"That's nice of you." Sloane sat on a barstool. Lore's hospitality seemed excessive. Whatever happened to leaving the keys under a doormat and a welcome basket on the counter, preferably one with a bottle of Jameson?

Lore sat on a counter stool next to her. "If you decide to stay longer, please let me take you on a village tour."

Sloane remembered Huxham's promise. She took a long drink and managed a nod.

"Of course, only if you want to. I'm just proud of our little town."

"Harold was too," Sloane said.

"Oh, yes. He was. He won several key lawsuits that made our village what it is today. He secured our heritage status, and won our most important petition, making the business block of Old Main a pedestrian-only street. It's a lovely place to shop." Lore sipped her wine and flushed.

"So how old is the village?"

"Well, let's see. Old Main's original businesses have been open since the mid-eighteen hundreds."

Sloane recognized an urgency in Lore that might trip her up if she continued to answer questions. "Which businesses?"

"My father's fish market, for one. It's three doors down from my flower shop if you're walking toward the coast." She drew a map in the air. "If you enter off Mallow Avenue, you walk under a beautiful arbor. My store is the first building on the right. The Keanes' Spotted Owl Inn and Pub is next. It's a great place to mingle with locals. Natty and Mary's gallery is between the pub and the fish market. The Grind is next to my dad's market. They serve wonderful coffee. And Huxham Law is at the end of the block."

"That's right. Harold did tell me the Wests had a gallery."

"Oh, yes. Your family has owned it for generations. Three artists are showing in it right now, not removing their work, a kind gesture of respect for Natty and Mary and the gallery's long history. They have always supported our local artists."

"What about the Huxhams' law firm?"

"It started in the late eighteen hundreds as well. And my brother's medical office is the newest of our families' businesses. But it's across the street from my shop. He has to rent, but he desperately wants to buy his space and the empty building next to him."

"A close-knit community, huh?"

"Basically, our four families, the Wests, the Huxhams, the Keanes, and the Reeds run Old Main. We make up the majority of the Old Main Commerce Community, the MCC." Her lip quivered, and she stepped down, walking to a counter behind them and bringing back a box of tissues. "I should have said we *did*."

Sloane looked at Lore empathetically while studying her face. "So you are all close?"

Lore dabbed her eyes. "We are. Oh, I can show you. I'll be right back." She stepped off the stool and rushed out of the room, returning with a photo. "Here they are. The Four Musketeers. Raymond Keane, Harold Huxham, Natty, and my dad, James Reed. They were best friends. We kids grew up in each other's houses." She passed the picture to Sloane. The Musketeers were likely teens in the photo, young with carefree, sunbaked faces and arms around each other's necks.

"So you and Charles grew up friends?" She set the framed picture on the granite.

"Yes. Charlie, Ken Keane, your mother, me, and my brother, Quinn. We were all close."

"Are you and Charles in a relationship now?"

"A romantic one? Me and Charlie?" She shook her head and said sympathetically, "Our friendship is complex but not romantic. Charlie isn't really partner material. He's struggled over the years. And now, with Harold's death. Well, he's a mess."

Lore wiped her nose. "The last time the Musketeers were together was at my mother's funeral. We say that Old Denwick is charmed. But in the last six months, we've been anything but. Alice, my mother, died of Alzheimer's last October, Sean Gildey—he was the patriarch of Denwick's original family— and your grandparents died in January, Jane in February, and now Harold. The losses have been a bit much to handle."

"I'm sorry about your mother."

"Thank you. Mother was special. Everyone loved her. It was hard. I took care of her during her decline. In the end, it was a blessing she no longer had to suffer." Lore wiped away the tears swelling in her eyes. "Listen to me ramble on. Here you've lost your mother *and* grandparents. And I'm taking up all the air in the room. I'm so sorry."

"No need to apologize."

Sloane stared at Lore over the rim of her wineglass. Lore was maudlin about Harold and her mother but still held her tongue. If she was lying about something, she was not showing any tells. "Listen, if you're not in a hurry, can I ask you a few questions?"

"Sure. I have plenty of time to chat."

"All right. Before Harold told me, I didn't know Jane was from here. And I'm curious if she'd contacted anyone after leaving?"

Lore looked down. "I'm afraid she didn't. Not even her parents. Unless Natty and Mary kept her secret, but they were so desperate to find her. I can't imagine it was an act."

"So no one from Denwick knew where she went after her holiday to NYC or about me?"

Lore lifted her gaze to Sloane. Her mouth opened and shut, and she shook her head slowly.

"It's okay. That's what I expected. Jane didn't tell me about any of you, either."

"I'm so sorry. We just had no idea Jane had had a child. Had you. But for what it's worth, I knew your mother. She must've had a good reason to keep you secret."

"A good reason?"

Lore winced. "I'm sorry for upsetting you. It's just that running away was so unlike the girl I knew. Ask me anything about her. She was my best friend. And even though I didn't know about you, I'm so glad you're here, a beautiful piece of her. With you here, our four families are still intact, despite everything." Her chin trembled, and she gulped the rest of her wine.

Sloane had trouble with melodramatic people, and Lore was hyperbolic. But she stayed calm, waited for Lore to finish blowing her nose, and launched another question. "Did Jane and her parents have a decent relationship?"

Lore stuffed the tissue in her pocket. "Of course, they did. You couldn't be more wrong if you think she left because of them. Natty and Mary were wonderful, supportive and loyal. They adored her. And for a good reason—she was the perfect daughter." She stared into the room, lost in memory. "I loved being over here when I was younger," she said finally. "I still do. I've taken care of Natty and Mary's houseplants for years."

Sloane tapped her finger on her glass. "I find it hard to believe Jane decided to leave such a happy home. Runaways are running for a reason. Did she ever say she was upset about someone or something?" She searched Lore's eyes.

Lore seemed to think back. "No, I'm sorry. Jane was happy. She had a loving family and friends. A boyfriend. And she was excited about going to university."

The doorbell chimed.

Lore jerked and clutched her chest. "Oh, my God, I'm sorry. I don't mean to be so jumpy. It's just Charlie. I'll let him in."

Sloane nodded, sat back, and braced herself. It had been two weeks since Harold had been murdered in her apartment, and she was about to confront the man at the top of her suspect list.

Charles Huxham entered the kitchen ahead of Lore, dropped a manila envelope on the island, and barely met Sloane's eyes. "You must be Ms. West."

Lore moved from behind him and smirked. "Of course, she is, Charlie. Just look at her. She's a mirror image of Jane." She filled the third glass with wine.

Sloane extended her hand. "Again, I'm sorry for your loss. Harold and I spoke for only a short time, but he seemed like a nice man."

Charles's lips drew tight, and he looked out a wall of windows into the backyard.

Lore held out the wine. "Here, Charlie, have this."

He frowned. "I don't want that."

"Maybe you should," Lore whispered and rolled her eyes. She sat down at the island and poured his share into hers and Sloane's glasses.

Charles looked at Sloane. "He was a nice man. Too nice. He was adamant you deserved to hear his news in person. Even though he could've just called you."

"Charlie, calm down. She was only giving her condolences."

"I don't need you telling me what to do, Emilie."

"Do you think now's a good time to fight?"

"Isn't it always open season with you?" he answered, his tone was harsh and accusatory.

Sloane listened to their voices' every nuance and studied the emotions flashing across their faces. Friends didn't fight this way.

"You're acting in poor taste, Charlie."

"Like Ms. West showing up in Denwick."

Sloane held Charles's eyes. "Listen, Mr. Huxham. I didn't invite Harold to New York. And maybe you don't know this, but Harold's killer tried to shoot me too. That wouldn't have happened if your uncle hadn't looked me up and knocked at my door."

Charles set his jaw, the muscles flexing. "This is the new paperwork." He slid the envelope across the island. "You need to read it and sign at the highlighted places. The copy of the

Wests' will is yours to keep. We can finish this on Monday at ten a.m. if that works for you."

"Wait a minute, Charlie." Lore's voice rose. "Invite Sloane to Harold's repast. She's a West, for God's sake."

He glared at her. "I wasn't speaking to you, Emilie."

"Oh, I need permission to talk?"

"Don't be late with the funeral's flowers," he said, ignoring her comment. "I'll let myself out."

Lore shouted after him, "For God's sake, Charlie, stop being so rude." The front door slammed, and she turned to Sloane. "I'm sorry. See what I mean, though. He's terribly wound up."

"Yeah. Pretty tight." Sloane swirled the wine in her glass. "So why does he call you Emilie?"

"He has since we were little. It's my middle name, a family name."

"I see."

Lore Reed and Charles Huxham might not be a couple now, but something still bound them. Why else would she put up with his arrogance? Sloane thought if she was willing to stay with him even now, chances were she wouldn't be a good informant.

"I brought you a few more things." Lore opened the refrigerator. "A baked lasagna for dinner. Just reheat it at three-fifty degrees for about thirty minutes. It'll be ready at dinnertime."

"I appreciate all your trouble. It's nice to have a friendly face in a new place."

"Oh, forget about Charlie. No one else is going to act like him, believe me. The rest of us are thrilled you're here." Lore gathered her purse from the back counter and slung it over her shoulder. "If you don't have any more questions, I'll let you get settled." She walked away and stopped. "Again, I'm sorry about Charlie. Please come to Harold's memorial with me. Sunday, ten a.m. at the Old Denwick church. You can meet all the people who love your family, okay? Charles can't deny you if you're my guest, now can he?"

"Thanks. I'll think about it."

Lore pulled out a business card. "Here's my number. Just let me know, and I can pick you up."

After Lore left, Sloane opened the French doors to the backyard. Three crows perched on the patio railing scattered. They flew in a circle and settled back in the same place. "I don't have any food for you, so scat." She stomped her foot. This time the birds dispersed into the yard.

She sat on a lounger and stared out at the Wests' garden. Its expansive lawn, soaring trees, and flower beds could pass for a park in NYC, except none of the boroughs had pines as tall. The sunset slipped through a wall of sky-scraping spruces bordering the back of the yard and washed the flower beds in a warm orange glow.

A meow came from the French doors, and Sloane turned. "Hey, you're awake. Are you hungry?"

Bear blinked her sleepy eyes.

"I apologize for drugging you. But I promise it would have been worse if you'd flown here awake." Sloane picked her up and went back inside. "Look at this counter. It's called an island. What do you think? Three times bigger than our counter, right?"

Bear lay on the white granite and purred.

"Looks like you'll have no trouble making yourself at home." Sloane petted Bear's head and opened the refrigerator. "We have lasagna, and I brought some canned tuna. You'd probably enjoy the tuna more." She searched for a can opener and a couple of plates.

After eating, Sloane opened the cabernet sauvignon, poured a glass, settled into the patio lounger again and opened the envelope Charles had given her. "Jesus. That's a fuck-ton of money."

Bear sauntered outside and curled up by Sloane's feet.

"All right. This is what we know so far. For over a hundred and fifty years, four families have owned property in common on Old Main. They have established businesses on the land. Unless one family's share in the jointly owned property is transferred directly to an heir at probate, it reverts to the other three families."

Bear looked up.

"Yeah, I agree. Motive. Just the Wests' business and share of the property is valued at six hundred and fifty thousand." Sloane sipped her wine and dropped the papers on the side table. "If Morris had killed me that's a lot of money to split between three families." She stared into the dark garden. "So who benefits from Harold's death," she whispered.

Bear bristled and hissed, crawling into Sloane's lap.

"They're just crows. You'll hear a lot of birds here, not just sky rats." As the sky darkened, they lounged silently, watching crows roost in a tree with sprawling branches. Sloane stroked Bear's back and said in a low voice as if the crows were listening, "I know Morris's employer is here, and he has a problem. I'm still alive."

# CHAPTER SIX

Sloane woke the following day and stumbled to the kitchen. She searched through the cupboards and groaned. No coffee. There was ibuprofen, so she took two tablets with a glass of water and stretched. Her muscles were sore from traveling and sleeping in a strange bed.

Bear sashayed through the kitchen with her tail in the air and leaped onto the window seat in the breakfast room, staring into the yard, perfectly still.

"More birds than you know what to do with, huh?" The moment she spoke, her memories of last night flooded back, and she hurried to the living room, searching the framed photos displayed on every surface.

"Bear, look at this." She walked back to the breakfast room. "It's a picture of Jane and her cat. You look exactly like it, especially your eyes. If I didn't know better, I'd think this was you." She studied the picture and her cat. "Jesus, is this you? Not that it would be. But you could be twins."

Bear meowed and leaped off the windowsill, padding out of the room.

"Is it your mom?" she shouted and laughed. Bear had an attitude, often leaving the room when asked questions as if she were human. Sloane looked at the ceiling and an overwhelming urge to search Jane's childhood bedroom came over her. Jane had always kept journals. She figured there were diaries up there and maybe answers.

Just then another vibration shook her as an older woman carrying a basket appeared at the back door. "I say, my scones will not stay warm much longer," the woman said in a polished English accent. The outside chill had reddened the woman's cheeks and her long, narrow nose.

Sloane set the photo on the breakfast table and opened the French doors. "Can I help you?"

The woman stepped inside and swooshed her rain-sprinkled indigo wrap past Sloane. Turning to Sloane, she eyed her head to toe. "At the moment, I believe you require my help. Here, take these. They are the only pastry I bake well. And I have made them for you." She removed her cloak, and entered the kitchen as if the cottage was her home.

With a thud, Sloane dropped the basket on the island. "All right. You barging in might be local etiquette, but I don't have time for a welcome-wagon visit. Let's just exchange names. I need to get to work."

"Welcome wagon?" The woman chuckled and stepped closer to Sloane.

Sloane found her scent—cloves and black pepper—oddly comforting.

"You have no idea who I am, do you?" They stood face-to-face. "I am Dorathea Denham."

Sloane recognized the name immediately from Harold's letter. "You're Dora? The Wests' friend. How are you?"

"For goodness' sake, who told you that nonsense was my name? Never mind, obviously Harold did. I abhor nicknames. They are absurd." She tutted. "The villagers called Nathaniel, Natty. What kind of name is Natty? It is ridiculous. Terms of endearment are fine, but you will call me Dorathea. Now, shall we have tea with our scones, pet?"

Sloane crossed her arms and rested against the island.

"Does your silence mean no, or is something wrong with you?" Dorathea gathered cups and saucers on a tray.

"You called me pet," Sloane said.

"I'm quite fond of the term, indeed." She moved to a cupboard opposite Sloane. "I suppose your mum called you pet, too."

"Yeah. She did."

"No surprise. It is what I called her." Dorathea retrieved a teapot and canister and placed them on the island.

"Wait. Where did you find those? I just looked through the cupboards. I didn't see coffee or tea."

"Oh, dear. Are you a coffee drinker like your grandfather?" She opened the cupboard again and pulled out a French press. "Nathaniel preferred beans to leaves, too. Obviously, he had no idea about civil hospitality. Luckily, your grandmother did. But do not despair. There is a canister of coffee here, somewhere."

"Harold said you knew the Wests well."

"My ancestors have lived next to yours since relocating here from England," she said, gliding to the sink. She filled a teakettle and set it on the stovetop. "I am your second cousin, twice removed. Your great-great-grandfather and my great-grandmother were siblings. My hair is graying, and my skin is no longer youthful. Even so, do you deny our family resemblance?"

Sloane recognized certain features in Dorathea's face. "Yeah, I can see it." But there was something else in her cousin's eyes. Something familiar beyond color and shape.

"And you favor your family in every way, except for the color of your eyes. I cannot recall anyone with those ice-gray eyes." She stepped away and gathered plates. "Let us have the truth, then. What did your mum say about your family?"

"She lied," Sloane answered. "Jane said she was born in New Jersey and her parents died when she was a baby, yadda, yadda, yadda."

Bear appeared next to her and meowed.

"Where'd you come from?" she asked the dark-gray cat. "Dorathea, this is my cat, Bear."

"Is it really?" Dorathea pursed her lips and pointed to the opposite countertop. "Please hand me that copper canister, pet."

Bear padded to a barstool and leaped on it, sitting alert on her haunches.

The metal container was behind a ceramic vase full of cooking utensils. It was decorated with a Tree of Life. Sloane handed it to Dorathea. "What is this? A talisman or something?"

"You have no idea?" Dorathea retrieved a necklace with a Tree of Life pendant from under her black tunic. "It is the West family heraldry." She handed Sloane a tray with three place settings. "Would you take these to the breakfast table and have a seat? I think you are going to need it."

"What's that supposed to mean?"

"You'll find out soon enough."

Sloane shook her head and set the crockery in front of three chairs. "Why three? Are we expecting someone else to show up at the back door?"

"No, we are all here."

"Who's the third? My cat?"

"She will join us, indeed."

"Jesus," Sloane mumbled to herself. Dorathea made Gary Prence seem like an ordinary neighbor. But she decided to indulge the odd woman. She could have some insight into why Jane ran away and lied about their family. Dorathea placed a platter with scones, marmalade, milk, tea, and coffee in the center of the table. She sat across from Sloane and spread a napkin over her lap. "Tell me, what do I call you?"

"You haven't already heard my name in the village gossip?"

"No, I am afraid not. I have been in seclusion since Nathaniel and Mary's accident."

Sloane pushed down the French press, poured a cup, and took a long swallow. "God, I needed that. My name is Sloane."

"Pshaw. Are you having a laugh?"

"No. My name is Sloane. Sloane West."

"You are a West, indeed." She poured a cup of tea and smiled. "Your cheeky mum. When she was young, I had a black Labrador retriever. Her name was Sloane. Jane spent more time with the dog during school holidays than with us."

"Seriously, Jane named me after a dog? Why am I not surprised?"

Dorathea added milk to her teacup. "You can consider your name an honor. Most people prefer the company of dogs. And Sloane, the Labrador, was exceptional. I suppose worse namesakes exist. Have a scone, and let's move on."

Sloane breathed in the familiar aroma of orange and cranberry. "Jane used to make these on Sunday mornings."

With a quizzical expression, Dorathea sipped her tea. "I find calling your mum by her given name quite disrespectful. Why do you do so?"

"Jane and I had a difficult relationship. I'd rather not talk about that."

"Hmm." Dorathea helped herself to a second scone. "Tell me, then, how old are you?"

"I'm thirty-one."

"Ahhh, a summer in New York City to spread her wings, indeed. I suspected many things when your mum did not return. But you were not one of them."

Sloane took another scone off the platter. "Yeah, I just figured that one out, too." They sat in silence until Bear strolled across the room, brushed against Sloane's legs, and jumped onto the table.

"I let her sit on counters and tables." Sloane expected a reaction from Dorathea, but her cousin filled the second teacup, added a splash of milk, and slid the cup in front of Bear. "But I've never given her tea."

"Well, I am sure your mum did." She looked at Bear. "Didn't she?" She set a dessert plate with crumbled pieces of scone beside the teacup.

"I definitely don't give her pastries," Sloane said.

"No? She asked me for a bite, and the dear is tired of canned tuna. Aren't you?"

Bear lifted her head and meowed.

"You see. She says she has never liked it."

Sloane was silent for a moment, studying Dorathea's face. Her only living family was reclusive, eccentric, and probably certifiable. "All right. You can tell Bear that I'll do better from now on. I'll serve her a variety of fresh fish. No more canned tuna."

"For goodness' sake. I haven't lost the plot." Dorathea sipped her tea. "I'm terribly disappointed in your mum. She hid you from us, but she also hid you from yourself. Foolish girl." She stared at the photo of Jane and her cat and then at Bear. "Why did she give you to Sloane, dear?"

"Gave who to me?" Sloane asked.

"Her *familiar*, pet."

"What's a familiar?"

"Your cat is not a cat. Her name is Elvina, not Bear. She is a spirit guide meant to protect and train you." She turned to the dark-gray cat. "Does your mother know what you and Jane did?"

Elvina's whiskers twitched, releasing drops of milky tea, and suddenly a deep, velvety voice filled Sloane's head. *There's no need to bring my mother into this, Dorathea. Jane asked me to protect Sloane. What was I supposed to do? Deny her?*

Sloane raised her hands. "Whoa, whoa. What the hell was that?"

"Well, you could have trained her," answered Dorathea. She set down her teacup. "This is going to be harder than I thought." Dorathea flicked her wrist, and a kitchen drawer opened. A knife flew from it, across the room, to her hand.

"Holy shit!" Sloane scooted her chair away from the table. She stared back and forth between her cousin and the drawer. "What the hell is going on?"

Dorathea spread jam on her scone and set the knife on the side of her plate. "For goodness' sake. Surely you are not so ignorant. I am *wiċċe*." Sloane scrunched up her face. "A witch, pet."

"And I think you're mad. Witches don't exist." Sloane burst out in nervous laughter.

"Yet, I sit before you." Dorathea frowned and twirled her finger, and the teapot floated through the air, refilling hers and Elvina's cups. "You know nothing of who you are, then?"

"Ah, Jesus, you think *I'm* a witch?" Sloane paced, a gravelly moan escaped her clenched teeth.

"You are a wićċe by birth," Dorathea answered. "Your mum's actions were inexcusable. She took too many risks. The biggest was raising you in a world that erases our existence. Even their naming reduces us to the other. Paranormal. Supernatural. Otherworldly. We are but fiction to the Nogicals' reality."

"Nogicals?"

*Naw-gi-cals,* corrected Elvina. *Non-magical humans.*

The familiar's voice floated through her mind, and Sloane realized that the answers she had desired for a lifetime were coming too fast, overwhelming her. The possible reason for her unnatural strength, her anger. Why Jane seemed to always know so many of her private thoughts. "All right." She gulped the last of her coffee. "It was nice to meet you, Dorathea. Thanks for breakfast. We'll have to do this again before I leave."

Dorathea's brow shot up. "What do you mean? It is time you learnt who you are."

Heat spread to Sloane's face. "I'm thirty-one years old. You had three decades to inform me if you wanted to. But today, I'm busy."

"You foolish girl. We searched every day for Jane." Dorathea's voice had a sadness that surprised Sloane. "You and your mum were both wrapped in spells strong enough to keep us from finding you. We are unaware of their source or how she accomplished them."

Sloane turned to Elvina. "What about you? I've taken care of you for years. Why didn't you tell me?"

Elvina lowered her head, unable to respond.

"Oh, now you don't speak. How convenient." Sloane turned to Dorathea. "You can show yourself out." She left the breakfast room and returned to the guest suite, slamming the door behind her.

Her mind raced. She was a witch? How absurd. Why did Jane and Elvina lie to her? Why did they have spells around them? She fell back on the bed and took several breaths. The diaphragmatic breathing Jane had taught her. She calmed her mind and thought, what or who the hell was Jane hiding them from?

Sloane pushed the thoughts out of her mind and put on a pair of jeans, a clean T-shirt, and her favorite cardigan. Now was not the time to get pulled into a spectacle of flying knives and talking cats.

It was time to catch a killer.

# CHAPTER SEVEN

The rain had eased to a light mist as Sloane walked to the historic district of Old Main. The block was lined with charming old-world, timber-framed buildings. She entered through an ivy-covered arbor and A Different Petal, Lore Reed's flower shop, was the first building on the right.

A delivery minivan idled in the lane on the side of Lore's store. The van's back doors were open, and it was crammed full of floral arrangements. Sloane could smell the lilies from the sidewalk. Lore emerged from a side door, pushing a floral-draped cart full of more bouquets.

Sloane ran to the side of the building. The last thing she wanted was a flower shop tour by the ebullient florist. When the van's doors slammed shut and it sped down the laneway, she slipped past Lore's shop and walked to Reed's Fish Market. It was closed.

She cupped her hands on the window and looked inside. The shop was empty, the display cases cleaned, and the lights off. James Reed kept a simple sign in the window with his business hours, eleven a.m. to six p.m. Sloane checked her watch. It was ten minutes to opening. In NYC, fishmongers opened early and sold their products well past closing. Businesses here were on Island time.

"No problem, Mr. Reed," she said out loud. "If you don't open today, I'll see you at the funeral."

Shoppers started to arrive on Old Main. Sloane watched a group walk through the arbor. The gray sky muted the evergreen surrounding it. They gathered in front of a dark timber-brick building next to Lore's shop, breaking into the silent morning with their chatter. Sloane casually headed back in their direction.

A wooden sign hung above the crowd. It had a hand-carved owl, brown with white dappling, a white X between its eyes. The sign read "Spotted Owl Inn and Pub, est. 1871."

Time to meet the Keanes. She followed the group inside and descended a dimly lit staircase filled with Scottish folk music. It led below street level. The pub resembled those she had seen on her whiskey excursions abroad. A long bar of polished wood ran the room's length on one side. Tables and chairs filled the dining room on the other side. She breathed in the familiar aroma of yeast and looked at the pictures hanging on every inch of the burgundy wallpaper.

The Spotted Owl's barkeep busied himself polishing glasses and said without looking up, "Breakfast is o'er. Lunch begins in ten minutes. Take a seat with the others."

"What type of whiskey do you keep in this place?" Sloane responded as she hung her tote on the back of a stool.

The bartender looked up. "Crivvens." He set down the cloth and glass. "Pure dead brilliant. Ye look just like yer mam."

Sloane sat on a barstool. "I'm getting that comment a lot. Call me Sloane."

He was too young to be Raymond Keane, but with the same curly ginger hair, he favored the man in the Four Musketeers picture. He reached across the bar and offered his hand, soft and gentle. "Ma name's Kenneth Keane. Call me Ken. My family is fifth-generation Keane on the Island. And we've known yer family the entire time."

"That's a long time off the mother island for that brogue." She grinned and pointed to the wall behind him where a framed tartan hung. It was burgundy with thick black stripes and thin yellow lines. "That must be the Keanes'?"

"Aye. My great-great-grandfather came to this Island from Scotland and built the Spotted Owl a hundred and fifty years ago. It may not be the oldest on the Island, but it's always been in our family. My da, Ray, passed it on to me when he and ma mam retired back to Scotland, which I often visit." He winked.

"Impressive." Sloane peeked over the bar. "Where's your kilt?"

"Ah, ma wife only lets me wear it during Hogmanay. I think she gets a wee jealous when I show off ma braw legs."

Sloane laughed out loud. Ken Keane was a charmer, old school, reminding her of Chief Detective Jacobson.

"What whiskey do ye fancy?" he asked and slid an old-fashioned glass in front of her. "We have Canadian, a few Irish, and Japanese. We also have Bourbon. Scotch."

Sloane feigned shock. "Only a few Irish whiskies? Doing your part to keep the feud alive?"

"Aye. Ye know yer history."

"I'll have a Redbreast neat."

He grabbed the bottle and poured. "My son, Oscar, runs a distillery west of town, in the mountains." His Scottish accent had disappeared. "His grandfather gave him the family's old rackhouse when he graduated uni. And he's built a fine business. He's even got a tasting room."

"Whiskey's a tough industry to break into."

"Aye. His first batch is doing well in the market, though. It's a quality product."

"I'm impressed."

"That makes two of us." Ken chuckled. "Would you like a taste?"

She rubbed her hands together. "Yeah, sure. My favorite is Hyde, but I'm always game for a new label."

He took down a jewel-green bottle and poured her a not-so-standard drink. "Here we go. Let me introduce you to Keane's Single Malt Whiskey."

Sloane sipped the amber liquid, letting it linger on her tongue. "Mmm. Smokey, a hint of vanilla and clove on the nose. A peppery rye finish. It's excellent."

Ken replaced the bottle, front and center. "I'll let Oscar know a true whiskey sommelier approves."

She glanced at a staircase in the back of the dining room. "How many rooms do you have?"

"Four. But two are booked. A couple fishermen are here early for chinook season. I expect the other two rooms will go tomorrow."

"Maybe I should rent one before any more anglers arrive."

He cocked his head. "Aren't you at Mallow Cottage?"

"Yeah, but I don't plan on staying there."

"The cottage was yer grandparents' pride," he said. "They'd be crushed if ye didn't."

Sloane sipped her whiskey. "What makes you think that?"

He picked up the cloth and wiped the clean, dry bar. "I guess akis they were first-rate. Two of the kindest people I've ever known."

"That's nice to hear. But I'm a stranger in their house. They never knew me."

He stopped and stared into her eyes. "Aye. But yer their granddaughter and yer sweet mam's lass. Sos ye belong in that house."

Sloane held his eyes. He seemed determined not to give her a room. She wondered if respect for the Wests was the real reason Kenneth Keane didn't want her staying at the Inn. Then she sat back, hard, and shook her head.

"Are you okay?" Ken asked.

"Yeah. I just got lightheaded. That's all."

"I'll get ye a glass of water." He shot water from his beverage gun and handed her the glass. "Ye know, I couldn't believe yer mam didn't tell us about ye. We were best friends until the day she left."

"Really? Did you stay in touch?"

He lowered his head. "She went on holiday to New York, and I never heard from her again. I assumed she made new friends in the US and moved on from the likes of us."

"I find it best not to assume." She knocked back the rest of Oscar's brand, and just as she set down the empty glass, a person appeared next to Ken, startling her.

"Jesus, people move quietly here."

"Sorry about that." The woman nudged Ken out of her way. "I wanted to make sure this old man wasn't bothering you?"

Ken laughed and put his arm around her. "Sloane West, let me introduce Rose Keane. Ma wee lass."

Ken was an average-looking man, but his daughter was flawless. The most striking woman Sloane had ever seen. A flood of energy coursed through her. She looked down, hiding the warmth on her face.

"Oh, God. I'm so sorry. He's using the Scottish bit on you." Rose sighed. "You only lived over there for schooling, old man. And twice a year is the most you've ever visited since."

Sloane looked up from her whiskey glass. Rose's voice was hypnotic. A silky cover wrapping around her and soothing her tingling skin.

"Now yer just bein' mean, Rose Mirren Keane. Our Highland roots are deep and strong. And yer mam and I'll be off to live there soon enough."

"Until then, how about you travel to the kitchen and get the glasses I washed."

"Aye. Keep the heid, lass." Ken turned and winked at Sloane. "Only the next landowner of the Spotted Owl could talk to me that way." He walked away and disappeared through the side door.

"I'm sorry for that. I hope my dad wasn't too much of a bother." Rose leaned over the bar. She smelled of sandalwood and neroli. And Sloane breathed in deeply. "He hasn't stopped talking about you since he found out you were coming to Denwick."

"I enjoyed our chat. Your dad's a funny guy."

"Now I know you're just playing nice." Rose tucked a loose strand of shoulder-length, tightly curled auburn hair behind her ear and extended her hand. "It's a pleasure to finally meet you."

Her hand was soft, and her grip easy. Sloane's face warmed again. "Nice to meet you, too."

Their handshake lasted longer than it should have. Rose pulled back her hand and smiled, removing Sloane's empty glass. "Pretty early for the hard stuff."

"Yeah. I usually wait until after I eat lunch, but this day already feels like a week."

"Sorry to hear that. This must be rough. Settling your grandparents' estate. I don't envy you." Rose reached across the bar and laid her hand on Sloane's. "If you need a friendly person here to talk to, come in and have lunch. I'm a good listener. Or just come in anytime. I can introduce you to some Canadian food."

"That's the best offer I've had in a long time."

"Good to hear. I know how lonely it can get around here." Rose squeezed her hand, grinned, and walked away.

Rose Keane was even more charming than her dad. Sloane leaned back and bit her lip. Focus on the case, West, she admonished herself. Rose might not inherit Harold's land just yet, but she was the next owner of the Spotted Owl. She had as much motive as Ken, and even beautiful women kill.

A few minutes later, Ken returned with a woman as tall as him. She had her slender arm wrapped around his waist. Sloane recognized the lithe body, heart-shaped face, and impeccable features. Rose's mom.

Ken planted a kiss on the woman's cheek. "Sloane West, this is Fiona Keane, my better half. We met at uni, and she agreed to marry me after several proposals."

Fiona extended her hand. "It's lovely to meet you. And don't listen to his foolishness. He exaggerates everything."

"It's nice to meet you, too."

Fiona's accent was Jamaican instead of West Canadian or a Scottish brogue, and her hand was ice cold. Neither of which Sloane expected.

"She's telling havers, lass. I proposed five times. Then I had to beg her to live on the Island. But now we wouldn't have wanted to live anywhere else before we retire and hand over to the wee bairn."

He pulled Fiona close, and her smile wavered. "Let's not be so amusing, love." She gave Sloane a compassionate look.

"How are you doing? I can't imagine how you must feel...at the cottage."

"I'm fine, thanks."

Fiona's empathy turned to concern. "It must all be such a shock for you. Has Dorathea come to see you?"

Sloane chuckled. "Yeah. You could say that. We had the pleasure of meeting this morning."

Ken laughed. "Aye, ye met yer neighbor."

Fiona shot him a stern glance and turned a motherly gaze to Sloane. "I'm glad to hear that. You probably don't know this, but she isolated herself after your grandparents' accident. We've been worried about her."

"Actually, I did know." She read Fiona's face. Trying to find an answer in her reaction to Ken's banter. But her face was blank. Her eyes revealed nothing.

"Well, if either of you needs anything, please let us know."

Sloane nodded at Fiona and took a long drink of water. Obligatory niceties always made her uncomfortable.

Fiona turned to Ken and spoke in a low voice. "I've checked in the wine and beer for Harold's repast. You need to take it to Charlie's tonight. And we need to talk about the margins."

"It's for his funeral, doll," he whispered.

"We only have so much to give, Kenneth. And this is the third time in six months."

He turned his back to her and grabbed his polishing cloth. "Let's discuss this later."

Fiona pursed her lips and left without saying another word.

Sloane took her cue and scooted the barstool back, pulling her tote over her shoulder. "It was great to meet you and your family, Ken. I'm going to head out before your lunch crowd shows up." She opened her wallet. "What do I owe you?"

Ken's eyes had become watery, and he held his hand over his heart. "On the house, lass. I'm just glad yer here."

# CHAPTER EIGHT

"Son of a—" Sloane shouted and clutched her bath towel tighter.

Elvina sat before her. *What's the matter? You've never cared about me seeing you after a shower.*

"Are you kidding me?" Sloane strode to her suitcase. "You need to leave."

*I'm not going anywhere.* Elvina curled her tail around her legs. *Dorathea and I have left you alone the entire day. But now we need to speak with you. We're waiting in the living room.*

Sloane glared at the familiar. "There's no way to get you out of my head now, is there?"

*You were always able to hear me. We first knew you had the ability when you were quite young. Too young to remember. That's when Jane made me promise only to speak if I needed to protect you. And of course I had to. Several times.*

"The warning voice before Morris kicked the door in? It's always been you?" She lowered her head and mumbled, "You gave me the advantage my partner didn't have."

*Yes. It has always been me. And I was truly sorry for your loss.*

Sloane threw a pair of jeans and a T-shirt on the bed. "Fine. Just go. I'll be out in a minute."

Dorathea and Elvina were sitting on the sofa. They had a fire burning in the fireplace. Its warmth and dancing shadows made the room comfortable even though it wasn't cold out. Sloane sat across from them in one of the armchairs, and they stared at each other.

*Tea, dear?* Elvina asked.

"Nope." Sloane popped open a diet soda and looked at Dorathea. "So, what do you want?"

"Do you believe in coincidences?" she asked.

"No. I'm a skeptic," Sloane answered. "It's my nature and good for my business."

"Quite. Neither do I." Dorathea folded her hands in her lap. "Your grandparents died in a car accident. Then, your mum died the same way a month later. And an attempt on your life followed a month after that." She paused. "Do you not find this chain of events suspicious?"

"Unfortunate, maybe. Now, if I had died in a car accident..."

"Do you drive?"

"Not in New York City."

"Then why would you have perished in such a way?"

"I could die as a passenger. Or be run over."

"You're being cheeky and avoiding the obvious."

"No. I'm here *because* of the obvious. A Musketeer or one of their kids planned to have Harold and me killed for a share of the West and Huxham business property on Old Main." Sloane set her can on a side table. "I'm pretty damn good at what I do. So don't you think I've already considered Jane and her parents dying were part of that plan? As long as Jane or I were alive, the West land wasn't reverting to the others."

Dorathea raised her finger. "Even if you had considered your mum and grandparents part of such a plan, you are unaware of important information. They could not have died from injuries sustained in a car accident."

Sloane looked out the front windows and mumbled, "Jane did. I was there. I saw her body."

Dorathea sighed. "I am truly sorry, pet. It is a horrific experience. I know. I was called to identify Nathaniel and Mary."

Sloane turned back and met Dorathea's eyes.

"I meant to say that Magicals only succumb to mortal ways of dying if sorcery is involved."

Sloane wrinkled her brow. "What does that mean? A witch killed them?"

"Wiċċe, not witch, dear. Such a common term. And, yes, possibly." Dorathea sipped her tea. "I need you to figure out who is behind their murders."

Sloane recognized the look on Dorathea's face. Her cousin had more to tell her. "Did anyone else have a reason to kill them?"

"The answer to your question is involved. We are a coven of Protectors. Our identities are hidden from Nogicals and other Magicals. Unless..." Dorathea stared straight ahead, her brow slowly narrowing.

"Unless what?"

"They have a Demon's help."

"Jesus. Demons are real?"

*Of course, they are, dear,* Elvina said. *Not the horned, red-skinned "devil" Nogicals teach their young to fear. Demons are malevolent supernaturals. Powerful like us. But they're not from some hell. They hide in the Nogical world, in plain sight, spreading evil.*

"All right. I'm going to need something stronger than soda. Why would a Demon want us dead?"

Dorathea sighed. "It is our greatest fear. *Wiċċan* Protectors are the only defense against Demons gaining control of the magical world."

A gravelly moan escaped Sloane's clenched teeth. Her head had not been this muddled since she was a child, and now Jane wasn't there to sway her back to stability. She closed her eyes and remembered the pictures in Morris's pocket. No one believed they existed. Hell, she had even doubted herself, but now they made sense. "Harold's shooter had photos of us in his pocket, nothing else. That's how I knew he was a professional."

*Repulsive,* Elvina said, wrapping herself in her tail.

"Thing is, as soon as I pulled them out, they disintegrated right there in my hands in a flash of bright green light."

Dorathea's eyebrow arched. "A *gedwínan* hex."

"A what hex?"

*To destroy, dear*, Elvina said. *And the green light could have indicated a demonic influence. Demons have an aura, an energy represented by a light within the people or things under their possession.*

"Jesus. So Morris was a wizard possessed by a demon with a thing for green? Makes sense. When we fought, he jumped up despite a hit I gave him that would have knocked any normal man out cold."

"*Wićċa*, dear, not wizard."

Sloane turned to Elvina. "What's the difference? Wizard, witch, wiċċan?"

*Wizard and witch are Nogical terms, dear. Wićċa is what Nogicals call wizard. Wićće is a witch. Wiććan covers both. You are wićće and your practice is wiććedōn.* Elvina smiled and nibbled on her scone.

"The green light indicated Morris was colluding with a Demon, indeed." Dorathea flicked her hand, and steam rose from the teapot. "You will help us, then?"

"Yeah. But why haven't you tried to find the wiċċan or Demon, or whatever they are?"

"Please tell me you have been listening?" Dorathea's voice was impatient. "I believed I was the last of our coven. None of us knew about you. Your grandparents and mother had been killed. I was isolating to protect myself."

"Can't you just get more wiċċan for the coven?"

"No, indeed, covens are hereditary. Only after intricate rituals can we receive nondirect bloodlines. There was no time," answered Dorathea.

"Wait. I'm the last of the West bloodline?"

"You are the last of the West Protector bloodline. Your great-great-grandfather's ability was to protect. When Protectors are born, they create a coven and live here, in the Nogical world. Their eldest sisters join them. From then on, the sisters are bound to the coven until their firstborn daughters are ready to take their place. My great-grandmother was your great-great-grandfather's eldest sister."

Sloane tilted her head. "All right. So your mother married a Denham and you took her place…" Sloane stared at her with a blank face.

"Obviously, I will be unable to continue that tradition," Dorathea said.

*Don't you mean unwilling, dear?*

Her cousin looked at Elvina with hard, stony eyes, and Sloane knew that was a subject for another time. "All right. There are two of us now. Are we safe? Can we go to Harold's funeral? Charles doesn't want me there, but I'm sure he wouldn't object if I turned up with you."

"Do you believe our killer will be there?" Dorathea asked.

"I know they'll be."

Dorathea looked at Elvina.

*We are safer now*, the feline familiar said.

"From the evil or whatever?"

"For goodness' sake, pet. Are you always so flippant?"

"Not always." Sloane tapped her fingers on the chair's arm.

"Yes. With Elvina we have greater power. But we need a coven of at least three wiccan to enable defensive spells to be strong enough against a demon. Two points, we are but a line with no form. Three points give us dimension—the triangle, a symbol of power. I have requested the Grand Coven prepare one of our cousins to assist us. Unfortunately it will take time. But you will meet him eventually." Dorathea stared at Sloane's tatty T-shirt, sweater, and jeans. "Harold's service is at ten a.m. I will pick you up at nine o'clock sharp. Did you bring something appropriate to wear?"

Sloane smoothed the front of her favorite T-shirt. "I've got a darker cardigan and black jeans."

Dorathea snapped her fingers. Sloane's clothes transformed into a black dress, and her wet hair slicked back behind her head into a twisted knot.

"Hey, what the hell?" She touched her body and hair. "Where are my clothes?"

*They aren't gone, dear.* Elvina's voice was calm and soothing.

"Then give them back. I don't wear dresses."

"Everyone is a critic." Dorathea admired the dress. "Shame." She flicked her wrist, and the dress turned into a black suit. "Better? I can do something with your face, too."

"Stop it. Stop doing that. Just—don't change things. I get it. You're a witch. Bear's a—"

*Elvina, dear. Your familiar.*

"Whatever. That's who you are. This is happening. But I'm capable of dressing myself. I don't do"—she flailed her hands around in the air—"these magical things."

*Not yet, anyway.*

"Elvina is correct, pet. You must learn."

"You want to teach me?" Excitement surged through Sloane.

"Yes, indeed. You will be a powerful wiċċe. Just like your mum."

*Oh, Dorathea. You have no idea. Sloane possesses strength beyond her control*, Elvina said. *Her promise scared Jane.*

"Is that right?" Dorathea's eyes widened. "This is a welcomed development and just in time."

# CHAPTER NINE

Promptly at nine a.m. the next day, a car honked outside the cottage. Sloane opened an umbrella and hurried through the rain to a small, black Fiat in the circular drive. "This is your car?" She plopped down in the passenger's seat next to Dorathea and shook the umbrella, tossing it in the back.

"You sound surprised. I've had dear little Onyx for several years. Longer than most. She performs nicely."

"I just figured when you wanted to go somewhere, you appeared there or rode a broom."

"Really, pet. Try not to be so cheeky today. I do not practice magic in public. And we are saying goodbye to a dear friend."

Sloane shoved her tote between her feet. "I know. It's all I can think about."

"Death cultivates memories of itself, indeed." Dorathea pulled onto Mallow Avenue, driving away from Old Main.

"Yeah. I've spent the morning thinking about Jane."

"Why don't you tell me something about what she was like as an adult?"

Sloane stared out the windshield. "She was a successful psychologist in Manhattan and worked as a profiler for the FBI."

Dorathea smiled. "Your mum was a rare telepath, one of our finest. I am sure she helped a lot of Nogicals."

Sloane scoffed. "You think using her powers was fair?"

Dorathea thought for a moment. "Did she hurt anyone?"

"I guess it depends."

"Maybe it does."

Sloane looked out the windshield again. "What do you do?"

"I write mysteries under a pseudonym—Ray West. You might have heard of me or even read one of my books." She turned, drove up a hill, passed through a rusty wrought iron gate, and parked.

They stood under the umbrella in front of Onyx, facing the church, a humble stone building. It had long, narrow stained-glass windows and a tall steeple looming over the gravestones and knobby trees like a conservator of the dead. Sloane lifted her chin at a steady stream of mourners entering the chapel's dark wooden doors. "Nine times out of ten, murderers hide in plain sight."

Dorathea pressed her lips into a thin line. "As does all evil."

Sloane pulled her tote's strap over her head, crossing it over her chest.

"For goodness' sake, can you leave the unruly bag in Onyx, please?"

"No thanks. I don't go anywhere without it."

Dorathea shook her head at the dark-gray sky. "Very well." She led them along an outer path that skirted the graveyard.

Sloane stared into the cemetery. "Are all the Wests buried here?"

"In a sense. Except for one." Dorathea ducked out from under the umbrella as they entered the church. "Keep me abreast of your suspicions."

At the front of the sanctuary, a plain silver coffin covered with a white floral spray was placed before a wooden pulpit. Sloane tugged on her cousin's black cloak and nodded toward the back. "I need to sit in the corner." Those already sitting turned their heads and stared at them.

Dorathea lifted her nose. "I am happy with that decision."

A few minutes later, the ancient reverend shuffled to the pulpit.

"This will take a while...I should know," Dorathea said with a hushed voice.

"Oh come on, what are you sixty-eight, seventy?"

"Not even close. And I have known him for over fifty years. That has been his speed for the last forty."

The murmurs faded, and except for Sloane and Dorathea, the old man gathered his flock's attention. Sloane watched the Musketeer families. One of them might betray themselves, display fidgety behavior, or sweat even though the sanctuary was cold.

Dorathea studied the faces around them. "I know everyone here," she whispered.

The reverend placed an open Bible on the lectern and rested his hand on its pages. "Friends, we gather here this morning to celebrate the life of Harold Charles Huxham. A man of gentle character. Kind and giving. He lived his entire life here in Denwick. He gave his time and expertise freely to those who needed it." His voice boomed through the intimate space.

Charles sat in the front pew with his head lowered, often glancing back at the entrance. Lore sat next to him. She held a kerchief and dabbed at her tears, never losing eye contact with the reverend.

Sloane nudged Dorathea. "Is that James Reed sitting behind Lore?"

Dorathea glanced at the front pews and nodded. James sat in the second row. Sloane watched him spend the better part of the service staring at the back of Charles's head. Ken, Fiona, and Rose Keane sat next to him. Ken and Rose kept their eyes forward, bodies motionless, but Fiona looked over at the side pews and behind her several times. Sloane wondered if Fiona was uncomfortable or looking for someone, maybe her son, Oscar. And the Reeds had a son too but his name had escaped her.

Dorathea elbowed her in the side, breaking into her thoughts. "The reverend has asked us to rise and sing." Sloane got to her feet and looked at the hymnal page Dorathea pointed to. At the same time, the congregation burst out in "Morning has Broken." Their collective voice made her jump, and she fought back a fit of nervous laughter.

Sloane and Jane had never belonged to a church. Quiet devotion unnerved Sloane. When Jane died, Sloane held a memorial outdoors in Strawberry Fields. It was Jane's favorite spot in Central Park. They would go there when she was little and watch people leave flowers on the mosaic. Once, Jane had whispered, "World peace is more complicated than any of these people can imagine, pet." She believed that that was one of the few truths Jane had told her.

The exuberant singing in the sanctuary finished, and a few prayers later, the funeral ended with the reverend's benediction. Charles Huxham, Ken Keane, and James Reed rose along with three other men to shoulder Harold's casket out of the church.

The mourners spilled into the yard behind the pallbearers and congregated around a long, black hearse. Sloane and Dorathea were the last to leave the church. The rain had turned to mist, and Sloane tucked the umbrella into her tote. A procession of mourners followed the hearse as it pulled away. Sloane and Dorathea joined the end of the line. They passed slowly through another weathered gate into the cemetery toward a white tent.

Rows of gravestones, mostly timeworn and blackened by lichen, spread across a meadow of rocky outcrops, Garry oaks, and Douglas firs. Atop another hill at the back of the grounds, a mausoleum's gleaming white exterior caught Sloane's attention. She nudged Dorathea. "Who's buried in there?"

"The Gildeys. And the old Denwick family tombs are in the crypt below. Including the Wests'."

At Harold's final resting place, the smell of wet, newly turned earth filled the air. There was only a handful of white folding chairs. Sloane and Dorathea stood in the back of the tent with several others. Dorathea leaned into Sloane and asked in a hushed voice, "Did you bury Jane in New York?"

Her cousin's bluntness punched Sloane in the gut, and she took a sharp breath. "Jane was cremated," she answered in a whisper.

"Then perhaps it might be easier to lay her ashes to rest with her beloved parents and grandparents, where her roots run deepest."

Sloane stood in silence, unable to respond.

The reverend's voice boomed as he began reciting the committal. Its volume refocused Sloane's thoughts on her possible suspects.

When he finished, Lore walked to a table and retrieved a basket of white long-stem roses. She stood at the end of Harold's coffin as the lowering device guided it gently into the ground. One by one, the funeral-goers tossed a single rose into his grave.

When it was Sloane's turn, she closed her eyes, thanked Harold for being truthful, and made him a silent promise to find his killer.

The crowd dispersed, and Sloane and Dorathea walked silently along the cemetery's edge back to Onyx. "I need to go to Harold's funeral reception," Sloane said as she tossed her tote in the back. "Our suspects will be there. It'll be a good time to get some answers."

"I question the decorum of such a plan." Dorathea pulled out of the parking lot. "Nevertheless, I will take you."

Sloane stared ahead, unsure how to behave with her cousin. She was used to investigating cases alone with no one questioning her. But now she needed someone's assistance. And not only someone but her newfound family. "Just so you know, high-stress situations are excellent times to interrogate. You might want to remember that for your books."

Dorathea turned Onyx onto a tree-lined street. "I thank you for the tip. But I prefer to have my protagonist read the room in such a situation."

Sloane chuckled. "All right. Have it your way. Did you see Quinn Reed or Oscar Keane at the service?"

"No." She turned down another street. "I will tell you, Quinn's absence surprises me, but Oscar's does not. He has little to do with the village."

"Interesting. Why do you think Raymond Keane didn't attend? Isn't that strange for a lifetime family friend?"

"Raymond and Elizabeth came from Scotland to attend Alice Reed's funeral last year, where they announced it would be their last trip back to Denwick. And so it seems it was. They missed Nathaniel and Mary's funerals, too. Of those in attendance, did you notice anyone acting unusual?"

"Yeah. Both Charles and Fiona seemed to be looking for someone, and I thought James Reed's impassiveness was strange, especially if he and Harold were close friends."

"It is not my place to judge. We all grieve in our own ways. But James's character is usually less staid, indeed." Dorathea parked along a curb in front of a modest house.

Sloane grabbed her tote and opened the door. "I'm going to hang back and observe before I ask questions. I need you to let me know if any strangers show up."

"We shall surveil together. But I will suggest again that you leave questions for another day." Dorathea got out of the car. "You might leave the luggage, too."

"That's not happening."

"In my novels, my protagonist has a holster and pockets to carry important items. I find it hard to believe she could carry such a bag as yours and pursue suspects on foot."

"That's why they call your work fiction."

Dorathea gave a short laugh. "Quite. Maybe I can sharpen her skills by observing your practice."

They walked up the path to the front door, and Sloane stopped beside a Mercedes SUV in the driveway. "Is this Charles's car?"

"Yes, indeed."

She snapped a photo of its license plate with her phone.

Inside Charles Huxham's house, he and the reverend formed a receiving line in the foyer. When Charles shook Sloane's hand, he refused to meet her eyes, looking away quickly and turning to Dorathea. "Thank you for coming, Dora," he said in a hushed voice. "Harold would be pleased to see you. He had missed you these last few months."

"It is Dorathea, dear." She patted his hand. "I am very sorry for your loss. And I will miss Harold, too. He was a dear friend."

"Ahem." The reverend held out his hand to Sloane.

"Nice ceremony, Reverend." She shook his hand and stepped out of line. Dorathea moved over.

The reverend grasped her hand. "Dora, we meet again. Three times in three months is lovely. I only wish it was under different circumstances."

"Please, Reverend, call me Dorathea. And yes, let us pray significant time passes before another friend in our village dies."

His eyes widened, and Charles interjected, "Refreshments are being served in the living room."

Sloane chuckled at her cousin as they walked away. "That was a little harsh."

Dorathea pinched her brow. "Since his first day in Denwick, that man has importuned to convert me. It has gone on for over five decades, and it is quite vexing."

Charles's living room smelled like an Italian restaurant, with garlic, onion, and basil permeating the air. Sloane glanced around. The room was sparse but comfortable, reminding her of her apartment before she inherited Jane's things.

They walked past Lore Reed. She was tweaking a floral arrangement, and its lilies made Sloane's nose tingle. She sneezed.

"Bless you, Sloane. Do you need a tissue?" Lore asked without turning around.

"No. I'm fine, thanks."

"That's good. Make yourselves comfortable. We'll have lunch out soon."

She and Dorathea walked to the back of the living room and stood beside a quaint brick fireplace with a plain wooden mantle. From there, they could see the entire room and the receiving line. Sloane lifted her chin at Lore. "Is she always so hypervigilant?"

"She has been her entire life. It is exhausting. An hour in her company takes a day of recovery."

"Yeah. I've known a few women like that."

Fiona and Rose Keane walked through the receiving line. Lore hastened them through a door to the kitchen. A few minutes later, the three women returned, carrying chafing dishes and crowding them onto a long table. When Rose noticed Sloane standing near the bar, a smile spread across her lips. In return, Sloane hid the warmth surging through her body behind a casual grin.

"Looks like lunch and drinks are ready." Dorathea looked out the window. "And just in time. Old Denwick has arrived." A large group of mourners walked up the front path and began making their way through the receiving line. Sloane was about to suggest they get some food, but then she saw Charles's mouth open in surprise. A man had entered alone.

"Do you know that guy?" she whispered to Dorathea. "I don't remember seeing him at the funeral."

Dorathea's eyes narrowed. "No. He is a stranger to me."

Sloane glanced around the room. Rose and Fiona Keane were staring at the man, too.

The stranger unzipped his dark leather jacket and tamed his blond hair, sweeping it back into a knot. He shook hands with Charles, who forced a smile, patted the reverend's shoulder, and walked into the living room. His hard blue eyes caught Sloane's, and he held her gaze before checking her out from head to toe and back up again.

What a douche, she thought.

A flash of anger ran through her, and she stepped in his direction. Dorathea wrapped her arm around Sloane's waist and stopped her, leading her to the buffet table. "Let us eat some refreshments and decide how to proceed with the stranger."

Sloane broke free. "What's there to think about? I need to find out who he is."

Dorathea handed her a plate. "We have plenty of time. And at this moment, you must temper your anger."

"Listen, forgive me if I do my job and pass on the church-ladies' pasta." She handed Dorathea her plate. "And I'm nowhere near angry yet." As Sloane drew closer to the man, he thrust out his chest. Then, when she was close enough to touch him, she tripped on the rug and fell into his arms. "I'm fine," she said, trying to regain her balance. "You can let go of me."

He smelled of hay and leather. "What's your hurry?"

She struggled, but the man held her tightly while pretending to help her get her footing. He leaned closer, his eyes fixed on her breasts. Then he froze.

Dorathea appeared next to her. "For goodness' sake, pet. You must control your flare for the dramatic."

Sloane worked her way out of the stranger's grasp and poked his motionless body. She looked around the room. An elderly man on the loveseat held a fork of dangling pasta to his open mouth. A glob of tomato sauce had fallen and hung above his white dress shirt. The woman beside him held a fork full of salad before her open mouth. Across from the old couple, two men crouched motionless in the air, their bottoms inches above a sofa.

She turned to the bar. Rose looked like a wax figure pouring wine, the stream had made it halfway to an empty glass. "Jesus Christ, what did you do?"

"I cast a temporal stasis spell. You suspect he might be involved in the murders, don't you?"

Dorathea slipped her hands inside the stranger's jacket, patting his chest and sides. Then she slid her fingers over the front and back of his pants, stepped back, and held up the man's keys. "He is carrying only these. Peculiar, don't you think?"

Sloane removed his wallet from her tote. "He had this in his back pocket, too." She opened it. "According to his ID, he's Gannon Ferris. Lives in Victoria. And I didn't need a magical spell to figure that out."

"Yes, but do you know if this man you so casually accosted is a Demon or a Demon's conduit?"

"How the hell would I know that?"

"Precisely. And it is a Demon that aims to end our lives." Dorathea put Gannon's keys back in his coat. "But he is not one."

"How do you know?"

"I just used a detection spell on his keys."

"You need to teach me how to do that." Sloane took a picture of Gannon's ID and shoved the wallet back in his pocket. She poked him again. "And I'd like to know how to do the temporal stasis spell."

"Very well. But right now, we must assume the exact positions we had before and resume time."

"All right." Sloane glanced around. "Why didn't we freeze?"

"The spell does not affect us, pet." Dorathea returned to her place in the buffet line, and Sloane wiggled back into Gannon's arms. A muffled noise sounded behind the kitchen door at the same time a snap echoed in the still room.

"Hey, how'd I lose your attention so fast?" Gannon said.

She turned her head back to him as his gaze made its way to her eyes. "You never had my attention." She freed herself and straightened. "The church ladies sent me over. Their pasta is the talk of the Island. Don't miss it." She patted his arm and returned to Dorathea's side.

"The food smells heavenly, Fiona," Dorathea said, her voice full of charm. "You have honored Harold well."

"Lunch is the least I can do. Next time you visit the pub, you'll have to thank Chef." Fiona pointed to the built-in bar. "Rose is serving drinks. Have a beverage with your lunch."

"I will, indeed, dear."

Sloane nodded and wondered what caused Fiona's change of heart. Did she close the margins, or did she figure she'd make up the loss soon enough?

Lore and another woman from the funeral walked through the kitchen door with more chafing dishes. "Lore, dear," Dorathea said. "I am sure Charles is most grateful for your help during this difficult time. Everything has been so lovely."

Lore managed a smile. "Thank you, Dot. That means a lot to me."

"Dorathea, dear. And you are quite welcome."

Sloane regarded her cousin's uncompromising personality and hid a smile. "I'm going to get a drink. Do you want one?"

Dorathea looked over at Rose. "No, thank you. Go on. I will join you in a moment."

Sloane walked over to the bar, surprised by a nervousness she hadn't felt in years.

"Hey, I hoped to see you here," Rose said as Sloane neared. She stopped unpacking wineglasses. "I brought you something." She disappeared behind the bar.

Sloane peeked over. "For me?"

She popped back up. "Yes, you. I heard your favorite whiskey is Hyde." She held out a bottle. "So I bought this and a case for the pub. You ought to have the honors of the first pour."

"I don't know what to say."

Rose looked toward the buffet table as she poured a double shot into a pint glass. "We're only supposed to serve beer and wine today. So don't say anything."

Sloane chuckled. "I'll do my best to stay quiet and swill it like a beer drinker."

Rose smiled, handed Sloane the glass, and leaned on the bar. "I heard you chatting with Dora Denham in the buffet line. What was she carrying on about?"

"Nothing really. She was putting names to faces for me."

"That's nice of her. No one has seen her since Natty and Mary's funeral." Rose looked in Dorathea's direction. "She and your grandparents were close. I felt so bad for her."

"They were related."

"What?"

"Dorathea is family. We're second cousins twice removed."

"Are you kidding? All these years, I had no idea." Rose tilted her head. "Just another surprise for you, eh?"

"Yeah. Two days ago, I didn't even know I had any family. Oh, and don't call her Dora. She hates nicknames."

Rose laughed. "Good to know." She poured two glasses of wine for an elderly couple and turned back to Sloane. "I've always liked Dorathea. Her eccentric outfits. That sexy long hair piled on her head. Is she as mysterious as she looks?"

"No. But she's as bossy and as odd as you think." Sloane took a drink. "Mmm. Thanks for this. You know your brother's whiskey reminds me a little of Hyde. I thought he'd be here today. What's his name again?"

"Oscar. He doesn't have time for anything but his distillery." She looked over Sloane's shoulder. "Crap." She grabbed the whiskey bottle and shoved it at Sloane. "Here, put this in your bag. My dad's coming. Beer, remember?"

Sloane nodded, shoved the Hyde in her tote, and turned to the foyer, rubbing the spot on her hand where Rose's fingertips had brushed. There was no love lost between sister and brother, she thought. Did it have to do with the pub? Ken said Rose was the next owner. Was Oscar angry? No. Ken said Oscar's whiskey was doing well. Was Rose angry? Was the pub in the red?

Ken Keane and James Reed left the receiving line and headed for the bar. After giving Rose a kiss on the cheek, Ken helped himself to a pint of ale and held one out to James.

But James's eyes were fixed on Sloane. "My God, you do look just like your mother. Lore told me you did. I just…we had no idea sweet Jane had a child."

"James, meet Sloane West," Ken said. "Sloane, this is James Reed."

"Nice to meet you," Sloane said.

James's smile faded as he looked past her into the foyer. "What the hell are *they* doing here?" he asked in a low growl.

An elderly woman and a younger man around Ken's age entered the living room. They were dressed like money. Tailor-fitted funeral blacks, and not the kind bought off the rack. She had red-soled, black high heels. And he hid behind designer sunglasses.

Ken patted James on the shoulder. "Today's not the day, old friend. Isobel's coming to Friday's meeting. Ye can say yer piece then."

James shook off Ken's hand and squared his shoulders. "I'll say my piece when I want. Harold would've approved. And if your father and Nathaniel were here, they'd understand."

Ken lowered his voice. "Today is for Charlie and all of us to say our goodbyes. Let's respect that."

"I could care less about Charlie," James said with a scowl.

"You don't mean that," Ken said.

James ignored him. "Isobel Gildey plans to ruin every business on Old Main. She's starting with mine. And she'll come after yours next. Mark my words. But she'll get her way over my dead body." By the time James finished, he was shouting, and Lore had hurried over. She grabbed her father's arm and led him away through the kitchen door as if he were a child throwing a tantrum. Another man, stockily built and blond, set down his plate and followed them. Quinn. She remembered the son's name. He must be Quinn Reed.

Dorathea approached the bar and slipped an arm around Sloane's. "A word?" She led her to the middle of the room. "I gather you've met James Reed."

"Yeah. Is he acting out of character?"

"James? No. He has always been an ill-tempered hothead."

"So who's the woman who set him off?"

"Isobel Gildey. She's with her son, Andrew." Dorathea stared at the Gildeys. "They are the first European family to settle the Cowichan Valley. Denwick's founders. Very wealthy and connected. Sean Gildey, her husband, died a few months ago."

The other guests lined up to shake hands with the Gildeys. Isobel was a tall woman. Her silver hair hinted at her age, but the skin on her face and neck didn't show much wear. Andrew appeared less pretentious except for his tinted glasses.

"Did Harold do legal work for them?"

Dorathea chuckled. "The Gildeys employ law firms with more than two solicitors."

"Do they own a business on Old Main?"

"They own all of Old Main except for the land the four families own."

Lore and James returned from the kitchen with the other man, and Sloane tilted her head toward them. "Is that Quinn Reed?"

"Yes, he's Old Denwick's doctor." Dorathea stared at him, a hint of fondness in her eyes. "When he and Jane were young, they were very close."

Lore returned to the buffet, and James stormed off toward the bar. But Quinn stayed by the kitchen door, watching his sister and father.

"Dorathea, who is this lovely young lady by your side?" a voice asked from behind.

Dorathea turned and faced the woman. "For goodness' sake, Isobel. You would be daft not to know."

"Well, from across the room, I thought she favored—" Sloane turned around, and Isobel fell silent, locking eyes with her, tapping a gloved finger on her chin.

"Jane West? Yeah, I know." She held out her hand. "I'm Sloane West, her daughter."

# CHAPTER TEN

After the repast, Dorathea pulled into Mallow Cottage's circular drive. "Shall we meet later?"

"All right," Sloane said as she grabbed her tote. She was only half-listening. The chatter inside her head dominated her attention. Inside the cottage, she grabbed a diet soda from the refrigerator and stopped.

The house was quiet except for a grandfather clock's tick-tock. "Elvina?" There was no response. Sloane drummed her fingers on the granite, trying to order her thoughts, to make connections among the conversations. What did they have in common?

The answer was Jane.

She bent her head back and stared at the ceiling. She had not checked out the Wests' bedrooms since she arrived. Not an excellent detective move.

The second floor smelled like her childhood. Incense and old rugs. She opened the first door in the long, narrow hallway. A guest room that lacked any personal touches. She shut the door and walked to the next one. A bathroom.

She immediately recognized Jane's bedroom behind the third door. Impressionist paintings hung on the walls. Not the masters but decent reproductions. Sloane found Jane's signature boldly claiming them.

Nathaniel and Mary had left Jane's room as it was thirty years ago. The bed was made with a plush lavender duvet cover and a stack of throw pillows. A jewelry box and perfume sat on her dresser, books were stacked on her bedside table. The room was a time capsule and hopefully it held some answers.

She paged through each book in Jane's bookcase and searched the clothes' pockets in her closet. No hidden love letters. She found a box of family photos with pictures of Sloane, the dog. There were also photos of Jane in a school uniform. And a photo of Jane, Charles, Quinn, and Ken that oddly resembled the Four Musketeer picture Lore had shown her. She flipped it over. Summer 1987. A year before Jane ran away. Whatever had caused her to run happened right before her graduation and had kept her away ever since.

Sloane put the lid back on the picture box and continued her search. Under the bed was clear. She stripped the bedding and examined the mattress. Then she checked under the box spring and around the sides of the sleigh-style frame but found nothing.

Jane's dresser drawers only held clothes. There were no hidden compartments behind the art on the walls. She lifted up rugs and examined the floorboards. None were loose. Frustrated, Sloane sat on the hardwood floor under one of the room's mullioned windows.

Jane had always written copious client notes. For everything. So why wouldn't she have kept journals as a teen? Unless Nathaniel and Mary found her journals and removed them. No, Sloane thought. Dorathea would have told her.

She stared at Jane's bed. It took up a good portion of the floor space. She shoved the mattress and box spring off the bed against the opposite wall, pushed the bedframe onto its side and rested it against them. The floorboards underneath looked untouched. Sloane tapped her feet on them. A section where the headboard rested was loose. She grabbed a nail file from her tote and pried off the boards, uncovering a hidden space. It was filled with books from the University of Victoria's library, some material from a heritage archive, and a few books that looked handmade and apparently from a library in a town called Tagridore.

Sloane reached her arm as far as possible under the floor and found a stack of smaller books. Journals. Her heart raced. She sat against the wall and started reading. The books dated from Jane's first year at school to her last. In the final one, Jane had compiled research about what seemed to be the original Old Denwick families—the Gildeys, Keanes, Reeds, Smalldons, Ilievs, Tindalls, and Emleys. She had starred a few names but didn't explain why.

Sloane set the journals aside and flipped through the books and archive material—research on the colonization of the Island, historical documents on land grants, business licenses, and old Denwick church records of births, deaths and marriages.

The manuscripts from Tagridore detailed supernatural creatures. As if they were beings we would see walking down the street. All she needed now was to discover vampires and werewolves existed. Witches and Demons do. Why the hell not, she thought and laughed out loud.

Jane hadn't included any information about her personal life or with whom she was involved when she got pregnant. Sloane was left wondering why Jane had hidden these things. Who would care if she had them in her possession besides the library in Tagridore?

She took the books downstairs, placed them on the breakfast table, and stood in front of the wall of windows, staring into the garden. What would Dorathea have to say about Jane's hidden stash? She thought about walking to the hobbit house next door and telling her cousin but decided to gather more information.

Dorathea had mentioned the original families were laid to rest in the crypt. She grabbed Jane's last journal off the top of the stack. "I don't know where you are, Elvina, but I'm leaving. I'll be back before dinnertime."

* * *

Sloane arrived at the Old Denwick cemetery and climbed over the locked, weathered gate, landing hard on the other side. The crows cawed and shattered the silence. It was late afternoon, and the sun had slipped behind the Garry oak canopies, leaving the headstones in shadows.

Sloane walked past Harold's grave, now marked only with the casket spray. The air was still thick with turned soil. She took a dirt trail covered with slippery ivy and decaying leaves. It diverged from a stone walkway and weaved around towering trees to the back of the cemetery and up a hill, ending at the opulent mausoleum. One name was chiseled above its door. GILDEY.

"Nice digs for the dead," Sloane said. She pushed on the door, and it creaked open. The waning sunlight entered the room through slit windows, revealing white marble walls and ornate plaques. The Gildey family's dead peopled the walls.

Sloane stopped in front of a wooden-slat door in the back of the room. It opened to a stone passageway and staircase leading down. It was pitch black, and a musty odor wafted up from below. She turned on her phone's flashlight and headed down to a second door opening into the crypt.

She stepped onto soft earth, and nothing moved in the room's total darkness, not even the air. Maybe, she thought, just maybe, the crypt could help her understand what Jane had been investigating before she left Denwick. She moved the light around. Four sarcophagi were placed in the center of the tiny space, and arched niches from top to bottom in the walls housed simple caskets.

Reading aloud the names from Jane's journal, Sloane searched for them on the walls. She found the Keanes, Ilievs, Tindalls, Reeds, Emleys, Smalldons, and the Wests. Except Jane had not included the Wests in her research. She examined the nameplates under each family name, the newest were still shiny gold-plated. *Alice Emilie Reed, Nathaniel D. West*, and *Mary L. West*. The last niche's nameplate read, *Beloved Daughter, Jane*

*West, 1970–*. She touched her mother's name. Was she supposed to add the death date now? She had never been superstitious, but the idea that her ancestors were looking down on her was unsettling.

She turned and pointed the light at the three stone coffins in the center of the room. A name and date were etched into the lid of each. They predated those on the walls, but the families were the same—Emley, Iliev, and Keane.

Sloane walked around a coffin and tripped. Her heart raced, and she steadied herself, aiming the flashlight at the ground. The dirt dipped several inches in the shape of what looked like a missing sarcophagus. She wondered if it was a fourth coffin, the original Gildey, now at rest upstairs away from the commoners. She gave a snort of derision, then imagined Jane sneaking around in the dark crypt, playing detective, revealing its answers. But Jane had never been brave like that, never took chances, at least not the Jane Sloane knew.

She shone the light into the back of the crypt. No niches. The wall was a solid light gray stone streaked with white crystallized material. The veins spread out from the center like tree limbs. Sloane smoothed her hand over the cool-to-the-touch rock, feeling several notches.

Jane's pendant warmed against her chest, and she pulled it over her head and held it in her hand. The silver star inside the glass bead began to glow. As she moved her hand closer to the wall, the star shone brighter. As if by instinct, she pressed the bead into the rock's indentations. After a few attempts, it slipped into a notch. A perfect fit. The cavity filled with light, and the veins around it luminesced.

The wall tremored, creaking.

"Jesus Christ," Sloane said, stepping back.

The crystalline mineral deposits transformed into shimmering branches reaching up and out, forming a solid tree whose trunk vanished into the malodorous ground. The wall gleamed like a silver veil. Sloane inched closer, holding out her hand. It trembled as she neared the wall, and she plunged it through. The air was crisp on the other side.

"Holy hell." Without hesitation, she stepped through the middle of the tree. Shocked, Sloane stood at the rear of a tall building in a laneway. She faced the stone wall from whence she came. The glowing tree had disappeared.

"No, no, no." She moved her hands over the wall and stepped back until she could see tree limbs etched into the stone. "All right. No problem. I got this." She ran her hands over the tree and searched for notches, but she could only see a wave, a pulse in the air, surrounding her.

Jane's pendant was back around her neck, warming against her skin, and it made her break out in goosebumps.

When she looked back at the laneway, she saw a man watching her. He disappeared around the building's side as soon as she made him.

"Hey!" She chased him to the front of the building, but he vanished into a crowd on a broad, brick road. There were no cars, no noisy honking or sirens, only people. She could chase down the man, but she didn't know where she was. Sloane looked up at the bright red awning above her and read, Silas Lamps, Enchanted Lighting for Discerning Tastes. Whichever direction she decided to go, this was where she needed to return.

On the other side of the street, a woman stood inside the front window of a whitewashed building with a lavender canopy. The sign on its awning read Steeped Café. She stared at Sloane, holding her gaze. She needed answers, and maybe the woman in the quaint café was up for some questions.

The ambrosial scent of bread dough filled the air, and customers sat at every table except one. The woman turned from the window and walked toward Sloane. She was tall and lissome, moving gracefully through the intimate space.

"Who are you?" Sloane asked as the woman approached her.

"It's Freya, pet," a voice answered from behind her.

Sloane startled and turned. "Jesus, Dorathea." She held a hand to her chest. "Why are you here?"

"Freya summoned me."

"You are the hidden one," Freya said, standing a hair's breadth away from Sloane's face.

"Yes, dear. This is Jane's child."

Freya swept Sloane's hair to one side. "I know who she is, my love. I've been expecting her." Her sensual voice smoothed over Sloane's nervous thoughts. She breathed deeply at the nape of Sloane's bare neck, across her chest, down her back, and back up to her trembling lips. Sloane's breathing quickened. She clenched her hands into fists, and when Freya's closeness overstepped her comfort threshold, Freya drew back.

"So quick to anger," she whispered.

Sloane shook her hands loose and glared at her. "Are you kidding me?"

"Please keep your voice down," Dorathea said. She looked at Freya. "Well then? What about the spells?"

"The concealment spell is strong. The protection charm is new. Yours I presume," Freya answered in a somber voice. Then, she turned and walked away.

Dorathea nudged Sloane to follow. They stopped at the open table and sat in overstuffed, orchid-purple chairs. "Is the older one impregnable?" Dorathea asked.

"I'll need time to discover its roots." Freya stared at Sloane's clothes. "The Nogical is buried, I suppose?" Her tone was gentler.

Dorathea nodded. "This morning."

"My condolences. I'll bring us tea and scones."

Sloane waited for Freya to disappear into the back of the café before dropping her tote on the side of the chair. She leaned as close as possible to her cousin. "Who is she, and why the hell did she smell me like that?"

Dorathea looked up and shook her head. "Are you at all capable of remaining phlegmatic?"

"Sure, when I'm not being accosted."

"For goodness' sake. You were no such thing. Freya is Elvina's mother."

"Her mom?"

"Yes. She is one of the wisest familiars and sensors of magic or evil in our world."

"She was sensing me? Like a cat does? Why? Did you ask her to?"

"I asked Freya to discern the concealment spell that had kept you and Jane hidden from us. We do not know its origins or why it is so powerful." She held Sloane's eyes. "Are you always so prone to anger?"

Sloane sat back. "Probably. I do tend to go from okay to anger fast."

"What did your mum do about this?"

"Well, now I know she used her abilities on me, getting inside my head. But she'd just calm me down. We'd sway, side to side. Sometimes in front of the *Moulin de la Galette*. I can still hear her. 'Relationships are like the dancers at the Galette, pet. You think you're safe in another's arms, but no matter lover, friend, or family, the light shifts and your understanding of it all changes.' By the time she was done talking, I had usually forgotten what I was mad about."

Sloane looked out the window. Across the street was a Beaux-Arts building that resembled NYC's Grand Central Terminal, except it was surrounded by an expansive lawn and gardens. "What's that building?" she asked.

"We are in Tagridore. The capital of magical communities in the Northwest Quadrant. That building is our Quadrant Hall, *Héahreced*."

Sloane turned back to her cousin. "What are quadrants?"

"Imagine the Earth flat, divided equally into four areas. We are in the Northwest Quadrant."

"All right. Makes sense. What's inside the Hehareeceed?"

"The Héahreced? Our Grand Coven and various Interspecies officials work there. The Grand Coven governs all laws of the Northwest Wiċċan."

"So, who are the other Magicals?"

"There are many creatures in our world. Each has its defenders, like us Protectors."

"Creatures like what? Fairies? Elves?"

Dorathea glanced around the café. "Lower your voice." She leaned closer to the table. "If you've learned about a creature in a myth or fairy tale, it probably exists. But we can only detect our own kind."

Sloane sat back, frustrated. "So, unless our murder suspect is a witch teaming with a Demon, how do we find our killer?"

"We request the Grand Coven's permission to pursue other magical beings."

"Permission?"

"I am sure it is not an unfamiliar concept for you. You are aware of warrants and court orders, are you not?"

"Yeah, intimately acquainted."

Sloane scanned the room, unsure what she was looking for. Nothing struck her as out of the ordinary except for how everyone dressed in jewel-toned cloaks and capes over matching tunics. Although after two days, her cousin's unusual outfits had grown on her.

"So you have to live in Denwick your entire life?"

"No. But Nogicals are quite fragile when faced with those who are different. We live among them, but it is an exhausting way to be. By our seventies, we go home and leave our covens to the next generation."

"But you're still living in Denwick."

"I had no choice. I have no successor." Dorathea peered out the window.

Sloane felt the familiar pull of a follow-up question, but she understood her cousin wasn't going to elaborate. She thought about the crypt and four generations of Wests. "Do you want me to put Jane's ashes with the others?"

Dorathea's brows drew together. "No, pet. Our ancestors are not in those tombs."

"Wait? You said they were. The niches have their names on them."

"I said no such thing. If you remember correctly, I said *in a sense* they were. You failed to question me further."

Sloane put her arms on the table and leaned forward. "Fine. Then where are they?"

"They are all buried in the Northeast Quadrant, our ancestral roots." Dorathea folded her hands. "We only buried your great-grandparents last year. Of course, they had lived in the magical world for years."

"Seriously? They'd have to be well over a hundred years old."

"We live a bit longer than Nogicals. I am unsure how your mum expected to explain that to you."

"I don't even know what to believe anymore."

"Well, I can assure you I am not a fabulist. You would be wise to trust me," Dorathea said.

Freya stole upon them unnoticed and placed a tray on the table. Sloane started. "Relax." Freya laid a hand on her shoulder. "You're safe with me." She placed a package next to Sloane. "Give this to Elvina, please. It's her favorite."

"Yeah, sure." Sloane put the warm package in her tote.

Freya turned to Dorathea. "Your favorite blackcurrant and thyme scones and Earl Grey tea." She placed a teacup and dessert plate in front of her.

Dorathea smiled and held Freya's free hand. "They smell delicious. Thank you, dearest."

They seemed to escape to another place, staring into each other's eyes. Sloane helped herself to the tea service trying not to interrupt their moment. When Freya walked away, Dorathea turned to Sloane with soft eyes. "I'm impressed you found your way here."

"Don't be." She retrieved Jane's pendant from under her shirt. "I was in the crypt, and this thing pretty much told me what to do."

Dorathea raised an eyebrow. "Why were you in the crypt?"

"I was going to tell you why this evening." Sloane poured milk into her tea. "After you dropped me off, I searched Jane's bedroom. And under her floorboards, I found some library books about Denwick's original families and a few from here about magical creatures. She also hid a stack of her journals. One was full of her research."

Dorathea set her teacup down. "We searched her room, every inch, for those."

"I don't know what to tell you. They weren't hard to find." Sloane sipped her tea.

"Your mother had caused tension with the Grand Coven with that research." Dorathea bit into the end of the scone. "Mmm. My favorite, indeed."

"The more you tell me about Jane, the less I think we are talking about the same woman. The Jane who raised me worked for the FBI for God's sake. She was a stickler for the rules."

"Age and experience change us. Sometimes into completely different people than we once were." Dorathea looked at Freya as she glided around the other tables, and the thought lines across her forehead smoothed. "Did you find any information about your father?"

"No. The early journals were about school. Friends. The last one was about whatever she was researching."

"That is regrettable," Dorathea said. "I know how important finding him is to you. Which is why I will help you in any way I can."

"You can start by telling me if you think my father put the concealment spell on Jane and me."

Dorathea turned her head, looking at Freya again. "We will know more soon."

Sloane stared out the window. A man was standing across the street under a lamppost. He looked like the one watching her earlier when she came through the Tree of Life. She jumped to her feet, and the man slipped into a shadow, disappearing down the side of the Silas Lamps building.

"What is the matter?" Dorathea followed Sloane's gaze outside. "Do you see someone?"

"Yeah, a guy. He was standing across the street, watching us. I think I saw him earlier, too. He knew I'd spotted him and ran down the alleyway."

Dorathea narrowed her eyes. "Sit. You are not going anywhere."

Sloane looked at her cousin. "Can Demons get into Tagridore?"

"Only if a wiċċan has given them access." Dorathea continued to stare out the window and said in a low voice, "We must be careful, pet. Even Tagridore will be dangerous for us now."

* * *

Sloane and Dorathea returned to Denwick through the Tree of Life and walked back to Mallow Avenue down quiet streets in the crisp night air. They added nothing to the silence until they reached the cottage.

"I'm meeting with Charles Huxham in the morning. About the estate," Sloane said. "But I'm also questioning him. He has as much motive as anyone else to kill Harold and me. Maybe more."

Dorathea nodded. "I suppose he does. Which is why you must be careful."

"Isn't that what Elvina's for?"

"She is not a bodyguard."

Sloane chuckled. "All right. I'll be careful. See you later." At the front door, she put the key into the lock, but it inched open on its own, and she jumped to the side, peeking in.

Nothing moved.

She slid her fingers along the foyer wall and flipped on the lights before slipping around the doorframe. Elvina sat before her, tapping the tip of her tail on the floor. "Jesus Christ. Why'd you scare me like that?"

*It's a bit late, and I don't have the hands to make my dinner.*

Sloane slammed the door.

*You might feel differently about me now, but while I'm protecting you in this form, you'll need to feed me at the very least.*

"I've had a mind-blowing day. So can you find some patience?" Sloane pulled out the parcel wrapped in brown paper. "If you're done complaining, we can eat." She held out the box.

Elvina's pupils enlarged, the yellow-green of her eyes vanishing. *You traveled to Tagridore.*

"Yeah. And I met your mother."

*Yes, I know, dear. That's my favorite dish.*

"I found the tree in the crypt."

*You did?* Elvina leaped onto the kitchen island.

"Yeah." Sloane pulled out the necklace from under her shirt.

*Jane's key.*

"It guided me to the lock. And the tree opened."

*Then it truly is your key, or it wouldn't have given you access.*

Sloane tucked the necklace inside her shirt and unwrapped Freya's package. She placed it on a dish and slid it over to Elvina. "So what is it?"

*Three-meat pie.* Elvina sashayed across the island and tried to bunt Sloane's chin, but Sloane backed away. *Oh, I see. No more affection?* Elvina sat on her haunches. *It's cramped in this body, and along with feeding me, I need you to pet me and scratch my chin, regardless of how you feel. It's only fair.*

"Fair?" Sloane opened a bottle of whiskey and poured a double. "I don't have a problem with you being a familiar. I'm pissed that you lied to me for all these years."

Elvina padded back to her pie. *I didn't want to, but I had no say in the matter.*

"Yeah. Right. Because you were bound to do what Jane ordered."

*Yes.*

Sloane's voice grew angry. "Do you know why she ran away from Denwick, and you're just not telling me?"

Elvina continued eating. *Jane never told me.*

"Did she order you to never divulge who my father is, too?"

Elvina looked up. *Your mother, my best friend, is dead. I'm no longer obligated to her orders. If I could stop your hurt and give you these answers, I would.* She hesitated. *Why are you staring at me like that?*

"You're obligated to me now?"

*I'm not a genie, but yes, I'm entirely your familiar.*

Sloane leaned against the island. Her anger slipped away. "That's very interesting to know."

*I'm sure I'll regret letting it slip.*

"So what form will you take when you're done protecting and training me?"

*I have no idea. But I know I should have finished my duties many years ago when your mother came into her full powers. For your sake, it's a good thing I didn't.*

Sloane continued to stare at her familiar. "Your mom's a beautiful woman."

*Yes, she is.* Elvina lapped up more of her meat pie.

"She's also scary as hell." Sloane sipped her drink.

*Again, you are correct.*

Sloane chuckled and held out her glass. "Enjoy your mother's meat pie. I'm taking my dinner to bed. I've got an early appointment with Charles Huxham."

Elvina raised her head and licked gravy from the sides of her mouth. *Try not to get angry and kill him, dear. We've all had enough death.*

# CHAPTER ELEVEN

*Please Ring Bell and Take a Seat.*

Together with an antique brass bell and an arrangement of wilted flowers, the sign in the Huxham law firm's foyer sat atop a table in the center of the room. Sloane reached for the bell but drew her hand back when Charles's voice, loud and angry, came from an office on the right. She snuck beside it and listened.

"You said Friday. And that's when I'll have it," he bellowed.

She peeked in. Charles was sitting on the corner of his desk. His hand on his head, pulling his hair back. "I told you I can't give it to you. The painting isn't mine." He held out the phone, stared at it, and slammed it on the desk. "Damnit."

Not speaking to a client, Sloane thought, and crept back to the table. She rang the bell and sat. Charles stepped out of his office, unrolling the sleeves of his sky-blue button-down shirt. "I'm late. Are we still on?" Sloane asked, standing.

He checked his watch. "It's all right. I've been busy with paperwork. Let's get this finished."

They walked toward his office, and Sloane stopped. "Beautiful portraits. You, Harold, and who are the other two?"

Charles pointed to the opposite wall. "That's my great-grandfather next to Harold. His father started the firm in 1898." Then he pointed at the painting next to his. "And this is my grandfather. Five generations. All lawyers."

Sloane stared at the door across the lobby. "Harold's office?"

"Yes." Charles coughed and wiped his mouth with a handkerchief. He stood at the entrance to his office. "Have a seat, Ms. West."

The office was a dump with piles of journals and papers everywhere, take-out containers stacked on a cabinet behind his desk, and a rotting floral arrangement on a conference table. Its stagnant water mixed with stale cigarette smoke in the air.

She tossed her tote onto a burgundy rug next to a chair at Charles's desk and sat while he searched through files in the cabinet. His phone lit up with a call. It was on silent mode, and the call went to voice mail.

Charles pulled out a file, closed the drawer, and sat in a leather chair behind his desk. He pointed at a box placed in the chair next to her. "Harold gathered together a few of your grandparents' things. Mostly old legal work, but there are a few pictures there."

"That was nice of him. I knew right away he was a quality person."

Charles cleared his throat. He stacked the scattered papers on his desk to one side. "I trust you found the paperwork is in order and where you needed to sign clearly marked?"

Sloane recognized the sleepless nights in his slumped shoulders and dark circles under his eyes. Was it grief? Guilt? Both? She took a manila envelope out of her tote. "Yeah. I haven't had a chance to open this yet."

The muscles in his jaw tensed, and he opened his file. "No problem. I'll walk you through the papers."

"This is beautiful." She picked up a miniature cloisonné scabbard and ran her finger along the threads of gold. "Does it have a sword inside?"

Charles put on reading glasses. "It's a letter opener from one of those cheap import stores in Chinatown. Now, if you'd turn to page three."

"All right, boss. No chit-chat, huh? What am I looking at on page three?"

"The Wests' financials. Harold transferred each asset into a trust for Jane. You probated Jane's will in New York, and I filed the trust and updated it in your name. All the necessary banking information is at the bottom of the page. We—I need you to sign on the highlighted lines."

Sloane skimmed the page. "It's a crapload of money. And Jane's Degas. I had no idea."

"Yes. I'm sure you feel like you've won the lottery."

She signed and dropped the pen. "It's not a damn thing like it. The only family I had and the family I just discovered are dead. How's that lucky?"

He looked up. "You're asking me that?"

"What's your problem with me, Charles?"

He peered over his reading glasses. "I don't have a problem with you."

"Then why don't you want me here?" She shoved the paperwork across the desk.

"I didn't think you should have come to Denwick. But now that you are here, I could care less."

"I mean here, here." She spread out her arms. "Alive."

He took off his readers and tossed them on the desk. "That's absurd."

"Is it?" Sloane paused. "If I had never been born, your uncle would still be alive, and you wouldn't be grieving for him. If Liam Morris had killed me, too, I'm guessing you'd be a much wealthier man."

He glowered at her as he pushed back in his chair and got to his feet. "I need to make a copy for your file." He stomped across the lobby's green marble tile, and Sloane grabbed his phone. "No password? That's just asking for trouble," she whispered and accessed his recent calls. The last two numbers appeared several times a day, going back weeks. She got her phone and took a picture of the screen. Then she dialed his voicemail. Charles's returning footsteps sounded in the lobby. She hung up and replaced the phone, wishing she knew how to do the temporal spell.

"Take this," he said, positioning the file near her. "That's your copy." He also held a large item draped in black cloth.

Sloane put the folder in her tote, and when she turned back, he'd revealed Jane's Degas. "Jesus, Mary, and Joseph." She got to her feet and stood in front of the painting. Three ballet dancers twirled with long elegant arms stretched out to each other, white tulle skirts flowing. Their movements blurred into a circle against a blue-green garden and sky.

"It's an original pastel, a small fortune as you now know," Charles said.

"It's stunning," Sloane whispered. "I've only seen reproductions of his work, except at the MET."

"My uncle helped Natty and Mary acquire it at auction."

Sloane looked at him. "Harold said it was Jane's sixteenth birthday present."

"Did he?"

"Yeah. He shared a little bit about Denwick. About his friends. You."

A flush spread across his face. "Did he instruct you to change the painting's insurance policy into your name?"

Sloane turned back to the painting. "We didn't get that far."

Charles coughed into a handkerchief until he was red in the face. A vein in his neck bulged. "I'll have to keep the painting here until you secure insurance. The insurer's contact information is in the folder."

Sloane stared between the Degas and Charles. "No, problem. I'll change the policy tomorrow. Do I need to settle the Wests' legal account with you?"

"Not yet. I'll figure billable hours and have an invoice delivered to you. I assume you're leaving in a day or two."

Sloane crossed her legs. "Why? In a hurry to see me leave?"

"Like I said, I don't have an opinion one way or the other." He turned and filed his copy of the Wests' estate.

"What will you do with the law firm now? Run it by yourself?"

Charles slammed the file drawer and turned to her. "I will absolutely keep it going. If anything, to honor my uncle."

"Is there another Huxham lawyer in the family, or does the legacy end with you?"

His muscular cheeks tensed. "What is that supposed to mean?"

"I just thought it would be a shame if, after four generations, it all ended with you."

"Nothing's ending."

"So the firm's doing okay, financially?"

"That's none of your business." His voice had become angry, and his composure slipped.

Sloane decided to push him a little more. "Harold also told me the four family friends hold their property on Old Main in common. You read the Wests' wills. You're aware they designated their friends contingency beneficiaries for their Old Main holdings. Did Harold leave this property to you?"

Charles sat as if she had shoved him down on the chair. He stared at her, open-mouthed.

"You understand how it looks, don't you? Harold dead. An attempt on my life."

"Are you accusing me of something?" He fumbled in his pocket and pulled out a pack of cigarettes. Then he lit a smoke and took a long drag. "You have no idea what my uncle's will says."

"Not yet. And I'm not alleging anything. Someone from Denwick hired Liam Morris to kill Harold and me. And I'm here to find out who."

He exhaled. "You think my uncle's murder was planned?"

"And the attempt on my life." Sloane leaned toward him. "We know it was."

Charles held up his hands. They trembled, sending up a plume of zigzagging smoke. "I don't understand. You were there. You stopped the maniac that shot him. I didn't have anything to do with that. I loved my uncle."

"Can you think of anyone who would want Harold dead?"

"No. Everyone loved him. My God, the very few times he lost a case, his clients sent him flowers."

"What about you, Mr. Huxham? Does anyone want you dead?"

"Me? No. I'm just a small-town lawyer. Who would want to hurt me?"

She observed him, waiting for his tell, but the smoke must have calmed his nerves.

"You might be surprised how easy it is to drive people to murder," she said. "If Harold left the land to you, who is your beneficiary?"

Charles took another long drag and stubbed his cigarette out in an ashtray. "I need to get back to work. So if we're done."

"I have a few more questions. Can you give me a few more minutes?"

"Actually, I can't. I'm busy."

"I just wanted to know when Harold told you about me?"

"He didn't have to. I helped him search for Jane for years. After she died, you were easy to find."

"Really? Did either of you tell anyone else in Denwick about me?"

"I didn't. But Harold spread the news on Old Main like a paperboy. Told anyone who would listen that he'd found you." He pointed a pen at her. "He could've called you. And done your business online. But he had to prove something. That's a side he didn't show anyone but me. He was stubborn. Rigid. He kept secrets. Hell, he hid a big one from everyone here for decades."

The bell in the foyer rang, and he jumped to his feet. "I'm done answering your questions. You need to leave."

Sloane made a mental note to follow up on Harold's alleged decades' old secret.

"Charlie, are you here?" a voice called out. It was Lore Reed. Charles hurried to the door as she waltzed into the office holding an armful of flowers, blocking Sloane's view of her face.

"Good morning, love. I'm changing out the flowers and watering your plants today. No more brushing me off. Look at your office. It's filthy. What would Harold think about this mess?" She shifted the flowers to her hip. "Oh, my! Jane's Degas. And you've been smoking? Next to her painting? For God's sake, Charlie."

"This isn't a good time, Emilie. You should've called first." Charles's voice was abrupt and harsh.

"I did. I left a message. What's wrenched your ginch?"

"I think I did," Sloane said.

Lore moved the blooms to her other hip, struggling to see around them. "Oh, hello, Sloane. I'm so sorry. I thought your meeting would be finished by now. Are you getting on okay? Please, let me know if you need anything. It really is my pleasure to help."

"Thanks. But I've got more help than I need from my neighbor."

Lore laughed. "I'm sorry. I shouldn't make light. I know Dotty can be a force of nature. But, even so, settling your grandparents' affairs right after your mother's? I mean, my God. If I can help in any way."

"For God's sake, Emilie, she said no thanks. Go put your flowers on the conference table."

"I said I was sorry for interrupting. Stop snapping at me, Charlie." Lore sat the flowers on the table. "I'll just wait out in the lobby."

"Don't do that, Lore. Charles and I are finished." Sloane swung her tote over her shoulder, picked up the box, and turned to him. "I'll call the insurance company tomorrow. And whenever your bill is ready, let me know. I'll swing by and pay it."

\* \* \*

Sloane sat on a wrought iron bench under a Garry oak, staring at the businesses down the block. Charles had lied and not very well. But she needed more than dishonesty to build her case for Jacobson.

It was time to call Mike Garcia, one of her contacts at the NYPD. They'd met when she graduated from the Academy. He stayed loyal to her through the incidents, investigations, and suspension, and his loyalty remained after she left the force.

She pressed his number. "Hey, Garcia."

"There she is. I knew you couldn't stay away for too long."

"Listen, I don't want to wear out my welcome—"

"But...Just kidding. I always got your back."

"Thanks. How are you?"

"I'm good. And you? How's Canada, eh?"

"Yeah. Nobody really talks like that." She laughed. "So Jacobson and Thomas are loud-mouthing my business, huh?"

"They broadcasted your shit over the radio."

"Great. Just like old times."

"That's about right. Jacobson also said you're thinking about joining again when you get back."

"Are you kidding me?" Sloane's voice grew testy. "Listen, I'm never working in the force again."

"Ahright. Don't get pissed at me. I'm just saying that's the rumor. Anyways, I heard you went up there on the Morris case?"

"Yeah. I have some leads."

"What do you need from me?"

"A drink at Stella's would be great."

"I'm always good for that, too. As soon as you're back in the city." He spoke in a hushed voice. "What do you need for your case?"

"Some record checks. I'll text you a list of names and a picture of two phone numbers. I need you to run them. Give me the usual."

"No problem."

"Today if possible. I owe you big time."

"I know that's right. The second round is on you."

"You got it. Wait. One more thing. Can you tell Chen I'm going to need some financials?"

"Ahright. Talk to you later."

Sloane leaned back and a sudden urge for pub food and more answers came over her.

The Spotted Owl was warm inside and smelled of deep fry, and without a room full of guests, the Gaelic instrumental was loud. Rose Keane stood behind the bar in a white button-down shirt and blue jeans. "Hey there, are you here to take me up on my offer?" she asked as Sloane approached.

"How could I resist?"

Rose's full lips turned up, and she tucked a few loose auburn curls under a head wrap. "Chef brewed more coffee. Would you like a cup?"

"Yeah, sure. Black."

"Coming right up." Rose moved to the back wall, where two coffee urns had begun to sputter and steam, mixing the aromas of fresh brew and Chef's lunch preparations. She placed two cups of coffee on the bar. "I've been thinking about where to begin your foray into Canadian cuisine. And I decided Quebec with poutine."

"What's poo-teen?"

"Your mom never made it for you?"

"No. Jane preferred bodega cuisine."

"What's that?"

"Whatever the corner stores had cooked up that day."

Rose guffawed out loud. The accidental laugh stole Sloane's breath. "I'm sorry. That was rude."

Sloane stared into her coffee cup. Rose mistook her reaction. "Don't apologize. Jane's meals were weird but a convenient way to raise a child, I suppose."

"I don't know about weird. Sounds fun to me. Every night a surprise, just like your first poutine. Which, by the way, you are going to love."

"Hmm. It's been a long time since I let food or anything else blindside me."

Rose tossed a menu in front of her and stood with her hands on her hips "You can check it out for yourself if you don't trust me."

Sloane held up her hands. "I'm good. I'll trust you."

Rose grinned and placed a silverware wrap in front of Sloane. "Smart move. You won't regret it." She winked and disappeared in back.

Sloane wiped the sweat off the nape of her neck. She hadn't taken part in electric banter like this since the early days with Jess. Waiting for Rose to return, she studied the photos behind the bar. They spoke of history and deep roots. Five generations of Keanes standing in the spot Rose had been, and hanging right in the center of the photos was the Keane family tartan. Same as in the photos. Not much in the pub had changed.

"Chef's making you his poutine special."

Sloane jerked. "Jesus. I didn't hear you come back."

"You need to relax. Get a massage. Spend the day outdoors. It would do you good."

"Yeah, you're probably right." Sloane stretched and nodded at the wall. "I was admiring your family."

Rose turned and looked at the photos. "Five generations. But I'm sure my dad told you that."

"Yeah. He said your family was one of the original settlers."

"We are. Are you becoming interested in our little village?"

"I guess so."

"I think that's great. It's good to know your roots."

"Maybe you can help me?"

Rose leaned closer and grinned cheekily. "What do you need?"

Her question was an open invitation to take their banter up a notch, but Sloane just wasn't ready to play. She pointed at a photo of four young men. It was the same one Lore had shown her. "I thought I'd start with the Four Musketeers."

"You know the name?"

"Yeah. Lore told me."

"This is my grandpa, Ray Keane, he's with Harold Huxham, James Reed, and Nathaniel West, and yes, they called themselves the Musketeers. Rumor is that our four families go back to when my great-great-grandfather built the inn. Well, except for the Huxhams. They came later."

"Did the Musketeers always get along?"

"I think so. I remember them meeting here a few nights a week until my grandparents retired to Scotland."

"The other three stopped coming?"

"Not right away. They met up once or twice a month for years. But then Alice, Mrs. Reed, died. After that, they hardly came in at all."

"That seems strange. You'd think James would need his friends even more, right?"

Rose stretched closer as if she needed to whisper. "All I know is Harold and James had a falling out."

"About what?"

"I'm not sure." Rose looked toward the kitchen. "And Charlie isn't welcome at the pub anymore."

"Really?"

She nodded. "Let me go check on your lunch."

Sloane dug out her phone and checked for an email from Garcia, eager to know as much as possible about Charles Huxham.

Rose returned with a steaming plate. "Here you go. It's hot. Be careful."

Sloane chuckled when Rose slid the lunch in front of her. "French fries?"

"That's right. Poutine."

Sloane inhaled. "Smells good. What's the catch? They're covered in—"

"A simple brown gravy."

"Okay, topped with green onion and…what's this?"

"Cheese curd," said Rose. "C'mon. Don't analyze it, just take a bite."

"Curds? The squeaky stuff?"

"Yes. And these are fresh. You'll love them."

Sloane speared a forkful of fries dripping with sauce and cheese. "Here we go." She shoved them into her mouth, and gravy dribbled down her chin.

Rose slowly wiped the gravy from Sloane's chin with a napkin and waited for Sloane to swallow. "What do you think?"

"About the fries?" She couldn't help but flirt while the feel of Rose's touch lingered. "They're delicious. But I can't eat all this alone? Here, you help me." She slid the plate over to her.

"No, thanks. Chef made me a huge breakfast." She watched Sloane take another bite. "Okay, I'll have one." She grabbed a fork.

"I thought Lore and Charles were a couple when I saw them in New York," Sloane said.

"Lore went there with Charles?" Rose picked her fork through the gravy, piling up cheese curd.

"You seem surprised?"

"A bit." Rose looked up. "I didn't think Lore liked Harold all that much. Or maybe it was the other way around."

"Why?"

"Just a feeling I got whenever they were in the same room."

Sloane watched, fascinated, as Rose ate forkful after forkful.

"Okay, I can't eat another bite." Rose stepped back.

"And you were right. It was delicious." Sloane wiped her mouth on the napkin. "You seem to like it, too."

"I have a healthy appetite." Rose looked at the entry. Light filtered in from the staircase, and voices followed.

Sloane stared at her profile. "Do you have a warning system, or is hearing your superpower?"

Rose shrugged. "Can't say. You'd know my secret if I told you."

"Guess I'll just have to find out." Sloane stepped down from the barstool. "Thanks for the poutine and the info." She pulled out a couple of bills. "How much do I owe you?"

"Keep it. And I'll let you pay for our dinner next time."

"All right. Dinner's on me."

"I'd like that. Just let me know when." Rose tucked a few menus under her arm and walked away.

Sloane picked up her tote and the box and ascended the staircase to Old Main, wondering why after two years of swearing off dating, did she agree to dinner plans with Rose Keane?

# CHAPTER TWELVE

Sloane lifted her face to the bright sun. The azure sky was cloudless, a nice change from the misty and rainy gray Vancouver Island it had been since she arrived. The nice weather brought shoppers darting in and out of the Old Main shops, their doors welcomely wide open.

She scanned the street and saw Lore's floral-draped cart blocking the fish market's door. Now was a good time to question James Reed. And she might as well get some salmon for Elvina. Through the plate-glass window, she saw the shop was empty. Moving Lore's cart, she slipped inside.

A bell chimed, but no one responded. The smell of the sea came from the walls, ceiling, and floor of the decades-old wet market. A long, polished wood case ran from one side of the store to the other. It was full of crushed ice. She stopped beside a fresh floral arrangement and a sculpture of an eagle catching a fish.

James's and Lore's voices spilled out from behind a set of swinging doors. They were arguing, and Sloane craned to see through the circular holes in the middle of each door, listening.

"Mother is gone. You must ask for help."

"I don't need your help. My customers are loyal," James said, raising his voice even more.

"People are only loyal to money, Dad. You need to get that through your thick skull." Lore's voice was shrewlike.

"Just go," James shouted. "I've got fish to prepare, or I won't make any money today." He burst through one side of the doors, waving a fishmonger's knife. He pulled a fish from a metal chest and slapped it on the cutting board.

Lore came through the door and stared at him with a pained expression, drawing her lips in a tight line. "Fine. Suit yourself. But don't say I didn't try to help you."

Sloane stepped behind the sculpture and out of sight as Lore stomped to the door.

James slammed the knife on the fish's head. "What the hell do you know about anything!" he yelled as she left. After the chimes died away, James steadied himself with both hands on the counter and took a deep breath.

Sloane moved around the statue and approached him. "Ahem."

He looked up. "None of the catch is out. My whole day is botched up." His attention went back to the fish. "Come back in an hour."

Sloane nodded at the fish on the butcher-block surface. "Is that salmon?"

"First chinook of the season."

"Could you sell me its head?"

He looked up again. "Are you making stock?"

"I was planning to—"

"Well, you can have the belly meat too, and I've got fish frames in the back." James put the knife down and wiped his hands on his apron before Sloane could finish speaking.

"Sure, I'll take them all," she said.

Happiness flashed in his eyes, and the tension in the room relaxed.

"It was a pleasure meeting you yesterday," Sloane said. "I'm sorry it was during such a sad time."

James nodded. "Harold was a fine man. Gone too soon. But he died righting a wrong. I imagine that's how he would have wanted it." He picked up his knife and with one strike, the salmon's tail came off.

"Do you mean finding me?"

He nodded, slit the fish's belly with a surgeon's precision, and gutted it.

"Do you mind if I ask you a few questions?"

James kept his eyes on his work, piercing the salmon's back and fileting down the spine. "About stock?"

"No, about Harold."

He flipped the fish, and it smacked the counter. The knife slid effortlessly between the flesh and bone as he fileted the other side. "What do you want to know?"

"Can you think of anyone in Denwick who might have wanted Harold dead?"

James looked up, surprised. "Harold Huxham? No. No one here would want to hurt him." He placed the two salmon fillets in the display case and pulled another out of the chest.

"What about him and his nephew, Charles? Did they get on?"

"I suppose. Harold was more of a father to Charlie, and they had moments like any father and son." He placed the fish on the board and stared at her suspiciously. "Why?"

"It's just, I heard they'd had some problems lately."

Whack. James's knife struck the fish's head hard. "I don't know anything about that. Harold and I didn't really speak about our kids."

"Oh. Since you two were close, Musketeers, I thought you might have an idea what the issues between them were."

He looked at her, "We were. But like I said, we didn't talk about Lore and Charlie. Our kids." He set down his knife to wrap the head and belly meat in white butcher's paper.

"I see. I was just wondering, if he and Charlie had trouble, maybe that influenced who he left his property to? Are you aware if it reverts to you and the other co-owners?"

Without looking up, he dropped Sloane's package in a bag of crushed ice, closing it with a knot. "I have no idea." He turned away and shoved open the swinging doors.

When he returned, he had another package on ice and handed both bags over the counter. "Your salmon pieces and fish frames."

"Thank you, Mr. Reed."

"Call me James."

"Okay, James. Call me Sloane."

The bells chimed. Sloane glanced at the new customer and back to him. "How much do I owe you?"

"I'll run you a tab. You can pay weekly or monthly."

"I won't be here that long. How about I pay you before I fly home?"

"That's too bad. I figured you'd stay awhile. Sure, pay me before you leave."

Sloane turned to leave but stopped. "Oh, one more question. Were Charles and Lore ever an item?"

Whack. The fish's head was off. "No," James growled. "Harold made sure of that."

\* \* \*

Sloane walked back to Mallow Cottage, passing a park and several well-heeled yards. The scent of cut grass and flower blooms cut the briny ocean air.

A constant theme had emerged during her interviews—Charles and Lore's relationship. Any question about Charles lead to Lore. Was Harold's murder a revenge killing with a financial bonus? Were they in it together? But where did her attempted murder come into it?

These were the type of questions she had once bounced off her old NYPD partner, Tom Hanson, before he turned out to be a lying son-of-a-bitch. She twisted the ring on her finger. Then she had shared her ideas with Bear, except now Bear is Elvina. Screw it. She'd brainstorm by herself.

Something moved ahead of her in the ivy cover below a tree. The leaves rustled. She stopped and bent her head back, looking through the early spring canopy, and an owl swooped down over her head, skimming past and back into the air.

"Shit," she whispered, covering her head and ducking. The owl glided away over the next block of rooftops and toward Old Main.

The cottage door was unlocked. She had locked it before she left. So either Dorathea or someone else was there. Sloane entered slowly, making her way to the kitchen. "Elvina, I'm back." Nothing moved. No noise. "I brought you fresh fish." No answer. She threw the fish into the refrigerator. "Elvina?"

*Out here, dear. We're having tea.*

Sloane groaned. Dorathea and Elvina sat on the back porch, a teapot floating between them. They had placed a third setting for her. "I'm going to need some Xanax if owls attack me out of nowhere and cats-not-cats keep speaking in my head."

Elvina flicked her tail. *It's doubtful to help, dear.*

Dorathea narrowed her eyes. "What kind of owl?"

"How should I know." Sloane looked at the trees. "It was huge and aggressive."

Her cousin waved her hand, and a patio chair slid back. "Have a seat. We're discussing your mum and grandparents' murders."

A few brave crows alit on the railing. "Jesus, the blackbirds here are as aggressive as our sky rats back home."

*Best be careful,* Elvina said. *Unlike pigeons, crows hold grudges.*

"Get!" Sloane stomped her foot, and the birds flew off to the old Garry oak in the back of the yard. She sat at the table and put a madeleine and a dab of cherry jam on her plate. The teapot lifted from the table and poured Sloane a cup.

She stared at her cousin. "Thanks, but I don't mind pouring my own drink."

Dorathea gave a slight head shake. "I did nothing."

Elvina stopped lapping tea from her cup and looked up. *Don't be unpleasant, dear.*

"Are you kidding me? You can do spells?"

*Obviously. How else would I train you?*

Sloane set her cup on its saucer, hard. "You've harassed me for seven years. Even last night, you told me you couldn't open a can of tuna. And all along, you could?"

*I should have said I wouldn't. My mistake. I could hardly feed myself without disclosing my identity, dear.*

"What about Harold? Why didn't you save him?" Sloane blurted out.

*It doesn't work that way. I'm bound to you, no one else. But, even so, I tried. I've known Harold for a lifetime, and his loss is painful for me, too.*

"Yeah, well, if you had told me the truth years ago, none of this would've happened."

"That is not a fair assessment, pet."

Elvina sat back on her haunches. *It's okay, Dorathea. I understand her pain.* She held Sloane's gaze. *I had no choice, dear.*

"I'm sick of hearing that. You chose to do what Jane wanted."

*That's not how our relationship worked. And not how ours works now.*

Sloane shook her head. "Listen, I don't want any more secrets or lies. You got it? Or you can go to Tagridore and stay with your mother. I mean it. You won't come back to New York with me, either."

*Stop bullying me and relax. Do you really think you're ever going back?*

Sloane's eyes opened wide. "Like hell, I'm not."

"Enough," Dorathea said. Her commanding voice made Elvina and Sloane snap to attention.

Sloane stared at her. "And you can't lie to me either. Or I'll leave, and I won't come back."

"I will always be truthful. However, there are unshared truths between us. These are not secrets, and I will not lie about them. I simply cannot disclose everything that you are unaware of at once. Will you give me that?"

Sloane turned to the garden, watching the crows. When Jess left her, she refused to continue any relationships built on lies. Bear and Gary Prence were all she had. But now it was just

Gary. "All right. I'll try." She turned to Elvina. "But you and me, we're broken."

Elvina's whiskers twitched, and she looked down.

"Even so. Elvina is correct. For now, you must remain in Denwick. Your life is in danger, and we will not risk losing you." Dorathea stared into her tea, grief on her face.

Sloane realized for the first time that she and her cousin had much in common. The killer had taken Dorathea's family and left her alone, too. "Okay," Sloane said. "You have my word. I'll stay until we solve our case." Now it seemed improbable Jane and the Wests' murders were two different cases.

"*Our* case," Dorathea repeated. "Does that mean you agree we are looking for the same person?"

Sloane pushed back in the patio chair. "Or persons. Yeah, I think you're right about that."

Her cousin lifted her nose in the air. "I'm seldom wrong. And when I am, you will know it has happened."

Sloane chuckled. "I don't doubt you can substantiate your confidence."

"Quite right. And for your protection, I suggest you learn a protection spell or two."

Sloane gulped the rest of her tea, grabbed another madeleine, and stood. "But right now, I need to go. Are there any office stores around here?"

"What do you need?" Dorathea asked.

"A whiteboard and markers. To work our case."

*Oh, yes. A lucky baby*, Elvina said.

"A what?" Sloane asked.

*Your board at home. You call it lucky baby.*

"No, I don't."

*Of course, you do. When we work a case, you say, let's get lucky baby. Ever since Jess and Tom—*

Sloane held up her hand. "Don't talk about them."

*Of course not. I apologize, dear.*

Sloane's frown disappeared. "I meant to get lucky. You know. Find a connection out of the blue." Elvina tilted her head to the side. After a few seconds, Sloane laughed hysterically. "But we can call it lucky baby if you want."

"Ahem. Will that suffice?" Dorathea nodded at a whiteboard on an easel next to the French patio doors.

Sloane walked over and knocked on its surface, picking up a pack of dry-erase markers. "Yeah. This is great. How'd you do that?"

Elvina licked cherry glaze from her paw and said, *Maybe you should start your training and find out.*

"I said I would. But not today."

"Of course not. The morning is over. We will begin tomorrow at my home before the sun rises."

"All right." Sloane set up the easel in the living room and returned to the kitchen. "Thanks for the tea, Dorathea. I'll see you in the morning." She turned to Elvina. "I got you some salmon. It's in the fridge. I won't be home for dinner."

Elvina's tail flicked. *Yummy. But don't be too late. We need to start on lucky baby right away. This is the most complicated case you've ever had—two murders in NYC. Two murders here. Possible Demon possession of a Magical. And a Main Street full of suspects.*

"I could not have written a better plot, indeed," Dorothea added.

# CHAPTER THIRTEEN

The following day at the blue hour, Sloane trudged through the dewy lawn to the hobbit house next door, eager to see inside and start her training in witchcraft. She had convinced herself any protection spells she learned would be fairer to any perps than her lethal strength.

Dorathea's porch was dark, and the drapes drawn. Sloane went to knock on the double doors when they slowly creaked open. She stepped inside the dark entry, and the strong scent of rosemary and clove rushed her. "Hey, I'm here," she called out. "Dorathea?"

A faint light flickered ahead. She followed it into a hallway, and it disappeared, leaving her to feel her way through the pitch black.

"C'mon. Stop messing." The light appeared again on the opposite side of a long, narrow room. "I'm not in the mood for games. I haven't had my coffee," Sloane shouted. The light shimmered again, bobbing its way to a second hallway. She followed it to a staircase at the end. Sloane took a deep breath and descended to the bottom of the stairs, whence the light disappeared, the door swung open, and she entered a cavernous space.

Dorathea and Elvina sat in two burgundy velvet-covered armchairs near a stone inglenook fireplace in a fire's warm glow. "Good morning. Come sit," Dorathea said.

Sloane tossed her tote against an empty third chair. "I don't think the childish games were necessary."

Dorathea glanced at the ceiling. "Thank you for bringing her to us, Alfred."

The door slammed shut.

Elvina tapped her tail. *You will find it best not to insult an enchanted house. They hold grudges just like the crows.*

"What the hell is an enchanted house?"

Flames shot up the flue.

*Delightful first impression, dear. I'm sure you and Alfred will muddle through splendidly.*

"Alfred is a spirit infused in every inch of my home," Dorathea said. "I would not survive without him."

"Well, your spirit likes to play games with people."

"He can be a bit impish, indeed. But play keeps life enjoyable."

"If you like that sort of thing." Sloane looked around. "What is this place?"

"This is the West Covenstead, where our coven has gathered since coming to Denwick. Elvina and I will train you here."

The room was dim, and floating candelabras bathed the space in soft yellow light. Shelves covered the walls, and tables were set about the floor. Each tabletop held glass containers with swirling, colored gasses and objects suspended in liquids of various viscosities.

Sloane tried to take it all in, but it was a carnival of sights. She tilted her head. "What's that sound?"

*The burning wood?*

"No, it's not that. It's a buzz. Can't you hear it?"

"Ah, you hear my library books." Dorathea snapped her fingers, and the room's far end lit up, revealing floor-to-ceiling bookcases full of gilded hardcovers in every color. Sloane leaned around the armchair and watched, unblinking, as several books pulled themselves out, floated through the air, and reshelved themselves in different places. "I've ignored them lately," Dorathea said. "They need to be read, or they become bored."

Sloane let out an involuntary laugh. "Bored?"

"Quite. Dreadfully."

"So they buzz around, swapping spots all day?"

"I would say they zozz rather than buzz." Dorathea observed them with an empathetic look. "I do wish I had the time to read them properly. Perhaps Elvina and you can take a few more lonely volumes to the cottage?"

Elvina swished her tail. *Oh, yes, that would be fun.*

"For reading, love. Not to bat around."

Sloane nodded. "Sure. They're amazing. Do they hold still in your hand?"

"Of course, pet. They only want to be read."

A familiar scent caught Sloane's attention. It came from glass tubes full of liquids on Bunsen burners, releasing trails of colored steam. "What are you burning?"

Elvina glanced at a table in the middle of the room. *Mostly angelica right now with some cinnamon and sage and a few other ingredients. It's a protection potion. My specialty. I'm making a batch and will give you a vial to carry in that luggage you call a purse.*

"Jesus. It's a tote. And it carries everything I need."

Sloane looked away and watched the bubbling liquids. They conjured the memory of a small saucepan full of leaves, roots, and bark that Jane always left simmering on the stove. It filled their house with the same scent. "Jane made the same potion." Her voice was matter-of-fact.

"That surprises me," Dorathea said. "I wonder why she felt the need for more protection. The concealment spell placed around you has proven impenetrable."

"Maybe she didn't think it was." Sloane shifted her attention to the books. "We need to figure out who or what Jane was afraid of. What made her leave Denwick." She looked at Dorathea. "It could be the same person responsible for the murders."

Dorathea furrowed her brow and seemed to consider the proposition. "But why let Nathaniel, Mary, and me live for so long?"

"Good question. Why not kill you before Jane and me? Unless the perp couldn't."

Dorathea got to her feet. "Indeed."

"I don't have any evidence Jane running away from Denwick was or wasn't connected to the murders." Sloane got to her feet, too. "We'll just have to see where the evidence leads us."

"Very well," Dorathea said. "Shall we begin your lesson?"

"All right. Let's do this."

Dorathea held out her hand, and a cane ripped across the room. She caught it and tapped the floor three times. A lectern appeared on the other side of the fireplace. On top of it was a thick tome.

"What's that? *The Witchcraft Bible*?"

"Your cheekiness is exactly why I chose to be a High Priestess and not a professor." Dorathea flicked her wrist, and the book's pages fluttered open. "This is the *Book of Hagorúnum*."

Elvina padded over to Dorathea and leaped on a stool. *It's the spell book for the Wiċċan of the Northeast Quadrant.*

Sloane rested against the side of the inglenook and crossed her arms. "I thought we were in the Northwest Quadrant?"

*We originated in the northeast, but evil brought us here.*

"And keeps us here. Now, for your protection, we will teach you three spells. You know their concepts as detecting, disarming, and moving your location without traversing physical space."

"Teleporting?" Sloane's voice almost stuttered in surprise.

"Yes, indeed."

"You're going to teach me all of that today?"

The familiar simpered, curling her tail around her haunches. *Your vibrations are strong, dear, but not that strong.*

"Elvina, please." Dorathea turned to Sloane. "We will start with a detection spell. It is quite simple, a one-word incantation. *Onwreon.*"

"What the hell language is that?"

"Must you be so captious?" A stool appeared beside Dorathea. "Sit here, please."

Sloane walked to the seat and mumbled, "I think High Priestess was the right choice."

Elvina laughed. *I see you're trying to be a teacher's pet.*

"I'm just saying don't assume I know different languages."

Elvina laughed harder and rolled off her stool, landing on all fours.

Dorathea ignored the familiar. "Onwreon is Old English."

Elvina leaped onto her stool again. *This is going to take a while.*

"You know what? I liked you better as a cat," Sloane said and turned to Dorathea. "Why Old English?"

"Wiccan exist everywhere. And we use all six thousand five hundred languages spoken in the world. Our Protection Coven uses the language of our ancestors." Dorathea tapped the floor with her cane, and a green plastic clog appeared in her hand. "This clog belonged to Harold. He wore it when he helped Nathaniel, Mary, and me work in our gardens." She held on to the shoe for a moment before passing it to Sloane.

Sloane wrapped her fingers around it. The bottom was caked in dirt. She thought of Harold slumped over her mother's armchair, and anger flooded her body, mostly anger at Liam Morris. And at herself. Sloane pointed the clog at her cousin. "Why are we detecting Harold?"

"Because his soul has been released. So you can look without mine or the Grand Coven's approval," answered Dorathea.

"Fine. But I've got a question before we start. If wiccan can sense each other, why can't they detect other magical creatures without using a spell?"

"We can detect most with the Grand Coven's permission. But Magicals who are defenders of their species in the Nogical world must conceal their identities," Dorathea answered. "We cannot detect each other unless the Interspecies Council gives consent."

Elvina licked the back of her paw. *If we stayed in Denwick, Dorathea and I could train you in Magical Creatures. It was your mother's favorite subject. You'd learn who lives among Nogicals. Interesting stuff. It's a shame you want us to return to New York.*

"And I might be alone, kitty-cat." Sloane looked at Dorathea. "Because he got into my building unseen, and had the disintegrating photos, we know Morris was a Magical and possessed, and we're guessing our suspect is also either a Magical, possessed, or both, right? So why waste time detecting? Shouldn't you teach me how to disarm?"

"You must trust I know what I am doing," answered Dorathea.

Sloane stared into the massive fireplace. The flames licked higher as if pulsing. Why should she trust this eccentric old woman? But then again, why shouldn't she? So far, Dorathea was the only family who hadn't lied to her.

"All right," she said finally. "What do I do?"

"Nothing yet. There are rules you must learn. You may only use the detection spell without permission if your life is in danger. Otherwise, as your High Priestess, if I am unable to grant consent, I take your request to the Grand Coven for approval."

"My life is in danger. Why would I waste time getting permission."

"Fair enough. I will clarify. To use the detection spell without permission, your life must be in imminent danger. Under attack. That is why I hope you would seek the authority to use the spell before our suspect resorts to violence."

"At Harold's repast, you detected Gannon Ferris. I didn't see you leave to get the Grand Coven's permission."

"As the High Priestess of our coven, I have the latitude to grant myself the right to protect us."

"Jesus. Fine. I'm seeking permission, now. I need to detect the Keane and Reed family members and Charles Huxham."

*Anyone else?* Elvina said.

"Not right now."

Dorathea nodded. "I will seek the Grand Coven's approval."

"All right. Good." Sloane looked down at Harold's green garden clog.

"Wiccan draw from our emotional and physical desires," Dorathea said. "We wield our internal chaos and harness the universe's energy through those desires."

"What desires?" Sloane asked.

"To protect," answered Dorathea. "When you have connected to the source, to the one you wish to keep from harm, you are ready to articulate an incantation. If you cast the detection spell correctly, your third eye will open. And it will reveal all you need to see."

"My third eye? Like my mind's eye?"

*Similar, but not the same. When your third eye opens, you will see the unimaginable.*

"All right. Doesn't sound too hard. Let's do this."

"Harness your feelings for Harold. Ask yourself why you need to glimpse his soul. Focus on your answer. I will say the incantation, and you will repeat after me."

"Do I say it out loud?"

"Yes, for now. Elvina and I have practiced our craft for decades. That is why we cast silently."

Elvina stopped grooming. *Even then, some wiċċan must always cast out loud. And some must use a wand.*

"True," said Dorathea. "Repeat after me. Onwreon."

Sloane shut her eyes and exhaled. Her fingers trembled. "On...wreh...on." Her mouth felt tortured, and she opened her eyes.

Elvina crossed her paws. *We need to work on your pronunciation.*

"It will come with practice," Dorathea said. "Repeat after me. Onwreon."

"Ohn...wree...oh...n."

*Better. But now faster.*

Dorathea nodded. "Yes, pick up the tempo. Practice it in your head a few times."

Sloane tightened her fingers around the green clog. She heard Harold's voice, telling her how he had held Jane when she was born. She focused on the love in his voice and her desire to find Morris's employer. "Onwreon." She dropped the shoe. "Holy fuck."

*What did you see?* Elvina asked.

"I can't describe it. Colors. In waves that just kept coming toward me."

"Anything else?" Dorathea asked.

"No."

Elvina's pupils dilated. *You opened your third eye.*

"Excellent, indeed," Dorathea said. "Now drawing on your desire to protect, peer through the veil of colors. You will see the last time Harold touched the shoe and his true essence will wash over you. Try again."

Sloane stepped off the stool and picked up the shoe, whacking it against her leg. Clumps of dried mud fell to the floor. She closed her eyes and, after a minute, said, "Onwreon." Her third eye opened, and she forced herself to gaze into the unfamiliar colors for as long as possible. "Damnit." She opened her eyes. "Nothing appeared."

Dorathea managed a smile. "Let's try another object." She snapped her fingers, and a silver brush appeared in her hand.

*Is that?* Elvina sat up. *I haven't seen it for ages. Jane was so disappointed she'd left it behind.*

Dorathea looked at the familiar in dismay and handed Sloane the brush. "What do you feel?"

Sloane passed it from one hand to the other. "It's vibrating."

"Yes, indeed. It was your mum's brush."

"Jane's stuff never vibrated before."

"I'm sure you stopped noticing your mum's vibrations after time."

"No. I never felt the vibrations until I arrived at the cottage, and you were spying on me from behind the roses. I felt it again in Freya's teashop. But never in New York."

Dorathea and Elvina stared at each other.

"What? Was something wrong with Jane?"

"There was nothing the matter with your mum," Dorathea answered. "You will always sense the presence of wiċċan unless a spell we cannot undo protects them. Possibly the protection charm your mum cast kept her vibrations from you, too. Do you have any of her items? Perhaps something she wore or touched recently?"

"Why? Do you want to detect her? You just said there was nothing wrong with her."

"I am not hiding anything. I thought I would make sure for both our sakes."

Sloane's stomach tightened. "I don't have anything here." She shoved Jane's brush in her back pocket, unprepared to see Jane or the version of her attached to it. "Why don't you just teach me how to disarm now."

Dorathea searched Sloane's face. "Yes. I agree. We will move on to disarming. But you must practice the detection spell. I have placed Harold's shoe and your mum's brush in your tote. You must be able to use them to detect both Harold and Jane by tomorrow."

Sloane patted her back pocket, and the brush was gone. "All right. But I also want to learn how to move things like you just did. That could be really handy in my line of work."

*A bit out of your league*, Elvina said.

"She is correct. You are unprepared for such a complicated spell."

Dorathea passed her hand over the pages of the *Book of Hagorúnum*, and they fluttered to a stop. She snapped her fingers. A dark leather-bound book floated out of the bookcase and whizzed across the room. She caught it without turning her head.

Sloane grinned. "So when I learn this spell, can I just take whatever I want from someone?"

"Absolutely not. We do not disarm for any purpose other than to protect."

"How loosely can we define protection?"

Elvina cackled. *You're so much like your mother.*

Dorathea's shoulders rose with a deep breath, and she exhaled slowly. "No more interruptions, pet." She held up the book in her hand. "This is the *Official History of Dracas in Europe*. I will summon a dragon from its pages, and you will disarm me of the book and close its cover before the creature can fully emerge, sending it back to its pages and protecting us from its wrath."

"Yeah. Right. The dragon's a hologram or something?" Sloane waited for a reply, but neither Dorathea nor Elvina answered. "Dragons exist?"

"They do, indeed," Dorathea said. "For your training, I will just call a wyvern. They are less dangerous than their cousins.

And rarely breathe fire." She glanced at the ceiling. "Alfred disapproves of firebreathers in the covenstead. But don't be fooled. The wyvern's swiftness and venomous sting make it deadly. It doesn't need fire."

Sloane crossed her arms. "Wait. You're serious right now? Why would you teach me with something that could actually kill us?"

*The danger must be able to compel your desire to protect*, answered Elvina. *It has to be real.*

Dorathea opened the book, and Sloane jerked. "Calm yourself and focus like before. The incantation for disarming an aggressor is *Āniman*." We will begin with your pronunciation. Repeat after me, ān-ee-mahn."

"Ān-ee-man," Sloane intoned.

*Not bad*, Elvina said. *Less cat and more aunt in the last a. Try again,* ān-ee-mahn.

"Ān-ee-mahn."

Dorathea nodded. "Very good. Repeat the word several more times in your head until I summon the wyvern. When I do, it will spring forth, headfirst, disoriented, but will quickly assess who its captors are. Our lives will be in danger. To cast the spell correctly, you will align the energy in your mind and body into a single desire to protect us and then say āniman clearly. Are you ready?"

Sloane planted her feet firmly to the floor as if bracing for a fight and asked, "What's our backup plan?"

*There is none*, answered Elvina.

Dorathea slid her hand over the open pages. The air above the book pulsated with expanding ripples. Then the foul scent of carrion emanated from the pages.

The first of the dragon Sloane saw was two leathery horns. Then a patch of dark brown and gray reptilian scales. She took a deep breath and braced herself. A second later, the top of the wyvern's head sprung forth. It flailed about and released a bone-chilling roar.

Sloane stuttered, "Ān...ān...Āniman."

The wyvern bore its fanged teeth and wielded its leathery horns. Its screeches filled the room while its serpentine neck pushed up, snaking out of the pages.

"Āh-ni-man!" Sloane shouted.

The beast looked around the room with beady, orange-red eyes, searching for the voice source.

Elvina rose on all fours, arching her back.

The wyvern locked its gaze on Sloane, and its leather wings emerged from the book. Sloane stumbled backward.

"Āniman!" she shouted.

The creature opened its jaws and hissed a forked tongue, its rough tip flicking Sloane's cheek, and just as she opened her mouth, the wyvern's spiked tail appeared, lashing forward.

*Belūcan!* Elvina shouted.

The wyvern's menacing force disappeared from the room, followed by its tail, wings, neck, and head as it slipped back into the pages. The book cover slammed shut.

Sloane bent over, her hands clenching her knees. "Jesus Christ, Dorathea. I'm guessing that wasn't one of your better ideas."

"Nonsense. That went as well as expected. Your iteration was correct. But you were unable to focus your energy. What did you feel when the wyvern poised to strike?"

Sloane shook out her arms and hands. "Nothing. Well, maybe shock. Seeing a wyvern isn't an everyday thing for me."

*Mhmm.* Elvina's tail twitched. *There's no shame in being scared.*

Sloane glared at the familiar. "I wasn't afraid."

*Your eyes told a different story.*

"Āniman!" The dark-brown leather book zipped through the air to Sloane's open hand. "Whoa. I did it." She surprised herself and looked at Elvina. "See, I can cast the spell. The wyvern just surprised me. I wasn't scared."

Dorathea snapped her fingers, and the book reappeared on her lectern. "You may have been unnerved before. However, just now, you were angry."

"No, I wasn't. I'm frustrated with Elvina. But not angry."

*Same emotion, different degree, dear,* Elvina said.

"Enough." Dorathea held Sloane's eyes. "I warned you, pet. When we cast spells out of anger, we open ourselves to evil. It can manipulate our anger and prehend our power. I fear you have already done so many times. But no more."

Sloane closed her eyes. The muzzle of Morris's gun flashed. An ache lodged in her throat, and heat spread from her neck. What if she had known how to disarm—

"My request is important." Dorathea interrupted her thoughts. "We must remain impenetrable to the evil that has come to Denwick."

Sloane opened her eyes. "Fine. I'll work on it."

# CHAPTER FOURTEEN

Sloane left after her first training session ended. She was hoping to leave the hobbit house on better terms with the house spirit, but she had forgotten its name, remembering only that it started with an A.

"Goodbye, Albert," she said, guessing. Alfred slammed the double doors behind her, unamused. "Hey. At least I tried," she said and laughed aloud at the absurdity of a house being mad at her.

The sun was bright in a cloudless sky, but the crisp spring air gave Sloane goosebumps. She scanned the street, fastened the middle button on her cardigan, and headed toward Old Main. It was time to make an impression on her suspects. Whoever hired Morris was a Magical or was working with a wiċċan and perhaps a Demon as well, so she needed to be ready for anything. In her head, she chanted the two incantations Dorathea and Elvina had taught her and considered the case.

What if whoever hired Morris was unaware of their actions because they were possessed? She needed to ask Dorathea if that was a possibility. Could there be more than one employer, perhaps even three? Maybe a Magical was controlling the suspect, and a Demon had possessed them both? There was so much she didn't know about the magical world.

Sloane stepped through the arbor entrance to the Old Main shops. A Different Petal was her first stop. When she opened the shop door, a bird alarm chirped a bright melody. The sweet scent of candles filled the air. A walk-in chiller ran the length of the store's left side, and gift and card displays were on the right. Lore's shop rivaled any Manhattan floral boutique.

Sloane heard Lore before she saw her. She was darting around the back, watering houseplants and tropicals and humming loudly. Sloane rested against the stainless-steel counter and waited for Lore to notice her.

"Oh, my! You startled me." She set the watering can down and took off her earbuds. "I'm so glad you've come to visit."

Sloane dropped her tote on the floor. "Your shop's beautiful."

"Thank you. I've worked very hard. You know, keeping up to date with the industry. And I love to decorate. When you visit my brother's office and my father's fish market, the décor comes from me."

A computer inside the service area dinged. "Excuse me. Just when I thought my day couldn't get busier. More orders. But I shouldn't complain." She mumbled, "Wish my father could see this." A printer underneath the cash register spat out several pages.

"Do you get a lot of Internet business?" Sloane asked.

She collected the pages. "Oh, yeah. The flower industry went digital years ago. At least sixty to sixty-five percent of my sales come from national and international orders. I spent a fortune on my website." She turned the computer monitor to face Sloane. "It's nice, isn't it?"

"Yeah, sure."

"I never asked what you do for a living."

"I'm a private investigator."

"Really? That must be exciting. I'm sure you have a website for your PI work, right?"

Sloane laughed. "No. My cases come by word of mouth."

Lore shook her head. "Good Lord, you and my dad. But you're too young to be a dinosaur."

"Speaking of James, are you guys all right? I don't mean to pry, but yesterday I was in the fish market, and you sounded like you were arguing."

Lore gave her an easy smile. "I apologize. Like father like daughter, I guess. Except I'm probably more stubborn. It was nothing, though. Just his finances. It got a bit testy."

"Is the fish market in trouble?" Sloane asked.

"Heaven's no. But he would be doing better if he'd advertise more. He refuses to. He's under the impression his customers are loyal to him."

"And there are better prices, huh? I heard him complain about the Gildeys' company trying to ruin his."

"The difference between their businesses is like whales and fish. The Gildeys provide exclusively to national and international markets. Dad's just angry because Isobel launched more trawlers after Sean died. He said he had an agreement with Sean. But Sean is dead, and Isobel can do what she wants. It's her business. Right or wrong."

Sloane thought Lore was downplaying her dad's anger. "Do the Gidleys' extra trawlers affect other fishermen?"

"Maybe. I'm not sure. The point is our father doesn't have to worry. Quinn and I won't let him go under. The market is his life. It's all he has left."

"These past few months must have been rough on him. First, losing his wife and the business slowing down. Then his best friend is killed. Not to mention the Wests. Is he coping okay?"

"He's grieving. But he's tough."

Sloane rested her arms on the countertop. "I don't want to take up too much of your time. But if you have a few minutes, could I ask you some questions about Harold?"

Lore looked at her watch and took a deep breath. "Talking about him is hard. But I'll try."

"I appreciate it." Sloane tried to catch Lore's gaze, but she was reading her new orders. "I came to Denwick to settle the

West estate. But I'm also here to investigate Harold's murder."
She waited for a reaction.

Lore remained perfectly still. "I'm sorry," she said finally.
"It's hard for me to hear those two things together—Harold
and murder." Her eyes filled with tears. "Detective Hanson told
us the horrible man who killed Harold was dead. What are you
investigating?"

"We have reason to believe someone hired the killer."
Sloane always said "we." Most people assumed she had a team
or a partner, which worked in her favor.

The comment seemed to surprise Lore. She turned to
Sloane, her mouth slightly agape. "Do...do you mean from
Denwick?"

"It's the only logical conclusion. Morris had pictures of
Harold and me. Only someone from Denwick would know
about our connection."

"Pictures? Oh my God...Charlie."

Sloane raised her brow. "What about him?"

"Nothing. I meant...well, he's been under a lot of pressure
lately. He isn't acting like himself. Your news will upset him
even more." She bit the nail on her thumb.

"I'm hoping he'll be eager to help me find who killed his
uncle."

"Oh, yes. Of course, he will." Lore placed an order on the
back counter. "And I am too. What can I help you with?"

"I was hoping you could tell me if everything was all right
between Harold and your dad?"

Lore frowned. "You can't think my dad had anything to do
with his murder? They were the Musketeers." She grabbed a
bag of ferns and eucalyptus stems off the cart and tore it open.
Then busied herself, unwrapping several bunches of lemon-
colored irises. The question seemed to annoy her.

"I'm just trying to understand Harold's last week here,"
Sloane said. "Did he and James spend time together? Was he
upset about what the Gildeys are doing like your father is? Have
they caused his law firm any financial problems?"

"Well, about Harold and my dad spending time together
I haven't a clue. They usually meet up once a week. But you

should ask him." She shook her head in frustration. "I've been at every MCC meeting. My dad is the only person who has mentioned financial trouble. Speaking of the MCC, our next meeting is Friday at the Huxham building. Are you coming?"

"What's the MCC? And why me?"

"The Main Street Commerce Committee. And of course, you. The West Gallery is yours now. I hope you're planning on reopening. It would be a huge loss for Old Main if you closed it. Your family business has a loyal following globally." She pointed toward the chiller. "Could you bring me the large white bucket, please?"

Sloane walked around a wall of planters. There were various sizes and colors of ceramic, metal, seagrass, and terra-cotta. The chiller was full of floral arrangements, smaller bunches, a variety of single blooms and filler greens, and a white bucket full of cornflower-blue hydrangeas.

She handed Lore the bucket. "I hadn't thought about the West Gallery. I suppose my options are selling it or hiring someone to run it."

Lore picked through some hydrangeas, adding three of the sizable blooms to each vase. "Of course, you have choices. I'm sure Charlie can help you figure out what to do."

"Charles? I'm not sure he's got time for me."

"Oh, he does. He comes across unfriendly, but that's only because he's lost without his uncle."

"Understandable. Did Harold and Charlie ever have problems?"

"Not any more than other fathers and sons. Harold doted over Charlie from the day he took him in. And when Charlie went to law school, my God, you would've thought he won the lottery, a child following in his footsteps." Lore opened a package of fragile sherbet orange peonies. Their fragrance smothered the air.

Sloane stepped back. "Jesus, those are as strong as trumpet lilies. No offense."

"None taken." Lore added the peonies to each arrangement. "You have a very sensitive nose. Most people love their scent."

Lore spun the first finished arrangement. The computer dinged several times.

"Sounds like you just got busier," Sloane said. "Do you ever get orders from New York?"

Lore looked up and tilted her head to one side. "You know, I don't recall. But I'm sure I have at least a few over the years. I receive orders from elsewhere in the States."

"Maybe we New Yorkers aren't the best at sending flowers. Who knows?" Sloane grinned. "Do you know why Charles was asked to stay away from the Spotted Owl?"

"Who in the world told you that? Ken would never ban Charlie from the pub. They're best friends." She sighed. "I shouldn't tell you this. But the truth is Charlie has a drinking problem. He didn't want it to affect his relationship with Harold or his work at the law firm, so he tried to stop. But he struggles. That's why he stays away from the pub."

"I see. Well, thanks for your time. I'll leave you to it."

Lore stepped over to the cash register area, retrieved a business card from a drawer, and handed it to Sloane. "This is my phone number. Call me any time. I want to help you catch whoever did this to dear Harold. To us."

"Thanks, I appreciate it." Sloane rapped the counter twice, picked up her tote, and dropped the card inside. "One more thing. Where do you live?"

Lore pointed up. "Above the store. You're welcome to visit me anytime."

* * *

Sloane stood on the sidewalk, staring at the smaller brick building on the other side of the Spotted Owl. The West Gallery. It had two tinted plate-glass windows and an elegant sign hanging above its door. Harold had placed Nathaniel and Mary's keys in the box Charles gave her. He had also labeled each key. She found the one marked with a G and unlocked the gallery's door.

The tinted windows allowed only faint light inside. Sloane turned on spotlights in the gallery's center. They illuminated a sculpture of a woman's bust in red marble. She had long, wavy hair twining down her shoulders and cupping her breasts. She walked over to the woman and stroked her face, feeling the marble's matte finish. A wall hung with a cluster of baroque oil paintings in water-gilded frames floated behind the sculpture.

She moved behind the installation. The wooden floors creaked under every step. "Jesus Christ," she said aloud, standing in the Wests' office area. Their desk, chairs, file cabinets, and even the knotted Persian rug on the floor were identical to those of Jane's. Except for the clean and organized desktop, she could have been standing in her Bronx apartment. Sloane stared at a picture of Jane as a teenager, then picked up a black lacquer pen. It vibrated in her hand, just as Jane's hairbrush had, and she wondered whose vibration it was. Nathaniel's? Mary's?

She tapped the pen's tip on the desk and then pointed it at Jane's photo. "You hid us from your family but wrote them hundreds of letters. Why? Why did you run if you weren't running away from them? You were getting away from someone else, weren't you? And you hid me. Were you running from my father?"

A scrabbling sound came from the back of the room, and she turned, holding the pen like a knife. "Who's there?" There was a loud thud against the floor. It came from the other side of the room. As she stepped from the center spotlights, the space became darker. She turned on her phone's flashlight and searched the back of the gallery.

A painting had fallen off the wall.

Sloane discovered a door on the back wall. It was ajar. The room behind was full of installation tables and shelves, with boxes stacked along the walls. She checked the exit door. It was locked. "Who's there?" she yelled again.

Silence.

Sloane searched behind boxes, old easels, cans of paint, and canvases. Then after a few deep breaths, she returned to the painting on the ground, rehung it, and straightened the art on either side that hung askew. The group of watercolors drew her in. Each was a shadowy nightscape with bold brushstrokes of indigo, charcoal, mahogany, wine, and black. The images were intense, dark, and the colors saturated. She searched for the painter's name and found a JW in the left corner. Jane West. These were not the bright Impressionist paintings she thought Jane preferred.

The Wests still hung her art in their gallery. Why did Jane hide from them for so many years? Or did she? Did she leave their New York apartment in the dead of night? Teleport and hide outside their windows, watching them?

Sloane became aware of the pen vibrating in her hand again. She closed her eyes and said, "Onwreon." Her third eye opened, and she focused on the veil of color until it cleared.

In her vision, Nathaniel appeared, sitting at his desk. The pen lay on a piece of stationery. He looked up at Mary, who held an envelope against her chest. Tears rolled down her cheeks. Mary reached up and pulled a gold pin from her hair. Long black and white strands cascaded over her shoulders, and she began to spin, moving faster and faster until her hair and dress swirled into one like the dancers in the Degas.

Sloane reached out to touch them.

Nathaniel smiled at Mary and spoke softly, "Dearest Jane, we have received your invitation and are overcome with joy to meet her." The pen lifted from the paper and wrote his words across the page. Without warning, he jumped to his feet, and Mary stopped spinning. The pen fell onto the desk. Sloane peered into the vision, searching for what they saw. Maybe they had heard something? Nathaniel and Mary had disappeared into the back of the gallery.

"Hello. I'm so happy someone's here," a voice called from the gallery's front door.

Sloane's third eye slammed shut, and she dropped the pen.

A woman stood inside the doorway. "I'm so sorry. I didn't mean to startle you. I saw the lights on. Has the gallery opened up again?"

Sloane caught her breath. "No. It's not. I'm just checking on things. And I'm about to leave." She walked toward the woman, waving her out.

"I'm so sorry. Should I keep checking back?"

"Sure, you do that." Sloane locked the door. She was drained as if she had pulled a three-day surveillance. She sat at the desk, replaying what she'd seen. Her mind raced. Not only had she been able to detect Nathaniel and Mary with a spell, but she had also discovered new evidence. Jane had invited her parents to come to New York. She was coming out of hiding. Introducing them to her daughter. Is that what triggered a Demon? If a coven of three is strong, a coven of five Wests would be indomitable.

"I need a drink," Sloane said out loud.

Immediately, she heard Jane's voice in her head. "Don't mask your feelings with alcohol, pet."

Sloane scoffed. "Why mess with the longest relationship I've ever had besides you, mother?" Sloane locked the gallery and headed next door. Besides a whiskey neat, she needed to clear up a few things with the Keanes.

* * *

Late-morning light pooled inside the Spotted Owl's front door, but the stairwell remained dark. Sloane stepped carefully to the bottom.

"Guid mornin', lass," Ken said as she rounded the corner. He polished glasses alone behind the bar, shoulders thrown back, perfect posture.

"You already know my footsteps?"

"Aye, a landlord's business." He smiled. "Fancy a swallie to get the day goin'?"

"Why not. Give me a shot of Oscar's neat." Sloane lifted her chin at the door leading to the kitchen. "You're risking Rose catching you in the act again."

He laughed and poured her drink. "Dinna fash yirsel. Me wee lass isnae 'ere."

Sloane tossed her tote against the stool and sat. "For what it's worth, I find your accent charming. Not sure what's wrong with your wee lass." She smiled. "Is Fiona here?"

Her name had no sooner left Sloane's mouth when Fiona appeared, walking toward them.

"Hello, Sloane. Are you okay? You look like something's upset you."

"I'm fine. Just an eager customer at the West Gallery. She thought I had reopened the place." Sloane knocked back half her drink. "Do you have a few minutes to spare before your lunch crowd arrives?"

"Of course, we do," Fiona said.

"Great. You know I came to Denwick to settle the Wests' estate."

"Aye," Ken said.

"I'm also here to investigate Harold's murder. But I didn't want to say anything until after his funeral."

Ken picked up his towel and grabbed another glass. "I thought an angry stranger killed Harold?"

Fiona rested an elegant finger on her chin. "That's what Charlie said. And the man's dead, right? You had to—well—it was self-defense." She adjusted the sangria silk scarf holding back her dark coils.

"Yeah. Morris is dead, but he didn't act alone. We know he was a hired hitman."

With one hand on the bar, Fiona steadied herself, grasping Ken's shoulder, her long fingers digging into his shirt. "My God. Do you think it was someone from here? That's impossible. We're all family."

"I know it's hard to believe, but can you think of anyone who might have wanted Harold dead?"

Ken halted his cleaning. "Maybe one of his clients?"

"We'll check his case files."

Fiona let go of Ken. "I've never seen Harold cross with anyone in town, except—" She hesitated.

"Except whom?"

"Well, I wouldn't say cross. But he and James Reed had been strained."

"Did they have a falling out over Lore and Charles?"

Surprise flashed across Ken's face. "Nah, I don't think Harold meddled with them. James might have thought he did. But I never heard them argue over it."

Fiona tapped her long fingernails on the bar. "I disagree, love. There was tension between Harold and James. It could have been because of Charlie and Lore." She looked at Sloane. "James would glare at Harold and Charlie whenever Lore was around." She looked back at Ken. "Don't you remember James and Harold's row in the pub?"

"Aye," Ken said, frowning. "But you don't think that was about a teenage breakup over thirty years ago, do ya?"

"Not at all, love. But I'm trying to answer Sloane's questions honestly. James was upset about something, and so was Harold."

"What about Charles's drinking? Did it create problems in his relationship with Harold?"

Ken hesitated and placed the polished glass on the back shelf. "You've found out quite a bit, eh?"

"It's my job."

"Aye. They had difficulties with it. Charlie has tried to give up the drinking, but the gambling's been harder for him."

"Gambling?"

"Oh, yes." Fiona lifted her chin at a corner table. "He even brought it in here. Sat right over there with his bet maker."

Ken patted Fiona's hand and said, "I made them leave immediately. And Charlie did without a fuss. And he hasn't been back since. But the disrespect for us and our business stung."

"And the disregard for Rose, expecting her to serve a criminal. The man even showed up at Harold's reception," she said.

"Did Harold ever mention Charlie's gambling?"

"He was furious," Ken said. "He said Charlie was out of the firm if he didn't give up the betting and the booze."

"When did Harold tell you that?"

Ken shrugged. "Well, he didn't say it to me."

"He told me," Fiona answered. "He came to the pub a few days after your grandparents' accident. Grief had overwhelmed him." She looked at Ken and back at Sloane. "I shouldn't say this, but he had had too much to drink and told me many other things."

"About Charles?"

"No. He was upset with James, and I think he was still grieving Alice's death."

"James's wife?"

"Yes. A beautiful, gentle soul. Kind. Easygoing. They were very close. Like I said. We're all like family. Anyway, I stopped serving him and made him eat. When it was time to close, Chef walked him home."

A group of customers came into the pub. "Looks like the lunch crowd is starting. I'll be off." Sloane placed a ten-dollar bill on the bar. "Could you tell Rose hello for me?"

Fiona answered, "Of course, we will. Let us know if you need anything else."

On Old Main, Sloane sat on a bench under a Garry oak. The sun was bright despite the tree's massive canopy. She didn't know Ken or Fiona Keane well enough to be sure if either one was lying, but she did have a gut feeling they had told her the truth, mostly. Still, she wondered if they kept as many secrets and lies as Jane had.

Could the Keanes be involved with a wiccan? Had Dorathea obtained permission to use the detection spell on them yet? She was at a standstill until she could detect their suspects. But then again, maybe Chen's information on the suspects' financials would reveal something.

# CHAPTER FIFTEEN

As she tapped Chen's number, a horn blasted, and a black Jeep Wrangler stopped in the lane beside her. "Hey. I've been looking everywhere for you." It was Rose Keane. She patted the passenger's seat and leaned across it, opening the door. "Interested in lunch?"

Sloane had not planned on having lunch or any other distractions, but then again, she hadn't met someone who made her stomach flutter since Jess. And how could a meal with a possible suspect hurt?

Rose backed out of the lane and turned on Second Street, heading away from the shore toward the mountains. "I'm taking you to my favorite spot. I told you time outside would do you good. I might even throw in a massage."

Sloane's body tensed. She watched the neighborhood blocks pass and the landscapes become open fields. "It's beautiful here. Is it always so green?"

"Even into the winter." Rose merged onto the Island Highway and pointed toward the mountains. "See the house over there?"

Sloane scanned the foot of a mountain. "Wow. That's some castle."

"Right? There are a few others in Victoria. You can tour them. But not that one. It belongs to the Gildey family. No one from Denwick has ever been inside. Not that I know of, anyway."

"Some digs," Sloane said. "Doesn't sound like they're a neighborly bunch."

"Not at all. The only time the Gildeys grace us with their presence is at special community events."

"Like funerals?"

Rose stared ahead. "No, not usually."

"So why Harold's?"

Rose shrugged. "Maybe he did legal work for them?"

"I don't know. Dorathea didn't seem to think he did." So why were Isobel and Andrew Gildey at Harold's funeral? Sloane thought she ought to pay the Gildeys a visit. Make herself the first person from the village to walk through their doors.

Rose turned off the highway onto a narrow back road. "This is the Nature Conservatory. It's a Garry oak ecosystem. Very rare. Most of the species in it are endangered. There's a meadow full of camas on the other side of those trees. Look." Wildflowers stretched to the horizon, a deep blue and yellow tapestry growing between lichen-covered boulders and moss-covered trees.

Sloane turned back and stared at Rose, the curve of her jawline and the warm glow of her skin. She wanted to reach out. Stroke her cheek. Cup the back of her bare neck and gently pull her into a soft kiss.

"It's beautiful, isn't it?" Rose asked.

Sloane stared ahead. "Yeah. The most stunning thing I've ever seen."

"And I bet you've seen your share." Rose merged onto a one-lane dirt road and drove into a dense forest canopy. "We're here." She parked inside the tree line and jumped out of the jeep. Sloane followed her to the tailgate.

"Here, take this." Rose handed Sloane a wool blanket and lifted a picnic basket out from behind her seat. "We have a short hike to my favorite spot. If we see any bears, just do what I do."

"Wait. Are you serious?"

"No." Rose tossed her head back and laughed. "We do have bears, but I've never seen one down this far."

"Ha. You're funny, Keane. Let's make the city girl sweat, right?"

Rose laughed harder. "Ah, I'm not cruel, but your expression was worth it. And making you sweat sounds like fun."

Sloane chuckled and trailed behind Rose through a thick understory of dank leaves, ferns, and shrubs. She pressed the blanket to her chest. With one word, she could use the detection spell on Rose. Remove her from the suspect list. But she heard Dorathea's warning in her head. They needed permission.

Screw it, she thought, and lowered her eyes and whispered, "Onwreon." Nothing. She stopped on the path, closed her eyes, and repeated, "Onwreon." Her third eye opened, and she concentrated, pushing through the veil. But no image of Rose appeared.

Above them, the birds made a ruckus, scattering from the trees.

"Hey. What's the matter?"

Sloane looked up the path. Rose had stopped, waiting for her. "I'm good. I just thought I heard something."

"Don't worry. I was kidding about the bears. Sort of." Rose grinned and sprinted toward a massive Garry oak. "Here we are. My spot."

"It's amazing." Sloane spread the blanket out underneath the tree. "Do you bring all the girls here?"

"I think you've seen enough of Old Denwick's population to answer that question." Rose opened the basket and sat with legs crisscrossed, her back to the sun.

Sloane kicked off her shoes and lay down, propping up on one elbow. She stared at the flowers and grasses in front of them and listened to water rushing in the distance. Rose was right. She did need a change of scenery. This spot was the best view she had seen since arriving in BC.

Rose unpacked the basket—a bowl of strawberries, a brie melting out of its skin, a crusty baguette, and a bottle of merlot. She poured Sloane a glass. "And half a glass for the driver."

Sloane sipped, letting the mild tannins and vanilla undertones linger on her tongue. "Have you always lived here?"

"I actually spent four years in Ontario, at McMasters University. Did my Bachelor of Commerce and came back. I've lived above the pub ever since."

"Do all the shops have apartments?"

"I don't know. The gallery does. When I returned from uni, your grandfather offered it to me. It's a great two-bedroom. He thought maybe I'd prefer something quieter than the one above the pub." She smiled. "He was such a nice man."

Sloane took a long drink and watched Rose finish cutting the baguette. "So you got your degree and came back to run the pub. Was that always your plan?"

"Ever since I can remember." She tilted her head back and closed her eyes. "There was a time at school, actually a relationship, when I questioned taking it over. But it passed. The relationship, not my desire to run the business."

Sloane swirled her wine. "Sounds like words drawn from a painful experience."

"It didn't end well," Rose said, spreading brie on the baguette. "Talia left at graduation. No goodbye. Nothing. Took a long time to get over that."

"Yeah. Relationships are hard. And breakups are harder. Might as well live alone, or at least with a cat."

"Oh, that's so cynical. How long ago did your relationship end?"

Sloane tapped her finger on the wineglass. "Almost two years. And this year, my ex-girlfriend and my ex-best friend are getting married."

"Ouch. I'm sorry."

"No, no. Don't be sorry yet. I haven't gotten to the best part." Sloane chuckled and drained the rest of her wine. "They sent me an invitation."

"No, they didn't. That's—"

"Dumpster-fire shit."

Rose burst out laughing. "I was going to say, really hurtful."

Sloane held out her empty glass. "Doesn't hurt if you don't care."

"I guess not." Rose poured a refill. "Helps to have a focus, though. The Spotted Owl is mine."

"I couldn't have worked for my mother. Hell, the idea makes me shiver." Sloane thought about Jane's office, the degrees on the walls, the welcoming sofa and her sleek leather chair, and what she now understood was her manipulation of hundreds of minds.

"Trust me. My mother isn't easy to work with either." Rose bent back and faced the sun.

Continuous caws erupted in the trees. Sloane looked behind them and saw a horde of crows move like a black blanket from one canopy to another. "So, what's wrong with Fiona?"

Rose filled a plate with strawberries and placed the food between them. "It's hard to explain. I'll just say she makes things difficult."

"Yeah. Moms do that. Is it the pub?" Sloane took a piece of bread, biting into the soft cheese.

"Mostly. And my brother, Oscar."

"Is the pub in financial trouble?"

Rose looked at her oddly. "No." She paused. "Okay, West. Enough of your interrogation. It's my turn. What are you really doing here?"

The comment surprised Sloane. "What do you mean? Here in Denwick, or here, here?"

"Here in Denwick. Although I'm not sure why you're here, here either." Rose grinned and sucked the juice from a strawberry before biting it.

Sloane sat up, spinning the ring on her finger. "You know I came to Denwick to finalize the Wests' estate. But I'm also here for work. Someone hired Morris to kill Harold and me."

Rose stared at her in disbelief. "You think someone from Denwick hired him?"

"We know someone did."

"We? Are you NYPD?"

"Not exactly. I'm a private investigator, following up on a lead."

"I knew there was a reason you asked so many questions." Rose lay on her side with her head resting in her hand and stared into Sloane's eyes. "A detective. Wow. Okay, I want to help. Ask me anything. One of the benefits of my job is knowing everyone's secrets."

Sloane fell silent. She had informants back in the city—Mel, street kids, drunks, and hoodrats. But none of them had eyes like mottled jade. Eyes that drew her in and held her, making it hard to turn away or concentrate.

The crows cawed again, and Sloane jerked her head toward the ruckus. She peered into the dense trees. The birds scattered and whirled around the sky until they decided in unison to take over another canopy.

She turned back. Rose's body was only a plate distance away. So close her skin pricked with arousal. She imaged pressing against the full length of her, spreading her legs with a knee… She bolted upright.

"What's the matter?" Rose asked.

"Nothing. I'm fine…my hip hurts. I need to sit up for a minute."

"Oh, no. Cramp? Want me to rub it out?"

Heat spread up Sloane's neck.

"No? Okay." Rose grinned. "So tell me detective, what do you want to ask me?"

"All right, Keane. Maybe you can help me sort out some conflicting information."

"Will that make me your mole?"

"Sure, you're officially my spy."

"How exciting. Should I get a burner so we can call each other?"

Sloane chuckled. "You watch a lot of TV, huh?"

"You don't use those pay-as-you-go phones?"

"No, Keane. The criminals use those."

Rose laughed. "Oops."

Sloane enjoyed Rose's enthusiasm for helping. It made it easier to sit across from her, less complicated. Less tempting to get into something unwise. "I usually pay my informants."

"That dinner you promised will do."

"That's an easy price."

"You would think." Rose grinned and sipped her wine.

Sloane rubbed her thigh. At least she thought a change of conversation would be easier. "I wondered if you knew the history between Charles Huxham and Lore Reed?"

"I actually do," Rose said, her voice taking on a serious tone. "A few months ago, James came in and had drinks with my dad. Pounding them back. Got drunk. Started complaining about what Charlie and Harold had done to Lore. Well, my dad had too much to drink, too. So I cut them both off and called Quinn to take James home. When my dad and I were alone, I asked the right questions, and the truth came out."

Rose bit into a strawberry, and its juice dripped over her full bottom lip. She wiped it off. "He said one night, right before Charlie left for UBC, Lore came into the pub hysterical and wanted to talk. They were all friends. She told Dad she'd overheard a conversation between Charlie and Harold that wrecked her."

"Did he say what she overheard?"

"No. But that isn't important. That's not what caused the problem between them. It was what happened next. My dad took a bottle from behind the bar and snuck Lore upstairs to the apartment. They drank and talked. One thing led to another, and they ended up sleeping together. The next day Lore broke up with Charlie right before he left for uni."

"Damn. I wasn't expecting that." Sloane paused. "Did your dad and Lore start a relationship?"

"He didn't say. If they did, I'm sure my mom stopped it as soon as Dad met her."

"How do Ken and Lore get along now?"

Rose thought for a minute. "They're still friends, but not close or anything." She spread brie on the last slices of bread.

"Did Charles ever find out about them?"

"No. My dad said Charlie never knew." Rose took a piece of baguette and brie. "Maybe Lore puts up with him over guilt."

"Could be. But why does he hang around with the girl who dumped him?"

Rose leaned over the plate of food. "That I don't know."

Sloane warmed at her closeness, finding it difficult to concentrate. "So, did your parents meet at UBC?"

"No. My mom grew up in Jamaica but went to uni in Scotland. My dad met her there."

"I see. I think Fiona misses the sun."

"Why do you say that?"

"When your dad introduced me to your mom, he said they wouldn't want to live anyplace other than Denwick. Let's just say the look on your mom's face conveyed he was wrong."

Rose bit into the last strawberry. "That doesn't surprise me. My mom's tired. I'm sure she wants to be retired by now. But they're younger than my grandparents were when they handed the business to my dad."

Sloane studied Rose's face. It was so stunning it confused her. The symmetry of her eyes. Her high cheekbones. The perfect line of her nose. But something simmered just beneath the beauty. She reached for more bread. The plate was empty.

"I better pack more for next time," Rose said. "I was hungrier than I thought."

"No problem. I'm thoroughly satisfied."

"I figured you would like a picnic."

"I'm a sucker for them."

Rose held Sloane's eyes and moved the empty plate behind her. She patted the blanket. "Relax with me again."

Sloane hesitated but then lay down and propped herself up on her elbow. She felt like someone had unbuckled her seatbelt in a runaway car.

"Intuition is a valuable trait in your line of work, don't you agree?" Rose asked.

"Yeah. It's important. But you have to back it up with evidence."

"And as an informant, I can help you with that." She reached across the blanket and touched Sloane's arm. "Maybe I'm what you need right now, a perceptive partner. How about it?"

Sloane looked down. "I'm sorry, Keane. I work alone."

# CHAPTER SIXTEEN

The smell of the outdoors was still on Sloane's clothes as she stood in Mallow Cottage's living room. Her afternoon with Rose had been great. She'd uncovered useful information. But Rose was becoming a distraction.

She stared at the room. Framed art hung on every inch of the walls, knickknacks covered every surface, and antique rugs and furniture filled the floor. Her grandparents were hoarders. Their home was crammed with stuff, three times as much as Jane had in her apartment. People who held on to things confused her. Why burden yourself? Now she had to dispose of Jane's *and* her parents' stuff.

She tossed her tote on the sofa. Being in Denwick was starting to feel too complicated. She hoped she didn't have to be in Canada to finalize property sales because she didn't want to return once she left.

Drowsy from the wine at lunch, she dropped to the sofa, her head falling back on the cushion. The truth was Rose's company was the best she had had since arriving. Hell, it was the best she had had in years. But Rose was a suspect until she wasn't, and the last thing she needed was to complicate her investigation with feelings.

Sloane walked to the refrigerator for a diet soda and rested her hip against the island, watching Elvina sleep on the window seat.

She roused and lifted on all fours, arched her back, stretching and yawning, and turned to Sloane. *Hello, dear. It's late. Did you have a pleasant day?*

Her smooth voice flowed through Sloane's head. "Yeah, it was good."

*Why so melancholy then?* Elvina leaped off the seat and padded to a kitchen counter, where a small fountain of water streamed down a fake rock into a ceramic bowl.

"I'm fine." Sloane drained the soda, crushed the can, and tossed it in a bin. "I have a lot of things on my mind. Like dinner. Are you hungry?"

*Depends on what you're planning to serve.*

"Watch it, or it's canned tuna for you." Sloane took a pack of chicken from the refrigerator. "I could grill these. Add some baby potatoes and peppers."

"Sounds wonderful. Am I invited?" Dorathea asked from behind the refrigerator door.

Sloane slammed it shut. "Jesus Christ. Stop doing that." She tossed the chicken into the sink. "Can't you ring the doorbell like a normal person?"

"Oh, your flair for the dramatic." She shook her head and stepped past Sloane. "I admire understated personalities, myself."

"Nice. That coming from the woman appearing out of thin air and wearing a purple cloak."

Elvina leaped onto the island. *So much for relaxation. I figured you'd be in a better mood after lounging in the sun all afternoon.*

Sloane glared at her. "How did you know that? Were you spying on me?"

*I don't spy, dear.*

"Your safety is Elvina's responsibility," Dorathea said.

"Was I in danger with Rose Keane? You said my ability is protecting, right? So I can take care of myself. No more spying on me, got it?"

*She said you could in time*, Elvina answered.

"You are untrained and reckless with your abilities. That makes you vulnerable." Dorathea sighed. "However, Elvina's presence had nothing to do with protection. You attempted the detection spell without permission."

"Yeah. But it didn't work."

"That matters not. Consequently, I spent most of the afternoon with the Grand Coven trying to call off the *Weardas* for your illegal use of magic."

"What's the Weardas?"

*Who, not what. They are our guardians*, answered Elvina. *Like the Nogical police.*

"Okay. The more important issue is my spell didn't work. I haven't had any problems with it during practice."

Dorathea shook her head. "Maybe it failed because subconsciously, you knew it was the wrong thing to do."

Sloane laughed. "I doubt that."

"And if you have forgotten, the Keane family is on our case board. Is it wise to spend time with Rose outside of the investigation?"

Sloane brushed past Dorathea and went outside. "It was for the case. Rose is a good informant. She's already given me answers that would've taken days to sort out." She lit the grill and scrubbed the grate with a wire brush as if it was a gang tag on her stoop. Her mind traveled back to New York. Jane on a slab in the morgue. Harold's body slumped over her armchair. Her heart pounded the air out of her lungs, forcing her to steady herself against the barbeque.

"Are you all right?" Dorathea appeared next to her with a platter of chicken and vegetable kabobs.

"I'm fine." Sloane looked at the platter. "Why did you do that? I said I would make dinner."

"As you know, Elvina can be quite impatient with her meals. So I decided to hurry things along." Dorathea handed the food to her. "Don't pull a face. Go on."

The marinade sizzled when the kabobs hit the grill. Steam spiraled up, diffusing Thai spice aromas through the air. Sloane stabbed at the chicken breasts.

Dorathea returned from inside carrying a stack of dishes. "Seems even cooking is aggressive in New York." She set plates and flatware on the patio table.

The aromas enticed Elvina, and she slinked onto the deck. *I want you to know, dear, familiars don't spy. I mostly slept in a tree when the crows left me alone.*

Sloane's thoughts returned to the picnic, the bright sun on her face, and the sound of rushing water. The crows, cawing.

Dorathea twirled her finger, and a bottle of white wine, a pitcher of water, two glasses, and a saucer appeared. "What did you find out from Rose?"

Sloane turned the kabobs. "She knew why Lore and Charles's relationship had been strained for thirty years. According to her, Lore broke up with Charles before he left for UBC."

"Lore?" Dorathea looked confused. "But why would she allow James to believe Charles broke her heart all those years ago?"

Sloane stacked the grilled chicken and vegetables on the tray. "It was easier than admitting she got drunk and slept with another guy."

*Ooh. Do elaborate*, Elvina said.

"Lore's sex life is not important right now, dear." Dorathea turned to Sloane. "What does that mean for our case?"

"I'm not sure. But if no one else knows the truth, then nothing changes. But then it begs new questions. Why would Charles stay in a relationship, whatever it is, with her all these years? Have they conspired to destroy the West Coven for years? Is that what keeps them together?"

Dorathea considered her answers, then sighed. "I am unsure. But I doubt either of them could have discovered us."

"All right. But I'm going to search for the truth about their relationship anyway. If you're right, you can say I told you so."

"Very well," Dorathea said. "When I met with the Grand Coven today, I returned with my own information. Our sensors do not detect a Nogical possession in the village or surrounding area."

Sloane placed the food on the table. "What the hell does that mean?"

"It means someone in Denwick is not who they say they are."

Elvina's pupils disappeared into thin black slits. *Other Magicals?*

Sloane thought about Jane's research. The graveyard and the crypt. The deep family roots in the village. They needed to use a spell to detect the old families.

Dorathea placed a kabob on her plate and one on Elvina's. "Unfortunately, they did not give me permission to detect—"

"Are you reading my mind?" Sloane interrupted, slamming down the wine bottle. "I was just thinking about that."

Dorathea furrowed her brow. "Are you daft? I am not telepathic and would not cast such a spell indiscriminately even if I wanted to." She narrowed her eyes. "I told you I would seek permission to detect our suspects."

Sloane took a long drink to temper her anger. "Yeah, well, excuse me if I'm cynical. Every time she needed to calm me down, Jane stole into my head. But I didn't know that then, did I? She lied. About herself. Me. You."

*Sounds like she kept a secret, rather than lying, dear.*

Sloane glared at the familiar. "They're the same damn thing."

"You are both wrong," Dorathea said. "What your mum did to you was unconscionable. And what Jane asked Elvina to do was unfair. She had secrets. And they turned into lies when they caused her and others to suffer." She placed her fork on her plate. "Perhaps during your investigation, you will discover your mother's truth, or maybe you will never know. Regardless, it is time to forgive your mum."

# CHAPTER SEVENTEEN

Sloane woke the following day to the aroma of cinnamon and coffee. It meant only one thing—Dorathea. Elvina was perched in the kitchen window behind the sink. Dorathea was hand-washing a pile of dishes.

"Can't you just snap your fingers and clean those," Sloane asked as she grabbed a coffee mug from a cupboard.

*Nice of you to finally join us,* the familiar said. *Your coffee's ready.*

Dorathea wiped her hands with a towel and turned around. "I often do the dishes like Nogicals. I find it relaxing." She eyed her. "I understand you had a difficult night after we left and sought solace in a bottle."

Sloane looked at Elvina. "What? Now you're tattling?"

*I only told her why you were still in bed.*

Sloane rubbed her temples. "Not so loud. My head hurts."

"Serves you right." Dorathea grabbed an oven mitt. "Elvina tells me you have grieved your past relationship for two years. And now your mum?"

"Are you kidding me?" Sloane stared at the familiar. "Elvina needs to keep my business out of her chitchat."

"Don't blame her. I asked what was causing your peculiar behavior."

"What's that supposed to mean?"

"I hardly need to spell it out. You drink into a stupor and dress in shabby clothes. You are a sad caricature, indeed."

"Good morning to you, too." Sloane stepped past Dorathea, wrapping her cardigan tight. "This happens to be my favorite sweater."

"Obviously," Dorathea said.

Sloane poured a cup of coffee and watched Dorathea retrieve a coffee cake from the oven. "I thought you only baked scones."

"Freya taught me a new recipe." Her face softened.

"Smells good. Stop nagging me like Jane, and I might stay for a piece."

"Hmm." Dorathea snapped her fingers, and the coffee cake, the carafe of coffee, and a teapot reappeared on the breakfast table. "Are you in a hurry to leave?"

"I have a meeting with Quinn Reed." She sat at the table. "Why? Did you want me to train this morning?"

"No. Not yet." Dorathea sent the teapot to Elvina's cup and back to hers. "Have you been practicing the detection and disarming spells?"

Elvina looked up from her plate. *Every chance she gets. It's annoying.*

Dorathea smiled. "I recall you felt the same about Jane's practicing when she was young."

Elvina returned to her coffee cake when suddenly the plate slid to the other side of the table.

"Well, well. You have learned to silently disarm. Quite impressive, indeed."

"Thanks. I guess."

*Thrilling, isn't it?* Elvina flicked her tail, and the plate returned to her.

Sloane's phone rang. "Listen, I need to take this call." She walked onto the patio. "Garcia, where've you been?"

"Hey, how about a great to hear from you or something."

"Yeah, yeah. Sorry. How are you?"

"Sorry?" Garcia laughed. "You've only been in Canada for a week. And they got you apologizing?"

"Funny. How about you give me the info I need."

"Okay. Okay. The number ending in zero seven is registered to Lore Emilie Reed. The number ending in twenty-two belongs to Gannon W. Ferris. None of your suspects have priors. I'm still waiting for Morris's records."

"Nothing on Gannon?"

"That's right. No priors, but he's not a choir boy. His known associates are doing time. His Uncle Scottie is head of a gaming syndicate. Got popped for money laundering and illegal gaming. He's doing a long haul in prison."

"All right. Email me everything you have," Sloane said.

"Just sent it. But if you go after Gannon, take someone with you, alright?"

"What? You're my mother, now?"

"Not likely. I'm just making sure I get my drink at Stella's."

"You got it. Thanks for everything." Sloane hung up and returned to the breakfast table. She read Garcia's email. "Change of plans. Going to have to cancel with Quinn. That was my contact in New York. I just got a break in Harold's case. Remember Gannon Ferris from the repast? Well, he's in imports. Has an office in Victoria's Chinatown. But it looks like that's not how he pays the bills."

Sloane picked up her tote and turned toward the door.

"Wait," Dorathea said. "When I detected him at the repast, I could see Gannon Ferris was not a Demon. But he is plain evil, in the Nogical sense. If you face danger in his presence, refrain from casting a spell in anger. Use what you have learned. Let Elvina protect you if need be."

The familiar's head popped up, and she licked cinnamon and sugar from her whiskers.

"I'll be fine," Sloane said. "I promise to seek peace before kicking anyone's a—"

"Sloane, please," Dorathea interrupted. "Shall I accompany you?"

"No. I'll behave. But you could let me borrow Onyx."

"I think not. She would never approve." Dorathea got to her feet. "I suppose it is time you met Pearl."

*Ooh, yes. It's been ages since I've seen her*, Elvina said.

"Pearl? I don't have time to meet anyone."

"Not someone. Nathaniel and Mary's car."

"Oh, of course. Their car has a name." Sloane smirked. Dorathea led them to the garage.

Sloane exhaled a loud, deep breath at the sight of lawn and garden equipment, sports gear, and holiday decorations hanging on every inch of the walls. A riding mower and several tool cabinets were crammed against the back wall behind a car covered by a tarp. "Jesus, more junk to deal with. What do a wizard and witch need with lawn equipment and tools?" she asked.

"Wiccan, pet. We use them to blend in. And honestly, I find gardening quite fulfilling." Dorathea flicked her wrist, and the car's cover slid off.

"Whoa," Sloane whispered.

"Nathaniel and Mary's first and only car, a white 1962 MGA Deluxe roadster. We created a lot of memories with Pearl."

*So did Jane.* Elvina purred and leaped onto the car's curved headlight.

Sloane moved closer to Dorathea. "Is this car like your stuff? You know, imbued with some spirit that I might piss off?"

"You have such a way with words," Dorathea answered. "Pearl's enchantment ended when Nathaniel and Mary died." Her voice lowered, and she ran her hand along the curve of the hood. "And now, she is yours. You might wish to enchant her at some point." She opened the car door. "Can you drive a manual?"

Sloane slipped behind the wheel into the buttery soft leather seat.

"I guess it's time to learn."

* * *

Sloane entered Victoria's historic Chinatown through the Gate of Harmonious Interest, an elaborate entrance of red and gold with a tiled hard-hill roof. Foo dog statues perched on each side. A female yin and male yang protected all who entered.

Sloane tried to pull into a parking spot, ramming Pearl's gearstick into first. It ground and squealed until the car finally rolled into the spot. "Sorry about that." She patted the dashboard and remembered the only time she had driven a standard. It was in the Catskills on a getaway with Jess, and after driving the rental Jeep for one day, she had stripped its gears. The memory made her frown.

She put Gannon Ferris's business address into her phone's GPS. His office was only a few blocks away, and GPS directed her back to Fisgard Street. The main drag was lined with cherry trees in full bloom. They filled the air with a faint scent of almond and rose. Red Chinese lanterns, hooked onto the roofs of two- and three-story brick and stone stores, hung on crisscrossed strings of lights up and down the length of the street. She entered the narrow lane, Dragon Alley, an unfriendly place to meet a suspect. But it was a brilliant place to do business if you had enemies.

Gannon's office was number ten, North Pacific Imports, the last business in the lane and leading to a courtyard around which the building was constructed. She walked to the end of the alley onto Herald Street and looked up and down the road. A decent escape route if she needed one. She returned to North Pacific Imports' door, and a cluster of tiny bells jingled when she entered. Gannon's receptionist sat behind a black lacquer desk. She was young, in her early twenties. She looked up from her computer and gave Sloane a perky smile.

"Good afternoon. May I help you?"

"I'm here for my twelve-thirty appointment with Mr. Ferris," Sloane answered.

The receptionist looked confused and turned to her computer. "May I have your name?"

"Sloane West." She peeked over the reception counter, scanning the desk.

"I'm sorry, Ms. West." The young woman turned to her. "There must be a mistake. You're not on Mr. Ferris's calendar."

"That can't be right. We set up the meeting weeks ago. You're Jules, right?"

Her doe eyes widened. "We did? I'm so sorry. Wait here. I'll see if Mr. Ferris is available." She disappeared and Sloane bent over the counter to grab a business flyer with Gannon's picture.

A few minutes later, Jules returned with Gannon Ferris. He was dressed in a navy suit over a crisp, teal-striped shirt. His dirty-blond hair was pulled back, and he wore fashionable glasses. He looked like a completely different character from the one she met at Harold's repast. He almost passed for respectable.

"Ms. West." He held out his hand. "I'm Gannon Ferris. I understand we've had a scheduling mishap." His mouth twisted into a smile. "If Jules had said how beautiful you were, I wouldn't have kept you waiting for even a second."

He pretended not to know her but had a shitty poker face. Sloane had already figured out his tell. She grasped his extended hand. "I promise I only need a minute of your time, Mr. Ferris."

"Please, call me Gannon." He held her hand as she pulled it back, then released his grip and turned to his receptionist. "Jules, hold my calls. Ms. West and I will be in my office."

"After you," he said, motioning her into his office, an intimate space with a set of French doors that opened onto the large courtyard. "Nice view, huh? The garden is the only reason I leased this suite, otherwise you only get natural light if you're in the front or back of the building. And believe me, I pay more for it here." He walked over to a bar cart, a retro fifties deal. "Would you like something to drink?"

"No, thanks. My visit isn't social." Sloane dropped her tote next to a plain wooden chair and sat.

He poured a drink from a crystal decanter and sat in a leather chair behind his desk. "How can I help you with your nonsocial visit?"

"I'm a private investigator from New York. I'd like to ask you a few questions about a case I'm working on."

Gannon leaned back and propped his foot on a cabinet. "You're a PI? Are you playing with me? I figured you for a lingerie model or something. But, hey, a detective's sexy, too."

He loosened his tie. "I've never been to the Big Apple. Maybe I'll plan a trip now."

"Do you have any business dealings in New York?"

He shook his head. "My operation is exclusively West Coast. That's why it's in the name."

She crossed her legs and rested a hand on her knee. "How do you know Charles Huxham?"

"Charlie? Oh, me and him go way back. But come to think of it, I haven't heard from him in a few days."

"Did you know Harold Huxham, his uncle?"

Gannon sat his drink on the desk. "No. Can't say that I did. I never got the chance to meet him."

"Yet you and Charles go way back? Why didn't he ever introduce you to his uncle?"

"You'll have to ask him that. But it might be because I've never been to Denwick. Charlie preferred to hang out here in Chinatown. He said the village nightlife at that geriatric pub bored him. Why are you asking me about his uncle?" His mouth twisted slightly, and he sipped his drink. He acted cool, but Sloane had already heard an imperceptible rise in his voice. Was it suspicion? Anger? "I was real sorry to hear he died. I felt bad for Charlie. He always had nice things to say about him."

"Actually, Mr. Huxham was murdered. And we're investigating a Canadian link to the crime."

"Murdered?"

"Yeah. We believe someone in this area hired the man who shot him. Do you know a man named Liam Morris?"

"Yeah, no. Never heard of him."

"All right." Sloane tilted her head to the side. "You said you've never been to Denwick?"

"Well, yeah. Except for the old guy's gathering at Charlie's. I went to pay my respects." He set his feet on the floor, lifted himself out of his chair, and pointed his empty glass at her. "Now I remember seeing you there. You wore a sweet black suit." He poured himself another drink and asked, "Are you sure you don't want to join me? I could clear my schedule for the rest of the afternoon."

Sloane's eyebrows pinched together. "Does that crap actually work on women?"

"More than you could imagine," he said and bit his lower lip.

"That's pathetic." Sloane uncrossed her legs and leaned on the desk. "Listen, I know you aren't the kind of company one brings home to meet the parents. You're a two-bit bookie trying to keep your uncle's illegal business going while he's in the slammer. I know Charles Huxham owes you money. I suspect it's a lot more than he's got. But you're still collecting. And there's only one way he's getting more money. I'd say that gives you a strong motive for hiring Morris to kill Harold and me."

Gannon rested with his forearms on the desk's top. "Look around. I'm in the import business. I'm not involved in anything illegal."

"No?" Sloane looked around. "Nice office. Cute receptionist. You're saying importing pays the bills, especially the best suite on Dragon Alley? I know Uncle Scottie isn't floating you anymore. Oh, unless you're running Scottie's business."

Gannon smirked.

"Your poor uncle. In prison in his late seventies. No chance for parole for at least ten years. That's a death sentence. And here you are on the outside. Running the ring he worked so hard to establish. You need to make him proud. Keep his confidence. A couple bullets can take care of the Huxham problem. Charles inherits and keeps the Degas. You get paid. Scottie stays happy."

Gannon stared at her, perfectly at ease. "I don't know what you're talking about."

"The only thing I'm unsure about is who hired Morris, you or Charlie? My hunch tells me you did. The chances Charles knows more sleazeballs than you are slim. But whoever it was, made a bad hire. Morris didn't finish the job. I'm in Canada, and the Degas is mine. You must be furious. I bet you counted on that pretty painting to give you a little class."

She picked up her tote and stood.

"Are all the good-looking bitches in New York crazy like you? Why would I put a hit on you? I didn't even know your name until today." He dismissed her with the back of his hand.

"You know me now. And Uncle Scottie's going to know me soon. I'll see myself out."

"Hey," Gannon shouted, and Sloane turned around. "If I were you, I wouldn't throw around accusations and threats. Not on this island. You're gonna make the wrong person angry."

She grinned, shut the door behind her, and said to herself, "What a total prick."

The sun had moved behind the top of the buildings, and Dragon Alley was left in the shade. Sloane shook off Gannon's slime and headed back toward Fisgard Street. A man in a shiny black tracksuit entered halfway down the laneway. He walked toward her with his hands in his pockets.

Sloane glanced behind her. They were alone. Not good. When she turned back, the man ran toward her, a knife in his hand. She stumbled backward, focusing on the blade. A dark shadow passed over them. And her flesh shivered.

"Āniman!" she yelled and held out her hand, expecting his knife to fly to her. But nothing happened. The spell failed.

*Keep trying, dear.* Elvina's voice, calm and collected, came into her head.

"Āniman!" she shouted.

Nothing.

She turned and ran. Near the courtyard the man caught her by the hair and yanked her back against his body. He held the knife to her neck just below her ear, shoved her into the garden next to Gannon's French doors and slammed her back against the brick wall. A moan escaped her, but she didn't struggle.

*I can immobilize him,* Elvina spoke in her head.

"No. I got this," Sloane replied.

*Remember to mind your temper.*

"I will."

"Say another word, and I cut you. Real bad," the man said. He reeked of cheap leather and hair gel, and Sloane turned her head away from his sweaty face.

"Listen, whatever your name is. I made a promise not to kick anyone's ass today. Keep pressing that knife into my neck, and you'll make me break my promise. And the only thing I hate more than a broken promise is a lie."

"No, you listen, tough girl." His breath was hot and wet on her cheek. "We walk out of here together, and when we get to my car, you climb in nice and quiet. We're gonna take a drive." He jerked Sloane from the wall and put his arm around her waist, pressing the knife against her side with his other hand.

Its tip cut through her cardigan and T-shirt, piercing her skin. A surge of adrenaline pulsed through her body. "You stupid son of a bitch. Did you tear my favorite sweater?" She struck the man's face with a back-side elbow. The force cracked his nose, spraying blood, and sent him stumbling backward. He shook off the blow, straightened, and lunged at her.

*Calm down, dear. Breathe.*

"Fuck that, Elvina." Sloane kicked him in the abdomen, slamming him against the brick wall. He collapsed to the ground, and she picked him up by his jacket. "Here's your trash back, asshole," she yelled outside Gannon's French doors as she flung the man into the glass.

She walked away, taking slow steady footsteps as she tried to calm her breathing. Back in the alley, she stopped, clutched her head, and fell to her knees.

# CHAPTER EIGHTEEN

A dark shadow descended over Sloane as she knelt on her knees in Dragon Alley. She plummeted into complete darkness. Her body tensed. Then an explosive light blinded her right before she opened her eyes.

She was sitting on the sofa at Mallow Cottage with Elvina and Dorathea by her side.

"Do you feel any pain?" her cousin asked. The lines across her forehead were more pronounced.

Sloane lay back and took note of her body. "No. I'm all right."

Dorathea held out a bottle of swirling smoke and released the vapors into Sloane's face. "Breathe it in, pet."

"What is that?"

"A protection against curse-binding." Dorathea held her hands at Sloane's temples for a moment. "There is no damage."

"What do you mean? What kind of damage?"

"The kind that happens when a wicce draws upon her anger," answered Dorathea in a stern voice. "Is this the first time you have felt pain in your head after protecting yourself?"

"Yeah. I've never felt that way before."

Dorathea sighed and turned to Elvina. "What did you sense?"

*Only the initial danger that summoned me, the man in Dragon Alley.* The familiar crawled over the sofa's top cushions and rested above Sloane's head.

"You know he pulled a knife on me, right?"

"And in return, you nearly killed him. Yes, I am aware." Dorathea sat in an armchair. "Elvina said you tried to disarm him first?"

"Yeah. But the spell didn't work."

*An incantation doesn't choose to work, dear. A wiččan makes it perform.*

Sloane looked up at the familiar. "Who asked you?"

Dorathea frowned. "You may have stopped his attack. But you drew from anger, not your desire to protect. They are entirely different sources. You have relied on anger for far too long without consequence. Something or someone protected you in New York. But here, you do not seem to have the same protection. I am afraid dark magic will affect your mind sooner rather than later."

"Jesus Christ. The guy tried to kill me." Sloane sat forward. "I'm sure you've laid someone out in self-defense."

Dorathea peered into Sloane's eyes. "I'm far too powerful to risk acting out of anger."

"Fine. I get it. I'll try harder." She looked up at Elvina. "So you teleported me?"

*We bestealced, yes.*

"Best-eal-ce—"

*Be-steal-ce-don. How hard is that to say?*

Dorathea tutted. "Elvina, please."

"Are you going to teach me to teleport like that?" Sloane asked her cousin.

"Yes. Your next lesson."

"Well, give me a day or two to wrap my head around it. That was a wild ride." She got to her feet and pulled the case board into the middle of the room.

*Excellent. We're working on your lucky baby*, Elvina said and crossed her front paws. Her tail hung languidly on the back cushion. *I've already explained to Dorathea how you and Thomas spent hours analyzing it, working through the night until the truth revealed itself. It was truly inspiring.*

Sloane scowled at her. "For Christ's sake. Why would you bring him up?"

Elvina's tail tapped the sofa. *How long are you going to carry such strong feelings?*

"Nice. You think I should be over their betrayal?"

Elvina looked away without answering.

"For goodness' sake, pet. Is there anyone in your life with whom you are pleased?"

"I'm happy with plenty of people. And for your information, I don't start out angry at anyone."

"Yes, I am sure. Do you feel up to working?"

Sloane nodded.

"Very well. Shall we have a look at our suspects then?"

Photos of Harold, Jane, Nathaniel, and Mary were in the middle of the board. Sloane pulled out the brochure she'd picked up in Gannon Ferris's reception area, placed it on the board and drew a red line to Harold. She stared at Jane's photo. It was easier to accept her death when she had thought it an accident.

She yanked the cap off a marker and pointed at pictures of Gannon and the family friends who owned businesses on Old Main. "These are our suspects. At first, I thought whoever hired Morris knew Harold was flying to New York to meet me. But there might be someone else. I was in the gallery, and I used a spell to detect Nathaniel and Mary. They had received a letter from Jane inviting them to visit us. And in my vision, Nathaniel was writing her back."

Dorathea straightened. "What? Jane asked your grandparents to come to New York? Why didn't you tell us this?"

"I didn't get the chance. At the time, you were harassing me about trying to detect Rose Keane and drinking too much. And then I forgot."

"Nevertheless, you must inform me of such discoveries," Dorathea said. "What exactly happened?"

"I found a pen on their desk and held it. It vibrated. In my vision, Nathaniel was using it to write a letter back to Jane."

*Then you saw the last time he used it,* Elvina said.

"The last time," Sloane mumbled. "How long has the exhibition in the middle of the gallery been there?"

"I have not visited the gallery since our holiday celebration. But the center showcase changes every quarter."

"So it would have changed in January, the month they were killed?"

"Yes, indeed."

"What was it last quarter?"

"In December, the exhibit was jewelry. Beautiful local gems. Red jasper. Flowerstone."

"It's a sculpture of a woman's bust now. So my vision had to be of them sometime in January." Sloane knitted her brows. "So, after thirty years, Jane was going to reveal everything. Why?" Sloane looked at Elvina. "Did you know anything about this?"

*No, dear.* Elvina's usually smooth voice stuttered in surprise.

"Could anyone have known that Nathaniel and Mary planned to visit us?"

"If I was unaware of their plans, Nathaniel and Mary had certainly kept it to themselves," answered Dorathea, frowning. She snapped her fingers and a tea service appeared.

"I think my vision was a few days before they died."

"Why do you think that?" Dorathea asked, sending a steaming teapot around to fill each cup.

"Nathaniel said they were overjoyed to meet her. I think he meant me. I was born on January twenty-first."

"They were killed on the nineteenth," Dorathea said.

"I wonder if Jane had invited them to meet me on my birthday." Sloane paused. "But why didn't the killer just follow them to New York and attack us while we were all in the same place?"

*If the four of you had been together, the West Coven would have been unstoppable.*

Sloane considered the familiar's comment. It made sense for Jane and her parents. But for her? Having been kept in the dark about being a wiċċan? Unable to cast spells?

She turned to the board and wrote MOTIVE on the right side. "All right. We have persons for the who. Let's narrow down the why." She turned back to Elvina and Dorathea. "We've discussed two motives. One is financial. We know Charles and the other family businesses benefit monetarily if I die. Charles or all of them possibly benefit from Harold's death. I believe Charles, Reed's Fish Market, and The Spotted Owl are all in financial trouble. I'll know for sure when my contact gets me their financials." She wrote FINANCIAL under motive.

*Charles owes this Gannon Ferris?* Elvina asked.

"Yeah. I think it's a substantial debt. Big enough to kill for. I also know Charles offered him Jane's Degas as payment. Gannon expects to collect it on Friday."

"Harold placed the Degas at the law firm for safekeeping. It is important to your family," Dorathea said.

"To the Wests?" Sloane asked.

"Yes, for you. You are a direct bloodline. We simply must not allow this exchange to take place."

"Don't worry. It won't. I told Gannon the art belongs to me, and I'm here in Denwick to collect it. Stirred the pot. We'll see what happens."

*Sounds dangerous*, Elvina said. She nodded at the coffee table and a platter of madeleines appeared.

"I'm not worried about it. After Friday when I meet with Charles, I'll bring the painting home to the cottage." Sloane sipped her tea and grabbed a cookie.

"Then I must place the Degas under a protection charm before then," Dorathea said.

"Yeah, okay. That's a good idea." She wrote COVEN beneath FINANCIAL. "The second motive is to end the West Coven."

Dorathea stared at the board and drew her mouth into a thin line. "Have we connected any suspects to a wiċċan or Demon?"

"Not yet. My contact is checking their phone records. One had to have called Morris, and we know he was a Magical or possessed." Sloane tapped the marker on the photos. "Has the Grand Coven given us permission to detect any of them?"

"Ours is a complicated request. It will take a while," answered Dorathea.

"Typical." Sloane paced. "Could any one of our suspects be wiċċan?"

"I have known everyone on that whiteboard since they were born, and no one has ever given me a vibration," answered Dorathea.

"But they could be hiding their identity from you like Jane hid ours, couldn't they?"

Dorathea held her finger to her lips, deep in thought. "You are correct," she said finally. "Or they could be defenders of their own kind. Nevertheless, they could not find our coven. Only Wiċċan Protectors can sense each other. And our numbers are few. I would know if the Weardas was investigating one of our own."

"Yet, someone did find us. The question is how?" Sloane stopped. "Maybe we're thinking about this all wrong. What if this wiċċan didn't need to discover our coven? What if they always knew it existed?"

"Hmm. That is unlikely. Under the Concealment Law, every species defenders live in complete anonymity. It is the only way to prevent magical collusion with Demons."

Sloane paced again and considered her cousin's answer. "When was the law enacted?"

"About the time our West ancestors arrived in Denwick. The four quadrants were becoming increasingly unstable. Nogicals and the original defender Magicals invited evil through acts of genocide and crusades of brutality, conspiring with Demons to amass wealth and power. Protector covens, like the Wests, as well as the Weardas were tasked with uncovering those magical families who had betrayed their communities and they were banished a long, long time ago." Dorathea placed her cup back on its saucer.

"Jesus Christ." Sloane sat in an armchair. "Revenge is a powerful motivation. It can last a lifetime. And I don't mean that saying, 'a dish best served cold.'"

Elvina lifted her head from a dish of madeleines. *What are you saying?*

"Maybe a descendent from one of the banished families has returned to avenge their ancestors. The Grand Coven should know what Magicals from here colluded with a Demon, right?"

"They would know, indeed. But I am afraid your theory is impossible," Dorathea said. "Banished Magicals go to *Drusnirwd*. They can never leave."

"If someone wants something bad enough, anything is possible. It would make sense…" she mumbled.

*What, dear?*

"Jane. Her research. Maybe she discovered something about the banished families. Say a member from one of them had somehow returned. And that knowledge made it dangerous for her. Maybe that's why she had to run."

Elvina sat up. *Do you think the killer has been here for over thirty years?*

Sloane looked at the faces on the board. "Maybe longer."

Dorathea shook her head. "Drusnirwd has held prisoners for millennia without incident. If such an escape had happened. We would know."

"Yeah. I get your skepticism. But after years in my line of work, I've found that what most people think is impossible is only improbable."

*Not this time, dear.*

"She is correct. But let us entertain your theory. Why would a descendant wait so long to inflict vengeance?" Dorathea asked.

Sloane leaped to her feet. "Maybe he or she couldn't risk being recognized. Or the West Coven was too powerful at the time." She wrote the names of Denwick's original families on the left-hand side of the board. "Keanes, Reeds, and the Gildeys are still here. Smalldons, Ilievs, Tindalls, and Emleys are gone. We need to track down these family lines. Were they magical? Do they have family branches that still exist in this world?" She capped the marker. "Dorathea, can you go to the Grand Coven again and try to persuade them to tell us what they know about them? And what about the Demon? Was it captured? Destroyed? See if they will tell us about it, too."

"I shall go at once." Dorathea wrapped her purple cloak around her and disappeared.

Sloane looked at Elvina. "I'm going to take another look at Jane's notes. There's got to be a clue in there. If her investigation forced her into hiding, she must have discovered something important. How about you visit your mother and ask if she knows anyone who might help us? Unless you're too scared of her."

Elvina bristled. *Very funny. While I'm gone, you might want to train more or avoid alleys.*

"Āniman!" Sloane shouted. The crystal dish on the sofa's top cushion flew to her. She caught it and ate another madeleine. "Looks like I'm doing okay."

Elvina flicked her tail, and her dish vanished. *Don't be too chuffed with yourself. We expect you to cast your spells when it matters.* She leaped off the couch, her nose and tail in the air, and sauntered away.

Sloane shouted, "You know what Jane used to say. Expectations only leave you disappointed. Hey, get us some of Freya's scones, too."

# CHAPTER NINETEEN

When Sloane woke the following day, the house was silent. This is how she liked her life, quiet and alone with a nonspeaking cat. A carafe of fresh coffee and a few hours to plan her day. She set the teakettle on a burner and scooped coffee into the French press. She had rescheduled yesterday's meeting with Quinn Reed to this morning, but first, she needed to track down Garcia. The case would crack if there was a call from a Canadian number on Morris's phone records. Of course, he could have used a burner, but there was a chance the initial call came to his regular phone.

And where was Chen? She was not complaining, but she'd never had to wait for more than a day or two for her information. Unless Jacobson had found out. No. Chen would have given her a heads-up.

The teakettle whistled and interrupted her thoughts. After several cups of black coffee and an unsuccessful attempt to get Katie Chen on the phone, Sloane walked to Quinn Reed's office. She breathed in the sharp medical air and approached the check-in counter. Quinn's receptionist was on the phone. She was an older woman dressed impeccably, with silver-gray hair in a blunt cut below a strong jawline. When Sloane called to reschedule, she had squeezed her in between Quinn's morning and afternoon patients. But she had not sounded pleased to do it. She hung up the phone, and Sloane coughed.

"Yes. I am aware you are there, Ms. West. Thank you for being on time." It was the same snippy voice she used the day before. "Dr. Reed will be with you in a moment."

Sloane walked around the waiting room and stopped at a sculpture of an owl in flight. Its magnificent wings were spread wide and talons flexed, with its powerful beak open as if its prey were directly below it.

Quinn finally appeared. He had a nice build and was a little shorter than Sloane. His once-blond hair was giving way to silver-white that offset his blue eyes handsomely. She thought Lore must have inherited her brown hair and eyes from her mother because she didn't favor James or her brother.

He extended his hand. "Hello, Ms. West. We finally meet." His palms were sweaty, and his forehead glistened.

"Hi, Dr. Reed. Thanks for seeing me. I know you're a busy man."

"Not too busy to meet Jane's daughter." He stared at her from head to toe and back. "My God, it's like visiting the past." His eyes darted to his receptionist. She was busy on the computer. "I'm sorry for not introducing myself at the repast. I didn't think it was the right time." He smiled. "You've met Betty Stewart. She opened the clinic with me. Hopefully, she'll stay until I retire. I'd be lost without her. She runs the place. Right, Betty? Didn't I say Ms. West and her mother looked like twins?" He rambled and coughed into his fist.

Betty nodded without looking up. "Yes, you did, Dr. Reed. Your next patient is at one o'clock. Time's ticking."

"See what I mean?" He raised his hands. "Would you like a cup of coffee? We could go to my favorite café?"

Sloane glanced at her watch. "Somewhere close, I hope. You're down to fifty-two minutes."

Betty looked up at them.

Quinn gave an awkward laugh. "It's not as fancy as a Manhattan coffee house. But it's the best on the Island and right down the street."

Old Main was busy with lunchtime shoppers, a helpful diversion for both of them. They crossed the street and walked past Lore's flower shop. Sloane broke the silence. "Seems Mrs. Stewart's upset about something. Did I offend her?"

"No, of course not. Betty's my mother-in-law, a real lioness, always piqued around strangers."

"If you don't mind, Dr. Reed—"

"Please call me Quinn."

"All right. And you can call me Sloane." She glanced at her watch. "I only have fifty minutes with you. So I'll be direct. I'm here to find who hired Harold's killer."

"I know. My father told me." He stopped before the gallery and shoved his hands in his pockets. "I only hope I can help."

She studied his face. "Did you know Jane lived in New York after she ran away?"

Quinn looked down. "I had no idea. I didn't even know Jane had had you or that she had died." He paused. "I wish I'd known before it was too late. I considered your mom my best friend when we were growing up."

"Have you ever visited New York?"

He lifted his head, and his charming smile faded. "No. And I don't know anyone who lives there either. Believe me, I could never hurt Harold or you." He stared into the dark gallery. "I'm so sorry you experienced such a terrifying attack." He turned back. "Are you okay?"

"Yeah. I'm fine. Liam Morris isn't the first perp to stick a gun in my face. And Harold Huxham isn't the first innocent person I've seen killed in cold blood."

"Mother of God, I'm so sorry." He met her eyes and held them for the first time. "Harold was a great guy. But you probably figured that out. Your mom, Ken, Charlie, and I always hung out at the Huxham's house. Harold stocked his cupboards with the best junk food. And he left us alone. It wasn't just lack of supervision that made it so good. He treated us with respect. Gave us privacy."

People sat at umbrellaed tables outside the coffee shop. Quinn opened the door. "Welcome to The Grind."

Sloane stepped inside and breathed in a smoky, herby aroma. People chattered. Bursts of steam hissed from the espresso machine. Her muscles relaxed. It was like a busy coffee house in the Bronx. Once served, Sloane followed Quinn outside and sat at an open table. She sipped her brew. "Mmm. You weren't kidding. This is smooth."

"I'm glad you like it." He poured two creams into his cup and tore open two sugar packets.

She stared at him. "Wait. Don't do that." The sugar went into Quinn's cup. "Ugh. How do you live with yourself debasing excellent coffee with cream and sugar?"

Quinn laughed. "A purist, eh? This is a regular coffee here."

"I'm hardly a purist. I just don't think we should complicate a good thing."

He stared at her, the lines around his eyes softening. "You remind me so much of your mother. It's more than looks. She was witty and tough, too."

Sloane sipped her coffee. Jane was funny, on the rare occasions she expressed it. But she had never considered Jane strong.

"I'm sorry. Talking about your mom must be painful."

"I'm fine," Sloane said. "I do want to change the subject, though. Do you know why your father's fish market is in financial trouble?"

"Trouble? He could be doing better, but it's hardly going under. I know why you're asking, and I agree money is a compelling motive for murder. My dad's cantankerous, but he's not a killer."

"Actually, I'm more interested to know if you thought the market's profitability, or even lack thereof, has anything to do with your dad's behavior toward Isobel Gildey at Harold's repast. His conduct surpassed cranky."

Quinn shook his head. "Well, my dad has a temper. Ever since Isobel took over the Gildeys' businesses when Sean died,

Dad has blamed her for everything that goes wrong in Old Denwick. It's nonsense. His problem is that he hasn't moved with the times. He doesn't advertise. He could double his sales."

"Lore told me the same thing. How about your practice? Are you profitable?" She waited for Quinn to react, but her question didn't faze him.

"I'd say. We're busy enough for a second doctor. Amy, my wife, has family money as well. My mother-in-law doesn't work for me because she has to." He chuckled. "I've been trying to buy my building and the building next to us for a pharmacy. The closest one is in Mill Bay or a drive-thru in New Denwick. We want to provide a closer, personal option for our Old Denwick families."

"What's the problem?"

"The Gildeys. They own the land and the building. It used to be a real estate office run by Sean Gildey's aunt. It closed three decades ago. But they refuse to rent or sell."

"That's very unneighborly of them. I don't know the Gildeys, but even at Harold's repast, it seemed they throw a lot of weight around." Sloane sipped her coffee. "What's James accusing Isobel of doing?"

He tapped his coffee cup on the tabletop. "The Gildeys began the European salmon industry here. They pretend to have sovereignty over the waterways. Fishing rights. But of course, they ignore that they stole the waterways in the first place."

"Yeah, well, every nonindigenous person in North America has that on their hands." Sloane crossed her arms on the table.

Quinn nodded. "My dad says Isobel is forcing the smaller fishers out of business, and that's why his overhead has increased. His suppliers charge more because they have less."

"I see. So Isobel really could put him out of business."

"Especially if she develops more fish markets in New Denwick. That's the way of a free market, I guess. But Lore and I won't let that happen to him."

"James is lucky to have a son and daughter like you." Sloane watched a young couple sit at the table behind Quinn. They hadn't let go of each other's hands. She looked at Quinn. He resembled Jacobson. And she wondered if he and Jane had been more than best friends. "Back when they were young, did the Gildeys have Harold in their crosshairs?"

"Not a chance. They associated with different people."

"I suppose they did." Sloane sat back. "Do you know any of the other original families? The ones in the crypt?"

"I can't say I do, besides the Keanes." He blinked hard and looked toward his office. "I'll need to head back now. Do you have any other questions?"

"Yeah, about a million." She set her cup down. "But for this case, just a few more."

"I'll try to answer anything." He pushed back in his chair. "Would you like to walk back with me?"

Sloane pulled her tote's strap over her head and got to her feet. "Do you know if Harold and Charles were having problems?"

"With each other?" Quinn thought for a moment. "When Charlie was young, he worked hard to make Harold proud. But when he came back from uni, they fought a lot. It wasn't Harold's fault, though. Charlie made it hard for him."

"Alcohol and gambling?"

"You have done your homework."

"Yeah. It's my job," Sloane said. "Do you think Charles could hurt his uncle?"

He sighed. "There was a time I thought I knew Charlie, and the idea of him killing Harold for money would be ludicrous. But that was a long time ago. Now I'm not too sure."

They crossed to the other side of Old Main. "Yeah. I get it," Sloane said and swigged the last of her coffee, throwing the cup in a bin. "Are you and Charles still friends?"

"We're friendly. But I wouldn't say we're friends. But Lore and Charles are still close. I don't know why. She even went to New York with him to identify Harold." He made a face. "I don't know what the hell's the matter with her."

His outburst surprised Sloane.

"I'm sorry," he said. "I just get angry. I can't understand what she sees in him."

"Are you sure Charles is the puppet master? I heard it was the other way around."

Quinn stopped beside a market with fruits and vegetables displayed outside. "Who fed you that load of crap? I was there when Lore and Charlie started dating. Lore never hung out with us before they did. She stayed home, her nose in a book. It was nice having her around, even if she was there because of him. Then one night, she came home, broken. He dumped her the night before he left for uni. After that, she was never the same."

"Just because they broke up?"

"He probably cheated on her, too."

"That's a big assumption," Sloane said.

"Well, he's guilty about something. She's given him grief for three decades, and he lets her."

They walked, passing a lunch crowd outside the Spotted Owl. "Were you and your dad furious with him for messing with Lore?"

"No. I didn't hold a grudge. We've all had relationships go bad. I've always been a bit upset with Lore for hanging around Charlie and not moving on. But my father never forgave him." Quinn tossed his cup in a bin. "He and Harold even had a few rows over it. I'm not sure why Dad couldn't let it go. Maybe it's too hard to see your daughter heartbroken."

Sloane stopped and looked across the street at the West Gallery. "So I own that entire building now."

"Every inch," Quinn said. They walked on. "You can do whatever you want with it. But you'll need the Main Street Commerce Committee's approval for any changes." Quinn stopped in front of the clinic door.

"One more question, if you don't mind."

"Go ahead."

"Do you know why Jane ran away?"

The question caught him off guard, and he shoved his hands in his pockets. "I've asked myself that question for many years. That summer, she seemed happy. Happier than I'd ever seen her." Betty appeared on the other side of the door before he finished. "She was dating a guy in Vancouver and took the ferry twice a week to see him. I provided cover."

"She didn't want anyone to know who her boyfriend was?"

Quinn shook his head. "I don't know why."

Betty opened the door. "Dr. Reed. Your one o'clock is here."

Quinn looked at Sloane apologetically.

"All right. I appreciate you talking with me. Is it okay if we chat again?" she asked.

"Absolutely. Coffee's on me."

* * *

A couple entered the Spotted Owl ahead of Sloane and held open the door for her. She nodded, too busy thinking about Jane to speak. Everyone remembered her fondly and described her as an intelligent, happy, beautiful girl. Why would she give up so much and run away?

The pub seemed dimmer than usual, and Sloane needed a moment to adjust her eyes. Ken was behind the bar serving draft beers to a couple of men in chest-high waders. He turned his head toward the entry and smiled. "Aye. Here's a fine lass."

"Hey. How's it going?" Sloane asked.

"Cannae compleen. Hou ar ye?"

"I'm doing okay. Could use a shot of whiskey. How about Oscar's brand? Neat." She peeked over the counter. "You need to put your foot down and don the kilt for the pub's sake."

Ken laughed. "I'm afraid I'll not win that battle." He filled a measure twice and slid the glass across the bar. "Rose is in the back. Should I fetch her?"

"I was hoping to talk to you first, if you don't mind."

"Aye. I'm here to help ye."

"I just had a coffee with Quinn Reed. And he seems to think Jane had a secret boyfriend."

Ken held up his hand. Then he turned to the fisherman. "You lot go on and sit at a table. Rose will be right out with your lunches." The two men grumbled, taking their pints and leaving the bar. Ken leaned closer to Sloane. "I wondered when you'd ask about the boyfriend." His Scottish accent disappeared. "Your mum told me very little about him, not even his name. He was at uni. I think UBC. She was still at her boarding school. She sneaked away a couple times during the week to visit him. Natty and Mary thought she was tutoring Quinn."

"Tutoring?"

"Aye. Quinn was her cover." Ken straightened and polished the bar. "Your mum was in love. But she refused to tell me who he was." He stopped, and his sad eyes held hers. "I should've told Natty and Mary what I knew when she didn't come back after her holiday. I mean, if you're in love, and you can't tell your best friend his name, something's not right, right? I don't know why I didn't tell them."

"Do you think her leaving had something to do with the boyfriend?"

"I've just always had a gut feeling it did." He lowered his head.

Sloane reached out and laid her hand on top of his. "Listen, it's not your fault. Jane lied. Not you."

"Aye, but I kept her secret, and the truth could have helped your grandparents find her."

"You didn't have a choice, trust me." Sloane patted his hand and released it. "Can I ask you another question?" The fishermen held up their pints and hollered for two more.

"Keep the heid!" Ken shouted back.

Rose delivered the fishermen their lunch plates and joined Sloane at the bar. She pushed her father toward the draft faucets. "Go on, old man, you have other customers to bug."

"Aye. I'm gaunnae. Why don't you lasses grab a table? Lunch is on me." He poured two ales and walked away.

Rose closed her eyes and shook her head while untying her apron. "He loves putting on a show for you. Are you hungry?"

"Yeah, sure. I haven't eaten," answered Sloane.

"Great. Chef's special is a traditional Québécois dish today. You'll love it." Rose walked around the bar. "Dad, a couple of specials and two pie slices when you get a minute."

Sloane followed her to a table tucked away in a corner. The blinds on the street-level windows were closed. "Are we hiding from someone? Or do you want your dad to get more exercise?"

"A little of both," Rose answered. "My parents are notorious eavesdroppers. They can hear anything said in this room unless you're back here with music playing and you're whispering."

"And you know this from experience?"

Rose flashed Sloane a grin, pulled a remote from her back pocket and turned up the volume on an airy, slow, and mournful Gaelic tune. Then she leaned closer to Sloane. "How's your case? Any leads?"

"Trying to sort out information right now."

"Do you have any questions for me?"

"Yeah. I was about to ask your dad what he knows about the other original Denwick families."

Rose thought for a minute. "I'm not even sure who the others are. Why?"

"Lore said the Keane and Reed families were friends right from the village's beginning. I'm just wondering if there were other friends."

Rose looked toward the bar. "I don't know. But I'll find out."

"Thanks. I appreciate it."

"That's my job, right?" Rose smiled and tucked a loose curl into her blue headband.

Sloane stared into her eyes, unable to look away.

"What did you find out about Charles?" Rose asked.

"His bookie works out of Chinatown." Sloane dug around in her tote for her phone. She scrolled through her pictures and enlarged one of Gannon Ferris. "Is this the guy Charles brought into the bar?"

"Oh, yeah. That's him. He was at the repast, too."

"Yeah, I saw him there. His name is Gannon Ferris."

Rose mulled over the name. "Never heard of him."

"He denied ever being in Denwick, except for Harold's repast."

"Well, he lied. He's been here in the pub."

"I know. He had a poker face when I told him someone from the Island ordered Harold's murder. But when I said we knew Charles needed money to pay back a debt, and I knew the debt was to him, he blinked."

"I thought you said you worked alone?"

"I do. I can't be responsible for what he assumes." Sloane swirled the whiskey around in her glass.

"So what happens next?"

"I wait and see. But I won't be waiting long. The news that the police consider him a suspect in Harold's murder provoked him."

"What if he tries to hurt you?" Rose whispered.

"I'm not afraid of Gannon Ferris."

Rose lowered her eyes and stared at Sloane's neck. "Turn your head." She ran her fingers along the cut below Sloane's ear. "Did he do this to you?"

Her fingertips made Sloane's skin shiver. Heat radiated from her core and rose to her face. "Not him. One of his men made the mistake of jumping me."

Ken walked across the back-dining area. "Sorry to interrupt, but lunch is served."

Rose pulled her hand back and smiled. "Thanks, Dad." When Ken was out of earshot, she fumed, "Did he try to kill you?"

"Nah. He only wanted to scare me. Make me drop my investigation. He was a lousy muscle."

Rose stared at the two-inch wound and bit her lip.

"Hey, up here." Sloane snapped her fingers.

Rose looked up and into her eyes. "You need to carry a gun."

"Trust me, Keane. I don't need a weapon."

"Why not?"

Sloane inhaled the aromas of her lunch. "Mmm, cinnamon. What is it?"

"It's slow-braised pork shoulder tourtiére. Chef also made a Saskatoon berry pie for dessert. You ignored my question. Why don't you need a weapon?"

"I can't tell you why. And I'm not going to lie to you." Sloane forked into the tourtiére. "What makes it a traditional Quebec dish?"

"It's Québecois, not Quebec."

Sloane ate another mouthful while Rose pushed food around her plate. "I'm telling you the truth, Keane. I can't tell you. And I hope you'll accept that."

Rose chewed silently.

"Well, whatever makes it a Québecois dish is delicious. Savory. Reminds me of the holidays."

"It is popular during the holidays," Rose said and took another bite.

They ate in silence until Sloane scooted her empty plate to the side. If Rose didn't want to participate in small talk, she would return to business. "Listen, I wanted to let you know my contact in New York is checking financials and phone records for me." Sloane glanced toward the bar. "She's checking the pub's accounts."

Rose put her fork down and narrowed her eyes. "Why? You don't think my parents had something to do with Harold's murder?"

Sloane sat back. "I just thought you wanted to know—"

"Forget it," Rose said, interrupting. "Forget I mentioned anything about my mother. We don't need to be a part of your investigation."

"I didn't say you were."

Rose looked at her phone. "I need to get back to work." She stood and picked up Sloane's plate. "I'll wrap your pie to go. You can pick it up at the bar on your way out."

# CHAPTER TWENTY

Sloane tossed the to-go container with the pie into her tote and left the Spotted Owl. She had upset Rose Keane, a free informant, the best kind, and broken a cardinal rule, keep your sources happy.

Pearl was still in Chinatown from the day before when Elvina had *bestealced* her home. She wasn't sure if Dorathea had even noticed, but she knew she'd better bring the car back before she did.

Walking toward Mallow Avenue to pick up an Uber, her phone rang. She hoped it was Garcia or Chen, but the number was Canadian. Rose? She answered quickly, "West speaking."

"Why the hell are you meddling in my business?" Charles Huxham was shouting in a frenzy. "I demand to see you immediately."

"Whoa, buddy. How about you settle down and tell me what's wrong?"

"My office, now."

The line went dead.

Sloane grinned at her phone and canceled her Uber. Gannon had obviously informed Charles about her visit. With his bookie due to collect payment the following night, Charles was panicked, and a panicky suspect was prone to mistakes.

Charles was waiting in the lobby and rushed her. "Who do you think you are asking Gannon Ferris questions about me?" he yelled. "And don't deny it. He just left me a message."

Sloane held her arms out. "You need to back up and calm down." She waited for him to step back. "Jesus. How many times do I have to tell you people, it's my job? I'm investigating your uncle's murder, and Gannon Ferris came up."

"Right. Just like that." He swore under his breath and walked to his office.

Sloane followed and dropped her tote on the floor next to a chair at his desk.

Charles white-knuckle grasped the back of his chair. "Gannon Ferris is not the type of person you want to anger, and you did. What did you say?"

"Really? I thought we got along smashingly." She sat and crossed her legs. "We talked about the weather. His lovely office." She studied his face. "C'mon, Charles. You know what we talked about. You owe him a lot of money, and he expects you to pay up. The only problem is you offered him something that belongs to me. And he wasn't too thrilled when I showed up."

"Son of a bitch." Charles dropped into his chair and buried his face in his hands. "You don't understand what you've done. I had everything worked out. I was stalling. Gannon was never taking your painting."

"Yeah, well, I don't believe you," Sloane said. "I think you told Gannon that Harold had found me in New York, so you couldn't pay out your debt with the painting. My guess is Gannon said a deal's a deal. My guess is he had a permanent solution."

"That's not true." Charles coughed and wiped away spittle with the back of his hand.

"You tried to stall him, but it didn't work," she continued. "He told you all you had to do was tell him when and where Harold was meeting me, and he'd take care of everything."

Charles's lower lip trembled. "I loved my uncle. I had nothing to do with what happened in New York. Someone called Liam Morris killed my uncle and tried to kill you. That's all I know."

"Yeah. The stranger-who-was-really-after-me cover story would've worked. But I'm alive, and I know Morris was a hired professional."

"I didn't have my uncle murdered. But if any part of what you're saying is true, Gannon Ferris could have. Except I didn't tell him about my uncle going to find you or anything about you. None of it." He lowered his head.

"Why didn't you tell the police about Gannon? You must have considered he might have had something to do with Harold's murder."

Charles looked up. "That would have been my death sentence." His eyes were bloodshot, and the corners of his mouth twitched.

"Tell them now. Tell them he's threatening your life. That you got mixed up in his illegal gaming. It's a crime, but it's not a murder wrap. Turn witness against his uncle's gambling syndicate, and you won't serve a day. They'll put you in witness protection."

He rubbed his face with his hands. "Denwick is my home. The law firm is my legacy. I brought Gannon to Denwick. I'll get rid of him."

Without help, Charles Huxham didn't have a chance of quitting Gannon. "Well, Harold's estate is enough for a clean slate. With no spouse or children, he probably left it all to you, right?"

Charles's face reddened, and suddenly, a stack of papers fell off a side table behind his desk. "Another one!" He jumped to his feet.

"What's the matter?" Sloane asked.

"Rats. I'm sick of this goddamn infestation," he yelled, chasing something to the back room.

Sloane could hear him behind the closed door stomping around and slamming objects against the walls. *Elvina, I need you.*

The familiar appeared beside her. *You spoke to me. It's a day of firsts, huh?*

"Yeah. Can you pause time for me?" Sloane whispered.

*Yes, dear. But only briefly.*

"I know, I know."

Elvina's tail flicked. Nothing moved. Even the air was still.

Sloane hurried to the back and found Charles, frozen, in midstride, his arm reaching out. She laid her hand on his arm and considered the detection spell. It would be easy to secure his guilt or strike him off her board. What was the saying, she thought? It's better to ask for forgiveness than permission.

*Not without approval, dear.* Elvina sat in the doorway.

"Fine," Sloane said and stepped past Charles. She searched behind stacks of boxes and around file cabinets and old furniture. Her head whipped to the back wall.

*What are you looking for?*

"A rat. Charles said he heard a rat. I want to know if he was lying because something else, maybe magical, is going on."

*Tick-tock, dear.*

"All right. Just a minute." Sloane returned to Charles's desk and pushed play on the answering machine.

One message. It was Gannon Ferris's voice. "Charlie, my friend. You and I seem to have another problem. I had the pleasure of meeting a friend of yours. Seems she's interested in our business. You know I don't like attention. I'd like you to make our new problem disappear by the time I collect. Or I'll make both my problems go away."

*He's arrogant for someone who doesn't fight his own battles.* Elvina's tail uncurled and tapped the desk. *When does he collect?*

"I heard Charles say Friday night." Sloane searched the files on his desk, in its drawers. She rifled through a large credenza and stopped to page through a file before putting it back. The cabinet's top left drawer was locked. "Where would he keep the key?"

*You'll have to find it later, dear.*

"But I need to get my hands on Harold's will." Sloane slammed a drawer shut.

*Even so, time needs to carry on.*

"Fine." Sloane sat exactly as she was before Elvina arrived. "I'll see you at home."

Elvina disappeared, and Charles's footsteps resumed.

"The bastard got away," he said as he entered the office. "We've tried everything to kill the rats. Nothing works. We haven't gone a day without their filthy messes." He picked up the papers and returned them to the side table. "I guess it's my problem now."

"You don't need to have quite so many problems."

Charles stared at her and rubbed his face with the palms of his hands. "I made a mistake calling you. I'll take care of Gannon." He walked to his office door and opened it. "Go. Please. Just go."

Sloane left with few answers and a whole lot of new questions. But mostly, she had a desire for dinner in New Denwick. She needed to figure out why Charles had a thick file in the credenza labeled Isobel Gildey.

\* \* \*

Sloane picked up Pearl, but instead of turning toward the cottage, she headed to the coast. New Denwick's shopping plazas had modern storefronts, bold signage, manicured gardens, and walkways to several piers, artfully woven into the Salish Sea's coastline. There was no doubt these businesses siphoned money from Old Denwick. This was Isobel Gidley's realm.

Sloane drove through the parking lots of each plaza and read the required building permits, safety, and legal postings at each of the active construction sites. Dorathea was right. The noted legal representation was a construction law firm out of Toronto. So why did Charles have a file with Isobel Gildey's name on it and dated January this year? That's when her husband died. What was his name? Sean. That's right. Did Charles suspect something nefarious in the Gildey patriarch's death?

After eating Dungeness crab at a quaint restaurant overlooking the Georgia Straight, Sloane drove Pearl back to Old Main. The quiet, dark night smothered her. She missed the city with its shrill car horns, sirens, and people hustling. She was gripped with longing. Once she found Harold's killer, she would hire an estate company, sell the Wests' things, and go home.

She could buy the brownstone and raise Gary's rent. Maybe she would turn the basement apartment into her own covenstead. The idea made her grin.

Mallow Avenue was empty and dark. *Creepy small towns.* She parked Pearl in the garage and went inside the cottage. She poured a measure of whiskey into a rocks glass, took the Saskatoon pie out of her tote, and grabbed a fork. She dragged the case board into the middle of the living room.

The night Tom Hanson made detective, she and Jess had invited him over to celebrate. He brought her a corkboard, her first case board. She had previously kept her photos and notes in a binder. He also taught her to organize suspect pictures in rows, but she now arranged them in circles, a new style she had developed.

"I understand Elvina assisted you today."

She spun around. "Jesus, Dorathea." Her cousin and Elvina reclined on the sofa as if they had always been there. "You're never going to stop appearing out of nowhere, are you?"

Elvina curled her tail around her feet. *You might as well adapt, dear.*

"At least until our case is solved," Sloane said under her breath.

Dorathea raised an eyebrow. "I understand you spoke telepathically with Elvina. Well done, indeed. And Elvina stopped time for you? What did you learn?"

Sloane waited for Elvina to gloat, but the familiar only lay on the top cushion, swishing her tail.

"Really, pet, your dramatic pause has me on the edge of my seat."

Sloane turned to her cousin. "Gannon wants me dead. Charles has until tomorrow night to get rid of me, or Gannon kills us both."

"That is absurd. The idea of Charles Huxham murdering anyone. Hire a murderer, maybe. But carry one out himself. Nonsense."

Sloane nodded and turned to the board. "I'm having a hard time believing it, too."

The doorbell chimed and they all looked toward the entryway.

"Don't move," Sloane said in a low voice and set the pie on the coffee table. She walked to the foyer. Charles or a hitman could be on the other side of the front door, and she would not make the same mistake twice. "Who's there?"

"Hey, tough guy, it's Rose Keane."

Sloane's grip on the doorknob relaxed as she opened the door.

Rose stood on the porch in a faded T-shirt tucked strategically behind the front button of her jeans. "Hey. Got time for a drink and an apology?" She held out a bottle of Hyde.

"You don't even have to ask. I always make time for gorgeous redheads and whiskey."

Rose laughed as Sloane led her to the living room.

Dorathea was on her feet, and the case board faced the wall, hidden from view. "Good evening Rose, dear," she said.

"Hello, Ms. West." Rose looked down at Elvina. "Aw, what a beautiful cat."

"Call me Dorathea, dear. This is Elvina. She lives with Sloane. But I am quite fond of her, too. In fact, the two of us were just leaving to dine on fresh salmon." She bent over and picked up the familiar.

*I'd much rather stay here*, Elvina said and jumped out of her arms.

"If you refuse, you will have canned tuna," Dorathea warned her.

Sloane stared at Dorathea and then Rose.

*Fine.* Elvina sashayed back to Dorathea's feet.

"Oh, wow. It's like she understood you," Rose said.

Dorathea swept Elvina up into her arms. "It is, indeed." She turned in a flurry of dark-green cloak. "Nice to see you, Rose, dear. See you in the morning, pet."

After the front door closed behind Dorathea, Rose turned to Sloane. "She's so eccentric, isn't she?"

"Trust me, more than you could imagine." Sloane picked up the plate with her pie, but her glass of whiskey was gone.

"I wouldn't be so sure about that. I can imagine some wild things." Rose followed Sloane to the kitchen. "Do you like the pie?"

"Yeah. It's delicious." Sloane pulled two glasses from a cupboard. "So what's this about an apology?"

Rose rested her hip against the island. "For earlier. I'm sorry I lost my temper. It's just the pub…I'm protective. It's my life. But you were only doing your job."

"No problem. I can be too blunt sometimes."

"This is the first time I've seen the inside of Mallow Cottage. You could get lost in here."

"Yeah, it's way too much house for me. How about a tour?" Sloane put the rest of the pie in the refrigerator. She walked Rose around the main floor, through a study, library, and an art studio, finally stopping in front of a large wooden door. "I haven't been in the basement. I'm not sure I want to. I'm guessing it's packed floor to ceiling with junk."

"Junk? I doubt it. If it's anything like the rest of the cottage."

"Maybe not junk but still crammed full of stuff." Sloane walked back to the kitchen, picked up the bottle of Hyde, and opened the French doors. "Join me?"

"Sure. But only for a few minutes. I have to be up early."

The light from the house barely penetrated the new-moon sky, and a mild, salty breeze drifted from the east, mingling with the scent of winter jasmine. Sloane left the porch dark, pulling two deck chairs together. "Have a seat, Keane." Sloane opened the Hyde and poured one for Rose and one for herself.

Rose eased herself into a lounger. "Let me guess, you live in a studio apartment decorated minimalist in the heart of Manhattan where all the action is."

"Even if I could afford to, I wouldn't live there. I live in the Bronx. Jane did, though, in a one-bedroom in Tribeca." She stared into her glass. "I need to put her apartment on the market."

"I'm sorry. I didn't mean to mention your mom. It must be painful. I don't know what it feels like to lose someone so close."

"You bury it deep, and the next death gets easier." She took a drink.

"That's cold, West. I should've brought food, too. You aren't such a grouch when I feed you." She sat up and laid her hand on top of Sloane's. "If you want to talk about your mom, I'm available."

Sloane expected heat from Rose's hand, a temperature to match the warmth of the whiskey. But Rose's skin was cool to the touch. She had a brief desire to turn her hand around and share her warmth.

Rose pulled back her hand and sighed. "I wasn't honest with you before. I think the pub *is* struggling. The thing is, I close almost every night and handle the daily closing reports. So I know what comes in, and I know what our expenses are. But my mom's month-end reports show us in the red, and she complains about finances all the time." She stared into the dark garden. "She's been acting strange these last few months. But I can't believe she could hurt anyone. She's lived here for over thirty years. The Huxhams and Wests are like family to her."

"I'm sure you're right. Besides, if your mom wants to retire and leave Denwick, why would she kill for money to keep the business afloat?"

"I guess she wouldn't," Rose answered, sounding hopeful. She turned back to the garden as if something startled her and peered deep into the black night, tilting her head toward the trees.

"What's wrong? Do you hear something?" Sloane was angered by the thought of Elvina out there, spying. "A few obnoxious crows roost in one of the big trees."

"I guess that's what I heard." Her face grew serious. "If your contact can find irregularities with the pub's financials, please tell me."

"All right. Are you sure you can't talk with your mom?"

"I'm not sure I can even fully trust her right now. But I might be able to help the pub if I know the true state of things.

I can't let my business fail. It's all I have." She swung her legs around and sat on the lounger's side.

"Are you leaving so soon?" Sloane asked.

"I open in the morning." She finished her drink and held up her glass. "One's my limit. I'll leave you to the bottle."

Sloane laughed and got to her feet. "I'll ignore the implication."

"I imply nothing." Rose grinned and held out a hand. Sloane helped her stand. She slipped her arm around Sloane's waist. "You realize we could consider tonight our third date."

"Really? Our third? We've been busy." Sloane placed Rose's hand behind her back, bringing their bodies together. Adrenaline shot through her. She exhaled and let her hand go, stepping back.

Rose released Sloane's waist and pushed her away playfully, downplaying the shift in emotion. "We have. And I like this kind of busy work. But I do have to go. Walk me out?"

"Where's your Jeep?" Sloane asked as they stood on the front porch.

"I walked. I love new-moon nights." Rose stepped closer to Sloane and asked teasingly, "Are you worried about me?"

"Of course, I am. There's a killer out there."

Rose took Sloane's hands gently and leaned into her body, her lips brushed against Sloane's ear, and she whispered, "If anything lurks out there in the dark, West, it should be more afraid of me."

# CHAPTER TWENTY-ONE

Sloane woke the following morning with a dry mouth and a pounding head. She shielded her eyes from the morning sun and groaned, rolling off the sofa onto her feet. The case board stood in the middle of the floor, and markers were scattered about, reminders she had worked into the early hours of the new day. She capped the Hyde bottle, grabbed her dirty glass, and staggered to the kitchen.

The aroma of freshly brewed coffee filled the air, and she felt Dorathea before she saw her. "Why did you open the drapes? Never mind. Why are you here?"

Dorathea washed dishes at the sink and turned to her. "Good morning to you, too. You are late for training, so we decided to wake you."

"Of course, you did." Sloane poured a cup of coffee and rested against the island. "Why didn't you get me up?" she asked Elvina.

The familiar sauntered over to her. *I left early to help Dorathea. You wouldn't have heard me over your snoring.*

"Me? The way you rattle the shingles. I should've known you weren't a cat."

Dorathea picked up a pastry box tied with a lavender string and eyed Sloane from head to toe. "When you are finished bantering like an old married couple, Elvina and I will leave to the covenstead while you change into something—clean."

They disappeared before Sloane could respond. After she dressed, she walked to the hobbit house. The front doors opened, and she slipped inside. "Thanks, Alfred." The door slammed behind her, and she stared at the ceiling. "Jesus, you make one wisecrack...I said I was sorry."

The covenstead was thick with incense and busy with zozzing books, whirling and whizzing gadgets, and beakers with globular bubbles popping open and releasing colored steam. Dorathea and Elvina sat in the velvet chairs by the fireplace. Its heat warmed Sloane's face. The familiar was licking a paw covered in powdered sugar.

"Those look delicious. Are they from Freya's?" Sloane sat next to Elvina. A coffee carafe floated in the air and poured her a cup.

"Yes, indeed. I met with the Grand Coven this morning. And Elvina visited her mother."

Sloane turned to the familiar. "Whoa. How'd that go?"

Elvina's whiskers twitched, sprinkling powdered sugar on the chair. *She hasn't brought herself to ask me where I've been for the last fifteen years.*

Dorothea raised an eyebrow. "Really? How curious?"

"Don't think you've gotten away with anything. I know mothers. The interrogation will come." Sloane let out a gruff laugh and helped herself to an almond croissant. "Oh, yeah. Before I forget, Rose heard you last night. I thought we agreed you wouldn't spy on me."

*Rose didn't hear me, dear. I had no reason to guard you. Dorathea and I were together until late last evening.*

Dorathea set her teacup on the table. "I believe I know who Rose heard."

"Who?" Sloane asked.

"The crows, pet." Dorathea peered over her glasses. "I suspected they might be *Gewende* defenders. The Grand Coven confirmed my suspicions."

"What the hell is that?"

*Gewende are shape-shifters, dear.*

Sloane stared at Elvina. "Seriously?" Sloane gulped her black coffee. "Why are they watching us?"

"I believe they seek to destroy the same Demon we have detected."

Sloane chewed her croissant slowly as she considered the ramifications. "So a Gewende is in Denwick."

"You are correct."

"And you don't know who it is?"

*No one does, dear,* answered Elvina.

"And the Grand Coven won't tell us?"

"They denied my appeal. They will not reconsider without evidence that the individual is involved. It is up to the Gewende defenders to detect the evil Magical or the Demon."

"That's bullshit. How the hell do we protect others or ourselves if we don't know who's here? I've studied Jane's research. I think she knew another magical family was here and was narrowing in on who it was. I think she suspected back then what is happening now."

"If she did, she did not tell us. But we must proceed along this line of inquiry carefully. As I told you before, Jane's interest raised suspicions among the Grand Coven. They summoned her to appear before them and forbade her to continue."

"Tell me exactly what happened," Sloane said.

"There's not much to say. The Weardas learned of her research and informed the Grand Coven. Nathaniel and I brought her before them. She was only seventeen, but they were ready to make an example of her flouting the Concealment Act. They demanded she relinquish any documents she had on magical families. But she told them she had destroyed everything."

"No surprise. She lied," Sloane said.

"Yes, indeed."

"We don't need to lie. We need to make our case to the Grand Coven again. I still think the guards at Drusnirwd may have made a mistake."

Dorathea looked up at the ceiling and shook her head.

"Just hear me out," Sloane said. "Does the prison allow visitors?"

*Of course. Banished families can have distant relatives visit them, but only one at a time. And no one else. The magical abilities of all who enter Drusnirwd are blocked,* Elvina said.

"She is correct. Banishment is a punishment felt as deeply as death."

Sloane paced in front of the crackling fire. "Let's explore the idea that one of the banished families had a child and hid the baby. Now, its descendant is back for revenge."

*Every magical species records the births of their children, dear,* Elvina said.

Sloane stopped. "Who recorded mine?"

Dorathea and the familiar stared at her. Then each other.

"Yeah. That's what I thought." Sloane paced again. "Only someone with a God complex would believe a plan is infallible. They aren't. We make plans as sound as we can. But someone smarter will come along and expose their flaws. Make them better. It's the natural order of ideas." Sloane paused before saying, "Can prisoners and visitors have sex?"

Elvina laughed. *I hardly think sex requires magical powers. At least not for most.*

"My point is it only takes one visit to walk out with the start of a new generation."

Elvina stopped laughing.

"There are rules in place to prevent such an event. Nevertheless, you posit an interesting theory. I will bring your questions to the Grand Coven," Dorathea said.

"What makes you think they'd tell you if they knew?"

"They have no reason to lie to us." Dorathea stood, wrapped her emerald-green cloak around her, and glided to the lectern.

"All right. You keep trying to get the Coven to cooperate. I'm going to take another look at Jane's research."

"Very well. Join me. It is time to begin our lesson. Today, you will learn to *bestealce*, the location spell." She waved her hand, and the *Book of Hagorúnum* opened.

Sloane climbed on a stool next to the lectern.

"We conjure the location spell through intense focus on place. *Place* is where we are and where we desire to be at any given moment."

"Oh my God, this is going to be unbelievably cool."

"You are learning to bestealce for protection, not so you can impress yourself or others. Indeed, if your life is in danger, you will no longer fight. You must bestealce to Freya immediately."

Sloane winced. "Why her?"

*She is the most formidable sensor of magic or evil in the Northwest Quadrant, and we trust her completely*, answered Elvina.

"I thought we were Protectors. Why do you want me to run?"

"At this time, you are no match for the evil that seeks to end us."

"Even with Elvina?"

*It takes a coven to eliminate a Demon, dear.* The familiar leaped into her seat next to the lectern.

"Yeah. Aren't we a coven?"

The familiar's tail swept to and fro. *More like half a coven.*

"Elvina, please," Dorathea said and turned to Sloane. "Trust me. We are unprepared to battle a Demon. Our priority is to keep you safe." She flicked her wrist, and the book's pages turned. "To bestealce requires splitting our vision. Do you find it easier to see from your third eye now?"

"Yeah. It's gotten easier," answered Sloane.

"Quite, right. Keep practicing."

Dorathea conjured a cloudy image between her hands. The image swirled into focus. In it, Dorathea stood at the lectern and sat in one of the velvet armchairs in front of the fireplace. She separated her hands, and the image split apart. "When I cast the spell, I simultaneously visualize myself standing here while also seeing myself sitting there."

Dorathea disappeared and reappeared in the armchair. "Now, you try." She glided back to the lectern. "Begin with your eyes closed, then open your third eye. See yourself here and by the fireplace."

Sloane closed her eyes. A palette of blurred colors, like the beginning of an Impressionist painting, slowly came into focus. "I see us."

*Excellent, dear,* Elvina said. *And the chairs?*

"Yeah. They're clear as mud." Sloane opened her eyes. "Is that all? No Old English to learn for this spell?"

*Of course, there is.* Elvina's snout disappeared into her teacup.

"The location spell's incantation consists of two words, *lecgan lāstas,*" answered Dorathea. "Repeat after me, Lek-gan lah-stos."

"Lakgahn lahstohs."

Elvina lifted her head. *Almost. You sound better. Are you practicing the language?*

"Old English?" Sloane laughed. "Not hardly."

*Try again,* Elvina said. *Lecgan lāstas.*

"Lecgan lāstas," Sloane said.

"Well done," Dorathea said. "Remember, our tongues have memories. Preserve this spell upon yours. Repeat it several times a day. But right now, continue to speak the phrase." She snapped her fingers and their tea reappeared on a table next to the lectern. She poured them another cup and listened to Sloane practice.

"All right. I'm done chanting like a Gregorian," Sloane said after a while. "What next?"

Dorathea placed her cup on the side table and pointed to the top corner of the page. "See here, spells with this sigil require our most intense focus. To divide your third eye's vision is no easy task and must be done precisely, or the consequences are severe."

Sloane thought about the dragon and held out her hands. "Wait a minute. Like what?"

Elvina shuddered. *Imagine if you tried to go next door but weren't focused. Parts of your body would remain here, and others would appear there.*

"Jesus. The spell can tear me apart? How do you fix that?"

"Our powers can heal most injuries, but not all, pet."

"Whoa. You think I'm ready for this?"

"I would not teach you if I did not."

"All right. Let's do it. Where first?"

*Nowhere, yet, dear,* answered Elvina.

"She is quite right. First, you will practice focusing your third eye until you see yourself here and there." Dorathea pointed to the armchairs.

Sloane stared blankly past the chairs for a few moments, then blinked, shaking her head. "It didn't happen. The colors in my head are overwhelming. I need sunglasses in there."

Elvina laughed. *You sound so much like your mother.*

"It will take time," Dorathea said. She waved her hand over the teapot, and steam rose from its spout. "Try to focus on different areas of the covenstead if that helps."

Nearly an hour passed before Sloane held an image of herself on the stool and in the armchair closest to the fireplace, but not without frustrated outbursts. And finally, she shouted, "I did it. I saw me here and there."

"Excellent," Dorathea said. "Now, hold the image again. This time when it is clear, articulate, lecgan lāstas. Remember, speak the words clearly, precisely, and only if your *place* is focused."

"All right." Sloane closed her eyes and concentrated. A few minutes later, she cast the spell, but nothing happened.

*Try again,* Elvina said.

Sloane repeated the words several times before closing her eyes. "Lecgan lāstas." She disappeared and reappeared in a chair. "Oh my God. That was incredible." Sloane turned to them, her heart racing.

The corners of Dorathea's mouth turned up. "Well done, pet. Now, think of yourself there and here, next to Elvina."

"All right." She took only a moment to clear the image in her third eye and visualize her place. "Lecgan lāstas." Her body jerked, and she fell into the dark void, but instead of her feet touching the covenstead's floor, she reappeared in her New York apartment beside the bay window. "Oh, shit," she whispered and patted her body. "Okay, I'm all right. No problem. I'll just go back before they notice I screwed up."

She closed her eyes and focused when whistling came from her bedroom. Her eyes flew open. She dropped to her knees, crawled behind Jane's desk, and peeked toward the hallway.

Wearing light-blue silk pajamas and a creamy face mask, an unlit cigarette dangling from his lips, Gary Prence sashayed into the living room. He set a watering can on the kitchen counter and strolled to the front door.

"Ahight, you beautifuls. I'll be back in a couple days to dust each of yus' precious tiny leaves. Keep growin' and stayin' gorgeous. Au revoir."

Sloane waited until the lock clicked and then rolled onto her back in a fit of muted laughter. She and Gary had emergency keys to each other's apartments. But she never considered her lack of a green thumb a crisis.

Lavender and sage still perfumed her apartment, masking the crime. She noticed the missing armchair and the bullet hole in the wall behind her desk. The apartment left her with a dull ache. Remembering Dorathea wanted something Jane had touched recently, she grabbed a photo and vase from her bookcase and closed her eyes, picturing where she stood and where she wanted to be in the covenstead. When the image was clear, she said, "Lecgan lāstas."

A floating book smacked her on the head. Elvina's laughter filled her mind.

"Very funny," she said as she joined Dorathea and the familiar. "Okay, I can bestel—"

Elvina shook her head. *Be-steal-ce, dear. It's not that hard to say.*

Dorathea took hold of Sloane's arm. "Where did you go?"

"At the last second, I messed up my image of Elvina and ended up in my apartment."

Dorathea released her. "Did you see or sense anyone?"

"No one important. Just my neighbor. But he didn't see me."

She exhaled. "Very well, pet. You must keep practicing but be careful. Only travel within the same room and do not focus on spaces that remind you of New York. Does that make sense?"

"Yeah, no problem."

*What are you carrying?* Elvina said, looking at Sloane's hands.

Sloane held up the picture. "It's a photo of Jane and me from this past Christmas. She gave it to me a few weeks before her accident." She stared at the urn tucked in the crook of her arm. "And this is Jane."

# CHAPTER TWENTY-TWO

When Sloane left the covenstead, a mist had crept in from the northeast, the sky a study in gray. She drove Pearl to Old Main and parked behind the Huxham building. Her gear shifting had not improved. "Sorry about that, old girl," she said.

She checked her phone. Katie Chen had promised to deliver the suspects' financials this morning. If money was the motive behind the murders, she had to know who needed it most.

No new messages.

She glanced at her watch. The MCC meeting started in five minutes.

Voices sounded from the second floor and filled the Huxham Law Firm's lobby. Sloane looked up. The double doors at the top of the stairs were open. She approached a middle-aged woman, perfumed in a concoction of oils. The woman studied her before handing her an agenda. "The meeting starts in five minutes. Please find a seat." She eyed Sloane into the room.

The conference room was decorated in the same dark traditional décor as the first floor. A substantial conference table was shoved against a fireplace on the back wall, replaced by a long buffet table and five executive chairs. Several rows of folding chairs faced them.

The room dimmed. Through the back windows, Sloane noticed the sky had turned darker. The members of the MCC milled about a sideboard full of pastries, coffee, and tea. The four Musketeer families were there. But only one original—James Reed. Raymond Keane was gone, now living in Scotland. Nathaniel and Harold were dead. Sloane shivered.

A mantle clock chimed. Ten o'clock sharp, and Isobel Gildey had just entered. Heads turned, watching the Gildey matriarch walk to the long table. She smoothed the sides of her tailored suit and rang a tiny brass bell. "We need to begin, please," she said and sat in one of the five chairs. James Reed, Fiona Keane, Charles Huxham, and another woman Sloane did not recognize joined her.

Sloane headed to the back of the room when an arm slipped around hers. It was Lore Reed. "You're here. I'm so happy. Natty and Mary would be pleased." She guided Sloane to the front row. "Come sit with me. Have you met anyone?"

"No. But I recognize a few people."

They sat, and Lore patted Sloane's leg. "I'd be happy to introduce you to anyone here."

Sloane stared at the five people before her and whispered, "Who's sitting next to Isobel Gildey?"

"That's Zara Patel. She and her husband own the Fresh Market across the street." She paused. "When did you meet Isobel?"

"At Harold's repast."

"Oh, yes. Of course. How did that go?"

"All right."

"Well, you did have Dorathea to temper Isobel's behavior."

Sloane nodded. Two aging, formidable women, heads of their families. They'd fit right in the Upper East Side.

Isobel rang the bell again, and conversations came to an end. She put on her reading glasses and picked up the agenda. "I call the Main Street Commerce Committee's special meeting to order."

"Excuse me, Mrs. Gildey." The thickly scented woman got to her feet. "Perhaps we need to ensure everyone present represents a business in the MCC before discussing any sensitive information." She gave a curt nod at Sloane, and whispers in agreement rippled through the room.

"Karen, this is Sloane West, Natty and Mary's granddaughter," Lore stated. "Not some New Denwick mole. She's here representing the gallery."

Karen's cheeks flushed, and she held her hand over her ample chest. "I'm terribly sorry, Ms. West. I didn't know. How thoughtless of me."

"You're fine, Karen. Sit down," Isobel said. "How would you have known? I apologize to everyone and Ms. West. Let me introduce our newest member." She gave a curt nod in Sloane's direction. "Ms. West. Would you care to say anything?"

Sloane attempted to meet Isobel's eyes, but the elderly matriarch refused to look at her. "Thanks, but I'm just here to listen."

"All right then. Let's return to the business at hand. The Community has two motions on the agenda. The first is a proposal for the MCC to align against any new development along Denwick's coast—"

"New Denwick," James said, interrupting huffily.

"—at the next district meeting," Isobel finished. "The second is to ask district staff to undergo an impact study of new development on Main Street businesses—"

"Old Main."

Isobel pulled off her glasses. "Mr. Reed. Will you please refrain from interrupting me?" She turned to the membership. "I'm sure you know I cannot support either of these items. The Gildey family has extensive investment in coastal real estate. It would be against our best interests. Therefore, I must recuse myself from discussion and voting. I hand over the chair to Fiona Keane."

James's face reddened. "Yet you're discussing." He drummed the tabletop with his fingers.

Lore straightened and whispered to Sloane, "It's primal, the way that woman perturbs my father."

Mrs. Gildey got to her feet and gathered her purse. "I haven't said anything that isn't obvious to everyone, James."

Something about Isobel's presence made those around her acquiesce, and Sloane wanted to know why. "Do she and James have a history?" she asked Lore.

"Oh, heaven's no. The Gildeys don't have a history with anyone in the village. They have other ways of getting what they want."

Sloane nodded and sat back, watching Isobel leave the conference room.

Karen stood again, hands on her hips. "The Gildeys' development at the coast has caused a steep drop in my customer traffic, even though I'm spending more on marketing." The other merchants mumbled in agreement. Karen continued, "Two weeks ago, Isobel rented to another gift shop, and it's undercutting my pure essential oils with cheap, toxic junk. If one more opens, I'll be out of business." She pulled a tissue from her bra strap and wiped her eyes. "Our family opened Denwick's Essentials over thirty years ago."

"Have you tried running an online store for more sales?" Lore asked.

Karen clicked her tongue at Lore and sat.

Zara Patel threw her hands up. "That's not the answer for everyone, Lore. What would you expect Raj and I to do, eh? Put our fresh groceries online and ship them here and there?" She shook her head. "No, the only thing we can do is a moratorium on further development until we understand how it's impacting us. That's what we need to argue at the district meeting."

The Community erupted in noisy agreement.

Fiona Keane rang the bell. "Calm down, please. The Gildeys' continued development of New Denwick has affected all of us. Let's move on. I propose if no one else wants to speak against the first motion, we vote."

The room was silent.

Lore shifted in her seat, and Sloane thought for a second Lore was going to stand and voice her dissent, but she didn't. Was she surprised there were more businesses on Old Main upset with New Denwick development?

"Good. Then we vote. Can I get a second?" Fiona asked.

"Second," Zara said.

"All in favor of aligning against the development at the shore at the district meeting, say aye."

"Aye," the members shouted. Lore remained silent.

"All against?"

No one spoke.

"Motion passes." Fiona stood. "Now, we will open discussion on our second motion, and I'll begin. The Spotted Owl has made a profit from the first day it opened. But that's not so any longer."

Murmurs spread around the room.

"That's right, the inn and pub are struggling," Fiona continued. "But we can't bring stories of personal loss to the district. We need to argue that the Gildeys, in particular, and big businesses, franchises in general at the shore, have created unfair competition for Old Main shops. We can't compete with chains. We need equity. We need some rules." Her voice became more assertive and louder as the Community agreed with her.

Sloane looked around. The other members hung on Fiona's every word. How deeply in the red had the pub gone for Fiona Keane to mount such a passionate battle cry against Isobel Gildey?

After a second unanimous vote, Fiona closed the discussion. "Charlie, will you please find Isobel and tell her we're finished?"

"She's going to be furious," Zara said.

The rest of the Community sat in their seats with heads down. A few minutes later, Charles returned with Mrs. Gildey.

They sat, and Isobel folded her hands on top of the table. "Well, I am surprised." Her voice was tight. "If it weren't for my husband's family, none of your businesses would have been possible in the first place."

"Point of order," Mrs. Patel called out. "Discussion is finished. And you—"

"I'm the Chair, Mrs. Patel," Isobel said, glaring at her. "If I choose to speak, I will speak." She stared at the rest of the Community. "Change is an inevitable part of life. Everything grows until it dies, and you can't stop that no matter how hard you try. You can only hasten it."

James pounded the table with his fist. "Isobel. I've had enough of you coming to these meetings, pretending you care about Old Denwick. Your people haven't had a business on Old Main for thirty years. And you've left 403 Main to rot when you ought to sell it to my son. Hell, you won't sell any property on your side of the street."

Lore clutched the scarf around her neck.

"Mr. Reed. What an astonishing thing to say. The Gildeys settled Denwick. Why wouldn't we want it to thrive?"

"Why the hell would you? Don't forget, Isobel. The Reeds have been here almost as long as the Gildeys. We know exactly what you did to establish yourselves on Cowichan land—"

"Dad," Lore called out, horrified. "There's no need to get personal."

"This *is* personal," James snapped. "Since Sean stepped down, Isobel has run off more fishermen than we lost during all his years in charge. And I want to know why."

"You're out of line, Mr. Reed," Isobel said. "My business operations and my family's success are not the cause of your struggle." She stared at the membership coldly.

"The hell they aren't," James growled. "As far as I'm concerned, your family doesn't belong on this board or in our community."

Lore jumped out of her chair and pulled her father to the back of the room. They stood at the conference table while Lore quietly admonished him.

Isobel rang the bell. "This meeting is adjourned." She tucked her purse under her arm and headed for the door.

Sloane stayed in her seat as the members gravitated into groups, talking quietly. Lore hurried from the back of the room, catching Isobel by the arm. Isobel pulled back, indignant. They exchanged tense words, neither backing down until Isobel finally left. Lore threw her hands up and walked out of the conference room behind her.

"Ms. West?"

Sloane turned to the voice beside her.

"Sorry. I didn't mean to surprise you."

It was Charles Huxham, standing like an awkward child. His hands jammed deep in his pockets. "Have you insured the Degas?"

"Yeah, I did. With the same company. They're emailing the new policy this afternoon."

"Good. That's good. Come by my office anytime today and pick it up. I'll be in until late."

Sloane glanced around the room. "I know you will. And I know why. Listen, Charles, I think meeting Gannon Ferris alone is a bad idea. Are you sure you don't want the police involved?"

Charles's face flushed. He leaned down and spoke in a low voice. "It's not a problem. My ex-associate won't be bothering me any longer." Then he walked away and shook hands with a few members before leaving.

Sloane walked over to the sideboard and threw her coffee cup in the bin. Fiona Keane stood next to the pastries with her back turned to the room, talking on the phone. Sloane poured herself a fresh cup and eavesdropped.

"I did my best. What I have now will have to be enough until I pay the pub's bills," Fiona whispered. She glanced at Sloane, and her voice became louder. "I must go, dear. I need to grab a few donuts for Ken and Rose and get back to the pub for the lunch rush. Talk later."

Sloane followed her out to the parking lot. Experience had taught her when someone was guilty, a certain attraction compelled her attention, and right now, she couldn't take her eyes off Fiona Keane. Fiona climbed into a Land Rover with black tinted windows, and Sloane ran to Pearl, sliding Pearl's gears in and out of place effortlessly for the first time.

She tried to stay a good distance behind Fiona. Pearl wasn't the best car in which to tail anyone. Hardly nondescript. Or fast. She could easily lose Fiona if she allowed too great a distance between them. Fiona drove the Land Rover over serpentine roads and up a mountainside.

"I guess you weren't going back to the pub," Sloane said to herself. "Who were you talking to? And what were you talking about?"

The dark-gray sky had opened up, and a steady rain fell. Thankfully, Pearl's wipers worked. Sloane recognized the drive. They were heading toward Rose's quiet place. She wondered why Rose hadn't attended the meeting. Was that why Fiona spoke frankly about the Spotted Owl's financial problems?

Fiona passed the forest line by the river, leading them farther up the mountain than Rose had. After a few minutes, the road leveled off in an expansive valley. They passed a rustic sign: "Keane's Distillery. Home of Keane's Single Malt Whiskey."

"Ah, we're going to see Oscar, huh?" Sloane slowed and allowed Fiona to pull farther ahead as they neared the entrance. The welcome center was an A-frame, redwood mountain cabin with floor-to-ceiling windows. The rest of the distillery's campus spread out on either side. Two copper stills. A mash tun and boiler. And an old rackhouse that still used a cooling pond. Sloane whistled. This was state-of-the-art equipment.

After Fiona disappeared inside, she eased Pearl into a parking space and entered the welcome center. A young man dressed in a black hoodie with a Keane's Whiskey logo on its front stood behind a U-shaped counter filing paperwork. Sloane glanced at his name badge. "Hi, Michael. Can you point me to Mr. Keane's office?"

He looked her over. "I'm sorry, we don't have tours or tastings on Fridays."

"Yeah, I'm not here for a tour. I'm here on business and need to speak to him."

"Do you have an appointment?"

"I wasn't under the impression I needed one."

Michael looked at his computer screen. "I'm sorry. His schedule is booked today. We can schedule one for next week."

"Listen, Michael. I know he's in his office with his mom, eating donuts. If you called him and told him Sloane West is waiting to see him. He'd come to get me."

"We don't do that," Michael replied.

"Well, I could yell for him until he hears me."

"Rude," Michael said under his breath. He pointed to the left. "End of the hall. Double doors."

"That wasn't so hard now, was it?" Sloane grinned and walked down the hallway, thinking she should talk to Oscar about his shitty security. The shale-tiled floor was unpolished and loud. Sloane lightened her steps as she approached the double doors, pushing them open as she knocked.

"Hello, Mr. Keane. Wow. Nice office."

Fiona and Oscar Keane stood behind a desk in front of a wall of windows. They turned to her, and Oscar subtly slipped a thick envelope into the desk's top drawer.

"Please, call me Oscar. And with whom do we have the pleasure?"

"Oscar, this is Sloane West." Fiona walked around the desk and placed a stone-cold hand on Sloane's back. "I'm delighted you've come to meet my son. I wish I had known you were coming. You could've ridden with me."

"I decided at the last minute."

"Yes, so did I." She forced a thin smile.

"I just came to ask Oscar a few questions." She turned to him. "If you have the time?" Sloane smiled and stared at Oscar and back at Fiona. Mother and son drew her in. They were stunningly beautiful. Like Rose. But Oscar took after Fiona with the same dark hair, golden-brown eyes, and high cheekbones. Their bodies were tall and lithe, and they moved gracefully.

Sloane's thoughts vanished, and the double doors closed behind her before she could remember what she'd said. She shook a dizzy feeling from her head.

"Are you okay, dear? Would you like something to drink?" Fiona asked. She stood next to a credenza against the wall opposite Oscar's desk.

Sloane turned to her, confused, and looked at Oscar, now sitting at his desk.

"Yeah. I'll take a black coffee. But I can get it, thanks." Sloane walked over to Fiona. "I don't want to take too much of your time, Oscar."

"No worries. What would you like to ask me?"

Fiona stepped away from the credenza. "I assume Sloane is here to ask you questions about Harold. Which is why I'd rather not stay. It is so dreadful, and I've already had a difficult day. I was up at dawn preparing for the MCC meeting." She walked back to Oscar. "I'm off to help your father at the pub. Don't be late for dinner tomorrow." She bent to kiss him on the cheek. "Have a lovely day, Sloane."

Sloane poured herself a cup of coffee and wondered what the hell had just happened to her. She remembered being suspicious of something Oscar did, but she couldn't recall what it was.

"You're exactly how my dad described you," Oscar said after his mother left.

"Oh, really? Ken told you about me?"

"Are you kidding? All he's talked about for weeks is Jane's daughter. And now that you're here, well, he's built you up so much, I couldn't wait for you to make the trip out here."

"So you assumed I would pay you a visit?"

"He said you were a whiskey enthusiast."

"That's fair." Sloane looked out the window. "Barley or rye?"

Oscar walked over to her and crossed his arms. "Both, actually. The new crop looks good, doesn't it?"

"Yeah, it does. You've got quite a place here. Was it hard to get started?" She remembered Rose said her brother chose to run a distillery rather than the pub and received his grandfather's rackhouse. She supposed he got the land that went with it, too.

"I started right out of university, almost seven years now. We'll release our second three-year batch from the lower racks in June. Our upper racks have four more years. And they're doing exceptionally well."

"So your first batch is keeping the lights on?"

"It received great reviews, which helped. I'll see an even healthier profit when our first ten-year batch releases."

Sloane noted he didn't answer her question. "That's good to hear. It's a cutthroat industry. Especially here in Canada. Not too many labels around and hardly any of those turn a profit with their first batch. Of course, I'm not looking to be an angel or anything."

"I don't need investors. We're holding our own." He rapped the windowsill with his knuckles. "I apologize. I got you off track. You came to talk about Mr. Huxham." He returned to his chair. "Dad said you are investigating his death."

"His murder," Sloane said and sat across from him, tossing her tote on the floor.

Oscar was calm and controlled. Maybe too relaxed and too rehearsed, Sloane thought.

"Sorry. Murder. It's horrible for the village. But I hardly knew Harold. Everything I know about him is hearsay. I'm not sure how I can help you."

"You might be surprised. I'm sure you hung out in the pub when you were younger. What did you hear about Harold, and James Reed?"

"Uh...supposedly, he and James had a feud. Ended in a friends-to-enemies relationship."

"Do you know why?"

"I think it was because of Lore and Charlie. Something happened between them."

"Yeah, I heard that, too," Sloane said. "Do you know of anyone who might have wanted Harold dead?"

"No, of course not."

"Have you ever had direct dealings with Charles Huxham?"

"Charlie's my solicitor."

"What did you think about Harold and Charles's relationship?"

"I didn't, really. They were uncle and nephew. Supposedly, Charlie's mother, Harold's sister, and his father were killed in a yachting accident. The grandparents were too old to raise him, so Harold did." Oscar's shoulders relaxed. "You don't think Charlie had anything to do with Harold's murder?"

"He's one line of inquiry we're following."

"Do you have others?"

"We do." Sloane sipped her coffee. "Have your parents ever talked about Harold and Charles arguing in the Spotted Owl?"

He leaned back. "We don't talk about what goes on at the pub." His voice was less composed. "If you want to talk about the Owl, you'll need to talk to them or Rose. Big sis is always there. She even lives in the second-story apartment, rent free."

"Sounds like you'd prefer to live there."

"Not at all. I just think my sister needs to understand how lucky she is. Life's easier when you get an established business handed to you."

Sloane cocked her head in mock concern. "I'm sure you've had your share of handouts."

A red flush crawled up his neck. "I'm sorry. I got us off-track again."

"No problem. I just have one more question. Do you sell your whiskey in New York?"

His charming smile faded. "No. I haven't broken into that market yet. But I plan to."

"Good luck with that." Sloane stood and pulled her tote's strap over her head. She stared at his desk, feeling she still had something to ask.

Oscar jumped up, scraping the chair legs against the tile floor. "Do you have time for a tour?" He walked gracefully around his desk.

"I can't today. Some other time?"

"Sure. Okay. But I'm going to hold you to it."

# CHAPTER TWENTY-THREE

Sloane was headed back to Denwick when Katie Chen called. "Hey, Chen. You're late. Make me glad to hear from you."

"Jeez, classy greeting. I broke a hundred rules and maybe a few laws for you, and that's how you say hello? And after all this time. You haven't called me since the Lewinsky case. How about you woo me a little before I give up the info?"

Sloane laughed and pulled Pearl into a turnout area. If she had anything close to a friend, Katie Chen fit the role. "I'm sorry. You're right. I've missed you, and hearing your voice makes my day brighter."

"Did you say you're sorry? Jeez Louise. What is Canada doing to you? Never mind. I don't have time for chitchat. Promise me our business doesn't get back to Jacobson."

"Have I ever divulged my sources?"

"No, but I need to say it. It makes me feel better."

Sloane heard tapping on a keyboard.

"All right, here's what I got. Only two businesses are in financial trouble, the Spotted Owl Inn and Pub and Reed's Fish Market. Oscar Keane is the only one in personal debt."

"Yeah, well, one of my suspect's debt isn't going to show up on a legal report."

"Whoever hired Morris is clever. I couldn't find any exchanges between US and Canadian dollars. But I did highlight some suspicious transactions in green. I'll email the records right now. Then they're gone, and you never saw them, right?"

"Got it. I owe you big."

"Just buy me a slice when you get back."

"You're on."

Her phone pinged, and she opened Chen's email. The transactions highlighted in green were on the Spotted Owl's business account and Oscar's personal bank account. Jesus, talk about amateur night, she thought. The patterns weren't just suspicious. They were blinking arrows saying "embezzlement here." Several payments from the Spotted Owl to Sunshine Coast Foods corresponded with cash deposits into Oscar's personal account. How long had Fiona been propping him up? Could the fear of two companies bankrupting drive her to kill?

She scanned the Keanes', Reeds', and Huxhams' personal finances, searching back five months. No transactions between the US East Coast and Canada in any reports.

Chen had also included the suspects' business financials and credit reports. She highlighted an entry in the Huxham Law file. Three weeks earlier, Charles had obtained an equity loan against the 414 Main Street property for three hundred and fifty thousand dollars. The funds were posted yesterday.

"Shit." Sloane shoved the papers under her seat and called Charles. Voice mail picked up. "Charles, it's Sloane West. I'm on my way to pick up the Degas, and I need to talk to you. I'll be there in ten minutes." She threw her phone into the passenger's seat and slammed Pearl into gear and pulled back onto the road.

She parked next to Charles's Mercedes in its spot behind the Huxham building. The sky was still dark, and the rain had been replaced by mist. Old Main hummed with lunchtime shoppers. Sloane walked to the law office's front door. It was locked, and Charles wasn't answering his phone. She parted a crowd standing outside The Grind and checked inside. No sign of him. Then she walked down to the Spotted Owl.

Ken was alone behind the bar, pouring drinks nonstop. Every table on the floor was taken, and Rose ran plates back and forth. On one of Rose's passes through the dining room, she noticed Sloane, dropped off the plates in her hands and walked over. "Are you here for lunch?"

"I can't today. I thought maybe I'd find Charles Huxham here. Have you seen him?"

"No. He's not that brave. Why? What's going on?"

"Hopefully, nothing. Is your mom here?"

"No. If she was, I wouldn't be running my ass off." Rose closed her eyes and smoothed back her hair. "Sorry. I'm pissed she left us alone on a Friday lunch rush."

"No problem. I understand. You're swamped."

"Totally in the weeds." Rose looked around the dining room. "Can you come back later? I'm off at five-thirty. You can interrogate my mom and have dinner with me. Don't say no."

Sloane smiled. "How could I refuse?"

Rose stuck a pencil into the mass of auburn curls piled up on her head. "Great. It's a date." Then she turned and greeted her new table.

Sloane snuck out of the pub without Ken seeing her. She scanned Old Main again. The fish market was closed and the lights off. Busy time to be closed, she thought. Next door, Lore Reed was pulling out her work cart. "Hey, Lore."

"Hello, Sloane," she said in a cheerful voice.

"Busy day, huh?"

"Oh, yes. This is your first Friday at Old Main, isn't it? We're usually steady, but we have a better-than-usual afternoon crowd today."

Sloane peeked around her into the shop's window. "Do you happen to know where Charles Huxham is?"

"Well, he's not here. He never comes to my shop." She glanced at her watch. "One thirty. I'm sure he's at work. At least he was when I cleaned up the conference room."

"I checked. His car is in his parking spot, but the front door's locked, and he's not answering his phone."

"Then he's hiding and doesn't want to be bothered. Trust me. Unless Harold was in the office, it was almost impossible to get a hold of Charlie. Almost. I have my ways. I suppose you do too, don't you? A credit card? Paperclip? Pop the lock? That sort of thing?"

Sloane chuckled. "If you see Charles, would you tell him I'm looking for him?"

"Of course. Would you like a bouquet? No charge."

"That's nice of you. But no thanks. Flowers really aren't my thing." Sloane walked back to the law office and pounded on the front door.

No answer.

She searched the building's front for security cameras. One was installed on the corner but pointed at the other side of the street and not at their front door. She walked down the side of the building. One more camera on the back corner of the building faced the parking lot. The back door had a blind spot.

Charles's car was still in its spot. No one was in the lot, so she sneaked to the back door. It was unlocked, and she slipped inside the storeroom. Boxes were opened and dumped all over the floor. She crept toward Charles's office. The door between the two rooms was also unlocked. Sloane pressed her back against the wall and dropped to the floor. Did Gannon and his men come early?

*Elvina. I'm at Charles Huxham's office. Am I in any danger?*
*No, dear. Why?*
*Looks like he had a break-in.*
*Do be careful.*
*Yeah. No worries.*

Sloane slid up the wall and eased the door open. Charles's office phone rang, and she froze, holding her breath. The answering machine picked up, and a woman's voice spoke. "Charlie, dear. Answer your phone—" It was Lore Reed leaving a message. "—Sloane needs to speak with you, and you're avoiding her. It's time to finish your business with the Wests. So stop hiding. Charlie?" There was a pause. "Fine. But you either call her back, or I'm coming over, and I'll use my keys."

If Charles was there, he wasn't making any noise. The building was silent, not even the sound of rats scurrying in the walls. Sloane slipped into Charles's office. His desk and file drawers, even the locked ones, had been ransacked. She stared at the mess for a minute, then dug plastic gloves out of her tote.

If it was Gannon's crew, what else were they looking for? They wouldn't ransack desk drawers for a painting. And where was Charles? Did they take him?

Chairs and stacks of papers were tossed on the floor. Sloane moved around the mess carefully but tripped in front of Charles's desk, landing hard on the Persian rug. She noticed the red on her gloves first before the leg that made her fall.

"Oh, shit."

Charles Huxham's body lay next to her. The cloisonne letter opener protruded from his back. Death had already clouded his eyes, and the bloodstain on his shirt had started to coagulate. There was no need to check for a pulse. He had been dead for several hours.

Sloane took off the bloody gloves, stuffed them in a plastic bag, and dropped them in her tote. Then she sat back and stared at Charles's lifeless face. "Damnit. I warned you." She closed her eyes, fighting back the tears welling. Swallowed the lump in her throat and laid her hand on his stiff leg.

"Onwreon."

An image of him appeared in her third eye. He was sitting at his desk in tears as he paged through a file. Then he looked past his desk and jumped to his feet, running around it, wielding the manila folder in his hand. The image pressed on her chest with an oppressive heaviness as if a black void was replacing life's color.

She pulled back her hand and retrieved her phone.

"911. What's your emergency?"

"My name is Sloane West. I need to report a stabbing at 414 Main Street in Denwick. The victim is deceased. I can't stay on the line. But I'll wait outside for the police to arrive." She ended the call, got to her feet and removed her shoes. She had bought herself at least five minutes.

She crossed the lobby to Harold's office and found his door unlocked. She put on another pair of plastic gloves and nudged it open. A black overcoat and hat hung on a coat rack in the corner of Harold's office. It made her remember Harold sitting across from her, his dark blue coat folded on the back of Jane's chair and his gray trilby on top of his briefcase.

Her anger swelled.

The killer had also rummaged through Harold's desk and cabinets. Files were strewn across the floor. Chairs were knocked over. The safe was hidden in a faux wooden cabinet inside the wall behind Harold's desk. Whoever killed Charles had left its doors open. The vault was unlocked and empty, and the Degas was gone. She slammed the safe shut. If Gannon wanted the Degas, why kill Charles? Why not just take it? And why ransack the offices? What would Harold and Charles have that Gannon would want besides the art? Did they keep a dossier on him? Leverage for Charles?

Sloane searched the cabinet drawers, running her hands along them for a hidden compartment, and along the rim of each drawer in Harold's desk until she found a bump. Click. A drawer dropped open. She yanked it out and dropped it on the desk. There was one file labeled 414 Old Main. She opened it and read. "Jesus, he'd cosigned the loan." The file held a personal contract between Harold and Charles.

There was also a photo, face down. The writing on the back gave a date and a single comment: *May 18, 1969, I'll never forget our night together. I will always love you.* It was a picture of Harold, about the same age as he was in the Four Musketeers photo. He was embracing a beautiful woman. They gazed at each other as if they were moments away from a passionate kiss.

At the sound of blaring sirens, Sloane shoved the photo into her tote, bagged her gloves, and made it outside as the two officers in an RCMP vehicle pulled to a stop between the Huxham building and The Grind. An unmarked car pulled behind them, and a plainclothes officer alighted. Her stomach lurched. The officer had an athletic build and short dark hair. She reminded Sloane of Jess.

The plainclothes sent the two uniforms to the back of the building and approached Sloane. "Hello, I'm Lieutenant Veena

Sharma with the Major Crime Unit." She spoke with unusual confidence for her age, which Sloane supposed was close to hers.

"I'm Sloane West."

The lieutenant removed her sunglasses and squinted brown-black eyes with long dark lashes, adjusting to the glare from the overcast sky. "You called in a stabbing?"

"Yeah. Inside. In the office."

The two officers returned to the front of the building. "All clear, Lieutenant."

"Seal off a perimeter," Lieutenant Sharma said to the officers. "When Ident gets here, bring them inside." She turned back to Sloane. "I'll need you to stay here to answer a few questions if that's okay, ma'am."

"Ma'am? Call me Sloane." Sloane gave the lieutenant a business card. "I'm a private investigator from New York. Here on a case."

"Call me Veena." She read her card. "New York, huh, Sloane? You're a long way from home."

"You have no idea." Sloane turned and walked toward the front door. "If you don't mind, I'll take you to the victim. I've got some information you might find useful."

Veena looked up and down Old Main and at the alleyway. "Yeah, sure. Then I'll need you to wait outside."

Sloane held the door open, and they slipped inside. "The body is that of Charles Huxham. I'm in Denwick on professional and personal business with the Huxhams," Sloane said, stopping outside Charles's office. "Harold Huxham, Charles's uncle and senior partner in the law firm, was murdered in my New York apartment seventeen days ago. The hitman also tried to kill me. I know the shooter's employer is from Denwick. I came to find him. I was convinced the victim was the perp." She pushed open the door and pointed at Charles's body.

Veena crouched next to him, using a pen to lift the lapels of his jacket. She looked up at Sloane. "Why would he order a hit on his uncle and you?"

"Greed or fear for his own life. I figured Charles wanted Harold and me dead for money. He was in debt to his bookie, Gannon Ferris."

Veena seemed to recognize the last name.

"My last appointment with Charles, I overheard a phone conversation between them. Gannon thought Charles was settling his gambling debt with a piece of art—*my* art, an original Degas. That's my personal business with the Huxhams. Harold Huxham was my grandparents' estate lawyer."

"So you were here today on business?"

"Yeah. I came to take my painting home. I was worried about Gannon stealing it. A couple days ago, I went to Chinatown. I met Gannon Ferris and told him the painting was mine. And that I was here to prove he hired the hit on Harold and me. I wanted to get under his skin, and it worked. He had one of his men jump me in Dragon Alley, but that didn't go so well for his guy. The next day, he called Charles and threatened to kill us if Charles didn't take care of me."

Veena walked around the office. "Are you working with the NYPD?"

"Detective Jacobson of the 78th Precinct knows I'm here. He sanctioned my investigation while Homicide pursues another line of inquiry."

Veena got to her feet and motioned to the three forensic identification specialists who had just arrived. "The entire building is a crime scene. Check the offices, second-floor rooms, and access doors." She looked at Sloane. "Have you touched anything?"

"Well, yeah. I tripped over his leg." She looked at her jeans. "That's how the blood got on me. He'd been dead a few hours. I called 911 and waited outside. I was careful not to contaminate anything else." She would let them discover Harold's office, the ransacked file drawers, the safe open, and her painting gone.

"Okay, let's step back outside," Veena said.

Sloane stared at Charles's body. The ornamental letter opener. Gannon made perfect sense for the murder.

Veena led them through the lobby and opened the door. They stood under a Garry oak. Sloane knew what the lieutenant ought to say next. It would shed light on how married she was to police procedure.

"Why didn't you contact the RCMP when you arrived in Denwick or when you found out about Gannon?"

Married, she thought. "You're right. I did ask Charles Huxham to contact the police, though. I warned him not to mess with someone like Gannon Ferris." She sighed. "I should have called for him."

Veena opened a notebook and jotted down information. "You said Charles was your prime suspect? Who are the others?"

"Sloane!" The shrill voice came from the pedestrian pathway. Lore Reed was running toward her. She grabbed Sloane's arm. "What's going on?" Her voice quavered, and she stared at the blood on Sloane's jeans. "Where's Charlie? Is he inside?"

"Lore, there's been an incident."

"With Charlie? Is he okay? Let me see him." She pushed Sloane aside and ran toward the front door. Veena outpaced Lore and caught her by the waist. She tried to shove her away, but she held her. "Let me go," Lore cried. "Charlie? I'm here! Charlie!"

Veena spoke to her quietly, and Lore collapsed against her chest, sobbing.

Not a moment later, Ken Keane rushed past Sloane and gathered Lore into his arms, walking her away from the building. "Is it Charlie?" he asked Sloane, his eyes full of worry. "Is he...?"

Sloane nodded.

"Oh, good Lord." He held Lore close as she let out a mournful wail. "I'll take her to her father's place."

Veena had disappeared inside, so Sloane headed to the parking lot. Halfway there, a firm hand squeezed her shoulder, and she turned with her fists up. "Sorry. I didn't mean to startle you." Veena took her hand and opened it, her touch warm and gentle. She placed a business card against Sloane's palm. "Take it. I'll question Gannon Ferris tonight and tell you what I find out. Call me if you need anything." She turned and rushed back inside.

Sloane read the lieutenant's card and smiled. Definitely not married. But indecisive. Another similarity to Jess. No matter. She needed someone on the inside of Major Crimes and Lieutenant Veena Sharma would work just fine.

# CHAPTER TWENTY-FOUR

Sloane poured a shot of whiskey and drained it. Then she poured another. She hauled the case board into the middle of the living room and stared at the pictures. Nathaniel, Mary, Jane, Harold, and now Charles. All murdered. And she was no closer to finding their killer or killers. "Fucking great," she whispered and downed the second shot.

Elvina sauntered into the room, leaped onto the sofa, and lay on the top cushion. *What happened?*

"Charles Huxham is dead."

*Dead?*

"Yeah. Stabbed in the back. Looked like through the heart."

*This is indeed a curious time.* Elvina swung her tail to and fro.

Dorathea appeared on the sofa next to the familiar. "Good for you, pet. You didn't even startle."

Sloane scowled. "Yeah. I expect you to show up whenever you want."

"I believe you mean when I am needed. Now, tell me what has happened to Charles Huxham?"

"Who told you?"

"Elvina. Just a moment ago."

"He was murdered." Sloane filled her glass with a double and turned to the board.

*Is it all wrong, dear?* Elvina asked.

"Yeah, it's fucked up. I was wrong. Charles didn't hire Liam Morris. I'm missing something. And it got him killed." She gulped her whiskey, firmly set the glass on the coffee table, and yanked Charles's photo from the center of the board, placing it next to the other four victims.

"Why have you come to that conclusion?" Dorathea asked.

"Charles secured a loan against the Huxham building a goddamn week before Harold came to find me. The money came through yesterday. That's how he planned to pay back Gannon."

*Maybe so. But that doesn't mean Charles didn't decide to kill you both when the opportunity presented.*

"I am loath to speak ill of the dead, but Elvina is correct. He still had motive and opportunity." Dorathea snapped her fingers, and a steaming teapot and a plate full of madeleines appeared. She poured two cups and a saucer.

"All right. That's a possibility. But he had stopped lying to Harold and had asked for his help. I found copies of the loan paperwork in a hidden drawer in Harold's office. He had cosigned. There was also a contract between them. Charles had committed to rehab." She looked at her cousin. "I think you were right all along. He loved his uncle." She picked up her glass. "I used the detection spell on Charles. He was emotional, grieving. Someone appeared in front of his desk, and he became angry, chasing after them. That's when I became overwhelmed with a darkness like nothingness. I had to let go of him."

"That was the moment his life ended, pet." Dorathea held out a cup of tea and madeleine to her. "Being right hardly feels important at the moment."

Sloane waved off the offer and took a sip of her whiskey. She tapped a marker on Gannon's photo. "He could have refused Charles's cash payment. Demanded the Degas. Maybe he already had a buyer for it. He could have killed Harold as a warning to Charles. Give me the Degas or else."

"So when Charles refused, Gannon killed him?" Dorathea asked.

"Yeah. Killed him and took the painting."

Dorathea's eyes narrowed. "The Degas is gone?"

"Yeah. But I told the Major Crime Unit about Gannon. If he stole it, they'll recover it."

"I can assure you Gannon Ferris did not take the Degas. Only a wiċċan could break the protection charm I placed on it. And a talented one, indeed."

"But I didn't feel another wiċċan's presence. Does that mean the wiċċe is a Protector?"

*Or the wiċċa,* said Elvina.

"Highly unlikely. Protectors like us are rare." Dorathea lifted her teacup. "The theft complicates our case, I am afraid. The artwork is another portal to Tagridore for your family line. It could be dangerous in the wrong hands."

"Why?" Sloane asked.

*A wiċċan could force the dancers to cooperate, dear,* answered Elvina.

"Opening access to Tagridore for anyone, Nogicals or Demon," Dorathea added.

Sloane looked at them in confusion. "The dancers?"

"The ballerinas, indeed." Dorathea set down her cup. "Securing the Degas is too important to leave to the police."

"All right. We'll get it back." Sloane turned and drew a new line between Gannon and Charles. "I've got questions about Charles's murder. A wiċċan could be directing Gannon. But why would they ransack Harold's and Charles's offices? And why stab Charles in the back with the letter opener? That's impromptu. Hired muscle bring their own murder weapons. And why a stabbing? That's dirty hands. Intimate." She tapped on Gannon's photo.

"Violence is irrational," Dorathea said.

"Yeah. I suppose so. But it seems to me if you're killing for a painting, you go in quick, neat, and get out. No mess. And

Gannon wanted me dead. Why not wait and ambush me as well?"

"Excellent points," Dorathea said.

*Do you have any more information on the other suspects?* Elvina asked.

"Yeah. I did find out why the Spotted Owl is in financial trouble." She drew a line between Fiona and Oscar. "Guess who's been stealing from Peter to prop up Paul?"

"Really?" Dorathea sipped her tea.

"Yeah. Fiona has jeopardized the pub, and the money she's stealing barely keeps Oscar afloat. He said his ten-year batch will see a healthy profit. But unless Fiona can continue embezzling for three more years. It's doubtful he'll see that day."

"Perhaps they realized their embezzlement could not last three more years," Dorathea said.

Just as Sloane opened her mouth to respond, her phone rang. "Hold that thought." She answered. "West speaking."

"Hey, Sloane. It's Lieutenant Sharma. I've got an update for you. Gannon Ferris left the country last night on a business trip to Los Angeles. His receptionist showed me Charles Huxham's account with the company. It was paid in full yesterday."

"Company account, my ass."

"I know. I know. But he settled his debt. Three-twenty K." She paused. "There's one more thing. Your art wasn't in Harold Huxham's safe. It's been stolen."

"Damn it." Sloane feigned a shocked voice and hesitated. "Did you search Gannon's office for it?"

"His receptionist opened every door in the place. We didn't find it. I'm really sorry. But he's got container space at the Port of Vancouver. We're getting a warrant to check it out. I'll keep you posted. I think Gannon still looks good for Charles's murder, maybe even his uncle's. He got his money, but he might have decided to double his payout. And he doesn't need to be in the country to order a hit."

"No, he doesn't. Thanks for the update." Sloane hung up. "Damnit. I was right. Charles paid his debt. Gannon left the country. And there's no sign of the Degas." She poured a measure of whiskey while Dorathea and Elvina watched. "What the hell am I missing?"

"Seems to me, nothing," answered Dorathea. "You have a case board full of people of interest." She flicked her wrist, and the tea and whiskey bottle disappeared. "It is time to use all of your senses and focus on a new suspect."

Elvina rose on all fours. *I'll tell you what time it is. Dinnertime.*

"Dinner?" Sloane checked her watch. "Oh, shit. Six o'clock. I stood up Rose Keane." She collapsed into an armchair.

"I am sure dear Rose will understand, considering," Dorathea said. "Call her and apologize. Then ask for a rain check. Now let us add some food to your liquid diet." She and Elvina walked toward the kitchen without saying another word.

Sloane shouted, "Ha! Liquid diet. You're hilarious. And no one says rain check anymore. It's archaic." She grabbed her phone and texted Rose an apology, rewriting it four times before pressing send.

* * *

A few hours after dinner, Dorathea and Elvina disappeared to the covenstead on a mission to create a location spell for the Degas.

Sloane dropped onto the sofa and studied the case board. She was angry at herself, at her myopic focus. She had too much experience for such a rookie mistake. Her head fell back against the cushion just as the doorbell rang. "Jesus Christ." Her heart leaped, and she got to her feet. Why could she handle a woman appearing out of thin air, but a doorbell sent her over the edge? Although, to be fair, someone or something wanted her dead.

Sloane stood to one side of the door. "Who is it?" Her voice was rough.

"It's me, Rose."

Sloane exhaled and opened the door. "Sorry. I'm still a little on edge."

"I understand. And I brought you food. In case you're hungry."

"Thanks, Keane. I ate with Dorothea. Sorry about dinner."

"Don't worry. I didn't expect you to make it after finding poor Charlie. I'm in shock myself. Another murder? Harold and Charles? What's going on?"

Sloane stuck the food in the refrigerator. "I thought I had a good idea. But I was wrong." She looked into Rose's jade eyes, her frustration subsiding, and a new surge of energy swept over her. "Can you stay for a drink?"

"Sure, but just one. My shift was long, and I have to open the pub in the morning." Rose leaned against the island. "Besides, I think you've had plenty."

"You're right. But don't tell my cousin I admit it." She poured Rose a drink. "I'm headed to bed after this one." She winked and lifted her glass in the air. On the patio, Sloane pulled two loungers together, inches apart. They sat on the edges, facing each other.

Rose searched her eyes. "I can't imagine what it was like to find Charlie dead. Are you okay?"

"Yeah. Just angry at myself. I knew his life was in danger. I should have been there to protect him."

"You couldn't have known what would happen or when."

Sloane stared into the dark garden and stretched out her body.

"I can't imagine who would want the Huxhams dead. An old client, maybe?"

"It's a possibility." Sloane turned her head, trying not to get lost in Rose's eyes. "I followed your mom to your brother's distillery. I overheard her on the phone after the MCC meeting. She told whomever she was talking to that she didn't have it all. Then she said she was heading back to the pub. But she got in her Land Rover instead and drove toward the mountain. I tailed her. When I walked in on them, I was sure I saw your brother do something that made me suspicious. But I can't remember what. It's like the entire moment was erased from my head."

Rose sat up. Her eyes narrowed. She laid her hand on Sloane's arm. "What exactly happened?"

Her touch sent a shiver through Sloane. "I can't remember. Maybe I imagined the whole thing. It's not important. Oscar had a lot to say when I asked about the Spotted Owl. I think he's not as happy with you getting the pub as you think."

"I never said he was happy. I said it's what he wanted." Rose tightened her hold on Sloane's arm and released her with a sigh. "When he realized how hard he had to work to build a new business, he fell out of love with it." She stretched out on the lounger.

"It seems to be his thing again. He was eager to show the entire campus off."

Rose laughed. "Thing? You call being in love a *thing*?"

"Don't tease me, Keane." Sloane put her hand over her heart. "I'm fragile when it comes to that thing."

"Fragile?" Rose laughed harder. "I wouldn't consider you fragile. But you are drunk and chatty. You're lucky I don't take advantage of you and ask about your mystery ex."

"That's just mean." Sloane grinned and traced her finger down Rose's bare arm. "Besides, there's not much to tell. I thought we would grow old together. And she didn't."

Rose frowned. "I'm sorry."

"Yeah. Me, too." She took a drink. "Doesn't matter. It's in the past."

"Aren't you still wearing *it* on your finger?"

Sloane balled up her right hand.

"I'm sorry. That was too nosy. But I'm a curious person. Especially about things I like."

Sloane met Rose's eyes, held them, then dropped her gaze to her full lips. She wanted to press them against hers. Feel the sensation in her core when they parted, and their tongues met. She looked back to Rose's eyes, but she had turned away, staring into the garden.

"What do you think my mom and brother were up to?" she asked after a few minutes of silence.

"Oh, I know what they've been doing. My contact sent me some information. Your mom pays monthly invoices to a food vendor called Sunshine Coast Food, but really it's money going to Oscar. The payments to Sunshine are the exact amounts your brother deposits in his personal account two or three days later."

Rose's eyes were wide with surprise. "Are you kidding me? She's draining the pub to prop him up? Of course, she is. If the Spotted Owl fails, she can force Dad back to Scotland." She sat up and threw back her whiskey.

"Your mom doesn't want the Spotted Owl to fail. She's fighting as hard as any other MCC business owner to stop Isobel Gildey."

"Damn them. They're all so infuriating. Letting Dad fret over the pub not turning a profit like it used to. Oscar pretending his distillery is already profitable."

"It's a shitty thing to do," Sloane said. "But now you know and can do something about it."

Rose nodded and placed her empty glass on a side table.

"Did your mom show up at the pub on Friday?"

"No. We both know that was another lie." Rose hesitated. "You don't think—"

"No, no. I'm not saying she had anything to do with Charles. But we need to know where she was before Major Crime starts asking the questions."

Rose sighed. "Good God, what a mess."

"It'll be okay. My investigation is at least a week ahead of theirs. I'll be done with the case before they figure out who to question. Your mom's okay."

Rose gave a slight smile and lifted herself out of the lounger. "Thanks for the drink. I need to get going."

"Why don't you stay a bit longer. We won't talk about the case." Sloane stumbled to her feet, and Rose steadied her.

"I meant it when I said I wouldn't take advantage of you. You're hurting right now and have so much grief to work through. But I'm not going anywhere." She walked Sloane inside and stopped before they reached the front door. "Thank you for telling me about my mother." She hugged her, loosely at first then pressing her body closer. Moving her mouth a breath away from Sloane's parted lips, she whispered, "We can all have more than one *thing* in a lifetime. Get some sleep, West."

# CHAPTER TWENTY-FIVE

"Thank you, Alfred," Sloane whispered as she entered the hobbit house. She tiptoed down the stairs to the covenstead.

*Good morning, dear,* Elvina said.

"Shh. Quiet in there. My head's pounding." Sloane dropped into a velvet chair, nursing a tumbler of black coffee. "I hope we aren't teleporting today."

*It's bestealce, dear.*

Sloane glared at Elvina.

"We are not training today. The Grand Coven has requested a meeting with you this morning," Dorathea said. "Unfortunately, we must attend."

"Why? Do they know I found Jane's research?"

"The Coven will reveal their reason when you arrive."

Sloane stared at her cousin. "They want to speak with me but won't tell us why. And you don't think that's a little sketchy?"

"Really, pet."

"And what do you mean, unfortunately?"

"Don't be daft. I can smell your spirit from here." Dorathea stood. "Follow me."

"Wait. Now? I'm all kinds of hungover. I barely got here. Let me rest for a few minutes."

*A few minutes isn't going to fix it.*

Sloane shot Elvina an irritated look. "Are you coming?"

The familiar was curled up in the chair closest to the crackling fire. *Not today, dear. It's drizzly and cold out there.*

Sloane groaned and got to her feet. "Fine. But if I'm going, I'm forcing their hand. They know more about the Demon and the Gewende than they're telling us. And what do they know about the wiccan?"

Dorathea walked toward the library. "You may try to get answers from them. But they will probably refuse."

They dodged bored books and stopped at the back of the library in front of an enormous painting. "This artwork is my portal to Tagridore. My great-grandmother enchanted it when she arrived in Denwick with your great-great-grandfather. Lavinia Fontana was her favorite artist. The painting depicts two women fighting the biases of Western history's male perspective." Dorathea raised her arms. "To enter our portals, we lift our arms and say, '*Onpenne.*'"

The two women in the painting turned to them. "Jesus!" Sloane jerked backward. The woman closest to them smiled. She turned and opened a door in the back of the painting. The other woman continued to guard the men.

Dorathea bowed and, taking Sloane's hand, they stepped forward and moved through the canvas as if it were a veil of fog. Their first step landed on a stone path on the other side of the opaque cover.

"Holy fuck. That was incredible," Sloane whispered. She looked around and recognized the white building with lavender trim and the aroma of bread. Freya's place.

A sudden chill overtook her.

"Are you all right?" Dorathea held her arm. "You're covered in gooseflesh."

"Yeah. I'm fine," Sloane answered, shaking off the feeling. "So your painting dumps you here. Why?"

"Because I can choose where my portal leads. And it leads here. To Freya."

"Where does the Degas take me?"

"Right now, to Tagridore's *Searugepræoe*."

"What the hell is that?"

Dorathea tutted her. "The art museum. But you may choose your destination."

"All right. That's cool." Sloane followed Dorathea to the front of the café. The sky was gray, full of mist making its way to the warm ground. "I'll wait for you here."

Dorathea stared up and down the street. "Very well. I will give Freya your regards."

Sloane pulled her cardigan tight around her chest and sat on a wrought iron bench. After a few minutes, a man dressed in dark clothing appeared across the street. The posture struck Sloane as familiar, but his face was obscured with a hat. And the mist didn't help.

When Dorathea returned, she stood before Sloane, blocking her view of the man. "These are fresh croissants, a peace offering from Freya. She is disappointed you fear her." Sloane ignored her, moving side to side, trying to see around her. "What is the matter with you?"

"I think the guy who was watching me the first time I came here is standing across the street. C'mon." Sloane jumped up and headed toward the Silas Lamp store.

Dorathea grabbed her arm. "No. We must not approach him. We need to reach the Héahreced at once." They ran across the pedestrian street toward the building that looked like NYC's Grand Central Terminal.

"Why are we running?" Sloane asked. "Is it because of him?"

Dorathea hurried Sloane up the stairs at the Héahreced's entrance. "Freya told me the Weardas had sensed a Demon during our last visit to Tagridore."

"Here?"

"Indeed. They believe it is the same presence detected in Denwick. If the Demon is here, we can be sure they are correct. And we can be certain it *is* following us." At the top of the stairs, Dorathea paused and looked at the street below. She led Sloane by the hand across a wide landing.

Sloane turned and stared at the rows of colorful shops and tidy gardens on the other side of the street. "What did we just pass through?" she asked.

"A protection charm around the building. Unless you work here, only those summoned to Héahreced can pass through it."

"A bit like a keycard to an office block." Sloane reached out with her hand, pressing her fingertips into the warmth. It felt like gel without the moisture or stickiness. "How does it know who you are?"

"Whoever requested you activates your registration with the *Brydranic*, a registry of wiċċan."

"Am I on a registry?"

"You are now. The Grand Coven made sure of it."

"So how do you get inside if you aren't summoned?"

"You don't."

Once inside the building, Sloane froze. "Jesus H. Christ." The Héahreced looked like Grand Central and Escher's *Relativity* had a love child. The celestial ceiling soared seemingly without an ending but paled in comparison to the myriad moving escalators where passengers rode right side up on the descending steps and upside down on the ascending steps underneath. The riders in both directions disappeared into thin air at either end.

The witches and wizards around Sloane sent vibrations through her body. She held herself tight.

"In time, you will grow used to sensing a large group of wiċċan," Dorathea said.

"Yeah. Okay." Sloane rubbed her arms. Her discomfort wasn't so much the vibrations as the other Magicals she saw. Some were nonhuman. Half-human, half-animal. Wings. Tails. Lots of hair.

"Stop staring, pet."

"All right. All right. I'm sorry."

Dorathea approached a short man with pointy ears and a hooked nose. He wore a smart suit, and his brown hair, tied back with a red ribbon halfway down, cascaded to his waist. His skin was the color of dried sage, and his eyes jaundiced yellow.

"What's your business?" he asked Dorathea in a nasal voice. "We are here to see the Grand Coven."

His eyes settled on Dorathea's face before he dragged a bony finger with a pointy nail down an open page and tapped a spot. He gestured to the side, and a gate appeared.

"Follow me," Dorathea said to Sloane. They approached an escalator coming down with one rider who disappeared as soon as his step reached the floor.

Sloane stopped. "What the hell?"

"There are many rooms in the Héahreced." She walked to the backside of the escalator. "We are going up."

Dorathea pulled Sloane toward the upside-down steps, moving up. When Sloane's foot touched one, the building seemed to rotate around them, and the escalator became upright. She clutched Dorathea's cloak.

A solid door materialized at the top of the ride and Dorathea led them into an intimate, resplendent auditorium. Sloane stared at three people sitting around a dark wood table in the center of the room. The two wiċċe and one wiċċa looked much older than Dorathea. She studied their faces, the placement of their hands, and how they positioned their bodies. Then her gaze shifted to the portraits of hundreds of men and women covering the walls.

Dorathea stepped up to a rostrum that faced the table, and Sloane stood beside her. "*Ealdormenn*," Dorathea said in a crisp voice. "May I present *Leornestre* West."

One of the women raised her hand. "Dorathea, there's no need for formality. We summoned you both here for an informal chat." She smiled at Sloane. "Hello, Ms. West. I am Polydora Nenge." She held her arms out to each side. "On my right is Cenric Verner, and Millicent Panas is on my left. We are your Grand Coven. Thank you for coming."

"Did I have a choice?" Sloane asked.

Polydora laughed. "I'm sure you have appreciated your cousin's propriety. And, Dorathea, I expect you have found her mordacity quite lovely." Cenric and Millicent hung their heads and remained silent. Sloane glanced at Dorathea. Her cousin's face was unreadable.

Polydora leaned forward, crossing her arms on the table. "Come closer, Sloane West. Let us look at you."

Dorathea nodded, and Sloane walked toward the stage, her hands shoved in her pockets.

The Coven combed over her, whispered back-and-forth, and sat back in their chairs.

"You are, no doubt, Jane's child," Polydora said.

"Yes, yes. You are a West." Cenric spoke in a breathy grunt, causing the wattle under his chin to flap. "We are pleased you're here. I knew your grandparents. Very fond of them, I was. They were in the last class I taught at the academy before sitting here. I'm deeply sorry for your loss."

"We all are," Millicent said. She lifted her hollow-cheeked face and prominent lapis eyes to meet Sloane's. "I understand you must be nervous but do try to relax. You can trust us. We are here to help you and only want to ask you a few questions."

Sloane's hands had balled into fists inside her pockets. She had learned from experience that people who broadcasted their trustworthiness were usually anything but.

Millicent held Sloane's gaze. "We only want to help discover who is trying to end your coven."

Sloane's fists relaxed as Millicent's silver voice lingered in her head, and a warm sensation spread through her body, soothing her muscles and releasing their knots.

Dorathea walked behind Sloane and squeezed her shoulders. Sloane's muscles tensed again. "Millicent. You may begin with your questions. Sloane will stand with me."

"I was only trying to help her, Dorathea. She might find our conversation difficult, and we don't want to upset her."

"You don't need to explain your actions, Millicent." Polydora glared at Dorathea and turned her attention to Sloane. "Were you and your mother close?"

Sloane shrugged. "Yeah. She was all I had when I was younger. Not so much as an adult."

"There was no one else in your lives? Was that hard for you?" Polydora asked.

"Not really."

"Even though Jane raised you alone in such a strange Nogical city?" Cenric asked.

"NYC is all I've ever known. It's normal for me."

"I'm pleased you were fine growing up without your coven," Millicent said. "But it must have been lonely not being around others like yourself?"

Sloane shrugged. "Jane kept this world hidden from me. She told me she grew up in a girls' home in New Jersey. That her parents died when she was a baby."

The Grand Coven stared at her, then at each other.

"Do you know why your mother deserted her coven?" Polydora asked. The question was abrupt. Polydora's voice was cold.

"I have no idea."

"Who else lived in your home when you were a child?" Polydora asked again.

Sloane learned through experience to pay attention to people's words, and practice made her economical with hers. "I already said no one." She grasped the rostrum's railing and leaned forward. "Is this a one-directional conversation? Or are you going to allow me to ask questions?"

Polydora smiled. "Go right ahead."

"One thing has bothered me since I found out about you, about the Grand Coven, about all of it, really. Why didn't you find Jane? You're the most powerful, right? I think you could find one missing witch and her hidden daughter."

Polydora's mask slipped slightly, and the corners of her mouth turned down. Dorathea squeezed Sloane's hand firmly.

"Our Weardas locate most wiċċan. But they failed to penetrate the spell around you, even with your coven's help," Cenric said.

"Has Dorathea informed you that we believe Jane had assistance in hiding from us?" Millicent asked. "The concealment spell that guards you is ancient. It's beyond our ability to detect at the moment. But we will, in time."

"Your mother was a gifted wiċċe. She hid that from you? Never trained you?" Polydora asked.

So that's their angle, Sloane thought. "She did hide it. But I had a feeling she was lying about her past. I would ask her questions. But she managed to distract me and change the subject." She gave Millicent a conspiratorial look.

"And you have no idea why she lied to you?" Cenric asked.

Sloane set her jaw. "None."

"Do you know who your father is?" Polydora asked.

Sloane scoffed. "If she refused to tell me who we were, what makes you think she'd tell me about the guy who knocked her up at seventeen?" Dorathea released a quiet breath of exasperation. Sloane wasn't sure if it was directed at her flippant answers or the Coven's questions.

"We see," Millicent said. "That's understandable. But could she have mentioned something about him, a clue to his identity you didn't notice as such at the time?"

Polydora added, "Were you not curious? Didn't you ask who he was?"

"Yeah, I asked. I spent my childhood asking. When Jane thought I was old enough, she told me I was the result of a one-night stand. She didn't know his name or where he lived. That wasn't really the answer I was prepared for. I didn't bother making her clarify the details."

Cenric and Millicent sat back, but Polydora continued to press. "Did you find any information in Jane's possessions? Any hints to our world or who your father was?"

Sloane's face burned with anger. "You know, our informal chat feels a lot like an interrogation. You are wrong if you think I know why Jane ran from your world. I don't. And I have no clue who my father is. She made sure of that. I thought *you* were going to help me find these answers." Sloane narrowed her eyes. "Help us by telling us what you know about the Demon and the Gewende in Denwick."

The Coven sat in silence, staring ahead. Then, after a long pause, Polydora spoke. "We have every intention of helping you. That is why we asked you here. Our questions are meant to determine if you might know something and not understand its relevance to our investigation. As a detective, I'm sure you understand."

"Yeah, well, you're wasting our time. I don't have any hidden clues. A month ago, I thought Jane was a psychologist who profiled occasionally for the FBI. A single mom who called me daily, wanting too much control over my life. And a notoriously bad driver." Sloane waved her arms around. "If I ever thought we might be different, she didn't allow those ideas to linger."

Dorathea, stone-faced, had seen and heard enough. Her restraint had gone. "Sloane has answered enough of your questions. We are leaving now, Ealdormenn."

Cenric grunted. "Wait, Dorathea." He snapped his fingers, and Sloane's cardigan appeared in his hands.

Crossing her arms over her chest, Sloane's anger swelled. She had no doubt he was using a detection spell on her. The Coven suspected her of something.

As soon as Cenric closed his eyes, his body jounced, and he dropped the sweater. "I cannot read this," he said, wiping beads of sweat from his forehead.

Dorathea grabbed Sloane's arm, and they left the rostrum.

Polydora's voice rang out before they reached the door. "Stop!" They turned and faced her.

"One more question for Leornestre West." Polydora's eyes were suspicious. "How did your mother's fictitious parents die?"

Sloane recalled the memory with ease. But the words stuck in her throat. Then, finally, she replied, "Jane said they died in a car accident."

Polydora raised an eyebrow. "How horribly prophetic."

* * *

Dorathea and Sloane returned to the covenstead through the Denham portal.

Sloane dropped into the chair next to Elvina and growled, "He stole my favorite cardigan."

The familiar woke with a start. *Who stole your favorite cardigan? The navy one? To be fair, it has seen better days,* Elvina said, lifting onto her haunches.

"You will get your sweater back." Dorathea sat on the other side of the familiar and summoned a tea service.

Sloane let her head fall back on the velvet chair. "When? After they harass me again?"

Elvina's whiskers twitched. *What do you mean they harassed you?*

"I do not believe that that was their intent, pet."

*Why did they harass her and take her sweater?* Elvina asked Dorathea, her voice getting louder in their heads.

"How would you know their intentions?" Sloane said to Dorathea. "They spoke to each other in their heads most of the time. I could tell. I might be new to this, but I'm not naïve."

Elvina flicked her tail, and Sloane and Dorathea began to mouth silent words. Dorathea turned to her in protest.

*I'll release your voices, but you must stop talking over me and tell me what happened at the Coven.* Dorathea nodded, and Elvina tapped the burgundy velvet seat with her tail.

"Do not make that a habit, dear," Dorathea said. "I disapprove of being silenced. Now, my apologies for ignoring your questions. I will answer them."

Sloane wondered what her cousin would say, the truth or a lie in line with the Grand Coven.

"They requested to see Sloane under false pretenses. Rather than an informal chat, they wanted answers to specific questions. They seem to believe Jane and Sloane are somehow a part of the plot to end our coven."

"Yeah. I got the impression the GC doesn't think I'm on the level."

Elvina broke out in a fit of laughter. *Who suggested that? Polydora? Certainly not Millicent or Cenric.*

"Yes, Polydora. But Millicent and Cenric allowed it," Dorathea answered.

Elvina hissed. *Outrageous. This isn't about Jane and Sloane. It's Polydora's pettiness.*

"What do you mean?" Sloane asked.

Elvina's pupils widened. *Dorathea was to take a seat on the Grand Coven, dear. But she turned it down.*

Sloane looked at her cousin. "You? On the GC?"

*Oh, yes, dear. Dorathea Denham.* Elvina curled her tail around her legs. "She gave it up for love."

"For love?" Sloane said with renewed interest, eyeing her cousin fondly.

"Enough, Elvina." Dorathea moved her hand over the teapot, and steam instantly trailed from its spout. "I believe the Coven thinks you and Jane may have had a turned Magical or a Demon in your lives who emboldened you to do evil."

*That's ridiculous. I was the only Magical in their lives.* Elvina's eyes suddenly turned into slits. *Did you tell the Grand Coven about me?*

"No. I did not. I am unsure how to explain your whereabouts for the last fifteen years," responded Dorathea.

*I'm not hiding anything. I was here in Old Denwick until Jane called for me and then New York with her and Sloane.*

"Exactly. You were there with them. And no one here knew. You will be accused of consorting with evil if we are not careful."

"Why would they blame Elvina?" Sloane asked.

"Because she is the only other Magical who was in your lives. And they do not believe Jane could have created the ancient concealment spell that surrounds you."

*When you say it like that, it sounds terrible for me.* Elvina hesitated. *Has my mother said anything about the spell?*

"She has yet to discover its source." Dorathea stared into the fire. "The Coven knows this as well."

Sloane blew into her cup and sipped the stout tea. "Ooh, I like this."

*It's a black tea only found in our world,* Elvina said. She looked at Dorathea. *What did Cenric want with Sloane's sweater?*

"I believe they hoped to gain insight into the concealment spell's source. But from Cenric's reaction, I do not think the sweater revealed anything."

"Then why the hell did he keep it?" Sloane asked.

"He had an odd reaction when detecting it. I suppose they wanted to examine it more," Dorathea answered.

She had no sooner spoken when Sloane jumped out of her chair, spilling her tea in her lap. Her cardigan had reappeared on her body. "Ouch. Damnit!"

"Take it off and give it to me quickly," Dorathea ordered. Sloane removed her sweater, balled it up, and tossed it to her cousin. Dorathea closed her eyes, and the muscles in her jaw clenched. "How dare they." Opening her eyes, she flung the cardigan into the fire.

Sloane ran to the fireplace, but the sweater shriveled away as the flames consumed it. "Why'd you do that? I've had that sweater for over a decade."

Dorathea held her hands up. "It is no longer yours, pet. It has a *séce* spell on it."

"Like a tracking device to watch me?"

*Your every move*, Elvina answered.

"What the hell?" Sloane watched the last of her cardigan turn to ash. "So much for their help."

"The Grand Coven is being foolish. They will learn of their mistake soon enough."

"Fine." Sloane slung her tote over her head. "Are we done? I need to follow up on a few things."

"We are," Dorathea answered. "Where are you going?"

"Old Main. Fiona Keane and James Reed weren't where they were supposed to be when Charles was murdered. And I need to find out why."

*Ooh, shall we have updates this evening?* Elvina asked.

"Yeah. And dinner?"

"That sounds lovely," Dorathea said.

Sloane turned to leave. "I forgot." She removed the photo of Harold and the attractive woman from her tote and handed it to Dorathea. "Do you know who this woman is?"

"Why, yes. That is a young Alice Reed. Most likely from her time at the University of British Columbia, where she and James met. They were foolishly in love. But poor James had to return home to run the market when his father died suddenly. Our dear Harold escorted Alice from school in Vancouver to Denwick on the weekends. And when Alice finished her studies, she and James married."

"This looks like Harold and Alice were the ones with a budding romance," Sloane said.

"Yes. But looks can be deceiving." Dorathea passed the photo back to Sloane.

"What if I'm right, though? Maybe James discovered the truth about Alice and Harold?"

"And therefore, James had another motive?" Dorathea asked. "You could be right. But James married Alice. They lived happily for fifty years. I would think his resentment would have faded long ago."

"Maybe he wanted to wait until Alice died. Or something else triggered his anger at Harold," Sloane said. "If Alice and Harold really did have a romance, I think it's time we make sure James got over it."

# CHAPTER TWENTY-SIX

Sloane left the covenstead. The drizzle had stopped, but the sky had turned darker and colder. She walked to Mallow Cottage and grabbed another cardigan out of her suitcase. Over a week here, and she hadn't unpacked. Oh, well, she thought, it's not like she ever put her laundry away, either.

Only one car passed her on her walk to Old Main. It put her on edge. She missed the busy streets of NYC, the thrum that pulled her through the day.

Sloane waited outside the door at Reed's Fish Market for it to clear before entering. The bells jingled. "Hello, James. Looks like a good afternoon rush, huh?"

He snapped back the head of a live lobster, pulling it away from its tail, and grumbled, "They came to see where the murder happened. Our businesses are afterthoughts. Terrible thing. I don't know what to think about it. Harold. Now Charlie."

"Listen, James. I'd like to talk to you privately for a moment."

James wiped his hands on his apron. "Are you here to accuse me of killing Charlie, too?"

"I'm not accusing anyone of anything," she replied. "I'm just doing my job."

James removed his apron and washed his hands at a sink against the wall. "What do you want to ask me?"

"I noticed the market was closed yesterday afternoon. Where were you when Charles was murdered?"

"I knew it. You are accusing me." He kept his back to her and dried his hands. "But you're wrong. I was with Alice in the crypt." He turned. "I close every second Friday of the month to visit her. We talked until about one o'clock. You can go see for yourself. I left her a bouquet of roses. Then I went home."

"Did anyone see you there?"

"No one alive. But Lore gave me the flowers on my way to the cemetery."

"What about at home? Did anyone see you there?"

"I was alone until Ken brought Lore to me after you found Charlie."

"How did you know I found Charles?"

He put on a new apron and tried to recall. "I don't know. Lore must have told me."

"All right." She stared at his knife. If she could just detect him, it would be so much easier. "I've seen your financials. I know how much debt the market carries. Has anyone ever suggested you do something illegal to make the market successful?" she asked.

James's face turned red. "How do you know that? That's private information. You can't—You—You, get out of my store."

"Fine. I'll go. I'm going." Sloane reached into her tote. "But just one more thing. Have you seen this photo before?" She tossed it across the counter.

James grabbed it. His brow furrowed, and his face softened. He studied the picture for several silent minutes.

"That's Alice when she was about twenty-one, isn't it?"

"Looks like it." He looked up at Sloane. "Where did you get this?"

"I found it in one of Harold Huxham's drawers."

James turned the photo over and read. His lips parted, but he didn't speak.

Sloane braced herself. Her following line of questioning might result in another attempt on her life. "Did you know Harold and Alice had a relationship at university?" she asked in a matter-of-fact tone.

He threw the picture back at her. "No. That's not true."

"Did you find out about their affair? Is that what came between you and Harold? Why you tried to keep Charles and Lore apart?"

"No. Those are lies." His eyes welled, and his rough voice cracked. "Leave. Now."

"Listen, James, if I can find evidence that you had any reason to kill Harold and Charles, Major Crime will. And they will be quick to arrest. If you're innocent, I can help. Are you sure you didn't know about their affair?"

"Get out!" He pointed at her, his thick finger shaking, and stormed into the back.

Sloane believed his anger, even his tears. But James's emotions had little to do with his innocence. The fact was James's alibi wasn't solid, and if she found a motive, the RCMP would too.

The cloud cover threatened real rain, not the misty stuff they had had off and on all week. The shoppers on Old Main walked up and down the pedestrian street without umbrellas, unconcerned.

Sloane bought a coffee at The Grind and sat on a bench across the street, watching the crime site. There wasn't much left to see. The detectives and forensics had gone. Only the caution tape and one uniform guarding the front door remained. There was probably another boot in the back.

It wasn't a coincidence the two financially sound families of the original Musketeers were of those dead. Well, except for her. But why kill Charlie? How would the Keanes or Reeds know who Charles's beneficiaries were? Unless he had told someone. Lore? Ken? She needed to know who benefited from his death, and there was only one way to find out.

Sloane tossed her coffee cup in a bin and walked to the back of the Patel's Fresh Market. She stood behind a stack of wooden pallets and opened her third eye, looked through the veil, and as instructed, imagined her *place* clearly.

"Lecgan lāstas," she whispered.

It was dark when she opened her eyes, but she recognized the smell of decades-old paper and felt her way past the storage boxes to Charles's office. After listening at his office door for a few minutes, she crept inside. Someone had ransacked it again. Even more file drawers were emptied onto the floor, pages scattered about, chairs overturned.

How the hell did they get inside? There were detectives on the scene and guards around the clock. Someone was looking for something and willing to take a considerable risk to find it. A wiċċan could have teleported themselves and Gannon inside. But what would Gannon want? It didn't make sense.

Sloane snapped on a pair of plastic gloves and got on her hands and knees. She flipped through every file folder on Charles's floor but found nothing. Then she checked for hidden compartments in his furniture. Damnit, she thought. He was not as clever as his uncle.

The room had dimmed with the late afternoon sun setting behind the row of old brick buildings. Sloane sneaked into the foyer. She needed to recheck Harold's office before the building was in darkness. The front plate-glass windows were uncovered, so she dropped to her knees and crawled across the lobby. The police had closed Harold's blinds, but it was light enough to see that his office had been searched again. She crawled across the floor, checking the contents of each manila file. She neared the window where the officer was stationed when her phone rang.

"Shit. Shit. Shit," she whispered. Her hand fumbled inside her tote and pulled the phone out. "West speaking."

"Hey, Sloane. It's Lieutenant Sharma. I got some forensics back. Do you have time to exchange info?"

"Yeah, no problem. When?"

"I'm in Denwick. Can you meet up now?"

She glanced at the window, and her heart quickened. "Sure. Where are you?"

"I just pulled into the parking lot behind the Huxham building. Do you want to meet here?"

"No, that's no good." She sneaked to Harold's door and peeked out the front windows, making sure no one could see inside. "I'm on my way to the Spotted Owl for dinner." She hurried across the foyer into Charles's office. "Why don't you meet me there?"

"Sounds good. Dinner sounds even better. Give me a minute to check in with my officers. And I'll be right over."

In the storage room, Sloane listened at the door and heard a car engine cut and a vehicle door shut. She threw her phone in her bag. Dorathea and Elvina would just have to understand Sharma's info was priority. She exhaled a deep breath and closed her eyes.

"Lecgan lāstas."

The gallery's back room was pitch black. Sloane patted her body, searched her tote for the Wests' keys, hurried out the back door, and locked it. A pungent stench of dead fish from the dumpster behind Reed's Fish Market filled the air.

She ran down the narrow lane between the two buildings and slowed down when she reached the front of the Spotted Owl. The staircase leading down to the pub was darker than usual, and the dining room was packed. Scottish folk music blared over the noisy chatter, and the smell of grilled meat filled the room.

Ken noticed Sloane right away and waved from behind the bar, gesturing for her to join him, but she pointed toward the dining room and gave him a thumbs-up.

Rose rushed through the kitchen door holding dinner plates. She dropped them off and hurried over to Sloane. "Hey. Is this a makeup visit for last night?"

"No, sorry. I'm meeting the detective in charge of Charles's murder case." Sloane glanced at the entry. "Can we have a table out of the way?"

Rose led her to a back corner below the old stage. "How's this?"

"Can your parents hear us from here?"

"Not with the music and the crowd. Why?"

"I need to make sure what she tells me stays between us." Sloane sat.

"Barkeeps hear a lot, but we don't spread gossip." She bent toward Sloane, and an auburn curl fell across her mouth.

Sloane brushed her fingers across Rose's lips, tucking the curl back into her headband.

"Mmm. Thank you. I'll be back with some waters and menus."

"All right. Thanks." Sloane sat back and regained her focus. Veena would be there any minute.

Ken approached the table and placed a whiskey neat in front of her. "I thought you could use this. On the house."

"Thanks, Ken." Sloane took a sip. "Ah, Oscar's."

"You know your whiskey," he said. "How are ye?"

"I bet we've all had better days."

"Aye. I don't know what to think about this business. Harold. Now Charlie. You know that lieutenant with the RCMP came around yesterday. Asked us if we saw or heard anything across the street. Rose and I were in the pub, and Fiona was at home nursing a migraine. We didn't hear a thing. I'm just sorry we couldn't help." He paused. "Can you tell me what happened to Charlie?"

"I can't say. The investigation's ongoing."

"Aye." Ken placed his hands on his hips. "She also asked about—"

"Hold that thought." Sloane waved toward the door. Veena had just entered and waved back.

"Sorry, Ken. What were you saying?"

"It's not important. I see your dinner date has arrived."

"Oh, no. This is work only."

Veena approached the table. "Nice to see you again, Mr. Keane. I've always wanted to have a drink in your famous pub, sir. I'm just sorry I waited until now."

"Aye," Ken replied. "What can I get you?"

"Pale ale?"

Ken nodded. "I better get back. Rose will bring yer drinks."

"How are you?" Veena asked her when they were alone.

"I'm fine. Charles isn't the first dead body I've found or my first murder investigation."

"Really? Detectives get a lot of murder cases in New York?"

"Some of us. And I prefer PI. So tell me more about the forensics."

Veena drummed her fingers on the table, then leaned in. "Listen, I have to answer to a real son-of-a-bitch inspector. You can't let anything I share with you get back to him."

"You can trust me."

The lieutenant looked around the dining room. "Okay. We got prints back. None of the preliminary findings flagged Gannon Ferris or his known associates. We only got hits on a few of the Huxhams' legal clients. The rest of the prints aren't known. But we're waiting for results from IAFIS."

"All right. That could just mean the killer wore gloves."

"True. But there's another problem with Gannon and his mates. We pulled CCTV footage covering the parking lot, the lane on the side of the building, and the front door. We couldn't find any security cameras covering the back door. Quite a few people entered the offices, including you. But everybody had left the building by eleven thirty a.m."

"Yeah. The local business group had a meeting. What did CCTV catch at the time of the murder?"

"Between eleven forty a.m. and one p.m., only a handful of people parked in the lot or went near the building. The back door was unlocked but hadn't been tampered with. And no one approached the Huxhams' front door at any time." She scooted her chair back and crossed her legs. "Except for you."

Sloane eased back in her chair. So, Major Crime had suspicions about her involvement.

"I told you, Sharma, we had an appointment. I was there to pick up my painting."

"Don't worry. I'm not accusing you. We tracked your movements on Main Street."

"Yeah. I wasn't on Old Main when he was killed. When I got there, I figured he was out for lunch. But I couldn't find him. I got nervous and tried the back door. It was unlocked."

Suddenly, Veena uncrossed her legs and casually leaned on the table. Sloane immediately recognized the woodsy scent behind her.

"Hello, Lieutenant Sharma. Here's your ale." Rose smiled, placed the pint in front of her, and turned to Sloane. She set down a whiskey neat and winked. "If I'd known you were having dinner with us, Lieutenant, I would've gotten these drinks out sooner."

"You remembered my name." Veena's face flushed and her mouth turned up in a self-conscious smile. "Call me Veena. And you're Rose, right, like the flower?"

She laughed. "That's right."

Sloane grinned at Rose. "What's the special?"

"Tonight, it's herbed Salt Spring lamb chops served with mash and green beans."

"Do you eat lamb?" Sloane asked Veena.

She nodded and stuttered, "Yeah…sounds delicious."

Sloane pointed at the menus under Rose's arm. "We don't need those. We'll take two specials."

"I'll have Chef throw in a piece of pie for the Island's finest," Rose said, and she flashed them a stunning smile.

When Rose was out of earshot, Sloane snorted in amusement. "Seriously? 'Rose, like the flower.' I'm sure she hasn't heard that since sixth grade."

Lieutenant Sharma lowered her head and shook it. "God, I know." She looked up and watched Rose disappear through the kitchen door. "If I'd known Rose Keane worked here, I would have come in sooner."

The muscles in Sloane's jaw tightened. She disliked the way the lieutenant eyed Rose, the tone of her voice when she said her name. A few minutes passed before she spoke again. "What other forensics do you have?"

"No prints on the dagger—"

"It's a letter opener from an import store in Chinatown." Sloane's words were harsher than she intended.

"How do you know that?"

"Charles told me the first time we met in his office. It was in an ornate sheath on his desk." Sloane tapped her whiskey glass. "Fingerprints are all your lab has for forensics?"

"So far. The lab's running DNA on possible multiple blood sources. And we recovered some fibers and hair on the victim's clothing. Other than that. None of the locks in the building were compromised. The killer may have forced Charles to hand over his keys before killing him."

"That could be." Sloane searched the lieutenant's face, deciding if her new acquaintance was telling her everything she knew. "Any leads on my painting?"

"No, sorry." She shifted in her seat. "Did you insure it recently?"

"Yeah, I did, Lieutenant. But I expect you knew that already. It was in effect yesterday. Which is why I had an appointment with Charles to take it home. But don't get any ideas. I don't intend to file a claim. I need the Degas back. My cousin's furious. I'm afraid she'll turn me into a toad if it's gone."

Lieutenant Sharma laughed. "We think Charles likely told more people than Gannon Ferris that he had an original Degas in the office. A painting worth that much could drum up a lot of interest." She swallowed the last of her ale.

Sloane considered this line of inquiry. "I don't know. Charles liked to party in Victoria, specifically in Chinatown. But I got the sense from Gannon that Charles only hung out with him."

Rose returned and set down their dinner plates. "Our special for the night. Enjoy Lieutenant Sharma. Sloane."

The lieutenant looked up with an air of confidence not evident earlier. "Thank you. And call me Veena."

"Okay. Veena. Let me know if you need anything else."

She watched intently as Rose stopped to speak with other guests. And Sloane had an overwhelming desire to yank the lieutenant's head back to center.

"You can call me Veena, too," she said, finally returning her attention.

Sloane held her glass up. "Good to know."

"Do you know Rose Keane well?" Veena asked.

"I wouldn't say I know her well. We just met last week." Sloane cut into her lamb. "Listen, back to the case. Did you contact Detective Jacobson?"

Veena nodded. "He said you don't think Harold was an innocent bystander in a shooting meant for you."

"Yeah. And that's one line of inquiry. But Morris didn't know Harold or me. He had a Nighthawk with a silencer and pictures of us on his person and nothing else. What does that say to you?"

"That he was a hired gun." Veena paused. "Detective Jacobson didn't mention any photos."

Sloane sat silent. "He didn't see them."

"How's that?"

"They got destroyed."

"How?"

"They…disintegrated. And don't ask me how. As for Morris, I'd never seen him before. And if I was his target, he would've shot me first."

"Why?"

"I have a reputation."

Veena stared at her, puzzled, and then she looked up and smiled widely.

Rose had returned. "How is everything?"

"It's the best I've ever had," Veena said.

Sloane smirked. "It's good. Compliments to Chef."

"I'll make sure to tell him." Rose brushed her hand across Sloane's shoulder, her fingertips lingering before pulling away.

"Okay. I'll keep an open mind about the employer angle. What information do you have for me?" Veena asked.

"Another motive. Someone hired Morris to kill Harold and me for money." She wanted to say more. But what would Veena do with the information that Morris's employer also conspired with an ancient Demon to end her family's coven?

"And I suspected Charles of Harold's murder because he owed a large debt to Gannon Ferris. I was wrong. But he wasn't the only one with a financial motive." Sloane filled her in about the land the family friends held in common.

Veena was intrigued. "Why only kill Charles? Why not take you out?"

"Too risky? One botched attempt on my life was too many?"

Veena nodded and pushed her empty plate forward. "Do you have any solid evidence that any of those four family businesses were in trouble?"

Sloane scoffed. "It's not like I can walk into a bank here and ask for someone's financials."

"You're right. But I can run them." Veena scooted her chair from the table and opened her wallet. "You haven't given me much to go on. But I'll look into it."

Sloane waved away her money. "Dinner's on me. Just let me know what their wills say when you find them."

"Sure. How about over dinner here again?"

"Yeah. Sure."

Veena went to the bar and shook Ken's hand. Then she waited by an old wood pillar in the middle of the dining room. When Rose returned from the kitchen, she stopped her. They spoke, and Rose nodded politely, then shook her head. Veena pulled out a business card, handed it to her, and left the pub.

Sloane watched Rose pick up a tray of drinks from the bar. There was a gracefulness to her movements. She was mesmerizing. A few minutes later, Rose placed a whiskey on Sloane's table and sat in Veena's seat. "What was tonight all about?"

"Charles's murder."

"Okay." Rose smiled. "She's not as perceptive as you. That's for sure. She asked me out."

Sloane chuckled. "You can't blame her for trying."

Rose bit her lip. "I'm going to take a five-minute break. Meet me in the back of the Inn. I have some information for you." Her voice was serious, and she stood and walked away abruptly. She held up a hand to Ken and disappeared into the back. Sloane put cash into the check holder, downed the whiskey, and walked up the stairs to the street above.

Rose stood underneath a metal staircase on the side of the building.

"Hey. What did you find out?" Sloane asked, leaning her back against a metal pole.

"It's about my mother. I know she's screwing me over. But she's not a murderer. She was at home on Friday, after you saw her at Oscar's. Dad and I knew. I was just pissed that we were so busy. But it wasn't her fault. The weather changed." She hesitated. "It gave her a migraine. She can't bear the light of day when she gets one. And she doesn't like people knowing her business."

"Did she call you from home? Did you call her there?" Sloane studied Rose's face. She seemed troubled.

"She didn't have to. Trust me. I know she was home."

"All right. I trust you."

"Thank you." Rose relaxed. "I better get back. Why don't I hire you a ride home?"

"Aw, now you're worried about me, huh? Like you said, if anything's out there, it needs to be more afraid of me."

"I was talking about myself, not you."

"Trust me. The same applies to me." Sloane pushed off the pole, and they stood face-to-face.

Rose's eyes had a look of longing that sent a surge of heat through Sloane's body, spreading from deep inside to her core. She encircled her arms around Rose's lower back and drew her body closer, gently kissing Rose's parted lips. Her legs trembled, her body ached with arousal. But she made the soft kiss linger, stroked Rose's back, untucking her T-shirt.

The touch of Sloane's hands against her bare flesh made Rose moan. And their kiss turned deep, hungry, a pent-up release of intense attraction. Sloane slid her hand up, fingering Rose's bra strap, sliding her hand underneath, cupping Rose's breast.

Rose groaned and slipped her mouth down the side of Sloane's neck. She nipped and kissed her way down to her collarbone. Sloane groaned and stumbled backwards against the pole. "Careful, West," Rose whispered, her voice husky. She lightly kissed her on the forehead. "I have to go back. This moment will stay with me for a long time." She delicately pulled the back of Sloane's hair, exposing her neck for one more nip. "I want you, to fully have you. Please be careful getting home."

# CHAPTER TWENTY-SEVEN

The quiet night sky and lamp lights reminded Sloane of midnight strolls with Jane. *Walking is best at night, pet. There are fewer people. You can hear your thoughts. Only stay aware of your surroundings.*

She stopped in front of A Different Petal. Rose's kiss lingered on her lips and neck.

Her thoughts changed to James Reed. His look of betrayal when she had shown him the photo of Alice and Harold. But was his reaction a memory or a fresh wound? His alibi was weak at best. Lore could have easily placed the roses on Alice's tomb for him. But why would she protect James if he had killed Charles, a man she obviously loved? Easy answer. She loved her father more.

Sloane's head raced. James was the most likely suspect. But were Quinn and Lore involved? Lore had keys to the Huxham building. And why kill Charles? The lights in Lore's second-floor apartment were on. She'd find out when Lore left Huxham Law on Friday and grill her about James's alibi.

She grabbed the staircase railing and stopped, telling herself it was a knee-jerk decision. It was too late and Rose and the whiskey had gone to her head.

*Never drink too much so that you lose control, pet. It can be dangerous.*

That's what Jane would tell her. Her mother approached every situation with the same level of restraint. However misguided, she had tried to keep Sloane from experiencing anger instead of telling her why she needed to avoid it.

The night had only a sliver of a waxing moon, providing little light on Mallow Avenue. The farther she walked, the more she felt a presence. No vibrations, just a sense she wasn't alone. She stopped and craned her neck, listening to the dark tree canopies. "Where are you?"

Nothing rustled the leaves. There was no answer, no swoosh of air, no owl above her head. She saw a movement come from the black blanket of grass beside her. "Who's there?" Something leaped past her and scurried into the ivy ground cover underneath a massive tree. Sloane jumped away from the tree. "Fuck me." Bent over, she put her hands on her knees and caught her breath. The ivy rustled again, and she straightened. Suddenly a figure stepped out from behind the tree.

A gun, Sloane immediately thought. She sprinted into the dark yard and spun around.

"Āniman!"

A shrill voice yelled, "*Ábýge!*"

Sloane's hand was empty. The disarming spell had failed.

The figure shouted, "*Amyrdrian!*"

Sloane heard *Move!* and everything around her flashed, monochromatic.

When Sloane opened her eyes, she was on the sofa in Mallow Cottage.

"Can you hear me, pet?"

"Yeah." Sloane tried to sit up but fell back, groaning in pain. Dorathea sat beside her, holding her hand. Her face slowly came into focus. "What the hell is that taste in my mouth?"

"You are back, indeed." Dorathea lifted her into a sitting position. "That is the remnants of an antidote. Luckily, Elvina absorbed the curse meant to end your life. But you still required a dose to counter remaining effects."

Sloane looked at the familiar curled up on the top of the back cushion right above her head. "Jesus, I'm so glad you were there. My spell didn't work."

*You're welcome, dear,* Elvina said, her voice weak.

"What happened?"

"A wiċċan attacked you." Dorathea waved her hand, and a water pitcher and glass appeared. "Did you sense them or see their face?"

"No, I didn't see anything, but I felt watched. Then I heard a noise. I couldn't tell if the attacker was a man or a woman. I tried to use the Āniman spell to disarm whoever or whatever it was, and the next thing I know, I'm waking up here."

"The wiċċan deflected your spell. Then they cast a death curse, Amyrdrian," Dorathea said, pouring Sloane a glass of water and refilling Elvina's saucer. "It is unacceptable magic." She helped Sloane sip from the glass.

"Death curse?" Sloane looked at Elvina. "Are you going to be okay?"

*I have more than one life, dear.*

Dorathea eased Sloane back against the sofa.

"I'm sorry you had to use one of them on me," she said to the familiar.

*Nonsense. I do have free will. I didn't have to. I chose to. We are family.*

Sloane reached up and stroked Elvina's silky, dark-gray fur. "Thank you."

"As much as I love a touching but rather maudlin moment, we must return to the attack," Dorathea said and patted Sloane's leg. She moved to an armchair.

"I don't have anything else to say. Everything happened so fast. I've never been caught off guard like that."

"A wiċċan inspired with evil has never attacked you before."

Sloane closed her eyes. "Maybe not, but plenty of bad people have come after me."

Dorathea sighed. "It is not the same."

"Yeah. I get it." She opened her eyes. "I'm sorry I stood you up for dinner. I met with Lieutenant Sharma at the Spotted Owl. She had some information for us."

*Then we'll need our lucky baby*, Elvina said.

Dorathea flicked her wrist, and the case board scooted across the floor. "Shall I document our new information?" Sloane watched her cousin glide to the board, amused at the delight on Dorathea's face. Not every crime writer had the opportunity to solve an actual crime.

"We'll start with forensics," Sloane said. "They found no fingerprints on the murder weapon or hits for Gannon or any of his known associates. Several unidentified prints were probably of village friends, at least those without records. And CCTV shows only me approaching the building."

"Not surprising now that we are sure a wiċċan is involved. They could have bestealced to enter the building."

Sloane reached for her water, but the glass began to float to her hand before she could move her body.

*Rest, dear*, Elvina said.

Sloane nodded and turned back to Dorathea. "The locks on the file cabinets and desks weren't tampered with, so the killer had access. I know Lore Reed has keys. She could've used them or given them to James or Quinn."

Dorathea wrote OPPORTUNITY next to Lore, Quinn, and James's photos.

"And I believe Fiona Keane has keys. At least for the front door and conference room. She sets up the MCC meetings."

Dorathea wrote OPPORTUNITY next to Fiona's picture.

"Lieutenant Sharma said they have no leads on the missing Degas. I'm guessing the wiċċan who attacked me tonight has it." Sloane tried to get up. "Damn."

Dorathea walked over and settled her back against the cushions. "Rest. The curse's effects will wear off by morning."

"We don't have until morning. We need to see the GC. They wouldn't give us the answers we wanted before, but they need to tell us now. The wiċċan outed themselves by attacking me and reversing my spell. We need to know if the Keanes or Reeds are working with a Magical or a Demon. They're ramping up. They know we're close."

"You have done enough for one day. Relax. I will speak with the Grand Coven. Elvina, are you able to put Sloane to bed?"

*I can manage.*

"Good. We shall meet again in the morning." Dorathea swirled her dark purple cloak around her and disappeared.

* * *

Sloane grumbled from underneath her blankets. Her face was buried deep in a pillow. "Not yet."

Elvina paced at the foot of her bed. *I'm sorry, but it's time to wake up. Are you feeling better?*

Sloane rolled over, wiping the hair out of her face, and scrutinizing her body. "Yeah. But I need ibuprofen and a pot of coffee." She sat up. "How are you?"

*Much better.* Elvina leaped to the floor and padded to the door. *Dorathea prepared breakfast at the covenstead. Get dressed and meet me in the kitchen. The Grand Coven is coming. We'll go together.*

"The GC? Here?"

Sloane threw the covers aside and got up. She pulled on a pair of jeans and a T-shirt and grabbed a sweater. The Grand Coven had the information they needed, and if they didn't give it to her cousin last night, they would give it to her today.

Elvina waited on the kitchen island. *Pick me up, dear,* she said when Sloane entered.

Sloane held the familiar in her arms, and they moved through darkness and returned to light an instant later inside the covenstead. Elvina disappeared from her arms and reappeared in a velvet chair next to Dorathea. "Jesus. That made my headache worse." Sloane looked up. "Hello, Alfred."

A stiff breeze made the candles in the room flicker.

Sloane nodded at the house's greeting and rested against a table. She stared at the bottles of dried plants, crystal containers with colorful liquids, and baskets of body parts and bones.

"Seriously, what do you need these for?" She held up a dried rat tail.

Dorathea turned to her. "They are an ingredient for many potions. Come join us. The Grand Coven will be here any moment." There were two extra armchairs beside the fireplace, making three on one side of the coffee table and three on the other.

"Oh, thank God there's coffee." Sloane sat next to Elvina and poured a cup. "Any pastries?"

Dorathea raised an eyebrow. "I see you are feeling like yourself again." She swiped the air with her hand, and a fragrant cinnamon cake appeared.

Elvina's tail twitched, and the logs in the firebox erupted into flames. The sitting area warmed quickly. *If you don't mind, I still have a chill.*

Dorathea snapped her fingers, and a blanket appeared underneath the familiar. "Are you sure you are unwilling to rest at your mother's?"

Elvina nestled into the blanket. *Yes. Now is not the time.*

"Very well, dear." Dorathea's care for Elvina seemed instinctive. "Are you going to be okay?"

*I'll be as good as new by tomorrow, dear.*

Sloane cut herself a generous piece of cake, but the Grand Coven began to arrive before she could take her first bite. Cenric appeared next to the fireplace and sat in the chair farthest away from it, beads of sweat forming on his pudgy face. Millicent arrived and sat in the center chair across from Elvina. She stared at the familiar sympathetically. Polydora materialized last near the covenstead's door. She strolled across the floor. "Your stead hasn't changed since the last time I was here, Dorathea. Years ago."

With a gush of air, the flames in the fireplace shot up the flue.

"It remains the same, indeed. But I am sure you have not taken time from your difficult schedule to discuss my interior design. Do you have an answer to our inquiry?"

Elvina's chuckle sounded in their heads, and Millicent stifled a smile, but it revealed itself in her eyes.

Polydora stared at the familiar and back at Dorathea. "I see, right to the business at hand. Surely we have time for pleasantries?" She flicked her hand, and a teapot floated off the coffee table and filled four cups. "Let's at least enjoy your refreshments."

Dorathea held her hand out. "By all means, help yourself."

Polydora cut a piece of cake. "It smells lovely. From Freya's café, I presume? The two of you have always been so close. I can't imagine what has kept you together for all these years. Well, of course, not *together*, together. Such a shame."

Elvina lifted her head, and the blacks of her eyes narrowed into slits.

"I would not expect you to," answered Dorathea as she sipped from her teacup. Her face was inscrutable, but Sloane detected the pain of loss in her cousin's voice.

Polydora grinned. "I thought you'd say it was because of Elvina. I assume she's lived with you since Jane abandoned her. That must have been humiliating, Elvina. Losing your connection with your wiċċe. After that, how could you possibly return to your mother, a foremost retired familiar, as such an utter failure."

She turned her head to Sloane, and her eyes seemed to encourage Sloane's intensifying anger. That was what the old woman wanted, Sloane thought. For her to lose control, let a secret slip out.

No one responded to Polydora's comments. "Well, then. I will also be brief. I'm afraid we're unable to oblige your request. The information you seek will remain sealed under the Interspecies Statutes. We have no right to seek the identity of other possible magical defenders. But don't worry. Our Weardas are working tirelessly to find who is responsible for the recent attacks. The West Coven is a top priority."

Sloane squeezed the chair's arms. Her knuckles turned white. "Attacks? You're calling five murders attacks?"

*Remember to breathe and remain calm, dear,* Elvina said to only her.

"This is an unacceptable decision, Ealdormenn," answered Dorathea.

"Whether or not you agree, it is our decision." Polydora set down her teacup.

"Why are you denying us their names? You know it had to be a wiċċan who attacked me last night, in your quadrant yet unknown to you. Evil right under your noses." Sloane's voice grew louder. "So who cares what the Interspecies Council says. The wiċċan has to be from one of the banished families. Tell us who they were so we can do our jobs."

Polydora narrowed her eyes. "We disagree."

Dorathea snapped her fingers, and an open tome appeared on Cenric's lap. The old wiċċa choked on a bite of cake. "Certainly, you know section six point four of chapter two thousand and seven?" Dorathea asked.

"Of course, we do," Polydora said.

"What does it say?" Sloane asked.

Cenric straightened, his lazy eyes opening wider. He cleared his throat, and his neck wobbled as he spoke. "According to section six point four of chapter two thousand and seven, the Grand Coven can provide the names you seek if the applicant is in pursuit of a Demon."

"Which is our only intention," Dorathea said. "Who but a Demon could facilitate our discovery and destruction?"

"And we disagree this situation falls under its purview," Polydora said.

"You are wrong. These murders and Sloane's attack are exactly why the article exists." Dorathea drank languidly from her cup.

Sloane felt the heat spread up her neck. The statute clearly applied. And she was about a day old in this world. "Give us the damn names," she shouted.

The Grand Coven deepened in their seats as if her voice had blown them back.

Elvina spoke in a calming tone. *Don't let them upset you, dear. They will see helping us is the right thing to do.*

"Then they need to fucking get to it." Sloane glared at Polydora. "There're only two of us left."

Polydora raised her brow. "I see you already communicate with the familiar. That's impressive." Her comment was more like an accusation than a compliment.

Sloane didn't know enough about the old wiċċe to understand fully why she refused to cooperate. Was it because of what Jane might have done or all those years ago? Was she exerting her power to put Dorathea in her place?

Dorathea set her cup on the table. "I agree with Sloane's hunch, and I have given you ample evidence a Demon hunts us and conspires with a wiċċan doing its bidding."

Polydora smoothed the front of her dark-red velvet cloak. "Well, this time, Dorathea, I know you are mistaken. The banished families' lines were extinguished inside Drusnirwd."

Dorathea shook her head. "Does Drusnirwd have protocols in place to detect *forbregdan*?"

"What's that?" Sloane asked.

"It is a spell to transform one wiċċan into another wiċċan." Dorathea held Polydora's eyes. "For example, a wiċċe could have easily transformed into a distant relative of one of the banished families and visited a male member of another banished family, couldn't she? Visitors are unable to perform spells within the walls, but this spell would have already been in place."

"And we don't need to explain what could have happened next. You have imaginations," Sloane added.

Millicent and Cenric stared blankly at her and turned to Polydora.

Dorathea continued, "This descendant may have groomed the next generation and the next for this very moment. Allied with the original demonic force that our own Weardas has detected."

Cenric and Millicent huddled together in hushed discussion. Their body language suggested agreement. It seemed Polydora's influence went only so far, Sloane thought.

They separated, and Millicent announced, "We reverse our decision."

Dorathea nodded. "Thank you, Ealdormenn."

Polydora flicked her hand, and the teapot refilled her cup. "I oppose Cenric and Millicent's reversal. We will have a great deal to explain to the Interspecies Council." She peered into Sloane's eyes. "If we sanction a breach of the Interspecies Statutes, the information you are given must only be held temporarily. We will erase your memory once you banish the wiċċan and destroy the source of evil."

Sloane held out her hand. "Whoa. Wait a minute. You're not doing anything to my memories."

"The Statute dictates it," Millicent said. "All magical Protectors no matter what species must remain anonymous. Known only to members of the Interspecies Council."

Elvina lifted her head. *Don't worry, dear. They only remove the memory you have about learning someone is a Magical. Nothing else.*

"Why should we trust them?" Sloane asked.

Polydora set her teacup on its saucer and frowned. "Dorathea, I think you need assistance in training your cousin. She ought to know basic rules. Her behavior in the presence of her Grand Coven is appalling. We are the most powerful of our world."

*And I think someone could use humility lessons*, Elvina whispered.

Polydora glared at the familiar.

"I am quite pleased with Sloane's conduct, considering our world was a figment of her imagination a week ago," Dorathea replied.

Sloane's expression hardened as she stared at Polydora. "Where I grew up, those in charge were the first to screw you over. So my skepticism is a consequential attribute."

Dorathea patted Sloane's hand and turned to Cenric and Millicent. "We can trust the Coven to do what they say and nothing more. Isn't that right?"

They nodded.

"Fine." Sloane watched Polydora's lips turn up at the corners. She would be hard-pressed to trust her.

"Maybe it would help my cousin a great deal if she understood why things are as they are," Dorothea said.

"Where do you want us to begin?" Millicent asked.

Sloane turned to her. "At the beginning."

"Ahem." Cenric straightened in his chair. "When Europeans colonized this land, they brought an ancient source of evil here. The Interspecies Council approved three Protector families to reside in Denwick. Two of the families were the Emleys, who were wiċċan, and the Ilievs, who were Ġewende, what I believe you call shape-shifters. But a powerful Demon compromised both of them, and they committed unspeakable crimes against the indigenes and set about destroying their pristine environment. We then sent two additional magical Protectors to stop them. The Reeds and the Wests. Your ancestors banished both families long ago to Drusnirwd."

"What about the third original family?" Sloane asked, pressing him.

"The third family remained impervious to the Demon's persuasion. They still live in Denwick, and we will only divulge their name with the knowledge that you will soon lose your memory of their true nature." He hesitated. "They are the Keanes, the *Blodaeters* and *Dhampyres*."

"Jesus Christ." Sloane slumped back as if hit in the chest. "What the hell are those?"

"Blodaeters is Old English for vampire, pet. And Dhampyres are half human, half Blodaeters."

"Fuck me." Sloane thoughts raced. The dark pub. Their intense beauty. It all made sense. Except Rose loved to be outside in the sunshine.

"Does that disturb you?" Polydora had been silent until that moment, and her sudden interjection drew everyone's attention, jarring Sloane out of her thoughts.

She refused to answer her and poured herself another cup of coffee.

Polydora chuckled. "So it seems."

"The Keanes' true identity makes them no more different than being a wiċċe makes you," Dorathea said.

"Yeah. I know. It's just a lot to take in." Sloane stared into her coffee cup for a few minutes, connecting the Grand Coven's information to Jane's research. Sloane turned to Dorathea. "So we're looking for a descendent of the Emleys or the Ilievs. Maybe the guy who's been watching us?"

"That is a possibility," Dorathea replied.

Sloane turned back to Cenric. "What kind of Magical are the Reeds?"

Millicent answered, "They are Ġewende. Predators. Birds. Owls, eagles, and the sort."

Sloane paced in front of the fireplace, her mind piecing together all she had heard and seen over the last week. She stopped. "What about the Ilievs? What type were they?"

"Prey. Rodents. Beavers, rats, etcetera," Millicent answered.

"That is all the information we are allowed to give you," Polydora said, watching Sloane. She looked at Dorathea. "I trust you will inform us immediately if you have any new developments."

"We will, indeed," replied Dorathea.

A moment later, the Grand Coven disappeared.

Sloane paced again while Dorathea and Elvina sat quietly. After a few minutes, she grabbed her tote and took out a business card. "This is Lieutenant Sharma's number. I'll contact Elvina if I need you to call her." She closed her eyes—

"Where are you going, pet?"

And Sloane disappeared as well.

# CHAPTER TWENTY-EIGHT

Sloane appeared beside the noxious dumpster behind Reed's Fish Market, patted herself, and thanked God she hadn't teleported inside it. The damp air seeped through her cardigan, chilling her flesh as she crept behind the buildings between the market and A Different Petal.

It was still early, and Old Main was quiet, but the flower shop door was open. Lore appeared, pulling a display out onto the sidewalk. Sloane jerked back. Good. Lore was at work, she thought and hastened down a tiny alleyway to the back of the building. She climbed the stairs by twos to Lore's apartment and pulled a pack of tools from her tote.

The front door unlocked with one try, and she slipped inside.

The living room was cozy. Sloane looked around and dropped to her knees, crawling over a plush rug and looking under side tables and a leather claw-foot sofa. She lifted sofa and chair cushions, searched behind tables and art on the walls, and rummaged through the kitchen drawers and cabinets.

A door slammed below, and Sloane froze, listening for footsteps. There was only one way out of the apartment and nowhere to hide. Had she thought this plan through? Should she call for backup? No. She didn't want to risk Lore refusing to talk and had questions that needed answering.

Sloane waited several minutes and snuck down a hallway to the rear of Lore's apartment. Incense impregnated the walls and floor. The scent grew thicker at the end of the hall. Sloane opened the door into Lore's bedroom, an intimate space, barely fitting the three pieces of furniture that filled every inch. She searched Lore's chest of drawers, under her bed, and the substantial wardrobe. Nothing. She ran her hands along the back of the massive piece of furniture, then pressed her body against it, pushing it aside and exposing a doorway covered in heavy drapes.

Sloane whispered, "What do we have here?"

Lore had turned her walk-in closet into a covenstead. There was a pot-belly stove and a stack of files on a small side table on one side. A center table full of bottles and a Bunsen burner, and a lectern with an open book on the other side. The *Book of Hagorúnum*. She turned the front endpapers. *Jane West, 1982.* Her mother's book. Lore must have stolen it and taught herself wiċċedōn.

Sloane yanked open the velvet shrouds lining the walls and found a collage of photos with the picture of the Four Musketeers displayed dead center. Nathaniel's and Harold's faces had been scratched out.

Throwing the drapes outward as if she were a stiff wind, Sloane found the Degas. Undamaged.

There was one more thing to locate, and she could hand Lore Reed over to Sharma or the Weardas, or whoever the hell needed to take her. Sloane leafed through the stack of files—Alice Reed's medical history and years-old financial records for the fish market. Halfway through the pile, she stopped. "Gotcha." She pulled out two manila covers, Harold's and Charles's wills, and dropped them in her tote.

* * *

The flower shop's back door was unlocked, and Sloane crept inside. She needed some answers before the RCMP got involved and slowed her investigation down. Lore Reed stood at the service counter in a simple cap-sleeve dress with splashes of spring-flower colors. A matching scarf held her hair off her face. Her back was to Sloane, but she asked, "Did you find what you were looking for?"

Sloane moved behind a group of parlor palms. "I did."

Lore continued to work on a floral arrangement. "I'm disappointed in Dora's training. I've heard your footsteps since you arrived. Hasn't she taught you to bestealce?"

Sloane kept her focus on Lore's back. "How long have you known about Dorathea training me?"

"Since she came to see you at Mallow Cottage. Of course, I can't cross her house spirit, but I know that's where she teaches you." Lore stuck a rose into the vase and turned the arrangement around. "What brought you to my humble covenstead?"

"I needed evidence." Sloane stepped away from the plants. "I've figured out who killed Harold and Charles."

"So soon? I mean, I assumed you would, but in only one week. I'm impressed." Lore replaced a eucalyptus stalk. "You really enjoy your work, don't you? That is admirable."

"Yeah, thanks." Sloane hid behind a column, scanning the shop for defensive positions when Lore tired of talking. "I suspect the same person also murdered Jane and her parents."

"You're a much better detective than I thought." Lore snipped a length of red ribbon and tied a bow around the vase's neck. "Jane tried her hand at investigation, too. But unfortunately, she wasn't clever enough to figure out my secret. Clearly, you didn't get your abilities from her. Your father must have passed them to you. But, of course, heaven knows who he is. Or maybe it's hell that does."

Sloane's body tensed with anger.

"Why so quiet? Cat got your tongue?" Lore added leatherleaf fern to the arrangement. "You must be pleased with yourself. Even though last night set you back a bit."

Sloane eased around the column, closer to the service counter. "Why not kill me when you had the chance? Is Elvina too powerful for you?"

Lore laughed. "Oh, I wasn't trying to kill you. I only wanted to summon sweet Jane's familiar. She has only so many lives. I'm surprised she didn't hide her face from me when we met last week on your arrival. But then again, you did drug her. Anyway, she hasn't changed a bit."

"No, she hasn't. She's still powerful, and you failed."

Lore grinned. "If my count is correct, she won't be fine *next* time."

"You're not going to find that out," Sloane said, her heart pounding. She tried to soothe her tensed muscles, to focus on protecting, but her anger was turning to rage. She spoke to Elvina.

*Have Dorathea and Lieutenant Sharma come to A Different Petal. And if you get a signal to protect me, ignore it. It's a trap.*

Lore turned the vase from side to side, judging her work. "I knew Jane could be cruel, but to hide you from your family and who you are. That's unspeakable."

"Sounds like you're speaking from experience."

"Don't pretend to know anything about my life."

Sloane stood just steps away. "Oh, but I know everything about you."

Lore turned around and faced her. "It's a pity your familiar needs to recuperate today."

"I can take care of myself. I've called the police. They'll be here any minute. I have all the evidence the RCMP needs to arrest you."

Lore scoffed. "So confident. Just like your mother." She turned back to her workstation and unwrapped another bunch of roses.

"Let's make this easy," Sloane said.

"I'm not resisting, am I? We're just having a conversation. You need answers from me, and I need answers from you. Besides, Elvina would have appeared by now if you were in danger, right?"

Sloane considered her next move. She knew Lore was capable of casting a death curse, Amyrdrian, which she couldn't deflect. And why the hell didn't she know how to?

"Should I take your silence as a sign of cooperation?" Lore snapped her scissors on another length of ribbon.

"All right," Sloane answered. "What answers do you need?"

"Has Dora taken you through the tree wall?"

Sloane recalled the mineral deposits in the gray stone at the back of the crypt, how they came alive, shimmering into a tree. Lore must know about the West Coven's passage to Tagridore. Did she follow them into the crypt and watch them pass through it? But how did she see them without being caught?

"Why?" Sloane asked.

"It's not your turn for questions. First, you answer mine."

"Yeah. She's taken me a few times."

Lore tightened the red satin strip around the vase's neck. "Did you enjoy yourself?"

"Wait. You had your question. It's my turn." Sloane backed away, moving toward a stack of potting soil bags. "I'm sure you and your family went all the time. Well, except for Alice. That must've hurt." She studied Lore's reaction. "But no, you and Quinn couldn't go either, could you? Is that why James and Alice lied to you and never told you about it?"

"My parents kept nothing from us."

"Oh, c'mon Lore. They've lied to you your entire life. Just like Jane lied to me. Let's at least be honest with each other."

Lore dropped the scissors and leaned forward with hands flat against the counter.

"Your father is still lying to you. He pretends it's normal that he and Quinn are different from you. They're Predators, right? An eagle and owl. Like the beautiful sculptures you bought them—the owl in Quinn's office and the sculpture of the eagle catching a fish in your father's market. But you're Prey. A rat. Just like Alice and the rest of your banished family."

Lore held herself steady, her arms trembling.

Sloane knew Lore was one push away from rage overwhelming her, and she knew just where to shove. "That wasn't their greatest lie, though, was it? When did you find out you weren't a Reed because you were *Rattus*?"

"Enough," Lore shouted. The sound of her fury spread through the store. She grasped a wooden stick and spun around.

"Amyrdrian," she screamed. A green light flew from the wand's tip.

Sloane dove out of the way as a dark blur streaked past her. It intercepted the flash and dropped with a thud. Sloane landed on her side behind the potting soil, immediately scrambling to her feet.

"Elvina!" she cried out and crawled to the familiar's lifeless body. "You're okay. It's okay." Lifting Elvina onto her lap, she stroked her dark-gray fur. "I'll take you to Freya. She'll heal you. Hold on."

"Don't move. Or the next curse will kill you and not your familiar."

"Hang on, please," Sloane whispered. Her eyes welled as she nestled her face into Elvina's back. She closed them and summoned her third eye. But before Sloane could see through the veil, Lore flicked her wand, and the chiller doors opened. Elvina's body flew across the room, slamming against the back wall.

"She's of no use to you now."

"No!" Sloane jumped to her feet, focused on Lore's hand, and yelled, "Āniman!"

"Ábýge!" Lore deflected her spell. "You're strong but too slow. And your eyes give you away."

Sloane gave a guttural cry and drove the stacked bags of potting soil into the service counter. Lore was trapped.

Sloane crouched behind a stack of planters. She wanted to hold Lore there until Dorathea and Veena arrived, but now all she could think about was getting Elvina to Freya.

Lore suddenly appeared on the other side of the counter, brushing the dirt from her dress. "My, you have extraordinary strength, an unusual ability."

Sloane stood. "I thought we were going to have a conversation. One tough question and you lose your shit? You kill again?"

"I have a schedule to keep. Killing that scrawny old cat was my first task."

"When did you find out who your real father was?" Sloane taunted.

Lore stepped closer without answering.

"I don't blame you for denying it. Your mother fell in love with Harold but still married James, already pregnant with you. Even when you developed feelings for Charles, in reality your first cousin, she still didn't tell you. That's why you had to break up with him, right? Not because you slept with Ken Keane."

"You're wrong!" Lore shrieked. She wielded her wand and cast a litany of incantations. Pots exploded, and broken pottery showered the area.

Sloane ran toward a long wooden fixture and dove as a jagged piece of ceramic caught the back of her leg. She crawled behind the display shelf, pain searing from her calf. She yanked the shard out, her anger flaring. Sloane limped to the other end of the card display. "How did you find out that your father was Harold? Did you shape-shift and scurry into his office? A rat in the corner eavesdropping, overhearing Harold telling Charles to stay away from you. Was that how Harold ruined your future? Your life with Charles?"

Lore screamed, casting a spell toward a chandelier above Sloane. The crystal and glass crashed onto the display as she ran to the far side of the work counter.

"Harold could've been mistaken, though, right? But then again, you got Alice's family name. Emilie, a variation of Emley, the original Denwick family, banished all those years ago." Finally, Sloane heard sirens in the distance. "You're out of time, Lore."

Lore cackled. "I don't fear Nogicals." The floral arrangement Lore had been working on exploded above Sloane's head and glass showered down. "Why don't you stand up and fight me? Hasn't Dorathea taught you more than a disarming spell?"

"You got the last laugh, though, didn't you? I've found Harold's and Charles's wills in your little covenstead. James gets a portion of their land when it reverts to what are now just three families. And you, well, you get revenge. Revenge for the banished families as well as for anyone who has ever wronged you. And all you had to do was sell your soul to a Demon."

Lore sneered. "You know nothing about revenge."

"I know it makes people do monstrous things."

"We're not ordinary people, Sloane. But then sweet Jane lied to you. Never told you who you really are, a wiĉĉe. You thought you were a Nogical." She slipped along the counter.

"That doesn't mean I have to be a monster."

"Of course, it doesn't." Lore's voice calmed as she stepped in front of Sloane. "I'm a bit disappointed in you. Where's the fight you gave Liam Morris? I didn't expect you to crawl about the floor like a coward."

Sloane jumped to her feet. Her leg throbbed. "Like you? Scurrying around. That's how you discovered the Wests were wiĉĉan, right? A little rat, burrowing into their home."

A police SUV and an unmarked car screeched to a stop outside the building. At the same time, a voice called from the door. "Lore, put down your wand." It was Dorathea.

Lore cackled and grabbed Sloane's arm, pulling her close. "You poor old woman, Dorothea. You can't stop me." She nodded toward the police cars outside. "You are bound to keep our secret from them. But I'm not. We're finished hiding in the shadows. Lying about who we are. There will be no more separation between our worlds. Lecgan lāstas!"

# CHAPTER TWENTY-NINE

"*Onlíhte*," Lore shouted.

Light spread through the crypt. The drizzle dampened the air, and the musty odor of the ancient ground mingled with the scent of roses. Sloane spotted James's flowers under Alice's niche. "Why are we here?" she asked.

Lore pressed the tip of her wand into Sloane's side, shoving her toward the back wall. "*Becnawan gemynd*," she whispered.

Sloane's muscles tightened, expecting a curse to bring her to her knees, but nothing happened. Her hands clenched. If she let the anger inside her go and drew on her desire to protect, she could stop Lore.

"Embrace your anger or don't. It doesn't matter. I will kill you before you have the chance to move."

"Get the fuck out of my head, you whack job."

Lore shoved the wand deeper. "My, my. A sore spot. Let me guess, Jane slipped inside your head whenever she wanted. Did she change the way you felt to suit her needs?"

Sloane refused to answer.

"Just imagine how different your life could've been if you had entered Jane's mind. Discovered the truth behind her lies. Decided for yourself who you would become."

"Yeah, well, unlike you, I happen to like who I am."

"Do you?" Lore laughed. "Poor thing. You're so used to lies that you even lie to yourself. I've watched you. Drinking every day. Probably so you can live in your own skin. Charles did the same. And he kept so many things hidden. You're so disillusioned that you're suspicious of everything and refuse to get close to anyone. You can't even call your mother, Mother. I can go on detailing the myriad ways you love yourself." She thrust Sloane toward the cold stone wall. "But I really don't care. I only need you to make the tree appear."

Sloane stumbled forward and stared at the stone. The tree. The Degas. Why was Tagridore so important to Lore? Why was she willing to kill to get there?

Lore pointed her wand. "Now!"

"You're just crazy enough to scare the hell out of me. But I'm not letting you through the portal."

"I see killing Elvina wasn't enough to motivate you. Perhaps I should set my sights on the last member of your newfound coven?"

Sloane scoffed. "Now, you're just making shit up. You aren't strong enough to battle my cousin. She would crush you."

"Who said I would be the one to kill the High Priestess?"

Sloane thought about Dorathea being exposed outside the hobbit house without Alfred's protection. She frowned and approached Lore until the wand's tip pressed into her chest. "Fine, you win, but leave Dorathea out of it."

"Wise decision. You should think about her safety. It's not as if you have anyone else left."

Sloane stepped backward. "But before I show you. I deserve a few more answers, don't you think?"

"There isn't anything left to tell. Like I said before, you're good at what you do."

"Yeah. That's why I know there's much more to your plan. So don't lie to me. I think we've both had enough lies. How about the truth. Let's start with the Precinct in New York when you accompanied Charles to identify Harold's body. You were surprised to see me. Why didn't you finish Morris's job?"

"I decided to change my strategy when I learned you had overpowered him. I had to find out just how powerful you were."

"Jacobson wouldn't have told you I killed Morris. Did you read his mind?" Sloane studied her face. "You did...But why? Who was Liam Morris to you?"

Lore narrowed her eyes. "Let's just say he was an associate in a more important endeavor."

"Ending the West Coven?"

"Good God. Self-importance runs deep in your DNA. You're just like Jane. Everything was always about her, too." Lore stepped forward, forcing Sloane to the wall again. "Destroying the West Coven is a means to an end."

"A hundred-and-fifty-year-old revenge plan?"

Lore's brow arched. "Something like that."

"So how did you figure out the Wests were wiċċan? I know Alice wouldn't have told you because if she was at all interested in any of it, she would have taken out her family's revenge years ago."

Lore jabbed the air with her wand. "Don't say my mother's name."

Sloane lifted her hands, palms forward. "Okay. Fine. Touchy subject. I get it."

"I didn't need my mother's help. Your mother's dishonesty and recklessness exposed your coven. When we were twelve, Jane told me she was leaving for boarding school. Just like that. No other warning. I came to see her the next morning to say goodbye. She was in a dark-green cloak and standing next to a trunk. She and Dorathea sat on the luggage and just disappeared. I looked at the ground thinking maybe they shifted, like me. But there was no animal in sight. They were gone. That's when I knew they were another kind of supernatural. That more existed."

"That must have hurt. All the lies. I understand that."

"Oh, please. I wasn't upset. My parents told us that we could never reveal our differences to anyone so I understood why Jane hid her secret from me."

"But you considered Jane your best friend. That must have hurt. Did you go against your parents' wishes and tell her you were a Gewende? Did you show her you could shift into a rat? But she still wouldn't tell you the truth about herself. You must have been so angry. Is that why you followed her? Watched her pass through the tree. Did you beg her to tell you where she went? But she lied again, didn't she? You were *both* different. You didn't know what was behind the wall, and Jane was not going to reveal anything."

"Enough!" Lore lunged and jabbed the wand at Sloane's heart.

Sloane didn't move. "I just can't figure out how evil turned you when you had Alice's protection and guidance. She forgave the Wests and gave up your ancestors' plan to kill the coven that banished them, right?"

Lore looked up into Sloane's eyes. "My, my. You do know more than I expected. But you're wrong. Alice was a deceitful coward, not worthy of her family name. She withheld her entire duty from my father and me."

"Harold?"

"James!" Lore thrust the wand under Sloane's chin. Her voice shrill. "My father is James Reed. And he thought he'd married a Nogical."

Sloane lifted her chin, unwavering. "He knew who Alice was." Sloane stopped speaking and searched Lore's eyes. "Oh, how tragic. You didn't discover Alice couldn't have been a Nogical until you learned your father was Harold, who *was* a Nogical. That had to mean it was Alice who passed her Magical status on to you. It was the only way you could be a Magical too, right?"

Lore shook with rage. "Alice let me believe I was a misfit. A mistake. A Prey among Predators. I spent years not knowing what I was meant to be."

"Your mother isn't the only one to blame. James is still lying to you. He knows you're Harold's daughter."

"You're lying." Lore thrust the wand's tip deeper.

Sloane felt a trickle of blood run down her neck. "Every magical creature has a passageway to Tagridore. The tree is my family's. James and Alice hid the Reed's from you and Quinn. They couldn't tell you. Or maybe they didn't trust you. Did you give them a reason not to?" Sloane paused. "They found out you were teaching yourself wiċċedōn. That's what scared them, isn't it?"

Lore pushed Sloane away and flicked her wand. "*Hete!*"

"Ábýge!" Sloane shouted, deflecting the curse.

Lore steadied herself. "Impressive. You are a quick study."

"And you have a volatile temper. From what I understand, Alice and Harold were easygoing."

"That's rich coming from you." Lore pointed her wand and stepped closer to Sloane. "No more questions."

"Oh, c'mon. That's not fair. I'm about to give you everything you've wanted since you took over for Alice, right? You can amuse me a little longer. How did your great-grandmother do it? Where'd she go after conceiving? And I still want to know how you learned about your mother's family obligation."

"My great-grandmother raised my grandmother alone here on the Island. She might as well have been banished. Alice's mother fared the same. They made sacrifices for a greater good. The plan." Lore stopped speaking.

"She refused to tell you, didn't she." Sloane glanced at Alice's tomb. "Until she couldn't resist you."

"Like I said, my mother was weak. She was unable to kill the Wests. We didn't have any use for her."

"Who's we?"

Lore ignored her question.

Sloane reached back, feeling the stone wall. There was only one way Lore could have forced Alice to tell her. "How did you kill your mother?"

"Let's just say, she had too many cups of my special tea blend. It didn't agree with her." Lore turned and pointed her wand at a sarcophagus. "*Undō.*" Its thick lid scraped open, releasing a cloud of ancient dust.

"So you drugged your mother to learn all about the revenge plan? Is that when the Demon found you? After you killed her?"

"No more questions. You seem to have all the answers you need. Now show me how to open the tree, or I'll summon Dorathea, and she will face my associate."

"Go ahead. We both know you have to kill Dorathea and me whether I show you how to enter the tree or not." Sloane carefully watched Lore's wand. "You're not as smart as you think you are."

"Oh, my. That hurts, dear," Lore mocked, and her lip curled up.

"It will." Sloane held Lore's gaze. "Haven't you figured it out for yourself? You and Quinn are also the only ones left. The last with the original Emley Protector's blood. The last of the Emley Coven."

"I am an Emilie, not an Emley! Quinn is not an Emilie! He is a Raptor. His blood is spoiled with the Reeds'. It is my blood we have an obligation to keep pure."

"Mixed with another Magical, yeah. But not spoiled. Emley blood is still flowing through his veins." Sloane glanced at Lore's wand. "Don't you know what happens when a Demon ends a Protector coven? Evil is unleashed upon the world. Why do you think it will let you and Quinn live? Whatever Demon you are conspiring with will end the both of you as soon as it gets what it wants."

Lore narrowed her eyes. "You're wrong. It fears us. I am not the only hidden one." She pulled a necklace from her pocket. "Recognize this? It belonged to your grandmother. I know it's a key. I know it grants access to the magical world. And you will show me how it works."

Sloane glanced down at her chest.

Lore flicked her wand. "*Āśćacan.*"

The Tree of Life tore from Sloane's neck.

Lore caught it and clicked her tongue. "Your eyes keep giving you away." She turned to the gray stone and pressed the pendants into several notches. "Tell me how these work. Now!" As Lore searched the mineral veins in a frenzy, jamming the pendants into every notch she could find, Sloane ran toward the door. Lore spun around. "*Bescūfe*," she shrieked in frustration.

The curse struck Sloane, a force that lifted her off her feet and slammed her inside the stone sarcophagus.

"Goodbye, Sloane West," Lore shouted. "*Clÿse*."

The slab ground shut, stone to stone, leaving Sloane in complete darkness. Her thoughts raced. Her breathing quickened, and she pushed on the thick stone top. Could the pendants work for Lore? Was she trying to open the magical world and give the Demon access to it?

Sloane's thoughts moved to Dorathea. Her cousin would fall into a trap if she entered the crypt, and she wouldn't let that happen. She slowed her breathing and opened her third eye.

"Lecgan lāstas," she whispered and appeared in front of the coffin. She reached out with her hand. "Āniman," she shouted.

Lore spun around and deflected Sloane's spell. "My, my. You've been a busy little wicċe, and you're a show-off, just like your mother. But you're nowhere near her speed." She stepped toward Sloane, barely moving her wand, but Sloane saw its tip twitch and dove behind a sarcophagus. "Amyrdrian," Lore shouted.

The deadly flash hit the coffin and evaporated in a green light. Sloane crawled to the farthest sarcophagus. A vibration spread through her. Dorathea.

"Perfect," Lore said. "Your cousin arrives."

"You're going to need backup, Lore." Sloane's voice sounded calm, but her heart raced. "You and your little stick are no match for her."

"Unfortunately for Dorathea, she has brought Nogicals to the party. Their presence will make her hesitate. And then, well, you know what happens next."

Sloane scrambled to her feet and reached out her hand. Āniman, she cast silently.

Lore had no time to react. Her wand flew to Sloane's hand. They looked up. Footsteps tromped across the floor above them. Lore turned to Sloane, and her mouth curved into a wicked grin. Her body began to shrink, her back curving, hair sprouting on her face.

"Sloane?" Voices called out above them.

Sloane thrust out the wand. She knew Lore was shifting.

"Bescūfe," she yelled, hoping the curse Lore had used earlier would stop her transition. The wand shook violently, releasing a torrent of light, knocking Lore off her feet. Her body flew across the crypt and crashed into the stone wall. The flash grew brighter, blinding Sloane, but she couldn't let go. The wand burned her hand before turning to ash.

"Sloane?" The voices were in the stairwell.

She ran to the other side of the dank room and found Lore. Blood streamed from her head, and her eyes were lifeless.

"Son of a bitch," Sloane whispered.

The old wooden door creaked opened. Dorathea was the first into the crypt, followed by Lieutenant Sharma, another officer, and Quinn Reed. "Oh, pet. Thank goodness you are okay."

More footsteps sounded on the steps and Rose ran through the door to Sloane. "Oh, my God, West, you scared us to death." She wrapped her arms around Sloane and held her close. Sloane breathed in the bergamot scent of Rose's thick auburn hair, and her eyes welled. Rose released her, looking her over from head to toe. "Are you okay? What happened?"

"Yeah. I'm good, Keane." She wiped her eyes with her forearm.

Veena spoke on her radio. "10-22. Missing person located." She crouched next to Lore and pressed two fingers on her neck. "She's dead."

Quinn lowered to his knees next to his sister's body.

"Radio for Ident," Veena said to the other officer.

"Yes, ma'am." He turned and moved to the back of the crypt.

Quinn laid his hand on Lore's arm, closed his eyes, and lowered his head. No one could hear what Quinn's moving lips were saying, but they watched him in silence.

When Quinn stood, Veena motioned to the door. "I need to move you all outside," she said.

Sloane glared at her. "Why the hell would you allow them inside an active hostage scene anyway?"

Veena opened her mouth but only stuttered a quiet apology.

"There will be time for arguments later," Dorathea said. She slipped her arm around Sloane's arm. "Let us go outside."

The sky had cleared, and steam was rising off the gravestones in the bright morning sunlight. Dorathea turned Sloane around. "Let me look at you. Cuts. Abrasions. The one on your leg is deep."

"We have a medic coming," Veena said.

"I will be taking Sloane for medical treatment," Dorathea said, uncompromisingly.

Veena shifted on her feet. "We'll need a statement from you before you go. It would be better for our medics to see you first."

"You can arrange a better time for your questions, can you not?" Dorathea lifted her chin, peering down her nose at the lieutenant.

Veena looked down and dragged her foot through the damp grass. "Okay. That'll be fine." She turned to Sloane. "Tomorrow morning. Nine a.m. I'll need to interview you."

The officer who arrived in the crypt with Veena approached them. "Ma'am, I found some jewelry by the back wall." He held out a plastic evidence bag holding the Tree of Life necklaces.

Veena held them up to the sky, examining them. "Now, what do we have here?"

# CHAPTER THIRTY

Dorathea and Sloane left the crime scene, walking down the hill, past the gravestones and police cars. Onyx was parked in the lot at the base of the hill. "We need to go back to Old Main," Sloane said nervously, opening the passenger-side door. "Lore had a covenstead in her apartment. The RCMP investigators—"

"The Weardas have already disappeared Lore's magical possessions. They also repaired the damage your battle caused inside the store."

"All right. Good. That's good. Did you see it? Did Rose and Quinn?"

"They did see the wreckage, but the Weardas will clear their memory of it."

"But not until we destroy the Demon, right? Isn't that what the GC agreed to?"

Dorathea waved her hand over Sloane's leg, and a bandage appeared.

"Ow. Shit. That hurts worse."

"Do try to be brave." Dorathea drove Onyx out of the church's parking lot. Her posture was erect, her carriage graceful. "The Grand Coven said they would allow *us* to retain our knowledge of the others until we've overcome the Demon."

"But Rose and Quinn can help us."

"Do you really want to put Rose in harm's way, pet?"

Sloane fell silent. Her cousin was right. She didn't want to put Rose in danger. But she also needed Rose to know the truth about her. She stared at Dorathea, her strong jawline and serene eyes. She'd heard and seen enough clues to know why her cousin had remained in Denwick, had never had a daughter to take over her position, and had relinquished her seat on the Grand Coven.

"Is that why you won't allow Freya to live with you at the hobbit house? To keep her safe?"

Dorathea's reaction was faint and fleeting. The same look of loss Sloane had seen in her cousin's eyes earlier. It was the loss of a life she wanted but couldn't have.

"Freya and I have been together long enough to know being apart matters not." She frowned. "But I would much rather we lived together."

"I'm sorry about that." Sloane looked out the passenger-side window, wondering how much of Dorathea's situation was Jane's doing and now hers.

"Do you want to tell me what happened in the crypt?" Dorothea asked.

Sloane turned back, unable to meet her cousin's gaze. "How about when we get back to the cottage?"

When they arrived, Dorathea waved the front doors open and helped Sloane inside. For the first time, the Wests' home felt familiar and comfortable. The roaring fire in the hearth warmed Sloane's face. She breathed in soothing scents of pine and cinnamon. "Did you start the fire?"

"Yes, when we left the cemetery."

"You can do that?"

"Of course."

"It's nice. Thanks." Sloane limped into the living room. "I was almost hoping I had a house spirit I didn't know about."

"That can be arranged."

"No, no. That was a joke." Her smile faded when she saw the top of the sofa. Elvina wasn't there, curled up, basking in the fire's warmth, only a folded blanket.

"She is still alive in Tagridore with her mother," Dorathea said gently.

"Jesus Christ. Why didn't you tell me that earlier?"

"Quite right. I apologize."

"Is she going to be okay?"

"Her existence is not of life and death. Whether or not she continues in her current form has yet to be determined. We can only hope she is back with us again in some manner."

"When will we know?" Sloane sat in an armchair and groaned, unaware of the extent of her injuries until that moment.

"I am not sure." Dorathea kneeled next to Sloane. "May I heal your deepest wound?"

"You can heal?"

"Injuries and torn sweaters."

"Are you kidding me?" Sloane poked her fingers through the holes in her cardigan. "All right."

Dorathea snapped her fingers, and Sloane's sweater was repaired instantly. She removed Sloane's jeans, the bandages on her leg, and slowly moved her hand over a deep gash. Sloane watched the torn skin mend as if Dorathea's hand was pulling a zipper. "That's amazing."

"I think it best to leave your less severe wounds until you have debriefed with Lieutenant Sharma." Dorathea flicked her wrist. "Why don't we enjoy a hot cuppa?" As the tea service appeared, the doorbell rang. Sloane started to get up, but Dorathea laid her hand on Sloane's shoulder. "Stay here. I will handle it."

She returned with Rose Keane and Quinn Reed.

"Hey. We're sorry for dropping by unannounced," Rose said to Sloane. "Quinn and I were walking back to Old Main talking about what just happened. And we realized our families share more things in common than we thought. Things we think you should know about."

"Please, sit down," Dorathea said. "I will get two more cups."

Rose sat in an armchair next to Sloane. Quinn perched on the sofa.

"I'm so sorry," Quinn said to Sloane, wringing his hands. "I should have known what my sister was doing."

"You can't think like that," Sloane said. "Lore was responsible for her crimes."

"You don't understand." His voice broke, and he looked down. "I could've prevented what happened today. Maybe even Harold and Charles's deaths if I had paid more attention to her."

Dorathea glided back in, filled all four teacups by hand, handed them out, and sat on the sofa next to Quinn.

Sloane pointed to the case board in the middle of the room. "Do you see those photos? Those are my suspects for the murders. Even I didn't seriously consider Lore. And it's my job. You couldn't have done anything. Trust me."

"But I knew more than you, and I didn't tell you. Lore returned from New York angry, obsessing about how you were just like Jane. If she were anyone else, I wouldn't have been concerned. But she's different. I've spent most of my life trying to avoid her. She's…was calculating. Ruthless. Especially if she thought you had done her wrong…And today, you witnessed her do things—"

"Unbelievable things, by the looks of it," Rose said.

"Exactly. And, well, we don't want to upset you any more than you are already." Quinn glanced at Rose and back at Dorathea and Sloane. "But we need to tell you how she did what she did."

"And we need you to know we, our two families, are like her. Like she was," Rose said.

Dorathea lifted an eyebrow.

"Not *like* her," Quinn said, rubbing his hands on his pants. "Not murderers."

Rose shook her head. "Right. Of course, my family would never hurt anyone."

"My dad and I wouldn't either. What we mean is, we're not entirely who you think we are." Quinn hesitated. "We are—I mean—I am…"

Rose blurted out, "West, the Reed family are shape-shifters, and the Keanes are vampires. I'm a vampire. Well, technically, a Dhampyre. Dad is a Dhampyre. My mother is a vampire."

"Our families have lived here since Denwick's beginning. We are defenders for our kind against evil. No one can know who we are," Rose said. Dorathea looked at her with a hint of remorse. "We're so sorry we've kept the truth from you when it could have helped."

Rose and Quinn stared at Dorathea and Sloane, wide-eyed.

"As hard as it was for the two of you to say that it was much more painful for us to hear it," Dorathea said. She snapped her fingers, and a tray of pastries appeared.

"Jesus Murphy, Dorothea. You're a witch." Rose's voice rose. "I always knew it." She laughed and turned to Sloane. "Are you?"

"Yeah." Guilt made her voice falter. "I'm sorry I didn't tell you."

Rose frowned. "You weren't supposed to. You're a defender, right?"

"Yes. The West Coven is. We're called Protectors."

"So Jane and Natty and Mary were all Protectors?" Quinn asked Dorathea.

"And many generations before them, yes, dear." She sipped her tea. "You realize we have all just broken many Interspecies laws."

"And it's about damn time," Quinn said.

"All this hiding. From our own kind. From other defenders. It's caused more harm than good. I grew up feeling different and alone. When all along, I lived around others like me. What a fucking waste." Rose's painful sincerity left them silent.

The late afternoon sun had dipped below the soaring Douglas firs in the front yard. The burning logs crackled and bathed the room in a warm glow.

Quinn finally broke the silence. "I knew Lore was troubled. That she was obsessed with you, Sloane. I tried to keep an eye on her. I followed her."

"You were the owl?" Sloane asked.

He nodded. "Dad told us there weren't others like us Gewende left. He said we couldn't let Nogicals know about our gift. My mother said she knew about my father and didn't care. She thought his ability to become an eagle and protect others was noble. I just don't understand why Lore was so angry. Why she wanted to kill the three of you."

Dorathea sighed. "She murdered more than Harold and Charlie, dear. Lore killed Nathaniel, Mary, and Jane, too."

Quinn's mouth dropped open.

"Oh my God," Rose whispered. "Why?"

Sloane's clients had asked the same question many times, but she had never distilled such a complicated response into three words. "Lore wanted revenge," she said.

Rose wrinkled her brow. "For what? A failed relationship with Charlie?"

"No. Not Charles. Lore's anger grew from generations of anger and lies," Sloane answered. "My ancestors, the West Coven, were sent to Denwick to banish two magical families, the Emleys and the Ilievs. They had conspired with an ancient source of evil, a Demon. Both families were imprisoned in Drusnirwd, the prison in Tagridore, a city in the magical world. They were your mother's ancestors, Quinn." Sloane stopped talking, observing his reaction.

"A magical world?" Quinn looked at them, eyebrows pulled together. "Ancestors? They couldn't be. My mother wasn't a Magical."

"Alice lied, dear," Dorathea said. "She was the great-granddaughter of those two banished families. She could never appear in our magical world for fear of imprisonment. That is why your parents kept it from you."

"Dorathea's right. The connection has always been there. In your mother's maiden name. Emley—Em and Iliev—ilie, Emilie. She was raised in this world to do one thing—enact revenge for them."

"Oh my God," Rose whispered.

Quinn's hand trembled, and tea sloshed in his cup as he set it on the coffee table. "This is too much."

"But why Alice? Why wait for generations?" Rose asked Sloane.

"I don't know. I can only speculate. Maybe because by Alice's time, no one in Denwick would recognize in her a resemblance to either the Emleys or Ilievs."

Dorathea looked at Rose. "Except for your family, dear. The Keanes would always be a threat. You are immortal."

"Technically, only Fiona is. I can die," Rose said.

Sloane looked at Dorathea. "Theoretically. But why would any Keane generation leave retirement and return to Denwick? And because of the Interspecies Statutes, the Keanes would not have known either James or Alice was magical."

Quinn sat forward with his hands on his knees. "Alice wasn't even from here. She told us she grew up in Alberta. She met Dad at uni."

"Alice lied to you. Her mom raised her here, on the Island. But your parents did meet at school. It was part of the plan." Sloane held his eyes. "Alice's obligation was to keep what had become Emilie blood pure from other magical blood. She needed to marry James Reed to hide the certainty that her children would be shifters while she masqueraded as a Nogical. Ultimately, as James's wife, she could get closer to the West family and kill them. So she had an affair with Harold Huxham, conceived Lore and married James. Your father knew Lore wasn't his child."

"Fuck me. Are you saying Harold is Lore's father?" Quinn lowered his head into his hands.

"He was, indeed," Dorathea answered. Dorathea waved her hand, and the teapot floated to each cup. "But the affair with Harold changed your mother's life. I was there and witnessed her transformation. With him she felt a bond of love she had never felt. I believe it was the love she experienced in Denwick that helped her cast off the evil that had held her and her ancestors for so long."

"Then why did Lore do this?" Rose asked. "The plan should've ended with Alice, right?"

"Exactly," Quinn said. "Why didn't it?"

"Because Lore discovered Jane was a Magical, and the deceit enraged her. It wasn't hard for her to realize your parents were lying to you both. That other Ġewende and Magicals did exist. Little by little, she uncovered the truth. She taught herself wiċċedōn with a book she stole from Jane. She became suspicious and mistrustful when Harold reacted so negatively to her relationship with Charles. She shape-shifted into a rat and stole into the Huxham offices, eavesdropping on them. That's when she found out Harold was her father. After learning the truth, it was simple for her to deduce Alice was a Magical. It was the only explanation for why she wasn't a Predator Ġewende like you and James.

"Your sister's anger grew and intensified for three decades while she plotted her revenge." Sloane paused and carefully chose her next words. "To put her plan in motion, while everyone thought she was caring for Alice's Alzheimer's, Lore poisoned her and invaded her mind. I don't think she knew about the Emilie plan to end our coven until she slowly extracted the details from your mother's mind. The knowledge gave her life real purpose. And she killed your mother to take her place."

Quinn sat stunned, horrified, eyes locked on Sloane. He got to his feet and paced between the sofa and front windows, holding a closed fist to his mouth.

Rose was speechless.

"Because Lore couldn't have penetrated my family's protection charms alone, we know she conspired with the same demonic presence that turned the Emley and Iliev ancestors from good to evil. Her next step was to spy on the Wests in their art gallery until she found out where Jane lived. A few months ago, my mother wrote to her parents and told them about me.

"Lore panicked. A coven of five would be all but impossible to kill. So she waited until Nathaniel and Mary left for New York and forced their taxi off the road. Then she organized for the same thing to be done to Jane. A sanitation truck blew through a stop sign and T-boned her car. But death curses actually caused their deaths. A few weeks later, Harold found me and decided to visit in person. Charles told Lore, and the opportunity was too perfect. She could order a hit on both of us, exacting revenge on the real father who had denied her all her life as well as another West. But, of course, Liam Morris failed.

"His failure worked in Lore's favor at first. Instead of killing Charles for keeping Harold's secret, she decided to set him up for Harold's murder. Lore told me Charles had drinking and gambling problems to make sure I considered him my prime suspect. What she didn't know was that Charles was in recovery. And his uncle had helped him settle his debt with Gannon Ferris. So when she learned he had come clean to Harold, and I would discover he was innocent, she stabbed him with the letter opener. Then she tried to make it look like Gannon killed him for my Degas. But Gannon couldn't have stolen the painting because Dorathea placed a protection charm on it. Only a wiċċan could have."

Rose and Quinn followed Sloane's and Dorathea's gazes to the Degas, now hanging safely above the mantle.

"Mother of God," Quinn whispered. He sat in an exhausted heap.

"But why murder Harold and Charles?" Rose asked. "Are they...like us?"

"No. They were Nogicals. But the secrets they kept about Lore's paternity deepened her pain and anger. She was an abandoned child and a ditched lover."

"Emley. Iliev. Em-i-lie," Quinn mumbled. "I'm so, so sorry." He struggled to hold his head up, to look any of them in the eyes.

"You are not responsible for your half-sister's actions, dear," Dorathea said.

"Is the plan over? Are you and Dorathea safe now that she's dead?" Rose asked.

Sloane hesitated. "Lore insinuated others were involved. She said she was part of something bigger than ending the West Coven."

"Do you believe she was telling you the truth?" Dorathea asked.

"I know Morris was a Magical and willing to kill for her, giving her the perfect alibi. Maybe there are more like them out there. Maybe there are Demons, and they are helping each other."

"What does that mean for us? For Denwick?" Rose asked.

"It means no more lies, dear." Dorathea's answer was unequivocal. "We must work together to keep our families safe."

"What's left of them." Quinn got to his feet. "I need to close the clinic for a few days. I have to get my head around all this, be with my dad."

Rose stood. "I better go talk to my parents. I'm sure they've heard their share of gossip by now."

"Good idea, indeed. Our families must address the Interspecies Council as soon as possible. Rose, dear. Have Kenneth arrange a time tomorrow for us to meet privately at the pub."

Quinn turned to Dorathea. "Will you help me talk to James in the morning, say eight a.m.?"

"Yes, dear. I will be there."

Sloane got to her feet and walked them to the front door. Rose held Sloane's hands, pulling her close. "Let me know if you need me later." She kissed Sloane's cheek.

"All right." Sloane rested against the door where Rose's woodsy scent lingered.

"Do you feel like an early dinner?" Dorathea called out.

She pushed off the door and walked back to the living room. "No, I feel like a double."

Dorathea turned away in a flurry of cloak. "Come with me. I insist we eat."

Sloane followed her cousin outside to sit at the patio table. The cherry blossoms had fallen, leaving the trees in frondescence.

Dorathea summoned two dinner plates.

"Mmm. Comfort food. Nice choice," Sloane said. "My mom made chicken and dumplings once or twice when I was a kid."

Her cousin smiled. "Your grandmother cooked it often. It was your mum's favorite. This is Mary's recipe. But I am sure it tastes nothing like hers did. I am a novice at cooking. Freya is trying to teach me."

Sloane chuckled and watched a couple of crows land on the railing. They hopped back and forth, their black feathers a dark iridescent purple under the patio lights.

"How do we know they aren't Ġewende?"

"It is not our right to know."

"I think that's bullshit."

"Yes, I know you do. And I agree. We will address the spying with the Interspecies Council."

They ate in silence. The taste of thyme, rosemary, and sage took Sloane back. She remembered when she and her mother watched the Macy's Thanksgiving Day parade on the street in the freezing cold. After Santa Claus showed up in his sleigh, they would walk home to a warm house with the smell of turkey dinner baking, watch football and the Westminster Kennel Club Dog Show. Her mother's friends would arrive and stay until late, eating and drinking.

"My mother was a lot like you," she said.

"Was she?" Dorathea's voice was gentle.

Sloane nodded and wiped the last bit of gravy from her plate with a warm yeast roll. "Did she have an affectionate name for you?"

Dorathea got a faraway look in her eyes, and then she smiled. "Your mum called me 'your majesty.'"

Sloane laughed out loud. "I can hear that." She set her knife and fork on her plate and sat back. "I guess I need a name for you, too. How about boss? Or 'my priestess'?"

"Do not be ridiculous."

"I'm only kidding. How about Denham? Last names are my thing."

Dorathea waved their empty plates away. "For those you care about? Like dear Rose?"

A crystal bottle with a smokey black label and two old-fashioned glasses appeared on the table. Sloane read its swirly pewter-colored label—*Fulsmécte*.

Dorathea poured two whiskey neats by hand and gave one to Sloane. "A gift to you. Our world's finest whiskey."

Sloane tipped her glass at her cousin.

"You saved us today." Dorathea sipped her drink. "You are a rare Protector, indeed."

"Five innocent people are dead, Denham. I think they'd disagree." She took a long drink.

"You could not protect them at the time. But with very little training, you stopped Lore. If you continue our work, you could prevent countless deaths."

"I understand what you're saying. But I need to get home."

"Is this not your home?" Dorathea set her glass down. "Your family is here. And you have made a friend who cares for you. And if I am not mistaken, you are fond of her, too."

"Oh, I am? What makes you say that?"

She glanced at Sloane's right hand. "You've taken off the past."

Sloane stared at the indentation on her right-hand ring finger. "I did. But not for Keane. It was just time."

"Wise decision. When it comes to love, we have many springtimes."

Sloane understood Dorathea's metaphor and stared into the garden, breathing in the sea air. Her grandparents' flowerbeds blended into the darkening light. The colors of purple crocus, yellow daffodils, and a wave of blue hyacinths created a scene worthy of Morisot. She turned back to her cousin. "I am worried Lore was a part of a bigger movement. Remember when she said *they* weren't hiding or lying any longer? What the hell do you think she meant by that?"

"Her connection with the Magical in New York concerns me, indeed. Who was Liam Morris?"

"And what about the other original families of Denwick? The ones in the crypt. The Smalldons, Tindalls, and Gildeys. Could they be involved?" Sloane asked. She thought about the file on Isobel Gildey that she found in Charles's office. "And we still don't know the identity of the man who was watching us."

"All good reasons you might consider staying to sort this out."

"Yeah. I guess." Sloane downed the last of her drink. "And I also want to find the man my mother was seeing in Vancouver."

"Do you think he is your father?"

"He could be."

"Then you will stay and discover the truth?"

Sloane held out her old-fashioned. "Pour me another."

Bella Books, Inc.
# Women. Books. Even Better Together.
P.O. Box 10543
Tallahassee, FL 32302
Phone: (800) 729-4992
www.BellaBooks.com

## More Titles from Bella Books

**Hunter's Revenge – Gerri Hill**
978-1-64247-447-3 | 276 pgs | paperback: $18.95 | eBook: $9.99
Tori Hunter is back! Don't miss this final chapter in the acclaimed Tori Hunter series.

**Integrity – E. J. Noyes**
978-1-64247-465-7 | 28 pgs | paperback: $19.95 | eBook: $9.99
It was supposed to be an ordinary workday...

**The Order – TJ O'Shea**
978-1-64247-378-0 | 396 pgs | paperback: $19.95 | eBook: $9.99
For two women the battle between new love and old loyalty may prove more dangerous than the war they're trying to survive.

**Under the Stars with You – Jaime Clevenger**
978-1-64247-439-8 | 302 pgs | paperback: $19.95 | eBook: $9.99
Sometimes believing in love is the first step. And sometimes it's all about trusting the stars.

**The Missing Piece – Kat Jackson**
978-1-64247-445-9 | 250 pgs | paperback: $18.95 | eBook: $9.99
Renee's world collides with possibility and the past, setting off a tidal wave of changes she could have never predicted.

**An Acquired Taste – Cheri Ritz**
978-1-64247-462-6 | 206 pgs | paperback: $17.95 | eBook: $9.99
Can Elle and Ashley stand the heat in the *Celebrity Cook Off* kitchen?